Suzanne looked at the envelope. Her name and address were neatly typed. She turned the envelope over. There was no return address. Using her knife, Suzanne sliced the envelope, opened it and took out a single sheet of paper.

The words on the letter were typed as neatly as her name on the envelope. But when she read the type, the blood drained from her face. Her stomach lurched and her throat began to close. "No," she whispered. "No," she said again, her voice barely loud enough to be heard.

Screaming the word "No!" she flung away the letter. She sat down and hugged herself, rocking slowly back and forth as chills raced through her.

Tears formed and spilled onto her cheeks. "Please," she whispered. "Please, no more."

The letter floated to the deck, face up. The words on it were clear and visible. Through the misty fog veiling her eyes, she saw Dana bend and pick up the letter.

She shook her head, but couldn't find the strength to speak aloud and stop Dana from reading the words that were burned in her mind: *"You should have stayed away! You should never have returned! You are a whore! You are a harlot! I failed before but I will not fail again. You will die soon. I promise that this time you will die!"*

MAKE THE CONNECTION

WITH

Z-TALK
Online

Come talk to your favorite authors and get the inside scoop on everything that's going on in the world of publishing, from the only online service that's designed exclusively for the publishing industry.

With Z-Talk Online Information Service, the most innovative and exciting computer bulletin board around, you can:

- ♥ CHAT "LIVE" WITH AUTHORS, FELLOW READERS, AND OTHER MEMBERS OF THE PUBLISHING COMMUNITY.
- ♥ FIND OUT ABOUT UPCOMING TITLES BEFORE THEY'RE RELEASED.
- ♥ DOWNLOAD THOUSANDS OF FILES AND GAMES.
- ♥ READ REVIEWS OF ROMANCE TITLES.
- ♥ HAVE UNLIMITED USE OF E-MAIL.
- ♥ POST MESSAGES ON OUR DOZENS OF TOPIC BOARDS.

All it takes is a computer and a modem to get online with Z-Talk. Set your modem to 8/N/1, and dial 212-545-1120. If you need help, call the System Operator, at 212-889-2299, ext. 260. There's a two week free trial period. After that, annual membership is only $ 60.00.

See you online!

KENSINGTON PUBLISHING CORP.

AND DOWN WILL COME BABY

BONNIE FABER

PINNACLE BOOKS
WINDSOR PUBLISHING CORP.

PINNACLE BOOKS are published by

Windsor Publishing Corp.
475 Park Avenue South
New York, NY 10016

Copyright © 1994 by Bonnie Faber

All rights reserved. No part of this book may be reproduced in any form or by any means without the prior written consent of the Publisher, excepting brief quotes used in reviews.

If you purchased this book without a cover, you should be aware that this book is stolen property. It was reported as "unsold and destroyed" to the Publisher and neither the Author nor the Publisher has received any payment for this "stripped book."

The P logo Reg U.S. Pat & TM off. Pinnacle is a trademark of Windsor Publishing Corp.

First Printing: February, 1994

Printed in the United States of America

Prologue

The wind whipped around the old Victorian house. An oak branch, long overdue for pruning, rapped upon the far corner of the slanted tile roof. A three-quarter moon hung in a desolate sky, surrounded by serpentine clouds coiling toward its pale yellow light.

Inside the house, a young blond woman picked up the telephone. She tried to dial, but there was no tone. The phone was dead.

She slammed the receiver down and ran to the rear door. Checking the lock, she nodded to herself when she saw that both the deadbolt lock and the lower lock were set correctly.

Returning to the kitchen, she went to the sink. She reached for the light switch and started to shut it off. But her hand hung an inch from the switch as the shape of a head appeared in the window.

She screamed.

Then she ran for the front door, but stopped when she heard someone trying to get in. She was halfway between the front door and the stairs leading to the second floor.

An instant later the door shattered, sending pieces of wood flying in every direction. Then, a large and dark oval shape filled the space where the door had been. The woman stifled the scream that tried to push out from between her lips, turned, and raced to the stairs.

Her eyes darted everywhere, seeking an avenue of escape, but there was none to be found. She reached the stairs and raced up, taking them two at a time. The intruder was coming behind her.

When she reached the top, she heard the loud sounds of *his* feet on the first of the steps.

A high-pitched mew bubbled from her mouth before she clamped her lips tight. She ran down the hallway and into a darkened bedroom, closing the door behind her.

Low moonlight came through the window and seemed to spotlight her on the wall as she tried to blend into the paint and the darkness.

She inched her way along the wall, all the while listening for the sounds that would tell her where *he* was. Seconds after entering the room, her right hand touched the edge of the night table.

She froze and listened intently. There were no sounds. She groped around the table until her fingers touched the ornate brass handle of the drawer.

Lifting the handle, she drew the drawer outward. The wood stuck. Footsteps echoed heavily in the hall. She waited until the sound died. Then she bit her lower lip, took a slow breath, and gave the handle a gentle tug. The squeak was loud. She froze again, her heart now pounding with desperation and fear.

When there was no further sound from outside the bedroom, she pulled harder on the drawer. It opened fully. She reached inside, her fingers seeking the object she knew was in it.

When her fingertips grazed across the cold hardness of the steel, she sighed, grasped the pistol, and drew it from the drawer.

Then the bedroom door opened and the light from the

hallway flooded in. She raised the pistol toward the door just as the bedroom light came on, momentarily blinding her.

She blinked away orange and red after dots, and tried to focus on the person standing in the room with her. She gasped when she saw the leather mask covering his face.

She swallowed hard at the sight of the mass of horribly twisted scar tissue covering his chest. In that instant, the dark eyes within the hood fell on her.

He howled with madness and hatred. Then he lifted the large axe over his head and turned completely to her.

"No!" she screamed.

He shook his head and took a step toward her, his dark eyes glaring malevolently at her.

She held the pistol with a two-handed grip, but her hands were shaking so much that the pistol moved in jerky arcs. "I'll shoot," she threatened.

The masked man snorted, gave vent to a loud blood-curdling howl, and charged at her. The upraised axe went all the way back in preparation to strike.

She pulled the trigger, once, twice, three times, but the masked maniac continued toward her. She pulled the trigger again.

With each shot, the madman grunted. Blood flew from his chest. Yet, he still came toward her, the axe held high.

She fired again and again and again. Blood sprayed at her, hitting her in the face and arms. He was almost on her when she fired the last shot. It hit him in the face, and knocked him off his feet.

He lay on the floor, blood pumping obscenely from the wounds in his chest. Dropping the pistol, she fell to her knees. Her sobs were loud in the silent room.

"And, cut!" came the amplified voice of the director.

Lights flared everywhere. People emerged from every

nook and crevice of the "room" which was part of sound stage three, on lot fifteen.

"Beautiful, Suzanne! Absolutely a perfect take!" called Sam Harding, the film's director, clapping his hands quickly in an offer of personal applause.

Suzanne Barnes smiled, wiped the gooey theatrical blood from her face, and walked toward the fallen maniac. "All right Larry, let's go," she said, smiling down at the leather-masked face of her co-star.

But Larry did not move; he lay perfectly still.

"Enough games," Suzanne said. "Let's go."

But something didn't seem right, and Suzanne bent closer. It was then that she saw that his special effect wounds were still bleeding.

"That's weird," she mumbled as she knelt next to him. "Larry." She touched his chest and pushed.

Then she looked at his eyes. They were open and glazed. Her throat constricted. Bile flooded the back of her throat.

"Oh! God!" she cried.

Still on her knees, she looked up at the director. "He's hurt! Larry is hurt! Get an ambulance. Hurry!" she pleaded.

Within seconds the director was at her side, feeling for a pulse. A moment later, he put the actor's unresponsive wrist down and looked at Suzanne. Slowly, he shook his head and called to someone standing behind Suzanne.

"Get the police. Larry's dead."

Chapter One

The scent of water from the Hudson River rose lazily up the face of the rocky cliffside palisade. The sun beamed down, warming everything it touched. A gentle breeze caressed all that lay in its path as Suzanne Grolier watched the two strong moving men carry in a long, flowered couch.

Suzanne looked at her watch. It was 2:20. The moving people were right on time. They'd arrived promptly at eight, and had started unloading the long red and white van. They'd worked steadily, taking only a single break for lunch, and were almost finished.

Yesterday, Suzanne had arranged for the telephone company and the electric company to come and hook up their services.

Suzanne had spent the afternoon in the house, cleaning and prepping for the move. While she'd worked, she'd gotten five telephone calls. All were in response to the advertisement she'd placed in the local newspaper.

After closing on the house, early last week, she'd arranged with the telephone company for her phone number. Then she'd placed an advertisement for a secretary/girl Friday to run in the Sunday paper. Yesterday—Monday—she'd gotten five responses. She'd had four of the respondents come by that morning, while the moving people were working. The fifth woman was due momentarily. She hoped the woman would be better than the morning's batch.

Two more moving men emerged from the truck carrying her bedroom dresser. A lump grew in her throat. It was one of four pieces of furniture she'd brought with her from France. Stop, she told herself as she closed her eyes, took a deep breath, and expelled it sharply.

She turned and started back into the house. When she reached the door, the phone rang. "Naturally," she muttered, turning and racing into the room off the living room. This was to be her office. She picked up the phone that was sitting on the carpet.

"Hello," she said.

"Hello, Suzanne. It's Arthur."

Suzanne paused a moment before responding to her stepbrother. "How are you?"

"Fine. I promised I'd call when I got back. I'm back," he added.

After returning to Springvale, and after buying the house, she'd called Arthur to let him and her stepfather know she'd returned to her home town. Then she'd invited them both for dinner. Arthur had been unable to accept because of business commitments.

"I also asked you and father to pick a date to come over for dinner."

"Whenever is good for you," he said.

"Sunday evening, seven o'clock."

"Will you be set up? I don't want to inconvenience you with the move and all . . ."

"Everything will be set up. And it won't be an inconvenience," she added, trying not to feel put out that she had to keep coaxing her own stepbrother.

"We'll be there," Arthur said.

"Wonderful. See you at seven, Sunday," she said.

After hanging up, she stood still for a few seconds, trying to understand why Arthur was being so hesitant. Could it be that he didn't want to come over at all? Or, she wondered, perhaps she had hurt him more than she'd thought.

She ended her lonely dialogue when one of the moving men came into the room with a desk chair. He placed it by the wall and went out. Seconds later, two men brought in her desk. She directed them to set it in front of the room's only window.

Fifteen minutes later, the rest of the office's furniture was in place. Suzanne nodded approvingly. The furniture was made of pale woods, and blended well with the off-white painted walls. The overall effect of the new office was light and airy.

Leaving the room, Suzanne went up to the second floor, and into the very large master bedroom. It was more a suite than a bedroom: there were windows along two of the bedroom's walls, and a large open sitting/dressing area that separated the bathroom from the bedroom.

One sitting room wall had two large windows. The other wall was the bedroom's only closet, and it ran the entire length of the sitting room.

Looking around, she saw that the moving men had followed her instructions exactly. They'd set up her treadmill and slant board in the sitting room. A small television was set between the two windows and faced the treadmill. A simple floral patterned chair was set against the closet wall.

The bedroom furniture was also positioned the way she had directed. The simple pencil post bed was in the center of the far wall. The matching night tables framed the bed. The large dresser was across from it, and her vanity was catty-corner between the dresser and the large window wall.

Again, Suzanne glanced at the furniture she'd had shipped from France. She steeled herself against the sadness that tried to slink into her mind.

"We're done, ma'am," called one of the moving men from behind her. "I need your signature."

Suzanne turned. The man extended a clipboard to her. She took it, read the disclaimer notice, and signed the receipt.

The man pulled off the second copy and handed it to her. "If you find any hidden damage fill out the back and send it in. The office will contact you and make arrangements for replacement."

"Thank you," Suzanne said, and followed the man down to the front door. When the man opened the door, Suzanne saw a woman standing there, just reaching toward the doorbell. She was petite, with short, dark hair framing an attractive face. She seemed to be around the same age as Suzanne, thirty-two or so.

For an instant, she sensed a tug of familiarity at the sight of the woman's face. "Can I help you?"

The woman's eyes fixed on her face for several seconds before she said, "Mrs. Grolier?"

Suzanne nodded. "Yes?"

"We spoke yesterday. I'm Dana Cody. We have an appointment."

"Yes, we do," Suzanne said, slightly uncomfortable at the way the woman was staring at her. All in all, it did not bode well for the interview.

"Come in, please," Suzanne said, stepping aside to let the woman pass. Inside, she brought the woman to the living room, pointed to the floral couch, and sat in the matching chair set across from her.

As the woman sat, Suzanne saw recognition flood her

features. Dana Cody's mouth opened, and her jaw hung slack for a second. Suzanne cringed inwardly, and waited for those old and familiar words to come. "You're Suzanne! You're . . . 'Baby.' Wow! I used to watch *And Baby Makes Five!* all the time. You were so cute. I loved you!" And no sooner had she thought it, than the woman's lips moved.

"You . . . Ya . . . You're Suzanne—"

Suzanne shook her head and started to push herself out of the chair. But before she could stand, the woman said, "Suzy! Good Lord, girl, don't you remember me? It's me, Dana. Dana Weiss! Suzanne, we—"

"We went to school together," Suzanne finished for her, suddenly remembering Dana as the pudgy little neighbor girl who she'd gone to school with.

"You've changed so much," Suzanne said, now able to recall clearly the Dana Weiss of her past. Dana had always been a cute, overweight, cheerful and friendly girl. She also remembered that even when Suzanne had returned to Springvale for high school, Dana had been the only one who had befriended her without question and had never talked about her "other life," unless Suzanne had brought up the subject.

"Me, change? I almost didn't recognize you at all," Dana replied.

Suzanne stood. "How about some coffee or tea while we get reacquainted?"

"Great," Dana said, standing at the same time.

Fifteen minutes later, after Suzanne had taken Dana on a tour of the house and the coffee was poured, they sat at the white formica table in the eat-in section of the kitchen.

"What brings you back home, this time?" Dana asked.

Suzanne sipped her coffee, set the cup down, and gazed at her childhood friend. "For some reason, I never think of Springvale that way. But, I have come home again, haven't I?"

Suzanne took another sip of coffee before she said, "I came back to write my autobiography."

Dana's cup halted in mid-air. "Your autobiography? A tell-all about being a child star in Hollywood? Suzanne, I . . ."

"Don't misunderstand," Suzanne said. "I'm not writing this for publication, I'm writing it for myself. Dana, I need to put my life in perspective. I need to get rid of the old ghosts . . . . And Dana, there are a lot of them. That's why I'm looking for an assistant."

"Well, I may be that person. Before I had my kids, I was the office manager of a real estate agency. Office manager was a euphemism for the only office worker in the place. I did it all, and I did it well. But I don't want to go back to work full-time, and your ad looked perfect. I can type, I'm adequate at dictation, and I can do any job that's necessary."

Suzanne smiled at her old friend. "Can you work for me? Would it bother you at all?"

A perplexed look tugged at Dana's features. "Why should it bother me?"

"Several reasons. It's not a regular office . . . . I'm a woman and some women prefer to work for men. There are no benefits, only a salary. And the job is temporary. When the book's finished—if I finish it—the job's over."

"Suzanne, I want to work, but I don't have to work. Permanency is not what I'm looking for. The hours are short, so I can be home for the kids when school is out. And I'm sure the pay will be fine. But a better question is, do you want me?"

Suzanne studied Dana's face for several moments. "Yes, I want you."

"Great!" Dana declared. "Now, tell me what you've

been up to since you disappeared from Hollywood . . . what was it ten, twelve years ago?"

"You were following my career?"

Dana nodded. "You were my friend, Suzanne, I was happy for you when you were able to act again."

"I was pretty bad in those horror movies, wasn't I?"

Dana laughed. "There were worse, but the guys sure loved it when one of those creatures would rip off your shirt."

"I'll bet," Suzanne snickered.

"Seriously, what happened?"

Suzanne took a deep breath. "Too much. After that last movie, the one when—"

"I know," Dana cut in when Suzanne's features went tight.

Suzanne swallowed. "I ran away to Europe, where no one knew me. In France, I met a wonderful man who helped me learn to cope with myself and who taught me how to live. We married. Jan-Michael was an author. He was a wonderful writer and a fabulous person."

The sadness that always seemed so ready to spring forth, did so. She took a deep breath and another sip of coffee. She screwed her face up at the cold and bitter taste. "More coffee?" she asked Dana.

Dana declined. Suzanne left the table and poured herself another cup. When she sat down again, she had herself under somewhat better control. "Jan-Michael and I had a baby, a boy. Dana, I can't describe how wonderful my life had finally become. I'd been a television child star but I lost my job because I had changed from an 'adorable kid' to a fat and ugly teenager.

"When I finally grew out of that 'ugly duckling' stage, and started to act again, that accident happened . . ." She paused to settle herself. "Anyway, Jan-Michael made my life more than bearable—he made it perfect. He even got me back into acting. I made several movies in France. They were real movies that I actually got to use my craft in, not the screaming tit and ass movies I'd been making in Hollywood."

Suzanne gazed at Dana, waiting to see if the woman would say anything. When Dana remained silent, Suzanne continued with her story. "Everything was going perfectly. My life was a story book, until a year ago."

Swallowing the lump that was already forming, Suzanne said, "A year ago, Jan-Michael, myself, and our son, Allan, were going to visit his parents for a week-long vacation before they started shooting my next movie. The night before we were to leave, the producer of the movie called. There was a problem and he needed to see me the next day.

"That morning, I went into Paris. Jan-Michael and Allan went to his mother's house. The police reached me at the studio that afternoon. There had been an accident . . . a blowout on the crest of a mountain. The car went over the side. Jan-Michael and Allan were dead . . ."

Suzanne closed and squeezed her eyes tight enough to stop her tears from spilling out. She felt Dana's hand take hers and press firmly. She took several deep breaths and then opened her eyes. "I'm sorry, I didn't mean to fall apart."

Dana shook her head. "Don't apologize. Suzanne, I'm so sorry."

Suzanne braved a shallow smile. "Now you know what I mean about old ghosts."

"Yes, I understand. When do I start?"

"Monday. I'll need the rest of the week to get this place together. Is nine alright?"

"Nine will be fine. The bus picks up the kids at 8:30. They get back home at 3:30."

"Nine to three sounds good to me. Now, tell me about you," Suzanne ordered.

Dana smiled. "I married Greg Cody two months after I graduated from college. We have two kids; Paul is eight and Trish is six. Greg is a hospital administrator, and I've been a practicing mother and housewife for the past eight years. And that really is it."

"Sounds nice," Suzanne said, her voice wistful.

"It is," Dana agreed, "but it's wearing a little thin now. I need more."

"Well, starting Monday you've got it."

"Suzanne, I appreciate this—"

"So do I. Now, didn't you say that your kids get home at 3:30?"

Dana stood. "They went to a neighbor's today. But I do have to get back and rescue her anyway. Suzanne, I'm glad you came home. I really am."

Suzanne stood and walked Dana to the front door. "I hope I'll be glad I came back, too," she said. "See you Monday."

An hour after Dana Cody left, Suzanne was in the living room, unpacking the third of five cartons. Two of the cartons contained small and medium-size paintings she'd brought back from Europe. She placed those paintings on the furniture or on the floor at the approximate spots at the walls where she thought they'd look good.

The third box she opened she'd mistakenly thought contained photographs. But when she reached into it, she found several of her award plaques for films she'd done in France.

Then she pulled out a slim, gold statuette. It was a Cesare, the French version of the American Oscar. She'd won this special award for her performance in her last motion picture. She took the statuette and placed it on the marble fireplace mantle.

Returning to the box, she took out another statuette. This one was different. The inscription was to Jan-Michael Grolier, and the award was the French Literary Critic's award for excellence in fiction. Her husband had won three of these prestigious awards in his twenty-year writing career.

"Jan, I miss you so much," she whispered as she placed his award next to hers. "How will I make it? How will I go on?" she asked him, seeing him in her mind as clearly as she had ever seen him in the flesh.

Wiping away a tear, she went back to work. She knew she would make it because Jan-Michael had taught her that her life had a purpose, and she had to fulfill that purpose no matter what it was.

Which was another reason why she would write her autobiography. Because within the pages of her life, she knew there would be a way to define her purpose for living. There had to be.

Chapter Two

"I truly am sorry," Arthur Barnes said as he accepted the Dewars and water from Suzanne.

"Why?" she asked her stepbrother.

Arthur shrugged. "He wasn't up to it. He's getting old, Suzanne, and he doesn't do much these days."

Sitting on the opposite side of the couch from Arthur, Suzanne tucked one leg beneath her and swiveled her torso to face her stepbrother.

The last time Suzanne had seen Arthur had been four years ago, at her mother's funeral. He hadn't changed a lot. He was still a tall and handsome man. His smooth face made it difficult to pinpoint his age, which was thirty-eight. Blue eyes and sandy brown hair complimented his deep skin tones, and he had managed to keep himself in a good and lean physical condition.

"How is your career going?" she asked in an effort to get the conversation rolling.

"Fine," he replied.

"Dinner will be ready in five minutes."

"I'm in no hurry," Arthur said with his first real smile. "And you don't have to force the conversation. Do you have a stereo?"

She pointed to a credenza beneath the living room's picture window. "Yes, over there."

"May I?" Arthur asked.

"Please," Suzanne replied. She sipped some of her wine as Arthur went to the stereo. He looked at the small CDs stacked next to the player and selected one.

He removed the disc, put it into the player, and pressed several buttons. A soft jazz tune floated from the speakers. Arthur returned to the couch. "That's better."

His words lightened the mood. A long-buried memory surfaced suddenly, and Suzanne remembered what it had been like as a child, growing up with Arthur. He had always helped her out. He had been the constant buffer between his father and Suzanne.

She favored him with an unfeigned smile. "Yes, it is better."

In accent to her words, the oven's timer went off. "Stay," she commanded as he started to rise with her. "I'll call you when everything's ready."

Working efficiently, Suzanne turned off the oven and opened the door. The scent of the Cornish hens rushed out in a vapor cloud. She pulled her head back and sniffed. It smelled wonderful.

She turned on two of the stove's burners, which already had pots over them, took the hens out of the oven to cool, and then got a chilled bottle of wine from the refrigerator.

Opening the wine, Suzanne brought the bottle to the table in the dining room. She poured wine into the two waiting glasses and, as she returned to the kitchen, called out to Arthur to go into the dining room.

After she lowered the flames under the two pots of vegetables, she retrieved the appetizer from the fridge and brought it into the dining room.

Arthur sat just as she put the small dish of four large shrimp at his place.

"I feel like I'm in an elegant restaurant," he said smiling. "The only thing I remember about your cooking was your peanut butter and raspberry jam sandwiches."

She laughed. "That and cereal were the only things I could ever make. Well, you could add frozen pizzas and TV dinners too. But when I settled in France, I learned how to cook, among other things."

"So I see," Arthur said as he speared a large shrimp, dipped it in the red sauce, and took a bite. "Perfect," he declared.

When the appetizer was finished, Suzanne returned to the kitchen and turned off the burners. Working quickly, she set the two cornish hens on a platter, and then surrounded them with the steamed vegetables.

She brought out the tray, set it on the table, and then returned for the gravy she'd made earlier. Finally, she served Arthur, herself, and then sat back down.

Watching Arthur's face was an experience in itself. He stared at everything, and then back at her. "You went to chef's school in France?"

Suzanne laughed again. "No. I learned to cook on my own, but Jan-Michael's brother is a chef. He taught me how to cook for real."

Arthur took a bite. "Yes, he certainly did!"

The rest of the meal went pleasantly, with the conversation centering on food, the theater, and music. After the dishes were cleared and Suzanne and Arthur returned to the living room, she said, "Now it's time for you to tell me about yourself. Tell me what you've been up to these last ten or so years."

Arthur comfortably draped one arm along the back of the couch. "A lot, but nothing earth shattering. I have a theatrical agency now. I'm also an artists' manager. I have quite a few acts whose careers I personally manage. I still play, but for fun, and primarily on weekends."

Suzanne held his gaze while she attempted to read from his features what was missing from his words. Although they sounded smooth and casual and natural, she found it hard to accept them.

"I had expected you to tell me that you had bookings to play all over the world. I had expected to hear about your playing with all the best of the world's orchestras."

Arthur's smile remained steady as he shook his head. "I like the path I've chosen for myself, because I chose it. I enjoy playing—jazz mostly, but with a fair amount of classical sprinkled in."

"I . . . he's never forgiven me, has he?" she asked suddenly.

Leaning toward her, Arthur reached out and took her hand in his. He squeezed it gently. "First of all, there is nothing to forgive. Secondly, Father was not feeling well tonight. Not at all."

"But I think—"

"Suzanne, please listen to me. Father wanted me to be someone I could never be. He pushed and fought and cajoled and harassed everyone around me, but what he wanted for me was not what I wanted, ever."

"But your talent. Arthur, you have so much talent. It shouldn't go to waste."

"Do you mean that by not becoming a world-class concert pianist I'm wasting my talent? Come on, Suzanne. I expect more from you."

Suzanne looked at her hand in his. She gripped his hand harder. "You're right. But Arthur, you were such a wonderful pianist. I used to lie in my room and listen to you play. I spent hours and hours listening to the way the piano responded to your touch."

"And it still does, but the way I want, not the way my father wanted. Suzanne, you have to believe me. I like who I am. It took me a long time to get to this point, but I like me, and I like my life."

"He still hates me, and he still blames me," Suzanne said stubbornly.

"Our father doesn't hate you, and he doesn't blame you for anything. He's sick, Suzanne. He didn't retire by choice; he was forced to retire because of his health. He's sixty-eight years old and he has a bad heart.

"He took his final business trip to England and Europe, just about a year ago. A month after returning home, he underwent bypass surgery."

"I didn't know," Suzanne said.

"He's been watching his diet, and he's been doing fine. Still, he gets tired quickly, and today wasn't a good day at all. He had wanted to come, Suzanne. I think he wants to try and make things better between the two of you."

Suzanne remained quiet. It was hard for her to imagine Raymond Barnes trying to mend any fence, much less the one between him and her.

"And you? Don't you think it's time to tell me what brought you back to Springvale?" Arthur asked.

Suzanne slipped her hand free. Then she interlaced her fingers together, placed her joined hands on her lap, and looked from them to him. "I needed to come to someplace that was familiar, but that was also safe."

She took a deep breath. "Arthur, I feel like I'm floundering in an empty sea with no boats or life preservers anywhere. I've lost almost everything I've ever loved and . . ." Suzanne paused to swallow her emotions. When she spoke again, her voice trembled slightly. "I just don't know where to go from here. So I've come home to put my life in order."

"It's a good starting place. I'd like to help you. What can I do?"

Suzanne smiled tightly. "You've always been there for

me, Arthur, even when I didn't know you were. But looking back, I see that very clearly now. And I want you to know that I've never considered you just a *stepbrother*. Arthur, you're the best brother I could have ever hoped for."

As she spoke, she saw his eyes fill with emotion. "Thank you," he said. "But you still haven't told me how you're going to put your life in order."

Inhaling deeply, Suzanne nodded her head. "My husband was a wonderful writer. He was able to put things down clearly and succinctly and make everyone understand what he was saying. I used to tell him that his ability to use words in that manner was a very, very special talent. But he said it wasn't. He believed his talent was nothing more than a desire to communicate with others, and with himself as well. He always said that writing was a way of making oneself clearly understood by oneself.

"After he and my son died, my world came to an end. But slowly, over the past year, I found that I couldn't will myself to die. There was something inside of me that was making me go on."

Pausing for a breath, Suzanne spread her hands outward in a gesture of frustration. "I've come to the point in my life where I have to find out whatever this thing is, inside of me, that is making me go on. Arthur, I've come home to write about my life. I'm going to do my autobiography. Perhaps somewhere along the way, Jan-Michael's words will prove correct and I'll find out what it is that I'm looking for."

Arthur stared at her, trancelike for several more seconds before visibly shaking himself out of his daze. "If anyone else your age had said that to me, I'd consider them an egotistical jackass. But you are one of the few people who have lived a lot of years and a lot of lives in just thirty-two years. Yes," he said, his voice becoming enthusiastic, "perhaps this is the best therapy of all. I hope it does work. I sincerely hope so."

Suzanne welcomed his warm words and support, because she sensed the love that was behind it all. "Thank you, Arthur."

Arthur looked at his watch, stood, and stretched. "You're welcome. And I have to go. I want to check on Father before I go home."

Suzanne walked Arthur to the door. There, they embraced and kissed each other on the cheek. "Thank you for coming tonight."

"Thank you for dinner. It was the best meal I've had in ages. And Suzanne, welcome home."

She smiled.

Later, after she'd turned off the light on her night table and settled herself into bed, she remembered the way Raymond Barnes had stared at her, at her mother's funeral.

His eyes had been hard and penetrating and accusatory. Had he really changed the way Arthur said, or did Arthur just want to believe his father had become a nicer person?

And what would it be like, when she and her stepfather finally did get together?

The news ended at the same time that the treadmill's timer went off. She turned down the speed, went from a run to a slow cool-down walk, and reset the time for two minutes.

The time showing on the lower left corner of the television was 8:15. Suzanne had slept until seven, which was an hour later than she'd expected. She chalked up her oversleeping to the fact that she hadn't had any of her usual dreams—the ones that woke her in the early morning hours and kept her from falling back asleep.

Dana Cody was due at nine, so Suzanne had been forced to cut her usual two hour exercise routine to a little over an hour. At 7:15, she'd warmed up and then done twenty minutes of exercises before hitting the treadmill. And now, forty minutes later, it was time to take a shower and get ready for her first day at work.

The timer went off again. Suzanne stepped off the treadmill, slipped out of her drenched body suit, and went into the bathroom.

She turned on the shower and while waiting for the hot water to come up, looked in the mirror. She was pleased with her physical shape. But she worked hard to maintain it. Tomorrow, she promised herself, she would do her full work-out routine.

In the mirror, she saw the steam filling the room. She turned from her reflection and stepped into the shower stall.

A half hour later, wearing jeans and a tee shirt, and having finished a light breakfast, she was in her office, waiting for Dana Cody.

She looked around to make sure she had everything they would need. The office was set up sedately. Suzanne's desk was under the window. Dana's desk, complete with a word processor, was off to the side. A beige loveseat style couch was against one wall. A coffee table was set before it.

On the table were a half-dozen yellow legal pads, two boxes of pencils, Number 2 of course, and a small tape recorder.

If there was anything else that Dana needed, she would have to tell Suzanne.

Dana arrived at exactly nine and, after Suzanne

showed her into the office, they sat down on the couch. "How do you work?" Dana asked.

Suzanne stared at her. She had no idea of how to work. Shrugging, Suzanne said, "I'm not really sure. Jan-Michael wrote in longhand, did his editing, and then had his secretary type the manuscript. He would go over that manuscript and make whatever changes he needed. But I can't even keep a diary. I'm an actress. I'm most comfortable talking."

Nodding, Dana set up the small tape recorder and then picked up a pad and a pencil. "I'll take notes as you talk, but I think it best if we use the recorder. I can type directly from that. Is that all right?"

Suzanne stood and started to pace. "That's fine. I've thought about when to start—the time period I mean. I'm not sure if I should start when we moved to California, or before. What do you think?" She paused in her pacing to glance at Dana.

Her old friend sat near the edge of the couch, her pencil poised above the pad. "How clear are your memories of that time? How old were you? Seven?"

"Very clear. They always have been. I was seven. We went to California just a few weeks before my eighth birthday."

"Is what happened before you went there that important?" Dana pushed.

Suzanne shook her head. "No, I don't think so. I was in school. Mom had married Raymond two years earlier. I hated the way he acted toward me, as if I was some sort of a bug that was always being shooed away.

"I also remember that almost every day after school I had to go to classes. There was dancing twice a week, gym once a week, and even fencing. Mom also had me going to a special acting coach on Saturdays. All my friends, even you, got to watch cartoons in the morning while I had to go to the acting coach's house. Boy! I used to be so jealous of you guys."

Dana laughed. "Not half as jealous as we were of you. Suzanne, you were a famous television star. To us, that was the best thing in the world."

"You should have tried it," Suzanne said. "If you had to make the rounds the way I did, you wouldn't have thought so at all. Every week Mom would take me on the rounds of the agencies. And when I got a job, I would be out of school for however long it took to finish. Commercials mostly, and a lot of newspaper ads and catalog work."

"Was it fun?" Dana prodded.

"Sometimes, but not usually." Suzanne sighed. "And then Mom took me for *that* screen test."

"And the rest is your autobiography," Dana joked.

Suzanne's smile was shadowy. "Yes, it was."

"What was it like, the move to California?"

"Different," Suzanne said as she went to the couch and sat down. "It was strange, in California. We moved into this large house with a swimming pool and almost everything a little girl could ever want."

Suzanne closed her eyes and, as she spoke, she was able to see herself when she was seven.

Suzanne's face was pressed to the window of the long, black limousine as it left the studio lot. The lot was a magical land of make believe turned real, and she was excited that she was a part of it. Next to her, her mother and Paul Driscoll were talking. Paul Driscoll was the director of the show that she was in.

It was kind of scary, she thought, but it was going to be fun. The show was called, *And Baby Makes Five*. It was what

Mr. Driscoll called a "sitcom." Her name in the show was Baby and she was the youngest sister.

In the show, she had a mother and father, two older brothers and a sister. But the show was mostly about Baby. On Suzanne's lap was the script. Mr. Driscoll had called it the "shooting script."

"Suzanne," her mother called, breaking into her reverie.

She looked up at her mother. "Yes?"

"Didn't you hear Mr. Driscoll?" When Suzanne shook her head, her mother said, "Mr. Driscoll said that he has a tutor all set up for you. The tutor will give you your school lessons on the set. That way you can keep up with your school work. Isn't that great?"

"Sure," Suzanne said. She was still upset about leaving her friends, and having to come to California. Whether she went to school or not didn't matter. She didn't want to have to make new friends. It was really hard to do that.

A half hour later, the limousine pulled to a stop at the large, white house that they had moved into the week before. Mr. Driscoll said goodbye to Suzanne and her mother, and told them that the limo would be by at six the next morning.

"So early," Lenore Barnes said.

Mr. Driscoll smiled. "You'll get used to Hollywood time. It's early in the morning when you work, and late at night when you don't. Well," he corrected himself, looking at Suzanne, "not everyone is that way. See you tomorrow, Baby!"

Lenore led Suzanne toward the house as the long black car drove out of the driveway.

Just as her mother opened the door, Suzanne heard the piano. "Arthur got his piano. It sounds good, doesn't it Mommy?"

"Yes," Lenore Barnes said.

"I can't wait to tell Arthur about today," Suzanne said as she raced inside.

She found Arthur in the salon, sitting at a magnificent grand piano. Beautiful sounds filled the room as his thirteen-year-old hands made magic on the keyboard. She ran over to him and joined him on the bench.

He finished a moment later and looked down at Suzanne. "Hi kiddo. Have fun?"

Suzanne nodded her head. "You like your piano?"

Arthur's eyes clouded momentarily. Then he smiled. "Yeah, it's cool."

"Yeah," Suzanne mimicked, "cool."

"What the hell's going on here!" shouted Raymond Barnes as he entered the salon. "You're supposed to be practicing. You have an audition tomorrow and I want you ready for it. You, little miss hotshot, leave him alone!"

"Dad," Arthur started.

"Quiet!" Raymond snapped. "Out, now!"

Unable to stop her tears, Suzanne slipped from the bench and ran into her bedroom, where she closed the door and dove onto her bed.

Burying her head in her arms, she cried silently. "I hate you!" she shouted into the puffy, down bedspread, which muffled her words efficiently.

A moment later her door opened and her mother came in. Lenore sat next to her and stroked her hair. "Easy sweetie, Daddy can't help it. The move was very hard on him. He had to leave his job and all."

Suzanne lifted her head and looked at her mother. "But why does he have to be so mean to me?"

"It's not his fault," her mother said. "Just try to forgive him, for me, okay?"

Suzanne sighed, wiped her eyes, and nodded. "I'll try."

"Good. Let's work on that script then, okay?"

"Okay," Suzanne repeated.

They worked until dinner. Then, after the meal, Suzanne took a bath and went to bed. Soon after her mother turned off the light and left, Arthur snuck into the room.

"Hey, kiddo."

"Hi, Arthur," she whispered back without picking up her head.

"Know your lines?" he asked as he sat on the edge of her bed. His face was backlit by the low, yellow light coming in from the hallway. He looked like an angel come to rescue her.

"I think so."

"Nervous?"

"Yeah," she admitted.

Arthur stroked her hair gently. "Remember one thing. They picked *you*. That means they like you. So if you make a mistake, don't worry. They'll understand. Okay?"

She smiled up at him. "Okay."

He winked at her and stood up. "Okay, kiddo, have fun dreams."

She waved goodnight as he left the room. She yawned. She was tired. And, she thought, she was lucky to have Arthur as her brother.

"And that was the start of my 'career,'" Suzanne said, opening her eyes and bringing herself back to the present.

Strangely disoriented by her reflections of the past, she focused on Dana who, having finished her last notes, was putting her pencil down.

"It sounds like it was a frightening first week," Dana said.

"It was, but Arthur helped to make it bearable. It's funny how adults think that children can accept and do anything as long as the parent tells them they can."

"In your case, it seemed to be true," Dana pointed out.

"Only to a degree. Yes, I became an actress because my mother wanted me to be one. But it was Arthur who really helped me to get through that first season."

"You were a lucky girl to have a stepbrother like Arthur."

"I was," Suzanne agreed. She exhaled and looked at her watch. It was almost two. "I can't believe the time. I guess I just got carried away with my memories."

"That's okay. It was fascinating," Dana said as she took out the micro-cassette from the recorder, numbered it, and set it with the other two she'd already removed. "And it was a good start. We got you from Springvale to Los Angeles, and even got you up to the point of going onto the set for the filming."

"And all without a tragedy, eh?" Suzanne said with a smile.

Dana's face turned quizzical, but Suzanne didn't elaborate; rather, she suggested they call it a day so that they could start fresh the next morning.

"Okay. But listen, boss," Dana added with a smile, "maybe we can take a lunch break tomorrow?"

Suzanne stared at Dana, realizing that she hadn't even given her old friend a cup of coffee or a chance to go to the bathroom. She started to apologize, but Dana stopped her.

"It's okay, it really is."

"Tomorrow at nine, then?"

"Nine," Dana agreed as she left.

Alone, Suzanne walked around the office. She picked up one of the tapes from the table, thought about playing it, but changed her mind. Jan-Michael always said you should never listen to your voice, only to the words which the voice gave birth to.

Deciding to wait until Dana transposed the tapes, Suzanne left the office and went into the kitchen. She was suddenly hungry and made herself a salad laced with bits of chicken.

She spent the rest of the day working on the house, and went to bed at eleven. At 11:30, the television's timer switched the set off. The only sounds that remained were those of Suzanne's deep and gentle breathing.

Chapter Three

The sun poured golden rays upon them, warming and lighting the way. The countryside was alive with the scents of the spring day. The sky was blue and cloudless and she could see almost forever, or so it seemed.

Turning, Suzanne looked in the back seat. Allan was sitting there watching out the window. Turning back, she breathed a sigh of contentment. Jan-Michael was driving. His large hands gripped the steering wheel firmly. She watched the play of muscles in his forearm as he maneuvered the car around a winding bend in the road.

In two hours, they would be at his family's home. She loved his parents' house, set high in the hills above the quaint thousand-year-old village of Alemare.

"I'll miss you." Suzanne put her hand on Jan-Michael's thigh. "A month is a long time."

"Not that long," he said, "And I must go. It is important that I do this tour. You know how Claude is about the release of a new novel."

Suzanne nodded. "I just get nervous when you're gone."

Jan-Michael momentarily covered her hand with his, before replacing it on the steering wheel. "I know. Perhaps you and Allan will come to Rome in two weeks and spend a few days with me?"

The scent of apple blossoms came through the car's windows. She inhaled the fragrance deeply before saying, "I'd like that. And so would Allan."

"Good! Then it is arranged. Now, after we get to the house, what do you think about leaving Allan with my mother, and we go for a little ah . . ." Pausing, Jan-Michael glanced into the rear-view mirror. He saw Allan looking at them. ". . . walk?"

She stroked his thigh lightly, using the tips of her nails. "That sounds like a very interesting idea," she said. "Especially after such a long car ride."

"Me too?" chimed in Allan. "I want to go for a walk too!"

Suzanne turned to him. Smiling, she said, "You want to go with Mommy and Daddy, or do you want to play with your cousins?"

Allan's eyes lighted. He adored his two older cousins, and was always asking for them. "Simone and Robert?"

"Yes, sweetheart."

"Yes!" Allan said excitedly. "Yes! Yes!"

Laughing, Suzanne turned to the front. They had left the moderately hilly country and were entering a more mountainous area. As Jan-Michael started onto a heavy upgrade, the road narrowed further. She hated this part of the drive. The old roads that laced through the French countryside were lovely, but they were narrow and hard to navigate.

But, she thought as she watched her husband, Jan-Michael drove them smoothly and with such confidence that she rarely was frightened.

When they reached the crest, Jan-Michael slowed the car. He stopped on the edge of the road, next to a sharp drop-off. "Allan," he called. "Look out the window."

Allan levered himself up and did as his father bid. The sight was magnificent. Because of the clear day, they could see so far into the distance that the greens of the trees and the ground finally blended together in a distant haze.

"That is what life is about, boy," Jan-Michael said. "Seeing something so beautiful that it takes your breath away. Do you understand?" he asked.

Allan lowered himself back onto the seat. "I don't understand, Papa."

Jan-Michael laughed. "You will, my son, one day you will."

He started forward, keeping the speed low as they descended from the crest of the hill. Ahead, the road changed into a series of cutback curves that wove along the side of the mountain. There was barely three feet between the pavement and the inadequate, ancient wooden guardrail set at the edge of the drop-off.

Suzanne refused to look to her right; rather, she concentrated on her husband's features so she wouldn't have to acknowledge her unusual attack of acrophobia.

When they came out of the first turn, Jan-Michael pressed on the accelerator. The car picked up speed. The next curve was a hundred yards away.

Fifty feet before the curve, Jan-Michael tapped on the brakes. The car slowed to a safe speed by the time they entered the turn. Then there was a loud explosion. She felt the car lurch to the right.

"Blow-out!" Jan-Michael shouted as he gripped the wheel tighter and fought for control. He twisted the steering wheel to the left as the car headed straight toward the edge of the mountain.

Tapping the brakes skillfully, he continued to fight the wheel. The tires squealed on the pavement. The car slowed, and Suzanne exhaled her held breath. But before

Jan-Michael could bring the car to a stop, the front fender struck the wooden barrier and shattered it. Then, as the car was slowed even further, the wheel reached the edge of the road and slipped off.

Suzanne was thrown against her seat belt. She cried out when the webbed material burned into her skin. Jan-Michael fought the wheel and, at the same time, jammed the shift lever into reverse. The gears ground in protest of what he had done; the tires spun and wailed. But it was all to no avail.

The car slipped further over the mountainside. The car held for another moment as Jan-Michael bellowed with frustration, stamped, and floored the gas pedal in a mad effort to get the rear wheels to back them onto the road.

But the car continued to slide forward.

Looking through the windshield was like seeing a slow-motion scene in a movie. Suzanne screamed as the car went off the mountain. She tried to turn back, to get Allan, but the force of the drop pinned her to the seat. She saw Jan-Michael rip off his seatbelt and, as the car did a flip in midair, he tried to grab Allan.

Just then, the front of the car hit a jagged outcrop and everything inside the car was torn loose. Suzanne's seatbelt snapped. Her head smashed into the roof of the car. Jan-Michael's heavier body rammed into hers, knocking the breath from her. Then Allan cried out in pain. Suzanne willed herself to fight the oncoming darkness.

Ignoring the battering of the car on the mountainside, Suzanne reached out for her son. She tried to grab him, but could not reach him.

The car hit something else, and then spun over again. From the corner of her eye, she saw huge limbs of trees seemingly reach out to swat at the car.

The car slammed into a huge old oak tree. Glass exploded everywhere and the front door burst open. The tree held, momentarily stopping the car, which swung in a pendulum movement until it slid off the tree. The car rolled over, tossing the semi-conscious occupants about, and fell downward again. It hit a long, stout tree limb. This time everyone was flung forward.

The car went into another airborne spin. Suzanne felt herself being sucked out. She grabbed whatever she could and, as she fell through the open door, held onto her son's light jacket.

And then she hit the ground. The force of the crash rocked her and slammed her into the earth. She tried to reach for Allan, but she had lost her grip.

Pain sliced through her when she tried to turn her head to look for them. With a superhuman effort, she turned her head and saw Allan inches from her. She willed her hand to go to him, and she put her fingers on his face. Then she saw Jan-Michael lying in a crumpled heap, not a foot from their son.

She tried to say something, but before she could find her voice, she was sucked into a deep, black and bottomless void.

She floated without pain or feeling. There was nothing around her; and, there was nothing within her. But, sometime later, she felt herself being pulled. She fought against the intrusion. She didn't want to be disturbed. She wanted to stay in the darkness. She wanted the peace that it offered. She did not want to be taken out of the newly found safety of this peaceful and dark void.

But the tugging and pulling and shaking would not go away. Her name was being called out, over and over even as she was being pushed about. She fought against it, shoving back against the hands that kept pawing at her.

And then her stomach cramped and a burning fire shot

upward from within her. She gagged, coughed, and spewed up spittle.

"Oh!" she cried, coughing again and trying to catch her breath.

She was lightheaded and nauseous. She blinked her eyes open and gulped at the air. "Allan . . . Jan-Michael, where are . . ." and then she stopped. Her family was dead. She was not in France, she was in Springvale. She almost cried aloud at the realization that she had been having another of her terrible dreams. It had been so real this time. She had been with them, again. And she had lost them, again.

Then she heard the wail of a siren from off in the distance, and looked up into Dana Cody's face. Her friend's features were pinched with fear. "Suzanne, can you breathe?"

Suzanne gulped more air. Her throat was raw and it burned. Her eyes were fuzzy. "What happened?"

Before Dana could answer, a lime-green fire engine and a white and red ambulance came to a screeching halt. Five black-clad men and two paramedics raced over to the women on the front lawn.

One of the paramedics carried an oxygen mask and tank. The other carried a first aid kit and blanket. The one with the oxygen equipment slipped the mask over Suzanne's face.

"When did she come around?" he asked.

"Just now. The house . . . the gas," Dana said to the firemen. "The back door is open. But the gas . . ."

As the firemen ran to the rear of the house, Dana turned back to Suzanne, who was now pushing away the oxygen mask.

"Please, don't fight it, you need the oxygen."

"What happened?" she asked before allowing the man

to put the mask back on. After the mask was on, he slipped the blanket over her shoulders.

Dana shrugged. "I'm not sure. There was a gas leak. I—" She paused as an unmarked police car, the red light on its dashboard flashing madly, pulled to the curb.

The driver got out and walked over to them. He was tall and lean, with dark hair and light eyes. "I'm Detective Peter Wilson," he said as he dropped to one knee next to Suzanne. "Are you all right?"

She nodded.

Wilson looked at the paramedic. The man nodded as well and then removed the oxygen mask. He knelt next to Suzanne and took the stethoscope from around his neck.

"Take a deep breath," the paramedic said as he placed the end of his stethoscope to her chest.

Suzanne did as he asked. As she exhaled slowly, the blanket dropped from her shoulders.

The paramedic withdrew the stethoscope and smiled at her. "Better?"

"Yes, thank you," Suzanne replied, realizing that all she was wearing was a very thin tee shirt and a pair of panties. She lifted the blanket and covered herself. Then she looked around. Behind the paramedics and firemen were a half-dozen of her neighbors. "How did I get out here?"

"I dragged you out," Dana said. "And Suzy, you may be thin now, but your not as light as you were when you were six."

"Can we go inside? I need to put on some clothes."

"We have to wait for the firemen to clear the gas from the house, and to check out the leak," said Detective Wilson.

"Ma'am," the paramedic said, "we'd like you to come with us, to the hospital. You should have a thorough examination. There could be some—"

"No," Suzanne said.

"But—"

"I'm fine. If I feel something later, I will go to the hospital. But I'm fine. I am."

"All right, ma'am," the paramedic said. "But please, be careful."

"I will," Suzanne promised as she started to stand. Both Dana and Detective Wilson reached out for her and helped her up.

"Pete," called a deep voice.

Wilson turned. One of the firemen had come out the front door of the house and was signalling to Wilson. The man wore the emblem of a captain.

"Excuse me," he said to Suzanne, and then started toward the man. "Jim?" Wilson said when he reached Jim Handley, the captain of the Springvale fire department.

"Since when does the assistant police chief come out to a gas emergency?"

Wilson smiled. "I was a few blocks away when I heard the call. I thought I'd check on things."

"That slow today?" the fireman joked. "Okay," he added, guiding the detective into the house, and then to a large utility room. A fireman carrying a toolbox walked past them. "Here's the scoop. A fitting in the laundry room came loose."

Captain Handley pointed to a pipe coming out of the wall a few feet from the side entry door that opened off the garage. "It looks as though it was hit. It was most probably done by the movers, when they brought things in here, or possibly into the house through the garage. The pipe was bent only a little, and the fitting was loosened."

"But she's been in here a week. Wouldn't she have smelled something?"

"Maybe not." He moved over to the washing machine, which was only a few feet from the gas pipe. "If she did a wash yesterday, perhaps the vibrations loosened the fitting and started the gas leak."

"I guess that's possible," Wilson said, bending closer to examine the pipe. He saw the spot where it was dented. It could be the way Handley said, Wilson thought. He looked at the fitting itself. There were scratch marks on the brass.

"We tightened it and set it properly. But I'll recommend that she get a plumber out to look at it as soon as possible."

"So you consider this an accident?" Wilson asked.

"In my opinion, yes. She's alive, and the house didn't go up," the captain stated. "She was lucky. Anything could have set the gas off. Damned good thing her stovetop is pilotless. But even so, just turning on a light could have . . ."

Wilson suppressed a shudder. "Yes, she was lucky," he said as they left the house and returned to the front lawn.

The neighbors had already dispersed; the paramedics were at their ambulance, putting their equipment away. The firemen were standing around their truck, waiting for their captain. Suzanne and Dana were in the center of the lawn, waiting for Wilson.

"Good job, Dana," Handley said.

"Thanks Jim. Everything okay inside?"

"Fine. We opened the upstairs windows as well. The gas should be all out by now. That was fast thinking."

"Thanks again," Dana said, her voice betraying that his words were making her uncomfortable.

"Ma'am, I'd recommend that you call a plumber and have him check the incoming gas pipe and fittings in the laundry room. We've tightened them down, but it would be a good idea to have a professional check it."

"I will," Suzanne promised. "Thank you."

After Captain Handley nodded, touched his hat, and

walked back to the truck, Suzanne looked at Dana. "You know him?"

"Greg is a volunteer fireman, so I know almost all of them. I usually feed them once a month or so," Dana added casually.

"We can go inside now, Ms. Grolier," Wilson said.

Suzanne studied him for a moment. He was a full head taller than her, and although she would not call him handsome, he was a striking man with strong facial features. He had dark hair just becoming laced with a little gray. His eyes were gray-green.

"How did you know my name?" Suzanne asked.

"That's my job," was all he would say as he motioned toward the house.

Inside, Suzanne excused herself and went upstairs. She could smell the gas, but only faintly. Shedding the blanket, she put on a set of sweats, rinsed the foul taste from her mouth with some mouthwash and, before going back downstairs, took a few seconds to gather her thoughts.

She was still shaken from the intensity of her dream. She had never before dreamt that she had been in the car with Jan-Michael and Allan. She'd always been a spectator to their terrible accident.

Taking a deep breath, Suzanne did her best to exorcise the old demons from her mind and went downstairs. She found Dana and the detective in the kitchen. Wilson was leaning against the counter, and Dana was just setting the teapot on the stove.

"Perhaps now someone can tell me exactly what happened?" she asked.

"Mrs. Cody saved your life."

"I think I figured that one out. I'd just like to know what the beginning of the movie was like."

Dana laughed and, ignoring Wilson's furrowing of his dark eyebrows, said, "I came by at nine and knocked on the door. You didn't answer. I tried several times. Then I went around back. I thought that you might be on the deck.

"You weren't. I went to the door and looked in. The kitchen was empty. I tried to open the door, but it wouldn't budge. Then, I got a quick whiff of gas."

Dana shrugged. "I wasn't sure, so I knelt down and sniffed around the bottom of the door. Whew, it nearly knocked me over. Then I knew why you hadn't answered the door.

"I didn't even think about it. I ran next door and had them call the fire department and an ambulance. Then I came back. I was lucky, because the kitchen window wasn't locked. I got it open, and slid inside.

"I opened the back door, went upstairs, and found you in your bed. I dragged you outside, and you know the rest."

"Yes, I do."

The pot on the stove started to whistle. Dana turned it off. "Tea?" she asked Peter Wilson.

"No, thank you, I have to get back to work."

Suzanne studied Wilson for a moment. "There are twenty-six thousand or so people living in Springvale. Do you make it a habit of knowing the name of every new resident, Detective Wilson?"

Peter Wilson smiled. A generous array of crow's feet radiated from the corners of his eyes. "Not really. But when I see a name that catches my eye . . . . We do have several celebrities living here in Springvale."

"And you consider me one of them?" she asked, her face tight with tension as she stared openly at him.

Wilson shifted uncomfortably, but did not take his eyes from her. "Indirectly. Mrs. Grolier, your husband was a wonderfully skilled writer—one of the best of our time. I am a great fan of his writing. When I saw your name in the weekly report of home sales, it caught my interest, immediately. I checked it out and discovered that you were indeed the wife of Jan-Michael Grolier."

Suzanne felt strangely relieved. Wilson had not known who she had once been. "I see. You . . . You enjoyed my husband's novels?"

"Immensely. His death was a loss to everyone," Wilson said.

Suzanne held her face stoic, but his words affected her deeply. So many things had happened to her in her life. So many.

"And I have to go. Are you sure you're feeling all right?"

Suzanne saw the concern on his face. "Yes, I'm fine, thank you."

"If there's anything I can do for you, please don't hesitate," Wilson said, extracting a business card from his shirt pocket and handing it to her. "Mrs. Cody," he added to Dana as he walked out of the kitchen.

When the policeman was gone, Dana sat at the kitchen table. "That was about as close a call as I ever want to have. I'm wiped out."

Suzanne looked at her old friend. "Dana, if you're going to be around me, get used to it."

Dana cocked her head to the side. "Excuse me?"

Suzanne wiped a hand across her eyes. "I don't know what it is, bad luck, or something, but these things happen to me, all my life. Accidents follow me. Things happen and people who are around me get hurt. Some of them die."

"Really, Suzanne," Dana said, waving her hand in a dismissive motion."

"Really, Dana. Really."

Chapter Four

Suzanne drank from a white porcelain mug. The coffee was strong and hot, made the way she had grown accustomed to while she'd lived in France.

The air was refreshingly cool. The day was clear and bright. She was sitting on the back deck, looking down at the Hudson river. A robin slipped from the tall Maple near the house, and glided elegantly to the lawn.

Landing, the robin dipped its head into the ground. Suzanne watched in fascination as the robin's body shook while its beak was buried in the earth. A moment later it flew back to the tree with a worm secured in its beak. Suzanne followed the bird until it disappeared into the leaves.

She felt better today than she had yesterday. The gas leak had left her shaken. Not because of the close call she'd had; rather, it was the fact that another "accident" had happened.

After Peter Wilson left yesterday, she and Dana had worked for a few hours, but she'd been unable to concentrate. Today, she hoped to get back on track.

She glanced at her watch. It was almost nine. Standing, she cast one last glance at the river. Its smooth surface rippled in the sunlight.

Inside, Suzanne put her cup on the sink and went into the office. Not two minutes later, Dana Cody let herself into the house with the key Suzanne had given her the previous day.

"Morning," Dana said in greeting as she entered the office and went over to her desk, gathering her pad and pencil. She checked the tape recorder and then asked, "Feeling better?"

"A little. But the whole thing still bothers me."

"You can't let it get to you. It was an accident."

Looking at it logically, Suzanne knew that Dana was right. Yet she couldn't let it go. "Yes, it was an accident, and thank heavens that no one was hurt. But I can't get it out of my head that I'm jinxed. Wherever I am, whatever I'm doing, and whoever I'm with, if I'm happy and things seem to be good, then . . . sooner or later, something terrible happens."

"Sooner or later something bad has to happen, it's natural. Life can't be perfect," Dana said.

Suzanne shook her head. Her voice was low and patient. "That's not what I mean. Really terrible things happen."

"What things? The only thing I ever heard about was on that movie. And when did these things start?" Dana asked, shifting from her desk to the couch. As she sat, she switched on the tape recorder and picked up a yellow pad. "Tell me about them. Start at the beginning if you want, or just talk about the first thing that comes to mind."

Suzanne smiled. "Are we working, or are you shrinking me?"

"Work," Dana said, her eyes wide and innocent.

"Okay," Suzanne laughed. The smile faded as she thought back over the years and tried to pinpoint the first of the "accidents" that seemed to follow her like a plague.

It had been in the third year of *And Baby Makes Five!* The

shooting season for the fall shows had just begun. It was the early summer.

"I was nine, almost ten," Suzanne said to Dana. "We were shooting the first show of the new season. I'd spent the winter going to private school, and was looking forward to going back to work. It was easier than school, and my tutor was a real pushover. I was also the princess of the whole place. Anything I wanted, I got. Whatever it was, it didn't matter. All I had to do was ask.

"Dana, you can't imagine what it's like to be in that position, and be only ten years old. The power is incredible, even if you don't recognize it as power; you know that you are special, and that when you talk, everyone else listens.

"Anyway, on the last day of rehearsals, Mr. Carlyle, one of the two executive producers, asked Mother if he could take us to dinner that night. He had some ideas he wanted to discuss."

Suzanne started to pace, as she had on the first day she'd worked with Dana. For some reason the physical activity helped her talk.

She stopped to look at Dana. "Shouldn't I try to do everything in order? Monday we just got me to California. Today I'm starting year three. Is that all right?"

Dana shrugged. "You're the one who would know better than me."

"You would think so," Suzanne said. "My husband was a writer, but when he wrote, he was alone. I do remember that he always told me that fiction worked best when the story evolved from its beginning. But," Suzanne added, "this isn't fiction."

"You're a novice and I'm not even in the ballpark. Suzanne, perhaps we shouldn't worry about what order you remember in. Why don't you just tell your story, and we'll sort it all out when it's finished?"

"That makes sense. Okay," Suzanne said after taking a deep breath. "Let's get to it. Buzz Carlyle was half of the team that produced the show. He was also the head writer for the show. When he asked Mother and I to join him for dinner, she couldn't refuse. It just wasn't done."

Suzanne knew about The Club, from listening to the talk on the set of *And Baby Makes Five*. It was one of the "in" places where all the "in" people hung out.

And it was real neat. The restaurant was set up like a maze. You had to walk by everyone's table in order to get to your table. There were no direct routes to anyplace in The Club, but that was the purpose—for one to be *seen*.

Still, Suzanne liked the place, and she also liked to be "seen." Tonight was especially fun, because Arthur had come with them. There were six at the table. She and Arthur, her mother and stepfather, Raymond, and Buzz and his wife Lena.

They had eaten their appetizer, and the next course had been served and cleared. The main course would be coming any moment, and Suzanne wasn't sure she'd be able to eat any more.

Then Buzz raised his wine glass, and the other adults did the same. He looked at Suzanne. "To Baby, who is making it all happen!"

Everyone clinked glasses except for she and Arthur.

"And it's because of how well we're doing that I asked you here tonight," Buzz continued after he'd set his glass down. "The show has been number one since the fourth episode was shown, three years ago."

He paused again to look from Suzanne to Raymond. "So, I've decided that the timing would be perfect to shoot a real movie!"

"Movie?" questioned Raymond Barnes. "When does

she have time to make a movie? She doesn't even have a chance to go see one in the theater."

"Ray," Carlyle said, his tone easy and placating, "in this business, you either do things when you're hot, or you never do them at all. I'm putting together a movie project and I want Suzanne in it. Her pay will be generous enough to be the cornerstone of a retirement fund for later in her life."

"That's all you people ever think of, isn't it, the money?"

Buzz Carlyle favored Suzanne's stepfather with a long and penetrating stare. "Occasionally, we think about our art and we even envision ways to make a better product for our customers. We also try to find actors and actresses who can be examples for those who will be influenced by what we've put on the screen. And Baby . . . I mean Suzanne, has that wonderful and rare ability to influence those who see her."

Mollified, Raymond Barnes spoke in a subdued voice. "I don't know. It would mean splitting up the family, again. Arthur is going to Boston in January. He's been accepted into the Boston Conservatory of Music."

"Wonderful," Carlyle said, reaching across the table to shake Arthur's hand.

Suzanne smiled. She loved her brother and was always glad when good things happened.

"Can we discuss this later?" Suzanne's mother asked Raymond.

"Fine," Raymond said and sat silently back in the chair.

"What's the movie about?" Suzanne asked, knowing that everything had been settled and she would make the movie.

"About an eight-year-old girl," he said with a wink.

"And don't you worry about it. It will be perfect, as will you," Buzz Carlyle added.

Suzanne turned to her mother. "Can I?" she asked, using her pleading puppy dog look.

"We'll talk about it at home," Lenore Barnes said with finality. Then she turned to the producer. "Do you have a copy of the script?"

Carlyle did not smile, although Suzanne thought she saw something in his eyes as he nodded to her mother. She felt a little tingle of excitement. She loved the movies.

By the time dinner was over, Suzanne was having trouble keeping her eyes open. She fell asleep on the ride home, and woke as her stepfather carried her into her room.

He set her on the bed and left as her mother came in to help her change into her pajamas. As her mother pulled the dress off, Suzanne asked, "Can I make the movie?"

Her mother smiled, and winked. "Yes."

"But Daddy—"

"I'll handle Raymond. Don't you worry."

She hugged her mother tightly. "Thank you, Mommy."

"Go brush your teeth," she said, giving Suzanne a little push toward the bathroom.

When Suzanne finished, she slipped into bed. Her mother bent over and kissed her. "Goodnight Mommy."

"Goodnight Princess," Lenore said, pecking at Suzanne's forehead. "Sleep well and sleep late, tomorrow's Saturday."

Her mother left, leaving the door slightly ajar to let the hall light filter in, as Suzanne preferred. She closed her eyes, and waited for sleep to come, but for the moment, she was unable to calm her thoughts.

She wondered what the movie would be like, and how

much different it would be than making a television show. As she let her mind fantasize about making a movie, she heard her parents' voices rise in a heated argument.

Slipping out of bed, Suzanne went into the hall. She stopped at the entrance of the living room and, pressing her back to the wall, she listened.

"You gave me your word that we would go back East for the hiatus so that Arthur could attend the conservatory," Raymond Barnes stated, his voice sharp.

"But this is a great opportunity for Suzanne. And we'll be there halfway through his quarter. Really Raymond, you're being selfish."

"I'm being selfish? What about you!" You make an agreement, and then you break it like that!" he said. The sound of a thumb and finger snapping together accented his last words.

"You're being unreasonable, Raymond. Absolutely unreasonable," Lenore said, her voice rising shrilly. "How can you deny her this? This could be the turning point. This could take care of her future, totally!"

"One movie will not make or break her career. Lenore, Suzanne is the biggest child star in the country today!"

"And she'll be a star when she's grown as well, if we keep her in the public's eye. Raymond, how long do you think this show will go on for?"

"Until it's over. But Arthur's musical education must go on schedule. If not, he will not have a career!"

"Bull," Suzanne heard Arthur whisper. Turning, she found her stepbrother standing next to her. She smiled at him and started to say something, but he put a finger to his lips, and motioned her to follow him.

When they reached her room, and went inside, Arthur closed the door. "Into bed, kiddo," he said.

She hopped into bed, and then snuggled under the covers. She was confused by her parents' fight. And she didn't want Arthur to miss his schooling either. She started to speak, but Arthur stopped her again.

"Don't you worry about it. It will all be okay."

"But I want to go with you to Boston," Suzanne said.

"I know. But even if you don't come at the beginning, you'll be there later. You heard what Mother said, didn't you?"

Suzanne nodded.

"Then go to sleep. We'll go out tomorrow morning and play. Okay?"

"Okay," Suzanne agreed.

Arthur left then, and a few minutes later her parents' voices faded away and she fell asleep.

It took another week before she found out that she would be doing the movie. It was scheduled to start the week after *And Baby Makes Five!* finished shooting and went on hiatus.

And it was a long week for Suzanne, who became more and more excited each day. Finally, they finished shooting the last show, and after the film was taken for processing, and the set cleared, they had their cast and crew party, as they did every year.

Near the end of the party, after all the little thank you speeches from the producers and directors and studio and network people, the cast and crew fell into its usual grouping. Suzanne was with her television siblings. Tim Randolf played her brother Bobby, and Carter Reynolds played her other brother, Tom.

They were hanging out in a corner of the set, drinking coke and eating pizza, ignored as usual by the adults, and able to eavesdrop on whoever they wanted. The older actors were near the center of the set, and the crew hung out along the edges. Everyone was talking, and a few people were dancing to piped-in music.

Buzz Carlyle and his partner, Aaron Kolstein, were

talking to Lenore Barnes. They were close enough for Suzanne and her TV siblings to hear Buzz excitedly telling Lenore that the shooting would begin in ten days, and that the press had already been notified about the movie.

Aaron Kolstein smiled at his partner and then at Lenore. "I thought I'd left the craziness of producing a movie behind me when I went into television, but Buzz talked me into doing this."

"You think movies are crazier than television?" Lenore asked him.

"Much more, but in a different way."

"They are," Tim Randolf said. Suzanne looked at Tim with large eyes. Tim had been in three movies already. He knew what he was talking about.

"Why?"

"They do things different. And they have so many more people working. It's harder. They want you to do everything three and four times so they can shoot it at different angles and with different light. It's a pain," he declared.

"I think it'll be fun," Suzanne said.

"Yeah, sure you do. But when we start shooting next season, you'll tell me I was right."

"Oh yeah?"

"Yeah," eleven-year-old Tim told her.

"We'll see. What about you, Carter?"

Carter, fourteen and stuck-up, shook his head. "I never wanted to make movies. You guys know my mother forced me to do this show."

His mother, both Tim and Suzanne knew, was Buzz Carlyle's sister. And Carter had always told them the same thing. She'd forced him into doing the show.

But he was good. He was a natural actor because he didn't even try to act, he just did what he was told, and it worked.

"Suzanne," Buzz Carlyle called, waving her over to them.

She walked the ten feet to the small group, and smiled up at the three adults.

"Ready to start learning your part?" Buzz asked.

"I already started," she told them. "I've been reading the script for a couple of days."

"You're a real trooper," the producer said with a wink. "And this movie is going to be a blockbuster!"

"And speaking of blocks, we're going to have our heads on the chopping block unless we get moving ourselves," Aaron reminded his partner.

Carlyle looked at his watch and then nodded. "We've got an appointment over at MGM in half an hour. Who's driving?"

"We're driving ourselves. I have to go out from there," Aaron told Buzz.

Both producers turned to Lenore and Suzanne. "See you a week from Monday. Be ready, Baby!"

"I will be," Suzanne promised.

"And give our best to Raymond, when you speak to him," Buzz said.

Lenore promised she would. Suzanne turned away momentarily. Arthur and Raymond had gone to Boston three days before, so that they could set up the apartment and get Arthur registered at the Conservatory. Suzanne missed Arthur. They hadn't been separated since they'd moved out to California from New York.

"And we should be going as well," Lenore said to Suzanne.

"I'll say goodbye." Suzanne said and went back to her two "brothers." She said goodbye to them, and to several other people she was close to and then met her mother at the exit to the sound stage.

They went to the parking lot, where Lenore's car was

waiting. As she got into the car, Buzz Carlyle drove past them in his black Porsche.

Suzanne knew it was a Porsche, because her idol, James Dean, had always driven one of them.

Lenore Barnes pulled behind Carlyle and followed him toward the street. Buzz's Porsche edged onto the street. As the front of his car moved onto the street's blacktop, there was the loud blaring of a horn.

Suzanne saw a large delivery truck bearing down on Buzz Carlyle's car. Its tires squealed loudly as it braked. But it wasn't able to stop in time. The truck smashed into the producer's small Porsche.

The little black car lifted off the ground. It went flying and landed on its side on the sidewalk. The car barely missed three people who were walking toward the studio's gate house.

Suzanne heard her mother scream. From the corner of her eyes, she saw the delivery truck speed up and drive away. And then she felt her mother's hand on her head, pulling her down to the seat. Then her mother laid on top of Suzanne and, an instant later, Suzanne heard a loud explosion.

When her mother finally let her up, all Suzanne saw were the flames and smoke pouring from Buzz Carlyle's car.

"My Lord," Dana Cody said. "And you saw it happen."

Suzanne took a sip of water to moisten her mouth. "My mother took me back into the studio so I wouldn't see everything else that would happen. Buzz had died almost instantly. They never found the truck driver. And I never made the movie. With Buzz dead, the movie was dead as well. No one had the heart or the desire to go on with it."

"It must have been hard on you."

"It was," Suzanne agreed. "Besides being the producer, I liked Buzz. He'd always treated me nicely. He never treated me like a kid, the way everyone else always did. When he talked to me, he didn't talk down. And even at my age, I knew that he was a real person in a make-believe world. The show wasn't the same after he was gone. I think that if he'd lived, the show might have lived longer as well."

"What happened after he died?" Dana asked.

"Not much. The show was in hiatus. Mother and I stayed for his funeral, and afterward, we flew to Boston to be with Arthur and my stepfather. I went to a private school for the spring semester. Then . . ."

Suzanne went on for another hour, detailing the time spent in Boston, and the family's eventual return to California for the filming of the fall shows.

They took a break for lunch at 12:30, and while they ate salad and drank iced tea on the deck, Dana asked about Suzanne's television brother, Tim Randolf.

Suzanne cocked her head and looked out at the river. "I haven't thought about Tim in a long time. You knew that we used to date when I was making those horror movies, didn't you?"

"Really? No, I didn't know that."

"Did you read the tabloids?" Suzanne asked.

Dana shook her head. "Suzanne, when I was eighteen it was all I could do to read a school book."

Suzanne laughed. She liked talking to Dana. "When I was making my comeback as a teen scream queen, Tim was in my first movie. We started dating. The tabloids made a lot out of it. You know the type of headlines *BROTHER AND SISTER LOVERS! BABY AND BOBBY TOGETHER, BUT THIS TIME THEY ARE MORE*

THAN BROTHER AND SISTER! The usual," Suzanne said with a shrug.

This time it was Dana who was laughing. "I think Tim Randolf must have liked those type of headlines."

"Why?"

"Because he does them all the time. Tim Randolf is the star of one of the hottest shows on local TV. It's one of those trashy interview shows. You know the type. It's called Tabloid Television."

But, when Suzanne continued to look at her with a confused expression, Dana said, "You know the type . . . . *Older women, teenage men!* Another one was, *Men who cry and women who love them!*" She paused to think, and then smiled. "There was one that was just a little too much. *Sexual slaves and their lovers.* Suzanne, it's like having the *National Enquirer* on television."

"I can't believe he's doing something like that."

"Believe it. His show is on from noon till one," Dana said as she looked at her watch. "It's ten to one, he's on right now."

"I've got to see this," Suzanne said as she set down her drink and led the way upstairs. She turned on the TV in the sitting area of her bedroom. "Channel?"

"Nine," Dana said.

No sooner did she change the station than she saw Tim Randolf's face. She was astounded at his appearance. He looked almost the same as he had when she'd dated him in Hollywood. Then she realized that he was made up for the camera and most of his age would be hidden.

There was a look of maturity about him. His face had broadened a little, and his eyes were older. But there was no mistaking that it was Tim Randolf on the television screen.

"I can't believe this," Suzanne said as a slight feeling of déjà vu crept into her head.

"Believe it," Dana said.

Suzanne shook away her emotions and, as the show ended and the credits came on, shut the set off. "Let's get back to work."

Suzanne set the brown paper bag on the kitchen counter. She looked at the telephone answering machine. There were no messages. She unpacked the groceries and put them away, leaving out the flounder filet for dinner.

Then she poured herself a glass of white wine. This time of day, as well as bedtime, were the loneliest for her.

In France, she and Jan-Michael usually ate dinner late, around eight. But the early evening time was family time. She and Jan-Michael and Allan would be together. In the winter, they would play games with Allan, or read books to him. In the spring and summer, they would always go on evening walks, enjoying the last of the day, and wishing a fond farewell to the setting sun.

Suzanne sipped at the cool white wine. It was becoming harder and harder with each day, instead of easier. Dragging up her memories of childhood only led her to think of her recent and greatest losses. She closed her eyes for a moment to stop the forming tears.

She had to do this, she told herself. She had to go through her life so that she could find a purpose to go on. And so far, there was no purpose.

Sighing, she opened the door to the deck and stepped outside. No sooner had her feet touched the wood of the deck than the phone rang.

She was tempted to let it ring, but decided to answer it. She picked it up on the fourth ring, saying, "Hello?"

"Suzanne?" came a vaguely familiar male voice. Who? she wondered.

"Yes?"

"I can't believe it's you."

"It is. But I don't know who I'm talking to."

"It's me, Suzanne. It's Tim."

Was coincidence stretching things just a little too far? she asked herself. "Tim?"

"Randolf. Tim Randolf," he repeated.

She thought of the boyish looking man she'd seen that afternoon on television. "How did you know I was here?" she asked.

"A surprised hello would have been nice. An 'Oh-My-God, Tim, it's been twelve years!' would have been even better," he said.

Suzanne's thoughts came free. She exhaled and smiled. "You took me by surprise. But how did you know I was here, in New York?"

"Do you really want to know?"

"Of course I do," she said. And she meant it. The only people who knew she'd come back were her lawyer, Dana Cody, Arthur, and her stepfather.

"Then I'll tell you. Tomorrow night. I'll pick you up at seven and we'll have dinner. I know a great place near you."

"Tim, let's not get crazy," she said.

"No craziness at all. Suzanne, I haven't had a chance to talk with you in twelve years. We've got a lot of catching up to do. Come on, I'll pick you up at seven and tell you my secret for finding out where my old girlfriends live."

She hung hesitant before deciding that seeing an old friend couldn't be all that bad. Besides, she reasoned, he'd be able to help her fill in some of the blanks in her memory. "Okay," she agreed. "Seven, tomorrow evening."

Hanging up, Suzanne felt some of her sadness lift away. She remembered the good times in Hollywood, between her eighteenth and twentieth birthdays. She and Tim had had fun when they'd dated.

It would be nice to see Tim again. Besides, she did want to find out who told him that she was back in New York. She needed to know if it was a coincidence that he called her, or if it was something else.

Chapter Five

Putting her fork on the plate, Suzanne pushed the dish away and exhaled with satisfaction. Within seconds, a black-jacketed waiter was at her side.

"Was it to your satisfaction?" he asked, speaking English with an accent as Parisian as the meal he'd served.

"It was superb," she said with a smile.

The waiter turned to Tim Randolf. "And yours, Mr. Randolf?"

"Excellent," replied Randolf.

"Dessert?" the waiter asked while motioning to a busboy to clear the plates from the table.

Tim Randolf looked inquiringly at Suzanne. She shook her head. "Demitasse, lemon, no liquor please."

"I'll have regular coffee," Randolf said.

The waiter poured the remnants of their bottle of wine into the glasses and left.

Suzanne took the opportunity created by the waiter's movements to study Tim Randolf again. His teenage handsomeness had matured into youthful good looks which had survived his twenties and brought him into his mid-thirties. Even without makeup, the lines around his eyes and mouth were those created by living, not by too fast an aging process. He had blue eyes and sandy brown hair that had been blond as a child.

"What?" Tim Randolf asked.

Suzanne blinked. "I didn't say anything."

"But you're looking at me so intently. What are you seeing?"

Shrugging, Suzanne said, "The past, the present."

"The future?"

"No. The future is the one thing I can't see. If I could . . ." she let her words die. "Tim, why are we here?"

"Because I wanted to see you again. Suzanne, it's been so long. We had a lot of good times together, when we were doing *Baby*, and when we made those movies, later on. And we did mean something to each other, once."

Suzanne smiled thinly. "We had fun, and we dated. But that was a long time ago," she reminded him as the waiter reappeared with their coffee.

He placed an empty demitasse cup before Suzanne. There was a lemon rind in the saucer. Then he set an individual sized espresso pot next to it.

After he served Tim Randolf, the waiter poured Suzanne's coffee and slipped silently away.

She added a half spoon of sugar before twisting and then dropping the lemon peel into the coffee. She stirred the coffee and then sipped the dark and potent brew. "It's time for the truth. How did you know where to reach me?"

Tim Randolf smiled again. "In order to do my show properly, I have a staff of researchers who comb the papers from every area in the country, looking for anything that can be used on the show."

Suzanne's brows furrowed. "I don't understand. How can reading newspapers help you?"

"The show is about things that happen to real people, but bigger. It's everyday things that get blown out of proportion. Or it's the things that people want to keep hidden from each other but love to read about or see. It's . . ." he paused, looking for the right words.

"Trash," Suzanne offered.

"Not really," Tim defended.

"I saw a little of it yesterday. Something about older women who seduced boys?"

"No. It was older women who married younger men for love."

"And the men married the women for their love? Or was it their money?"

"That's the difference. None of those women are rich. The best of the lot was an executive who earned seventy thousand a year. The men genuinely love these women."

"Perhaps, but a psychiatrist might have a different explanation."

"That's the point. What I try to do is to show different views of not quite taboo subjects."

"And taboo subjects as well. From what I've learned, it's the *National Enquirer* on television."

"Again, yes and no."

"You still haven't answered my question."

Tim drank some of his coffee. "My researchers read everything. One of them came across a small article in your local paper. It was about you and the gas leak and the miraculous rescue. She recognized your name and brought the article to me, because of our old ties."

"And then you found out my phone number and called," Suzanne added.

"Exactly."

"Again, why?"

Tim Randolf gazed at her for several long seconds. He clasped his hands together, and then separated them. "Okay, the truth," he said. "It's really simple. I wanted to see you again. Suzanne, a year and a half ago, I took my show to Rome. We were there for two weeks. One night, with nothing to do, I was walking along a street. I don't even know which one. I was passing a movie theater. There was a poster out front. It was huge. I took one look at it and almost fell down. It was you.

"I went inside, and I had the shock of my life. You were the star of the movie. I didn't understand one damned word, but it didn't matter. I watched you for two and a half hours, and I couldn't stop myself. Ever since then, I haven't been able to get you out of my mind."

She looked deeply into his wide, blue eyes and saw no deception. "Tim, I'm here because we were friends a long time ago. I'm not looking for a relationship."

"People who look for relationships rarely find them," Randolf said. "Besides, what's wrong with looking up an old friend?"

"Nothing," she admitted.

They finished their coffee silently. When the waiter came to the table, Tim Randolf asked for a check.

The waiter smiled at him, and then at Suzanne. "It has been our pleasure to serve two such distinguished people as Monsieur Randolf and Madame Grolier. There is no charge. And may I say," he added, looking at Suzanne and switching to his native French, "My wife and I are fans of you and of your husband. We regret his loss, greatly."

"Merci, Monsieur," she replied, moved by his simple words.

Standing, they left the restaurant and went out to the car. Tim put on a classical station, and drove silently. The dashboard clock showed that it was ten.

When he pulled into the driveway, he did not turn off the engine. "Would you like to come in?" Suzanne asked as she opened the car door.

Tim Randolf smiled. "I would, but it's getting late. Perhaps another night?"

Although her invitation had been offered out of courtesy, she had expected him to say yes. She was pleasantly surprised when he declined.

"Another night would be nice," Suzanne replied.

Tim walked her to the door and, after she had it open, took a single step back. "Thank you for tonight. I enjoyed it," he said.

"I did too," Suzanne admitted. "It was fun."

"When shall we do it again?"

"Call me," she answered before stepping all the way inside and closing the door.

"We finished yesterday with Buzz Carlyle's death. What happened after that?" Dana asked, turning on the tape recorder.

Suzanne walked to the window and looked outside. The sun's morning warmth washed across the front lawn, turning the grass into a swath of shining emerald.

"The movie was canceled. No one had the heart to go on with the project without Buzz. As I said yesterday, after his funeral, we flew to Boston and met my stepfather and Arthur. Raymond had found a large apartment, and they'd put me in a private school."

Suzanne left the window and went to the chair across from Dana. Sitting, she said, "I hated that winter. It was cold and boring and the only two things that made it bearable were Arthur and the fact that I knew I would be leaving no later than the beginning of April.

"And of course Mother never let up. There were acting lessons every day, and commercial shoots at least once every two weeks. On one of those shoots . . ."

Suzanne talked on for almost two hours. Dana interrupted only when it was necessary to clear up a point.

At twelve, Suzanne stopped talking and declared it lunch time. They sat at the kitchen table and ate a salad Suzanne had prepared that morning.

"So, are you going to tell me or do I have to die of curiosity?" Dana finally asked.

Puzzled, Suzanne stared at her.

"Didn't you go out with someone last night? Tim Randolf, wasn't it?" Dana said. "Jeez, Suze, are you putting me on?"

Suzanne laughed. "I'm sorry. I . . . . It was very nice."

Dana cocked her head to the side. "Oh, it was very nice. Suzanne, Tim Randolf is a pretty big personality in this part of the world. Do I have to read about this in the *Enquirer* or are you going to tell me about your date?"

"It was nice," Suzanne began. "We went to La Fontaine du France, had a wonderful meal, and talked. He told me how he learned where I was, and asked me out again."

Dana's eyes widened. "And?"

Suzanne laughed at her expression. "I told him to call me."

"Is he like he is on his show?"

"I haven't the slightest idea. I've seen him on the show once, for ten minutes, remember? But he seemed to be like he always was, just a little older."

"His show today is housewives who hook part time to supplement the family income."

"What?" she said, not sure she heard her friend correctly.

"Exactly. He's doing a show about housewife hookers."

"I don't think I could handle that one."

"I brought my husband's Watchman television," Dana

said, opening her purse and taking out a little portable radio size television set.

She put it on the table, raised the antenna and turned it on. After adjusting the tuner, Tim Randolf's face filled the screen.

"And now, let's talk with Mrs. ah, Smith," he said as he turned to a woman seated next to him. There was a fuzzy dot centered over her face.

"Because of the delicate nature of today's show, the faces of all our guests will be disguised."

Randolf paused a moment, and then said, "What made you turn to prostitution, Mrs. Smith?"

"My husband had been hit with several setbacks at work. We were getting into deep financial trouble." Her voice was electronically distorted as part of her disguise, but her words were those of a well educated person. "We were about to lose our home. I could not allow that to happen to my family."

"Give me a break. This is even sleazier than I thought it would be," Dana opined as she turned her full attention to the screen.

They'd finished lunch twenty minutes ago, and had moved from the kitchen back to the office. But Suzanne could not stop thinking about the show she'd seen during lunch. To call it trashy was not enough. It was worse than trashy, and it bothered her that this was the fare that people actually wanted to see and hear.

But she knew better than to let it bother her, for it was only a natural extension of what had been going on all over the world for years. Gossip tabloids had been and would probably always be the biggest selling magazines, because people wanted to know what happened to other people. They didn't want to know about the good things and the nice people; they wanted dirt, any kind of dirt.

"Suzanne?" called Dana.

Shaking her head, Suzanne turned to Dana. "Yes?"

"You were starting to talk about the next season," Dana reminded her.

"Yes. But there wasn't much happening that season. It was our fourth year, but with Buzz gone, some of the magic had been lost. It was good, but nothing spectacular. We dropped in ratings from the number one sitcom, to number eighteen, which was still good."

"None of those 'accidents' happened that year?"

Suzanne shook her head. "No accidents. It was an easy season. But during the hiatus between the fourth season and the fifth, things changed for me. When filming started again, it all went downhill."

"How? Was it still because Buzz's leadership was gone?"

"No. It was because of me. Baby was gone."

Dana frowned. "I don't understand."

"You will. I had just turned twelve. And I was changing, physically. I was entering puberty and becoming an adolescent," Suzanne said, as she led Dana back to the fifth season of *And Baby Makes Five!*

"Nothing fits!" Suzanne snapped, flinging the too small dress away. It had fit the week before, but she couldn't close it over her budding breasts this week.

She fell to her knees and started to cry. Her mother sank on the carpet next to her. "Easy sweetheart. It happens to everyone. We talked about this just a few months ago. It happens to everyone."

"I know. But why now? Mommy, I don't want this!"

"Suzanne, it's not a matter of wanting or not wanting. Women menstruate. That's all there is to it."

"But they don't get fat, and I'm getting fat! I can't help it. And look at this," she added, pointing to her chin, where a large and angry red pimple stood out.

"They usually come together," Lenore said. "Look, sweetheart, just put on some jeans and a top. We'll go to the studio, and they'll fix you up."

"Like always. But it isn't working!" she snapped and started to cry again.

It took her mother fifteen minutes to get her to stop. When she put on her jeans, they were also tight, and her belly paunched out over them.

When they finally got to the studio they were a half-hour late. The wardrobe mistress and the makeup artist worked for another hour before they declared Suzanne ready for the set. By the time she reached the set, everyone's tempers were raw.

The ratings had been slipping ever since the first show, and if things weren't pulled back together, she knew that the show would be canceled at the end of the season.

Suzanne sensed that the show's downward drop was her fault. She was changing, every day, and she was changing for the worse. She was on a diet, but it didn't help. She was always hungry. And she was growing taller and wider, with every passing day.

And her face was broadening as well. She didn't look like *Baby* any more. She looked . . . ugly, she told herself as she stepped onto the set.

"Come on Baby, we're all waiting for you. You do know those lines, today, don't you?" asked Paul Driscoll, who was still the show's director.

"Yes, sir," she said in a low voice.

They did a quick rehearsal, and then started filming. Halfway through the first scene, Paul Driscoll shouted to cut. He yelled for makeup, and when the woman stepped onto the set, he told her to fix Suzanne's face.

She went over to Suzanne, and then looked at Driscoll. "What's wrong?"

"Her face is too big. Make it smaller."

"I do makeup, not plastic surgery," the woman snapped sarcastically.

Suzanne's face flushed crimson with embarrassment. "You . . . I . . ." Unable to find the words to express herself, she spun from them and ran off the set. Tears fell freely, ruining the hour of makeup that had preceded the event.

Not a minute after she reached her dressing room, Paul Driscoll came in. "Baby, I'm sorry. I shouldn't have said what I did. I—"

Turning to him, her embarrassment feeding her self-hatred and her anger, Suzanne said, "I know I'm fat and ugly. I can't help it. It's not my fault. And I quit!"

The director put his hand on her shoulder. "Baby—"

She pulled away from him. "My name is Suzanne. My name isn't Baby! My name never was Baby!" she cried.

Her mother came in then, pushing past the director and taking Suzanne into her arms. "Get out," she ordered the people who were all gawking openly through the door.

"Easy, sweetheart," Lenore cooed, holding her daughter close.

She held Suzanne until she stopped crying. And then, when she was calm, Lenore Barnes stepped back and gave Suzanne a long hard stare. "All done now?"

Suzanne nodded.

"Good. Now, I'll say this only once. You will never, ever, do something like that again! Do you hear me, young lady?"

Suzanne stared at her mother. She couldn't believe her mother was scolding her.

"I—"

"These people have been like a second family to you. They have supported you, emotionally and with their love, for the last four years. They have worked with you, and they have been your friends. They are trying to help you now, as well. Don't you dare show your ingratitude by acting like this. You are a professional. You may only be twelve years old, but you are a professional."

Lenore took a breath. "You have things that any girl in the country would give her eye teeth for. You are famous. You are rich! Yes, you are rich because I've invested your money for you. And you owe all the people you work with your gratitude and your devotion for helping you become wealthy and famous. There isn't another child, anywhere, who doesn't know who Baby is. And there isn't another little girl, anywhere, who doesn't want to be you!

"And if nothing else, you will finish the last three shows like a professional. I don't care what you think you look like. You will play your part, and you will play it like you have for the last four years. You are part of this show, and you will continue to be a part of it. You owe that to everyone who has worked with you, and you owe it to everyone who watches this show. Now get yourself together and get out there!"

Suzanne stared at her mother, the words still ripping through her head. She felt betrayed and let down. Now she had no one. Arthur was in college. She hadn't seen him in three months. Her mother was the only person she thought she could trust, and now she found out she couldn't.

"When this season is over, I will not come back."

She saw her mother's face change. A shadow of sadness crossed Lenore Barnes's features. "Suzanne, the reason everyone is so . . . short with each other today, is because they were informed, this morning before we got here, that the show was canceled. This will be the last season."

"Whew," Dana said. "That was pretty intense."

"To say the least. But it had its effect. I went back out and ignored the way I looked and the way I felt. I finished that show, and the next two. And that was the end of the five-year run of *And Baby Makes Five!*"

Suzanne crossed the room and sat down on the couch with Dana. She glanced at Dana's writing pad, and saw that it was filled with notes.

Leaning back, she rested her head on the top of the cushion and closed her eyes.

"When the last show was filmed, I was twenty pounds heavier than on the first show of the season. I was only an inch taller, but I was wide as a kite. And dear Lord, I was ugly. And I kept getting uglier.

"It was like living the story of the ugly duckling, except in reverse. I'd been a beautiful child—that's not ego speaking, either. I was beautiful. There were always pictures around me to show me how pretty I was.

"But in my case, when I started to menstruate, it truly became the 'curse.' I turned from the little swan into the ugly duckling. And it lasted for a long time.

"All that summer, after the show had ended, Mother kept taking me on rounds, but no one would hire me, for commercials, films, or anything else."

Suzanne paused. The painful memories were easy to dredge up, but hard to voice. "I got one job offer all summer, and that was to model 'big' girls clothing. I threw such a tantrum that my mother gave in. But, she also put me on a special diet that the doctors set up.

"That summer was one of the worst of my life. My periods were killers. And besides becoming fat and pimply, my allergies grew worse. I couldn't even use regular makeup any longer.

"We—"

"Hold up," Dana said after a loud click had sounded in the room. Suzanne looked at the tape recorder that Dana was picking up. The tape had ended. She looked at her watch. It was almost three.

Dana put a fresh tape into the machine and leaned back, ready to take more notes.

"It's late. Your kids will be home in a few minutes. We can continue tomorrow."

Dana shook her head. "You're going strong. And I don't mind staying today. Paul has baseball practice, and Trish is playing at a friend's after school. I'm free until five, if you want to go on."

Suzanne smiled. "Great. Okay, I followed my mother's diet, and I lost a lot of weight. But I hated the way my face looked. It was broad, and round, and . . . . It just wasn't me any more.

"Anyway, Mom never stopped being the 'stage mother' and even if it was only once a week or so, she took me out on agency and studio rounds. Nothing ever happened, though. Then, in the middle of the winter, I got a call back. A month before, I had gone on an audition for a TV series. It seems that they wanted to take another look at me. This time with a full screen test.

"I was really excited for the first time since *Baby* ended. I felt better about myself, and I was really ready for this. They sent me a script, and I memorized it, completely."

"Just remember to relax," Lenore told her daughter as Suzanne went into the prep room and Lenore was taken back to the waiting room by the page who had been escorting them.

Entering the room, Suzanne went over to the first chair and put her makeup case on the counter. All the cosmetics were specially made for her, and were completely hypoallergenic. She even had her own special set of brushes that the allergist had made for her.

After setting out the cosmetics and a special can of hairspray, she sat on the chair. A few moments later the makeup artist and hairdresser came in. The hairdresser was a woman in her forties, but the makeup artist was barely out of her teens.

The hairdresser worked first. The younger woman waited off to the side while the hairdresser brushed out Suzanne's hair. Then she gently teased it into the look that the show's producers wanted. Suzanne liked the style. It fit her face.

"Aren't you . . . Baby?" asked the younger makeup artist who had been watching Suzanne in the mirror.

"Yes, I played Baby."

"That was a great show. I loved it," she said.

"Good luck, Miss Barnes," the hairdresser said as she misted Suzanne's hair with the hairspray that Suzanne had put on the counter with her makeup.

The makeup artist took over next. The first thing she did was to push Suzanne's makeup out of the way. "Those colors are a little out of date," she said. "I've got better ones."

"You have to use them. I'm allergic to anything else. My face will swell up badly if you use anything else. And you have to use my brushes too."

"Too bad," the makeup artist said, setting her own tools down and picking up Suzanne's.

She worked for another ten minutes and then stepped back. "Not bad, even if I say so myself."

She raised Suzanne's chair so Suzanne could look into the mirror. She gasped at the results. She didn't recognize herself at all. She looked stunning! She looked . . . older and prettier and her face seemed much thinner.

"It's . . . . You did a great job, thank you."

The girl winked. "Hey, you get the job, you put in a word for me. I could use a series to get a leg up."

She was only thirteen, but she'd been in the business for a long time. She knew exactly what the makeup artist was saying and understood her.

"If I get the part, I'll put in more than just a word. You're great!"

"Thanks. I'm Janie Morse," she said.

"Suzanne Barnes," Suzanne said, shaking the girl's hand.

"Good luck, for both of us," Janie said as she helped Suzanne out of the chair. "I'll put your makeup together, you go ahead out there."

Suzanne took her script, and left the makeup room. She found the page who had brought her there, just coming down the hall. "Follow me, they're ready for you."

Two turns and three doors later, she stepped onto an empty sound stage. A cameraman was seated on a swinging boom camera, and another cameraman was standing behind a rolling camera.

There were several spotlights on, all directed on a stool that was set in the middle of the set. She saw two other people sitting in director chairs near the edge of the set.

"Hi, Suzanne," came a disembodied voice. "My name is Walter Harmon. I'll be directing your screen test. Please sit on the stool, get yourself comfortable, and give us five more minutes. Go over your lines if you'd like."

"Okay," Suzanne said, looking toward a darkened glass booth.

"She's perfect," she heard a low voice say over the

speakers. A moment later there was a loud click and the sound system went dead.

Trying to ignore what she'd heard, Suzanne opened the script and turned the pages until she found the marked-off area. Although she'd memorized it, she started to read it again.

After a few minutes under the lights, the heat began to bake her. Then, a moment later, an itch started in her left cheek.

She tried to ignore it. She didn't want to spoil the perfection of the makeup. But the harder she tried, the more it itched.

Carefully, she used the back of a knuckle to pat at her cheek. It didn't help. Then she rubbed with the back of the knuckle. The itch turned into a burning sensation.

She tried to pat at it again, but it continued to get worse.

Then the other cheek started to burn. Suddenly, her face was on fire. She dropped the script and tried to rub at her cheeks with her fingertips, still trying not to mess up her makeup.

But it didn't help. All she knew was that every time she moved her fingers, the burning grew worse. And then it became painful, like someone was stabbing her with sharp needles.

The pain was incredible. She heard someone screaming loudly, but didn't realize it was her. All she felt was the pain on her face; all she heard was the way her fingernails were tearing at the skin on her cheeks.

She fell off the stool and landed on her side. She was kicking and writhing in pain, and fighting off the hands that were suddenly clutching at her arms and legs.

"Hold her hands," she heard her mother's voice shouting. "Someone get me ice and a bowl of water. Hurry! She's having an allergic reaction."

"Good God," she heard someone say when her hands were pulled from her face. "The blood. Look at the blood."

And then she passed out.

"What happened?" Dana asked in a hushed voice.

"I had an allergic reaction. To this day, no one knows how my makeup had gotten contaminated. Perhaps it was one of the colors I'd never used that wasn't as pure as it was supposed to have been, but something in the makeup gave me a reaction. My face had swelled to twice its normal size before my mother had been able to get the makeup off and my face iced down.

"I didn't get the series, needless to say. The swelling went down in two weeks, and the producers tried to hold off casting the part until my face was back to size. But it took four months for the skin on my cheeks to heal enough to take pictures."

Suzanne sighed with the memories. "Naturally, they couldn't wait that long. They had to cast the part. I was so upset and so disgusted with myself and my life that I had eaten myself up three dress sizes. I was past being chubby; I was fat."

"And then?"

"We moved back to Springvale. That following September, Arthur started his second year at Julliard, and I started ninth grade, with you, remember?"

Dana made a face. "Yeah, we were called the tubbo queens."

"And that's another chapter," Suzanne said. "Anyway, I guess we're through with *And Baby Makes Five!*"

"Not quite," Dana said, smiling. "My kids watch you every day. You've been in syndication for the last fifteen years."

Chapter Six

The car reached the peak of the road, and Suzanne took her foot off the gas. "Perfect!" she declared, motioning to a restaurant set back from the highway.

"The Overlook Cafe." Dana read the name from the sign at the entrance to the parking lot. "It must be new, I've never heard of it . . . but really, Suzanne, the Overlook Cafe?" She rolled her eyes, dramatically. "Do you think it overlooks the river?"

"You've become such a cynic, Dana. It may be a lovely place for all we know. Let's see."

"You're the boss," Dana replied as Suzanne pulled into the parking lot and went around the side of the restaurant.

She maneuvered the car into a parking space between two larger cars. The parking lot, she observed, was more than half filled.

The view was outstanding. The green mountains rising from the river bank on the far side were staggeringly beautiful. A multitude of small boats dotted the deep blue water, their pale decks and white sails combined to look like the Mad Hatter's version of dotted highway lines.

"Not bad," Dana admitted.

"I think you should bring the recorder. We'll work over lunch."

After Dana gathered her note pad and tape recorder, they went inside. The interior of the restaurant was light and airy. Three of the four walls were glass.

The Overlook restaurant lived up to its name, Suzanne decided. "Not bad?" she asked Dana.

"No," Dana admitted, "not bad at all."

A smiling hostess led them to a window table. After they were seated, Dana excused herself. Alone, Suzanne savored the view.

She felt good. An hour earlier, she'd felt trapped. She'd been spending too many hours cooped up in the house. She remembered when her need for getting outside had started. It had been during the first year of doing *And Baby Makes Five*. As a young child, she hadn't understood her intuitive need to escape the interior set for a few minutes a day. But as she'd grown older, she'd learned that her need to go outside was the need to have a few minutes of sanity amidst a life of fantasy.

Today, not five minutes after she'd started to talk about her past, she'd gotten that closed-in feeling she used to have when filming. The sensation had grown so strong, so quickly, that all she'd been able to do was to tell Dana that they were going out, and for her to bring her pads and recorder.

Leaving the house, Suzanne had driven north on Highway 9. As she drove, she'd gone back to that last year in California, and to the terrible time it represented in her memory.

She'd been able to bare all, and had done so with a strong voice that seemed to deny the heartache that still lingered inside her. So many bad things had happened to her over the years that she just could no longer trust what appeared to be good.

That last summer in California had been the worst ever. Following the incident at the screen test, and in less than three months, she'd gained twenty-six pounds. Her acne grew to monstrous proportions, and her allergies had gotten progressively harder to contain.

By the time they'd moved back East, her mother had stopped pressuring Suzanne to go on interviews. And when they returned to New York to live, Lenore Barnes didn't even set up a single interview; rather, she let Suzanne be a girl again.

Her mother had even given in to Suzanne's pleas that she be sent to a small, local private school, rather than the artistic specialty brand of private school where the wealthy sent their children. That too had been a small oasis of salvation in a terrible time.

"Suzanne?"

Suzanne blinked and found Dana sitting across from her. "Sorry. I was in the past."

"No problem," Dana said, opening a menu and reading it.

Suzanne did the same and decided on a cold lunch of smoked trout and vegetables.

After ordering their lunches, Dana said, "Where were you, in the past I mean," she added when Suzanne favored her with a puzzled expression.

Nodding, Suzanne said, "I was thinking about that summer in California and when I got back here."

"Ninth grade, right?"

Looking out the window and across the river to the rolling green mountains, Suzanne nodded. "Ninth grade. The Country School."

"That was a good time in the bad time, wasn't it?" Dana asked. But before Suzanne could speak, Dana went on. "But only to a small degree. After all, we were the two fattest kids in school. Yuck!"

Suzanne gazed at her friend. She tried to picture Dana as she'd been all those years ago. She had been even fatter than Suzanne. But at least Dana hadn't had the curse of that terrible acne.

"Yuck is right! But we survived, didn't we?"

"We survived because the kids at that school didn't pick on us the way they would have in a public school," Dana stated.

Suzanne laughed lightly. "They couldn't. The teachers wouldn't let them get away with it."

"It didn't take that long for you to change either," Dana reminded her. "By the time we were juniors, you had changed again. You went from ugly duckling to swan. Suzanne, you were gorgeous!"

Hearing both adoration and sadness in Dana's voice, she studied her friend's face. "What?"

Dana shrugged her shoulders. "It was hard for me to watch you change. You were my closest friend. But when you started losing weight, and getting pretty again, I started to lose you as a friend."

"No you didn't. I never turned my back on you. We were always friends."

"That's not what I mean. It was in my own head, and I knew it even then, but you were changing and I wasn't, and . . ."

The waitress appeared with their plates and Suzanne did not miss Dana's sigh of relief at the interruption.

They ate silently. Then, halfway through the meal Suzanne said, "Were you jealous of me when I lost all that weight?"

Dana shook her head in denial, then smiled shyly. "What do you think? I loved you like a sister, and I hated you at the same time. I tried diets and exercise and everything, but nothing worked for me. So I'd get discouraged and eat even more."

"But you did change," Suzanne reminded her. "You

changed so much I didn't even recognize you when you rang my doorbell."

"Yes, I came to terms with myself in college. Maybe it was being on my own that helped, but somehow I learned how to accept who and what I was. After that, the physical part was easy."

"Which is what we all want to do, somehow. How is your lunch, by the way?"

"Very good." Dana said. "I'll have to pass the word about this place."

The waitress returned and both women ordered coffee. When the waitress brought the coffee, she also left the check.

Ten minutes later, Suzanne laid several bills on the table. "I needed this," she said. "And I feel good. Really good for the first time in a long time. Let's go home and finish up for the day."

"Yes, ma'am," Dana replied, giving her a semi-salute.

Outside, the day had grown even warmer. There wasn't a cloud in the clear, blue sky. Suzanne drew in a deep breath of fresh air, and then unlocked the car. She backed out of the parking space, and drove slowly out of the lot and onto the highway.

Looking ahead, Suzanne saw that the crest of the next mountain was at the same level as the one they were on. Her acrophobia reared its ugly head, but she clamped down on her fear. Then, as they followed the sloping road, she began to marvel at the way the highway turned into a long, black ribbon winding down for almost a half-mile. Two thirds of the way down was a section of twisting turns that looked far more curvy than they'd felt like when she'd driven up the mountain.

"I'm not big on heights," Dana said.

"Me either, but it sure is pretty."

"It is," Dana agreed, "but would you mind keeping it under sixty?"

Suzanne looked at the speedometer and saw she was doing almost seventy. She'd been so taken by the view that she hadn't realized how fast she was going.

She tapped on the brake pedal with her right foot. Nothing happened. She pressed harder. The pedal went to the floor without any resistance.

"Dear God," she whispered aloud as she began to pump the brakes.

Nothing happened. The car was picking up speed and was almost screaming down the side of the mountain. The road curved. She worked the steering wheel while telling herself that this wasn't happening. She must be dreaming.

Panic seized control of her mind. Flashes of all the nightmares she'd had streamed through her thoughts. Her husband and son had died in a car. And now she would die too.

"Suzanne!" Dana shouted.

Dana's voice cut through her panic and fear and freed her vocal chords. "There are no brakes. I can't stop the car."

Dana turned in her seat and grasped the handle of the emergency brake. She pulled it up hard. The handle snapped back without any resistance at all.

"Jesus," Dana swore as the tree trunks lining the side of the rode turned into a blurred line that looked more like a dark picket fence than a copse of trees. "Suzanne!"

"What do I do?" Suzanne cried out, trying to control the now hurtling car. She glanced at the speedometer. The speedometer registered ninety. She tried the brakes again. Nothing!

She looked ahead and gasped when she realized that they were about to enter the section of road made up of the series of double S curves that she'd seen from above.

Releasing the useless emergency brake, Dana grasped the transmission lever and shifted the car from drive to low. The engine screamed in protest. The two women were slammed against their seat belts as the car slowed.

But the maneuver didn't slow the car enough, and the speed hovered around seventy.

Suzanne made herself think. Then she realized there was only one way. Without hesitating, she grasped the ignition key and shut off the engine.

The instant the power died, the steering wheel turned into a sluggish instrument that acted as if it were mired in cement. Belatedly, Suzanne remembered that a front wheel drive car was close to impossible to steer without power from the engine.

"Help me steer!" she cried to Dana while she tried to keep the car on the road.

Dana released her seatbelt and leaned next to Suzanne. She gripped the steering wheel, her hands next to Suzanne's, and worked with her friend to keep the car on the road.

They were down to fifty when they entered the first turn. Somehow, they managed to turn the car. Suzanne's shoulders screamed in pain as she fought the steering wheel and kept praying for the car to slow more.

Seven seconds later they were out of the first part of the turn. The car was coasting at forty miles an hour. The second part of the S cutback was coming fast.

Suzanne attempted one more drastic measure. She tried to put the car into reverse. But the automatic transmission would not allow it. The gears ground, but the lever would not stay.

She pulled the lever back into low just as they started the turn. The car leaned hard to the left as she and Dana fought the almost immovable wheel.

They turned. The car went wide. Suzanne thought

they were going off the road. Then, suddenly, another car was coming at them. They tried to turn the steering wheel more.

"Left!" cried Suzanne.

The car shifted slightly to the left. But, thankfully, the other driver turned at the last second, and went to the inside of the road. The car missed them by a fraction of an inch.

"God that was close," Dana said as she worked frantically to keep the car on the road.

Suzanne's heart pounded. "Right!" she shouted as the last part of the curve came upon them. They managed to get the car into the turn.

The car drifted further left as they fought to get it to turn right. Then the front wheel left the road and dipped into the softer earth of the shoulder. Suzanne bit down on her lower lip as she fought to turn the wheel. "Harder," she shouted, talking to herself as much as to Dana.

The left front wheel came back onto the road. And then they were out of the turn and heading down the road again. The speed started to pick up.

The car was angling right now. Off to that side was the granite rock of the mountain. She knew she had to keep the car away from that.

Ahead of them was the lowest portion of the road. Hold on, Suzanne told herself as they rolled toward the nadir of the road.

"Left!" Dana said, grunting as she tried to help Suzanne turn the wheel.

Together, they forced the wheel to turn another fraction of an inch. The car straightened. Then they reached the bottom of the road and as soon as the car started on the upgrade, it slowed and stopped.

Suzanne let the car start to roll backward. At the same time, she and Dana turned the wheel enough to get it off the road. The instant the tires left the pavement, she slammed the shift lever into park, ignoring the grinding protest.

Exhaling, Suzanne slumped into the seat.

"My Lord," Dana whispered a few moments later. "We could have been killed. That car back there. It almost hit us head on."

Suzanne closed her eyes. It was happening again. Would it ever end?

"It must have been frightening," Arthur Barnes said after Suzanne told him about her car's brake failure.

"It was. I'm just glad that no one was hurt," Suzanne added as she continued to tell Arthur about the afternoon's events. She was lucky as well, because the car that she'd almost run off the road had turned back to see if she was okay.

The driver had a car phone, and had called a tow truck. The rest of the afternoon had been spent in getting the car towed back to the dealership. By the time she and Dana had gotten to her house, it was time for Dana to leave.

The people at the car dealership had been upset. The owner himself had come out to check on her. He'd promised to have the car inspected thoroughly, and to find out what happened.

He'd also told her that the dealership would take care of the towing bill, and then he insisted that she take a loaner car to use until her car was repaired.

"Arthur, why does this always happen to me?"

Her stepbrother reached across the kitchen table and patted her hand. "Suzanne. These things happen to everyone."

She stiffened at the words, and their tone. "I would have thought you would know better."

"Don't do this, Suzanne—"

"No! You think I'm paranoid, don't you?" she demanded.

Arthur shook his head quickly. "Please, think about this. Unlike most people, who have to leave their homes to work, you're usually home. This is the way it's always been for you. Even when you were a kid, doing the TV series, you had a different life. You went to work, and went to school at work.

"After that, when you were older, you made movies, and then you stayed home. When you left California and moved to France, you stayed home almost always. And when you did make movies again, you still took over a year off between films."

Arthur's relaxed tone helped to ease Suzanne's anger. "What has that to do with these accidents?"

"I'm not a psychologist, but I do have an idea about this. Suzanne, what happens is that you have no buffer between you and the events that surround you.

"You go along peacefully and steadily, for a while, and then something happens—an accident, or even a tragedy. But there are no changes in your life to get you accustomed to negative events. If you went to an office, where you would interact with others every day, you would have their experiences to think about as well as your own. You would see that different things happen all the time.

"But because you move along in a straight line, going from A to B without taking any detours to visit F or X, things seem to always happen to you. But, Suzanne," Arthur said, leaning toward her and taking her hand, "you're no different than anyone else. People have tragedies, and accidents, and good times. But they also have other things in their lives that break up the routine of just going along with the flow of time."

"Is that what you think I'm doing? Going with the flow of time?"

When Arthur nodded, Suzanne laughed. The sound was almost bitter. "When Jan-Michael and Allan died, I cried for days. I prayed for my own death. But I stayed alive, Arthur. I lived and two of the most gentle and beautiful people on the face of the earth died. Now you're telling me that their deaths are affecting me only because I didn't have anything else going on in my life?"

Arthur shook his head slowly. "That's not what I'm saying. I'm saying that you view these accidents and tragedies as something that is vindictively directed at you."

"How else can I see it?"

"Logically. Suzanne, if there is nothing to take your mind off a misfortune, and a few months later some other type of adversity occurs, of course you will feel that these are things that always happen to you—that you have bad luck, or that you are a victim of . . . whatever. But if there were other things in your life to occupy you, the misfortunes wouldn't always be so monumental."

Before she could react, Arthur cut her off. "I'm not saying that the loss of your husband and son was not a terrible tragedy. I'm just asking you to look at your life and put everything that happened to you into perspective."

Suzanne let her anger blow away. Arthur was trying to help, trying to do what her big brother had always done—help her.

"I'm sorry. I don't mean to get angry. And I do understand. And I am doing exactly what you're saying I should. I'm trying to put my life into context. I'm trying to find out why so many," she started to say bad, but stopped herself, "unfortunate things seem to happen to me. I'm trying to learn enough about myself to understand what my life is about."

Arthur's smile warmed her. "And that's good. But try something—and if not for yourself, for me. Try to stop looking at these accidents as if they were personal attacks on you. They're the happenings of life and only that."

"I'll try. And thank you for coming over," Suzanne said.

"My pleasure. I'm only sorry that I returned from the city so late. I would have been here earlier."

"You're here now. That's what's important," she said.

The doorbell rang. Suzanne looked at the clock. It was nine. She wondered who would be at her door. "I'll be right back," she told Arthur.

Rising from the chair, she went to the front door. "Yes?"

"Detective Wilson," came the muffled reply.

Puzzled, Suzanne opened the door. "Detective?"

"May I come in?" he asked.

Suzanne stepped back to allow him entrance. "Is something wrong?" she asked.

"Possibly. May we talk?"

Momentarily confused by both him and his words, she nodded. "This way," she said, taking him into the kitchen.

"Mr. Barnes," Wilson said, acknowledging Arthur Barnes's presence.

"Chief Wilson," Arthur said, rising and offering his hand. "How are you?"

"Assistant Chief, and I'm fine, thank you. How is your father?"

"Good," Arthur said. "Is something wrong?" he asked, looking from Suzanne to Peter Wilson.

Wilson shifted from one foot to the other, "Actually, I need to speak with Mrs. Grolier."

"Detective Wilson, Arthur is my stepbrother."

Peter Wilson openly stared at Suzanne. "You're . . ." He smiled. "I'm sorry, I didn't recognize you when we met the other day. You've, ah, changed."

Suzanne returned the smile. "Would you like some coffee?"

The Assistant police chief shook his head. "Ben Jeffries called me late this afternoon. He's the owner of Springvale Motors. Where you bought your car."

"Yes, I know who he is."

"Ben called me to look at your car. He was concerned about what had happened."

"I don't understand," Suzanne said. She looked into his eyes and was pleased that he met her stare openly. Most men had a habit of blinking or turning slightly away when she looked at them for too long.

"Neither do I," Arthur added. "Why would he call you for a mechanical problem?"

"Partly to protect himself from a lawsuit. A brake failure could lead to a major lawsuit if his dealership was found responsible for that failure, because of the negligence of a mechanic. But—"

"But to call the police?" Arthur interrupted.

"In this instance he did exactly the right thing by calling the police. Mrs. Grolier," Wilson said, shifting his gaze from Arthur to Suzanne, "the brake line leading to each wheel was cut. The mechanical emergency brake's cable was severed as well.

"Every time you pressed down on the brake pedal, you were draining the fluid from the brake system," Wilson finished.

Suzanne became lightheaded. She took several deep breaths in an effort to control herself.

"Are you saying that someone deliberately sabotaged my sister's car?" Arthur asked.

Wilson nodded. "The evidence seems to point in that direction."

Suzanne exhaled slowly. "Detective Wilson, do you think someone is trying to kill me?"

She felt Peter Wilson's gaze as if it was a physical touch. "Either that, or someone is trying to scare the hell out of you."

Chapter Seven

Suzanne crossed the backyard, stopping at the wooden gate set on the very edge of her property. Glancing down, she traced the steep wooden steps that ended on the cement embankment of the river.

Watching the water lap at the embankment, she thought back to the little girl who had played along this same river. She remembered too, the high school girl who had sat for hours along these very same palisades. She had always wanted to live here. And, when she'd been in high school, she'd promised herself that one day she would have a house set on the edge of the palisades so she could see the Hudson River every day.

Some dreams do come true, Suzanne told herself. She looked up and to her left. In the distance, cars streamed over the Tappan Zee Bridge on their daily trek to Westchester and points beyond.

Was Arthur right? Did her life seem plagued more because there was nothing substantial enough to interrupt and soften the crises? She hoped not, because that would mean that her life had been no more than a series of misfortunes separated by a few good events.

No! He was wrong. And Peter Wilson had been the carrier of the news that disproved Arthur's theory. Yet, she did not like the substantiation that Peter Wilson had offered her yesterday. The assistant chief of police believed that someone had tried to kill her. Why? And who?

Peter Wilson had asked that question himself, last night. But neither she nor Arthur had been able to come up with anyone who would want her dead. It just didn't make sense.

She closed her eyes and pictured Jan-Michael and Allan as she would always remember them. So much had passed, so many things had been taken from her. Why?

"Hello," came Dana's voice.

Suzanne pulled herself from the grip of her emotions and turned to face her friend and assistant. "Good morning. Ready for work?"

When Dana nodded, Suzanne came abreast of Dana, and the two women walked back to the house. Inside, they went directly to the office.

"What's on today's agenda?" Dana asked. "No joy rides, I hope."

"No, thank you," Suzanne said, keeping her tone as light as Dana's. "I guess we could go to the first of the horror movies. I don't think we have to spend any time on the high school years. Nothing really happened then."

"Then we're finished with the TV series?" Dana asked.

Pausing, Suzanne cocked her head thoughtfully to one side. Were they finished with that period? She sensed that there was more, but she wasn't quite certain of what more there was.

"I don't know. But, we can always go back. I think that there's—" The phone's ring interrupted them.

Suzanne waited while Dana answered the phone. A moment later she said, "Hold on," and covered the mouthpiece with her palm. "Tim Randolf. Want me to leave?"

Suzanne shook her head as she took the phone. "Hi, Tim, how are you?"

"Fine," he said.

"To what do I owe this pleasure?"

"I enjoyed myself the other night, and since we agreed to do it again, I have a one word question for you: when?"

Suzanne hesitated. Although she liked Tim, she wasn't sure she wanted to go any further than their single date. But, she did remember that she'd told him to call her, and she didn't want to insult him by saying no. "Hold on a second," she told him.

She put the phone down and went to her desk. Looking at the calendar, she saw that she had set up an appointment with her attorney for tomorrow afternoon.

She picked up the phone and said, "How about dinner tomorrow evening?"

"Perfect. "I'll pick you up and—"

"I'll be in the city tomorrow. Where shall we meet?"

"There's a great little restaurant on Fifty-sixth and Third. Corky's. About six?"

"Six is fine," Suzanne said. "See you then." She hung up the phone, and turned to Dana, who was staring openly at her.

"I thought you didn't want to get involved with Mr. Trash and Brash?"

Suzanne shrugged. "I don't, but he is an old friend, and I promised that we'd go out again. Besides, I can take care of two obligations at the same time. I do have to be at my attorney's office. There are some matters about my husband's estate that need to be settled."

"A lot of women get themselves into situations they don't want to be in because they 'can't say no' to someone. Be careful, Suzanne. I don't trust Tim Randolf, no matter how nice he was twenty years ago!"

Suzanne smiled fondly at Dana. Even in high school, Dana's maternal instinct had been well developed. "Don't worry. I know how to say no, when it's necessary."

Dana smiled sheepishly. "I didn't mean to sound so . . ."

Suzanne waved away Dana's words.

"Did you hear from the dealership? What happened to the car?"

Suzanne caught her lower lip between her teeth. She debated the wisdom of telling Dana the truth. "There was nothing wrong with the car."

Dana's jaw dropped. "Nothing wrong with the car? We were almost turned into stone ground wheat, and there was nothing wrong with the car? Bull!"

Suzanne watched Dana carefully. "It wasn't the car. Somebody cut the brake lines."

Dana's eyes widened. The blood drained from her face. "Someone cut . . . . Jesus, Joseph, and Mary. Suzanne, do you know what you're saying?"

"Peter Wilson came by last night. He told me about it."

"Suzanne, I . . . I'm sorry. I didn't believe you yesterday, when you kept telling me about all those terrible things that keep happening."

"You aren't the only one," she said. Then Suzanne took a deep breath. Exhaling forcefully, she added, "But that doesn't matter now. What I'd like to do is get to work. Okay?"

"Okay," Dana agreed. "Where do we start?" she asked, repeating the question she'd asked a few minutes ago.

"The horror movies," Suzanne said, repeating what she'd said just a few minutes earlier.

"Why would someone want to hurt you?" Dana asked suddenly.

Suzanne shook her head. "I don't want to talk about it."

"But isn't that an element of everything else? Isn't it all tied into why you're writing your autobiography?"

Suzanne swallowed back the sharp retort she was about to use, because Dana was right. She was trying to put the past to rest. How could she if she wasn't willing to face every aspect of it? Was there a single person who had been haunting her all her life? Was that possible?

"Dana, I don't know. I . . . I don't think I've ever considered the possibility that there was a person behind the bad things that have happened."

"What about the makeup?" Dana asked suddenly. "Do you think it's possible that someone contaminated your makeup for the screen test?"

The question tugged at her mind. She tried to come up with an answer for her friend, but she realized that there was no ready answer. "Why would someone do that?" she asked aloud. "It doesn't make sense."

"I read an article a few months ago, about how fans do strange things to the stars that they become obsessed with," Dana said. "Maybe that's a reason for what happened."

"I was a fat, ugly, pubescent girl. I wasn't an object for obsession. Besides, that's no reason to kill me."

"You don't know that. Did anything happen when you were doing *Baby?* You talked about Buzz's death, but did anything ever happen to you? Were there any strange incidents, or fans who did crazy things?"

"There are always unusual things that happen to celebrities. People are always watching them." But, as she spoke, the memories of several events, from when she was a child actor, came quickly to the surface. A few were so minor they didn't merit mentioning, but there had been two very specific incidents that she recalled clearly.

"Yes," Suzanne said, "there was one really wacky lady who had been coming to the studio—she waited outside the main entrance every day—to say hello to me. She started doing it in the second year of the show.

"She even got to the point where everyone knew her name. She told everyone that she 'just loved me to death,' and would spend hours waiting to see me. She showed up after lunch, every day during the season. She would wave at me when my car drove out of the studio lot."

Suzanne smiled. "She was a funny lady. She always wore a wide-brim hat and a flowered mumu dress. Her name was . . . Theresa," Suzanne said, dredging up the woman's name. "Theresa James."

"Sounds harmless enough," Dana said as she looked at the counter on the tape recorder and made a small notation on her pad.

"She was, at least that season. But the next season things had changed. She was there again, on the first day of rehearsal. But this time she was there at six in the morning.

"When we left that afternoon, she was still there." Suzanne paused. She moistened her lips and shook her head. "She did that for a solid month. And then, one day in the middle of shooting, the television production company's attorney interrupted the shoot and informed us that we would have to close down the set, temporarily. It seemed that papers had been filed, claiming that I was not who my parents said I was. In fact, the lawyer told us, they claimed I was actually the daughter of a woman by the name of Theresa James."

"The old woman," Dana said.

"Exactly. It seems that she became totally fixated on me. She built an entire fantasy that I had been her daughter, kidnapped just after my birth."

"And the lawyer believed her?"

"She had a birth certificate to prove I was her daughter."

"How . . . ?" Dana began but stopped.

Suzanne smiled at Dana's confusion. "It looked like a

real birth certificate. As I said, the woman was obsessed with me. And she wasn't just some whacked out poor old lady. She had a lot of money and lived in a very fashionable area of Bel Air.

"She paid someone a lot of money to have the birth certificate forged. It even had my real baby footprints on it. But, all it took was two days to prove that I wasn't her daughter. Everyone felt bad for her, and the judge didn't send her to jail, but he did tell her that she was barred from being within a thousand yards of me, at any time, ever!"

"And that was the end of it?"

"Uh-huh. Never heard from her or saw her again."

"Anything else?" Dana asked as she jotted down another note.

Suzanne stared over Dana's head, to a spot on the wall, as another memory grew sharply in her mind. Her mouth went dry, and she had to swallow several times before she could speak. "Yes, there was another 'thing.' It happened in the final season of the show."

Sitting in her chair, Suzanne watched the crew getting the set together for the filming, later that morning. She'd gotten in early, to rehearse her new lines with the director, but Mr. Driscoll was stuck on the freeway.

"Want your mail now?" Judy Klinger asked. Judy was a studio aid. Her job was to run whatever errands the cast needed while they were on the set.

"Sure," Suzanne said, shrugging. She shifted in the canvas chair, and scratched at a small blemish on her cheek that she knew would grow into another of those large and ugly pimples that had been plaguing her for the past three months.

"Here ya go," Judy said, putting down a small box of mail.

Suzanne glanced at the box. It was filled with open envelopes. In the last two years, Suzanne had read almost all her fan mail. Before that, her mother used to read her the letters. She liked reading the letters from other kids. The letters were her friends: she didn't have time for real friends because her mother kept her much too busy for that.

Oh, there were acquaintances. There were the children of the other actors in the show. And when she was off season, she had some kids she played with. Then there was Arthur. And, until he'd gone to school in Boston, he'd been her best friend.

She read a half-dozen letters, drinking in the praises and smiling at the way they all told her how great she was. Didn't they see the way she was changing? she wondered. Yet, none of the mail ever said anything about that.

Yes, she knew that her mail was always screened, but she'd asked if the mail room kept back any of her mail before she'd read it.

The man in charge of security had explained to her that they always opened all the fan mail sent to all the actors, because there were crazy people who sent dangerous things through the mail. But they always gave all the mail out.

Suzanne glanced at the set. It was almost finished. She looked at her watch. It was 8:30. Then she reached for another envelope. She went to separate the top, but couldn't.

She looked at the envelope and realized that it was still sealed. She glanced quickly around. No one was watching her. She felt a shiver of excitement. The letter had never been opened. Somehow, the mail room had missed this one.

She read the handwriting on the outside. It was done in script, and it was sloppy. Suzanne decided that the writer was either very young, or a boy.

Slipping her finger under the edge of the flap, she opened the letter. The tearing sound that the paper made seemed very loud. She paused to look around. No one was watching her.

Extricating the letter, she breathed easier. She unfolded it slowly, and looked at the writing. It took her a moment to adjust to the large block letters written in crayon. But, as she read it, her heart began to pound loud and painfully.

SUZANNE! BABY! CHILD OF SATAN! YOU MUST DIE! YOU MUST BE WIPED OFF THE EARTH! YOU ARE THE CORRUPTOR! YOU ARE THE EVIL ONE BROUGHT UP FROM THE DEPTHS OF HELL! YOU ARE AN ABOMINATION! YOU SHOULD NEVER HAVE BEEN BORN! YOU MUST DIE! YOUR HEART MUST BE TAKEN FROM YOUR BODY AND BURNED SO THAT IT CAN BE SILENCED FOREVER! AND I WILL BE THERE SOON TO DO WHAT I MUST! YOU MUST DIE! YOU ARE THE SPAWN OF SATAN AND THE WHORE OF THE NETHERWORLD! I MUST TAKE CARE OF YOU AND I SHALL! YOU WILL DIE AND THE WORLD WILL BE RIGHT AGAIN!

Suzanne's hands trembled. Her eyes misted and tears formed. She couldn't catch her breath. She closed her eyes and forced herself to breathe deeply.

The instant her eyes closed, she saw the words again. They were like burning arrows piercing her lids. She understood every word. She knew someone was going to kill her. That someone was going to cut her heart out and burn it. She started to cry, and then she began to scream.

"How awful," Dana said when Suzanne finished the story.

Suzanne blinked away the memory, and the remembrance of the fears it had brought with it.

"What happened then?" Dana asked.

"Nothing. The police were there in a half hour. They called the FBI. The letter was examined and . . . . I don't know what all was involved, but they told us, a few days later, that there were no fingerprints on the letter, except for mine."

"Whoever it was, was being very careful, wasn't he?" Dana asked.

"Yes. There was something else. But it couldn't be proven. The letter had not been postmarked."

Dana looked at Suzanne, confused. "You mean it hadn't been sent?"

"They weren't sure. It seems like it hadn't been sent, but it was possible that the letter was under another one in the post office machines. There were a lot of fingerprints on the envelope itself. So many, that they couldn't get any full sets. The police said it was as if it had been handled at the post office.

"And if it hadn't been mailed, it could have been left by a delivery person, or even someone on the studio tour. That happened all the time. As the people leave from their tour, and go through the main entrance, they pass a large drop box for after-hour deliveries."

"So it could have been anyone."

"Anyone, and that's a lot of people," Suzanne summed up.

"Were there any more letters from him?"

Suzanne shook her head. Then she made herself think. "I don't know. I never saw any other letters. Not then. But my mother always double checked the studio people after that incident. She would read my mail, and pass the letters on to me. If there'd been any more letters that season, I wouldn't have known."

Dana was nibbling on the eraser of her pencil. She pulled it from between her teeth and said, "Now, let's see if we have a pattern anywhere. Forgetting the crazy lady who wanted you to be her daughter, we've got what? A death threat letter, and a possible sabotaged makeup case."

Suzanne couldn't stop her smile. "Are you playing detective or shrink?"

"Detective," Dana said, returning Suzanne's smile. "Seriously. Let's look at it all. You've always had ill fated things happen. There's the letter, and the makeup . . ." Dana paused in thought. "And don't forget that accident when your producer died. That was a hit and run. Could that be connected?"

Suzanne exhaled loudly. "It all seems pretty thin. And you can't possibly connect Buzz's death with the letter and the makeup."

"It's connected by you. Remember what you said. These things follow you," Dana argued.

Is that what they do? she wondered. Am I some sort of a magnet for misfortune? The thought was unpleasant and made her search for other incidents that had happened in that last year of the television series.

Walking over to the window, Suzanne looked outside. A blue and white van pulled up to the front of her house. She watched, as the mailman reached out of the truck, opened her mailbox, and stuffed several white envelopes into it. When he closed the mailbox's cover, he drove on to the next house, where he repeated the process.

"I don't know if it's significant, but there were a few minor things that happened that season," she said, and explained several incidents that she'd never thought of in that light.

She spoke slowly, reliving the memories as she explained them. One incident grew clearer in her thoughts. "I remember the last Christmas show we did for *Baby*. We were filming it just before Thanksgiving, and Arthur had come home on semester break. In fact, my whole family had been at the filming, and I was having all sorts of trouble with the scene."

She had been rehearsing all morning, and had been messing up her lines. She was supposed to be on a ladder, decorating the Christmas tree. But each time she went up on the ladder, she concentrated more on holding on than on her lines.

The director had worked with her, on the stage level, until her lines were perfect. Then he had her climb up and down at least ten times, until she felt comfortable doing it. Then they worked for another half hour with Suzanne on the ladder.

By the lunch break, Suzanne had become confident enough to do her part on the ladder without flubbing her lines or looking like she was on a floundering ocean liner.

After lunch, and after she was dressed and made-up, they did one run through. It was perfect. Then they started filming. Suzanne picked up the Christmas bulb she was to screw into the empty light socket, so that the tree would light up. Once the bulb was in, she was supposed to deliver her lines.

With the cameras running and quiet called on the set, Suzanne had picked up the light bulb and climbed the ladder. She went up to the next to last rung, and leaned toward the tree.

She grasped the wire with the empty socket in it, and then started to screw in the light bulb. She turned it three turns, and as she started to turn the final turn, there was a flash and a little explosion.

Electrical shocks raced through her hand and she was knocked backwards. She lost her balance on the ladder and fell. Luckily, one of the light men was standing nearby. The man reacted instantly, and caught Suzanne before she hit the floor.

"I ended up with a slightly burned hand, and a sore back. But I was all right."

"What happened?"

"Everyone believed it was a bad bulb. But the stage electrician had looked the wiring over, and had even taken out the bulb that had blown. When he examined it, he found that the base was damp."

"There was water on it?"

"That's what he said. Then they looked at the dish that the bulbs had been in. There was a small pool of water in it. All the bulbs were wet."

Dana's eyes widened, momentarily. "You could have been electrocuted."

Chapter Eight

The city stretched out like a lithograph whose frame was the Hudson River on one side, and the East River on the other.

From her vantage point, high up in her lawyer's office in the World Trade Center, Suzanne was able to appreciate the way in which New York City was laid out.

She also appreciated being above the street level, and free from noise and pollution that always accompanied a trip into Manhattan.

Behind her, her attorney spoke on the telephone. His voice was politely low. Suzanne did her best not to listen to the conversation. Instead, she concentrated on keeping her emotions in check.

Today she had signed all the papers necessary to begin administering the Jan-Michael Grolier Foundation. Because her mother had wisely invested all of Suzanne's earnings, she had been wealthy in her own right, even before she had met and married Jan-Michael.

The money she'd earned from the five years of *And Baby Makes Five* had been the basis of her future. That money, invested carefully by Lenore Barnes, had turned into a trust fund that would keep her comfortable for the rest of her life. The money she had earned while making the four horror movies had been icing on the cake.

She would never lack for anything, as long as she was not foolish about living. And no matter what anyone had said about her mother, Lenore Barnes had been more than just the proto-typical master stage mother, she'd also been unselfish when it came to Suzanne and Suzanne's earnings.

Suzanne exhaled gently. Her breath misted the window near her mouth. Her mother had been a powerful manipulator. She had manipulated Suzanne, and her husband, Raymond, and Arthur, so that they all did "their" jobs in her life. And while Lenore took a commission as Suzanne's agent and manager, she also discharged her obligations and kept Suzanne's career going, until Suzanne herself refused to do any more.

Money had never been a problem for Suzanne. And Jan-Michael had been wealthy himself. His earnings from his novels and published essays had always been in the upper echelon of French writers.

After his death, and according to the wills that both he and Suzanne had drawn several years before, a special trust was to be established, to help those in the arts who had been less fortunate than they.

Today was the day that Jan-Michael's wish would come true and the Jan-Michael Grolier Foundation would become a reality.

Suzanne looked up. The sky was pale blue, with small puffs of white clouds drifting casually over the earth.

I miss you, she said to Jan-Michael. *I miss you and Allan so very much.*

Blinking away the onslaught of tears, Suzanne turned from the window and returned to her seat. Just after she sat down, Oscar Duvall hung up the telephone.

"I'm sorry for the intrusion," he said.

Suzanne waved aside his apology. She was certain that there had been times that she had interrupted another client when she needed to speak with him. "What's left to do?"

"You need to sign the checks, so that the new account can be officially opened. And then you need to tell me who will be the first recipient of a Grolier grant."

"I haven't taken it that far yet. How should we go about choosing who to give the grants to?"

"The usual method," the attorney said, "is by application. You advertise in the area you want to gift a grant, and then you choose by application."

Suzanne shook her head. "Wouldn't that put a writer of fiction at a disadvantage against say, a technical writer? One is used to manipulating words to fit a specific objective while the other uses words to describe that objective."

"Grants could be given to both," he suggested.

She shook her head. "Until I'm sure about how to proceed, I want to do something else first. Jan-Michael belonged to an organization of writers. I want this year's grant to go to that organization, to be used to help novice writers. These writers should be able to apply for small loans, to help them survive while they try to get published."

"That creates another problem. How should the organization decide on who is qualified for these loans?"

Suzanne didn't have an answer. She had not expected to be making decisions about who gets what, at this stage. "It will take a while to iron everything out, won't it?"

"I'm afraid so. Mrs. Grolier, I know this is difficult for you. Why don't we wait a little longer before you make any decisions. Let's set up an appointment for next month. At that point, we'll try to work out the methods to obtain the objectives you and your husband wanted to attain."

As the lawyer spoke, Suzanne recalled something out of her past with Jan-Michael. "All right, we'll do that, but for next year's grants. This year I would like a grant to be given to Rene Abourne. He is the Dean of Students at Jan-Michael's old university. This grant is to be distributed by Monsieur Abourne. He will give it to those students he deems worthy."

"Are you certain?" Duvall asked.

"Absolutely. Rene Abourne is above reproach. Jan-Michael admired him greatly. He once said that Rene could spot a writer even before that person knew he could write. I am comfortable that the grant will be well used by Rene Abourne."

"I'll see to it. He will have the funds next week."

Suzanne stood and went to the desk. "Thank you, Mr. Duvall."

The attorney stood and shook her hand. "I'll call after the first and set a date to meet. I will also send you materials as soon as possible, on the way similar sized grants have been distributed by other organizations."

"That will help, thank you."

"Shall I have a car called for you?"

"No, thank you. I'm meeting a friend. I think I'll do some walking."

"Very good. Be careful though, please."

"I will be," Suzanne said. She smiled and then left the office. Looking at her watch, she saw that she still had three hours before meeting Tim at Corky's.

She didn't mind the wait. She hadn't walked around New York City in years.

Suzanne had been pleasantly surprised that the restaurant Tim Randolf had chosen was so casual. But as she'd looked around, she'd found that the casualness had a very studied air. And on further inspection, she'd realized that it was very much like all the places she used to go to in California—a celebrity hang-out.

Even though the restaurant typified the exclusive type of place she was not very fond of, she'd been enjoying the last two hours that Tim Randolf had spent talking about his show.

While there had been a few breaks in his conversation, so that they could eat some of the more than ample portions of food and wine, she'd been so completely entranced by the enthusiasm Tim displayed when he talked about his show, that even now, with the food gone and only a short time left before she had to leave for the station, she couldn't help but be drawn deep into Tim Randolf's web of tabloidism.

When Tim finished another of the anecdotal stories he'd been entertaining her with all evening, Suzanne poured more Evian into her glass.

"You're sure you don't want more wine?" Tim Randolf asked.

"Positive. One glass is more than enough. You're forgetting that I still have to take the train and then drive home. But not for a little while yet. So, tell me more about the show. So far you've painted a very fascinating picture."

He took a sip from his wine glass. "It truly is a fascinating branch of show business. The type of show I do is a cross between show business and journalism. It's a genre that stands all by itself."

"So I've come to understand."

He favored her with an exasperated look. "Tabloid news sells. It's worked for newspaper tabloids for decades. And it works even better for television. People want to see the people behind the bizarre stories they read or hear about, every day."

"Do they? Or have we created this desire by pandering to the voyeuristic side of people?" Suzanne asked without a hint of humor or sarcasm.

"I'm not qualified to answer that, nor am I sure there is one specific answer. But, whatever or whoever created this craving for the inside knowledge of others, it's becoming a monster—at least in relationship to the money it creates. And the amount of shows and papers that are devoted to gossip and trash throughout the world grows larger every day."

Suzanne shook her head. "But what about the people you exploit?"

"I don't deal with anyone who is not willing to come forward on his or her own," Tim stated fiercely.

Suzanne was surprised by the vehemence and undercarriage of anger contained in his tone. "Couldn't these people be coming forward to you out of peer pressure, or even from some need to be seen by others when they confess to whatever it is that makes others want to listen and see?"

Tim studied her for several long seconds and spoke, finally, just before Suzanne became too uncomfortable under his gaze.

"These people want the recognition. They want their friends and their families to see them. They want to be on television and they are willing to do whatever is necessary to get there."

"That's very sad," Suzanne commented.

"But very true. Did you enjoy the meal?" he asked, changing the subject.

Suzanne smiled at his ploy. "Yes, it was delicious."

"I've never had the trout here, but I've always found everything to be good." He paused for a breath. "Don't rush back. Let's spend the evening together. We can 'do up the town,'" he offered.

She held his gaze for several silent seconds. "I'd like that, but not tonight."

His features tensed. And while he didn't look away from her, she sensed him draw back. "Tim, don't rush me, please."

A moment later his face softened. "You're right. It's been so long since we've spent any real time together. I mean, really, one evening out of the last twelve years?" And then he laughed, lightly.

Suzanne laughed with him. "I guess I'm just a bit edgy these days. Strange things seem to be happening around me."

"What kind of things?"

"I don't want to talk about it, not right now."

"All right," Tim said, his entire demeanor changing. "But you must tell me when you want to come into town to see my show. I'd love to have you on it."

"You mean in the audience?" Suzanne asked. "I would enjoy that."

"I'd like to have you on the show as well. I think you'd enjoy it and I know the viewers would too."

"No way," Suzanne stated, emphatically. "It's . . . it's not my kind of show."

"It's not the *Enquirer,* Suzanne."

"Your offer is very kind, but—"

"No. I knew you'd say that," Tim told her without any rancor in his voice.

"I don't like feeling exploited or being exploited. But please, Tim, the waiter is coming."

The olive-skinned waiter appeared at the table and asked about coffee and dessert.

Tim ordered coffee, as did Suzanne. Fifteen minutes later, they were in a cab, heading to the train station. Tim sat close to her. Their shoulders touched at every bump.

Suzanne was very much aware of Tim. She could smell

the faint traces of his cologne, mixed with the scents of tobacco and a hint of perspiration.

A strange thought occurred to her. This was the closest she'd been to another man since Jan-Michael had died. She stared ahead, looking at the street in front of them and avoiding further contact with Tim.

When they reached Grand Central, Tim paid for the cab and led her inside. At the windows, Suzanne checked the track for her train. And then, she turned to Tim and said goodnight. "And thank you for a wonderful dinner."

"I'll walk you to the train. I don't mind and I don't like this place at night."

Looking around Suzanne quickly agreed to his company. At the train, Tim took her hand in his. "You can still change your mind. You can still stay."

"I can't, Tim. I have work at home."

"I don't want to lose you again. Please, Suzanne, don't walk out on me. Let's try to pick up from where we left off."

She stiffened at his comment. Why did he have to keep pushing her? Forcing herself to stay calm, she said, "That was a long time ago. Tim, I'm not the person you used to date. I . . . I'm no more that Suzanne Barnes than I'm that innocent little girl who played Baby. Please Tim, I'm not ready yet for another relationship. Don't make me keep saying no."

"I never said that we had to be lovers. I just don't want you to disappear from my life again. Suzanne, before we dated, we were friends. I'd like to be your friend again."

Her cheeks burned scarlet. She was embarrassed at her assessment of his intentions. She had taken it for granted that he wanted a romantic relationship.

The call came for her train. "I'm sorry, Tim. Yes, I'd like to be friends. I'd like that a lot."

* * *

The train pulled into the Tarrytown Station at 9:15. Suzanne disembarked and maneuvered her way from the station to the parking lot.

The air was filled with the scents of water, humidity, and the machinery from the giant automobile plant nearby. It wasn't as hot in Tarrytown as it had been in the city, but it was still pretty warm.

She walked slowly through the parking lot. She had left her car in a remote area, because it had been the only space available. But as she walked from the more lighted area to where her car was, she found herself growing uneasy.

She heard several sets of footsteps behind her, but slowly, each faded until there was only a single set tapping behind her on the blacktop.

She moved faster, but couldn't determine if the footsteps increased their speed. She tried to tell herself that she was imagining things, because of what Wilson had said to her the other night. But she could not halt her rising fear.

Just as she was about to break into a frantic run, the footsteps that had been closing in on her stopped. A second later the double chirp of a car alarm echoed in the night.

Exhaling, Suzanne stopped to look around. She could not find her car even though she knew she'd parked it somewhere near this spot. As the panic began to build again, she remembered that she didn't have her car; rather, she was driving the white car that the dealership had loaned her.

She laughed at herself. She was standing two cars away from it. She took a step forward and stopped. There was a man standing in front of the car parked directly across from her car.

The car's hood was up. The person had his back toward her. He was bent over, looking into the engine with a flashlight.

Suzanne went to her car, unlocked the door, and slid behind the wheel. Locking the door, quickly, she started the engine.

The man straightened at the sound, turned, and looked toward her. She could not make out anything about him. But when he started forward, her heart began to race.

He was almost to the car before she got her brain working and turned on the headlights. Pinned between the twin beams of the headlights, the man stopped to shield his eyes from the glare. But Suzanne had seen his features before he'd completed the gesture, and exhaled in relief.

She opened her window just as he reached her. "Good evening, Detective Wilson."

Wilson blinked. The surprise on his face seemed genuine. "Mrs. Grolier, how are you?"

"Better than you, I think. Engine problems?"

He shrugged. "I can track down a criminal, but I'll be damned if I can track down a problem with my car."

Suzanne laughed. "Serious?"

Peter Wilson rolled his eyes. "It won't start, so I guess it is serious."

"Can I give you a ride somewhere?"

"Thank you," he replied. "If it's not too much trouble."

"No trouble at all," she said, reaching across the car to unlock the passenger door.

"I would think that the police department in a well-to-do place like Springvale could afford to give its policemen decent cars," Suzanne ventured as he sat down.

He smiled ruefully. "They do. That's my car, not the department's." He closed the door and the interior light went out.

Suzanne decided that she liked Peter Wilson's smile. It had been friendly and open, and completely unguarded.

She put the car in gear, backed out of the space, and left the parking lot. "This was very lucky," the policeman said.

"Your car breaking down is lucky?"

"No, your being here is lucky. If you weren't, then I would have had to take a cab across the river. It isn't cheap."

"What about having the car fixed and then driving it across?" Suzanne asked.

"What, and miss getting a ride with you?"

Suzanne almost hit the brakes. But she laughed instead. "A detective with a sense of humor. That's nice."

"At this point I have to joke about it," Wilson said. "But, there's not much anyone can do at night. I'll have the car towed to a garage tomorrow, and then get a verdict."

Suzanne nodded as she turned off of Route 9, and onto the Tappan Zee Bridge ramp. A few minutes later she blended into the light traffic and was halfway across the bridge.

She took a quick glance at the detective, and saw that he was staring out the window. She nibbled on her lower lip before hesitantly saying, "Have you heard anything more about . . . about what happened to me the other day?"

He looked at her. "No, I'm sorry, there's been nothing further. We talked to the people at the restaurant, and even spoke to a couple of their customers who'd been there around the same time as you."

"No one saw anything?"

"No," he agreed. "But that's to be expected. Investigations always take time."

Swallowing, Suzanne gripped the steering wheel tightly. She had a lot of questions, but wasn't sure if she should ask them yet. As she tried to form a question, the detective spoke.

"Mrs. Grolier, I know that what happened has unnerved you. And it should. But you're a strong woman, and I'm sure you'll understand that you must not let this wear away at you."

"Are you trying to patronize me?"

From the corner of her eye, she saw the policeman's features tense. Instantly, she regretted her words.

When he finally spoke, his voice was low. "If I wanted to patronize you, Mrs. Grolier, I would find a way to do so without paying you a compliment."

"I'm sorry," Suzanne said. "Sometimes my mouth works faster than my brain."

"And a woman who did not have your strength would never have apologized to me," he added. "So, let's let that issue pass. Instead, tell me why you came back to Springvale."

Suzanne put on her turn signal and changed lanes as the sign for the first exit appeared. "I'm from here, originally."

"I know."

"But you didn't know who I was the other day, did you?"

"No, but since then there have been quite a few people who've taken the job of enlightening me."

"Detective—"

"Peter."

She paused a beat. "Peter, should I be afraid?"

"I don't know. Perhaps. The truth is that a little fear is a good tool, because it will keep you alert. But there is a very narrow line that can't be crossed over, for if you do give in to that fear, it will debilitate you."

The exit came up fast. Suzanne maneuvered the car onto it, and followed the wide curving exit road around until it recrossed over the thruway, and then came to an end. After pausing at the stop sign, she turned left, and drove the two miles to Springvale.

"Which way?" she asked when she reached the outskirts of the village.

"Left at the third block. I'm the fifth house," Peter Wilson said.

Following his directions, she pulled into the driveway of a modest Cape Cod house. The lights were on over the door, and there was a light coming through one of the windows.

"Thank you for the ride, Mrs. Grolier," the policeman said, opening the passenger door.

She heard a dog start to bark. "You're welcome, Peter, and call me Suzanne, please."

He smiled and nodded.

"Would you do me a favor?" Suzanne asked before he could get out.

"If I can."

"Please let me know what you learn about what happened to my car. I . . . I don't want to be kept in the dark."

He met her pleading gaze with a strong and direct stare. "When I learn something, you'll know it, too."

She believed him. "Thank you. And you'd better get going before that dog wakes up everyone in your house."

"There's only the dog and myself," Peter said. "Good night, Suzanne. I'll speak with you soon."

"Good night," she said as he left the car and closed the door. He bent once to wave before he went to the front door.

Suzanne returned the wave and backed out of the

driveway. She drove back to the main road and then turned toward home.

On the short drive home, she thought about Peter Wilson. She instinctively liked the policeman. Peter had a pleasant demeanor, and he appeared to be a very easy going and laid back man. Intuitively, she knew that he was worthy of her trust.

By the time she let herself into the front door, she was exhausted. She locked the front door, went into the kitchen, poured herself a glass of water, and started upstairs. On the way to the stairs, she caught sight of the blinking red light on her answering machine.

She stopped and pressed the playback button. It quickly rewound and began to play. She recognized Arthur's voice immediately.

"Sorry I missed you, Suzanne. But I've good news. Father is feeling much better, and would very much like to take you up on your dinner invitation. Please call me so we can arrange the day and time. And how are you doing?"

The message ended, and the machine shut down. Arthur's had been the only call. Arthur . . .

She took a deep breath. She'd enjoyed having dinner with her brother the other night. And she'd like to do it again, but . . . . Suddenly, Suzanne was not as sure as she'd thought she was about seeing her stepfather again. A chill raced along her spine. She shivered.

She had to do it, she told herself. She'd been the one who'd extended the invitation. She'd been the one who had extended the olive branch.

She inhaled deeply and started up the stairs. "Can I do it?"

Chapter Nine

The gentler hues of blue were giving way to cinnamon skies as dusk edged into the last of the daylight. The heat of the day was lessening; the breeze from the Hudson River cool and fresh on her bare arms.

Turning and leaving the deck, Suzanne entered her kitchen. There were pots on the stove, ready to be turned on, and a roast, covered with a loose sheet of aluminum foil, sat on the oven door. It had finished cooking fifteen minutes ago.

Myriad memories assaulted her. Most of them reminding her of the meals she'd prepared in France, and of the enjoyment that had always been a part of her cooking for her family. A tendril of nostalgia threatened to jar her carefully prepared mindset, but she willed it away.

She'd spent every minute from the time she and Dana finished working, earlier that afternoon, getting ready for tonight. She knew that this dinner was a landmark event in her life. And she was determined to make it work.

After the deaths of her husband and son, Suzanne had become acutely aware that the only family she had left was her stepbrother and stepfather.

For a moment, Suzanne pondered the peculiar path into which her thoughts were leading her. She had no living blood relative. Her family consisted of a father and brother brought to her by her mother's marriage when Suzanne was four. Yet, she had never viewed her stepbrother and father as anything but her real family, not even through the years of their estrangement.

"Perhaps that will be over now," she said aloud as she looked at the clock and saw that she had a little more than three-quarters of an hour before they would arrive.

Leaving the kitchen, Suzanne went upstairs. She took a quick shower, and then began to dress. She almost put on a demure, pale blue dress, but stopped herself. She did not want to create a particular image in Raymond Barnes's mind.

After looking through her closet, she decided to wear a pair of white linen pants and a beige short-sleeve pullover top. The outfit was neutral. It was not overly feminine, and it certainly did not give the impression of demure obedience.

Satisfied with her clothing, Suzanne brushed out her hair and then applied a minimum of makeup. When she finished, she stepped back to give herself a critical once over.

"Not bad for someone in the over thirty set," she told her mirror image. Then she smiled. One very good thing about life with Jan-Michael had been his ability to make her look at herself as a person, not as an object inside a camera lens.

It had taken her a long time—years—but she'd finally learned how to like herself, for herself, not for the image she'd always been expected to be.

Suzanne drew in a deep breath, held it for a moment, and then exhaled slowly. "Showtime," she said as she turned from the mirror and went into her bedroom.

She slipped on the white gold watch that had been a birthday present, three years before, and then started out of the room. The phone rang before she reached the door.

She went back to her night table and picked up the white receiver. "Hello?"

There was no response.

"Hello?" she said again. "Is anyone there?"

The receiver remained silent. But the low crackling in her ear told her that the line was open and there was someone on the other end. "Who is this?"

The silence continued. Suddenly, Suzanne sensed a dark and malignant force at the other end of the telephone. Her throat closed, and her thoughts became murky and sluggish.

The only sounds in the room were the crackling of the receiver and her own loud and ragged breathing. She was paralyzed within a grip of unreasonable fear, unable to move or react.

And then, somehow, she forced herself to think. In that very instant, her muscles were freed.

She slammed the phone down, and sat on the edge of the bed. She told herself that the call was from a kid pulling a prank, and that it was a random call and would not be repeated.

But she could not rid herself of the silently malignant force that she'd sensed directed at her. "Stop!" she told herself, knowing that she had to get a grip on her emotions. She could not let something like this undermine her ability to cope with the evening ahead.

Closing her eyes, Suzanne took several deep and calming breaths. Could it be that her mind was playing tricks on her? Could the phone call have been a simple teenage prank that had released her fears about seeing her stepfather again?

Suzanne decided that it must be that. The mind, she told herself, is a very complex and tricky thing. With her thoughts settled, Suzanne returned to the kitchen to check everything.

Ten minutes later, and right on time, the doorbell rang. Reminding herself that she had to keep control of her emotions, Suzanne opened the door. What she saw was not what she'd expected.

"Arthur," she said as her stepbrother came in and kissed her cheek. "Father," Suzanne added as Raymond Barnes followed his son inside.

Her stepfather was thirty pounds lighter than Suzanne remembered from their last encounter, at her mother's funeral. His face was more heavily lined, and his eyes seemed to have become duller. She recalled what Arthur had said. Raymond Barnes had been sick, and he was getting old. But, Suzanne thought as she took in his full countenance, he seemed much older than he actually was.

"Hello, Suzanne," Raymond Barnes said. When Suzanne lifted and bent slightly forward, as she had when she'd kissed Arthur, Raymond held still, as if he was unaware of her intentions.

Suzanne accepted his gesture without bitterness, and stepped back to let him pass. Once they were all inside, she closed the door and led them into the living room.

"Drinks?" she asked as she motioned them to the couch.

"Wine, if you have it" her stepfather said. "Red."

"Arthur?"

"The same, or scotch. Whichever is easier."

She favored them with a smile, and went to the credenza by the window. She set up three wine glasses and took out a bottle of light Claret from the rack. She deftly removed the cork, let the bottle breathe for a few seconds, and then poured the wine.

After she served them, she sat down in the chair across from the couch. "To a memorable evening," Arthur said.

Suzanne smiled at her stepbrother and raised her glass. She saw her stepfather look at her. She barely tasted the wine when she sipped it, conscious that Raymond was watching her.

"How is it going?" Arthur asked. "Your work with Dana?"

"Good, thank you." She nodded, grateful for the break in the silence. "I keep remembering more and more."

"Mostly the good memories, I hope," Arthur offered.

"Both. There are a lot of both." She sipped the wine again, and stood. "I have to check dinner. I'll be right back."

She walked swiftly into the kitchen and turned on the first of the four pots. Then she uncovered the roast and slid it into the oven. She turned the oven up to three hundred, and closed the door. Fifteen minutes would be enough to bring the meat and the potatoes surrounding it to the right temperature.

Although she rarely ate red meat, she'd made the roast in deference to her stepfather, who had always preferred meat to anything else.

She heard Mozart drift into the kitchen and realized that Arthur had turned on the stereo. She had another of the nudges of déjà vu that sent her mind stumbling back through the years, returning her to the time when she used to help her mother in the kitchen, while Arthur practiced piano in the living room.

She thought of that as she went into the dining room and opened the bottle of Merlot she'd put on the table earlier. The rich wine, with its fragrant bouquet, needed a little time to breathe before they drank it.

She smiled at herself. That was another of the things she'd learned about in France. The way to drink wine, and what wine worked with what types of food. Wine, she'd always believed, was wine: red with meat and white with fish, but mix and match as she wanted.

Over the years she'd lived in France, she'd discovered how the various wines complemented certain foods, and how they also enhanced the flavor of the food, if used properly.

As she returned to the living room, she wasn't sure if her thoughts were making her seem like a wine critic, or a wino. She laughed under her breath.

Her laugh ended the instant she stepped into the living room and saw Raymond Barnes staring at a photograph of her mother. The picture was fifteen years old. Suzanne had taken it just before she'd left Springvale and returned to Hollywood.

"We can go inside," Suzanne announced.

Raymond turned and stared at her. "I don't remember that photograph."

"I took it the day after graduation. It was printed in California, when I did that first horror movie."

Her stepfather nodded his head. "I think I remember now. You had it in the apartment, on your bedroom dresser."

Suzanne shrugged. She didn't remember where she'd kept the photograph. "Shall we?" she asked the men.

Arthur started forward with Raymond following behind. She wasn't sure if Raymond was just hesitating about everything he did, or if somehow, he and Arthur had traded places and that it was now Arthur who controlled Raymond.

But she knew that could never happen, for Arthur had never been one to stand up to Raymond in their face to face confrontations.

In the dining room, Raymond went over to the red mahogany breakfront and studied the crystal objects within it. After a moment, he nodded and sat at the place Suzanne had shown him.

"I'll be right back," she told them and walked into the kitchen. *Was he going to do that all night? Was he going to scrutinize everything in that silent overbearing manner of his? Am I going to keep overreacting?*

"No," she told the soup as she ladled the clear consommé into the waiting bowls. At the bottom of each bowl was a grouping of julienne carrots. When the consommé was poured, the thin orange slices floated to the surface. Before going further, she turned on the burners beneath the other pots, and then turned off the oven, but left the door closed.

"Can I help?" Arthur asked, appearing behind her.

Suzanne jumped. She hadn't heard him come into the kitchen. She looked over her shoulder at him. "If you insist." She smiled, handed him a bowl, and then led the way back to the dining room.

She set a bowl before her stepfather, and the second bowl at Arthur's spot while he set the third bowl at her place. When everyone was seated, she picked up her soup spoon. "Please," she said and began to eat.

Her two guests did the same. The only sounds in the dining room were those of Mozart and the utensils being used to eat the soup. Suzanne managed a third of her serving before she put her spoon down. She watched Raymond, hoping that the coldness emanating from him all evening was coming from her imagination.

"I understand you've retired. It must be nice to finally be able to relax instead of always being on the run," she said.

Her stepfather put down his spoon and stared at her. "It wasn't by choice. Very little in my life has been done by my choice," he added in a strangely low monotone.

"I . . . Father, I," but she couldn't finish saying she was

sorry, because she wasn't; not for his choices in life, at least. Instead, she stood and brought her bowl inside.

Alone, she heard Arthur speaking in a low voice. While she couldn't make out what he was saying, the tone was enough to tell her that he was having an argument with Raymond.

Ignoring the voices, she turned off the burners on the stove, took the roast out of the oven, and set it on a cutting board. Then she sliced enough for three, and set it on a platter.

She took the roasted potatoes from the pan the meat had been in, and set them on the platter as well. Then she finished off the platter by surrounding the sliced beef with steamed green beans and broccoli.

"Arthur, would you pour the wine?" she called as she lifted the tray and brought it inside. Arthur was just pouring the first glass when she set the platter down and served her stepfather.

"As I said the other night, you are a wonderful chef!" Arthur said when he finished pouring the wine.

"You haven't even tasted it."

"I don't have to. It will be perfect," he stated as he cut the first piece and slipped it into his mouth.

"Thank you," she said. Arthur's compliment was so unfeigned that she felt some of the tension begin to ease.

"I was right," he added after swallowing. "Listen, you forget this writing stuff, and I'll forget my agency and the piano and we'll open a gourmet restaurant. We'll be the sensation of the county."

Suzanne laughed. "I don't think so."

Arthur shrugged. "Hey, it was worth asking."

"Enough!" Raymond Barnes snapped loudly. "I won't sit here and pretend that things are sweet and pleasant any longer. And I don't have to! Why did you leave the way you did? Why did you run out on your family?"

Suzanne's smile locked on her face. Her fork was halfway to her mouth when her stepfather had spoken. She blinked and lowered her fork to the table.

Her stomach twisted, and her breathing turned shallow. Intellectually, she knew that this was bound to happen tonight, but she had naively hoped it wouldn't.

Moistening her lips, she answered his challenging stare with one of her own. "In part, I left because of you. You ruled everything with an iron hand. You would never give an inch, and there was no reasoning with you. You frightened me. You made me afraid to talk to you or to ask you for something. And when that actor was . . . . When the accident happened and I ran to you and Mother, you turned your back on me.

"You refused to help me, and you finally won your battle with my mother. You made her turn from me as well." Suzanne paused to catch her breath. "That was when I ran away. And I ran until I found a place where I could live and not be haunted by all the bad things that kept happening in my life!"

"Your mother was devastated by your desertion!"

"Stop, Father," Arthur asked.

"It's all right," Suzanne said, giving Arthur a quick glance before returning her focus to her stepfather's face. "This has to be dealt with. And yes, at the beginning my mother was devastated, but no more than I. Don't think for a moment that it wasn't one of the most difficult decisions I'd ever made.

"I was twenty. I'd been making movies for over two years, and I was taken care of in every aspect of my life. Someone did my hair. Someone regulated my diet. Another person picked out my clothing, and another person told me what my schedule would be, every single day. I was pampered, and I never had to make a decision that was more important than how I would look in what outfit."

Suzanne took another breath and tried to control her speeding thoughts. "Yes," she repeated, "Mother was devastated in the beginning. But later, she forgave me. Which is something you seem incapable of doing! But then, there are a lot of other reasons for your anger toward me, aren't there?" she challenged.

"No!" Arthur shouted suddenly. "No! We're not going to drag up that old horse again."

Suzanne turned to him, the brother who had always come to her defense. "But it's true."

"It's also in the past. And it's more than time that we put the past to rest," he said. "Father," he added, looking at Raymond.

Raymond's gaze went from Arthur to her. He started to speak, stopped, and then started again. When he finally did speak, the words came out low and were filled with a grainy and emotional timbre.

"Being pushed out of my work. . . . Growing older and becoming sick has made me think a lot about the life I've lived. It's forced me to think about what I've accomplished, and what I failed with, in my life.

"I always loved your mother. I'm different than most. When your mother and I married, we made a commitment for life. Neither of us wavered in that commitment. Everything I did was done in an effort to keep my commitment to your mother. Looking back, I've come to see that I was a hard and sometimes unforgiving taskmaster. But that was because your mother and I wanted so much for both you and Arthur."

"We knew that," Suzanne interjected. "But you never gave me . . . us, any latitude. There was no balance to your rule. It was all or nothing."

"And I was wrong," Raymond Barnes stated. "I was wrong. But there is nothing I can do to change what happened then. All I can tell you is that the last years I spent with your mother were hard ones. She blamed me as much as she blamed anyone else for what had happened."

Pausing, he took a drink of water. "I didn't mean to come here and argue with you tonight. I didn't want to challenge you, to accuse you of doing wrong in the past. I . . . . It just got away from me."

Suzanne stared at her stepfather. For the first time in the twenty-eight years that she'd known Raymond Barnes, he had apologized to her. More than anything, she wanted to believe him. She hoped she could.

"And I'm sorry for fighting with you as well," she said. Then she looked down at her plate. "We . . . we should eat, the food's getting cold," she added, inanely.

Suzanne drank coffee and watched a pair of sparrows dip and swerve across her backyard and into the leaves of one of her neighbor's massive oak trees.

She couldn't get last night's dinner out of her mind. She'd fallen asleep thinking about her stepfather, and she'd awakened the same way.

His spoken admission had hit her strongly. Yet, after all the years of living with and fighting with him, she just could not lower her guard all the way. She wanted to believe him, but something held back her full belief.

She tried to analyze what was stopping her from embracing his apology. Perhaps, she reasoned, it was all the years it had taken to get him to speak the words.

"Good morning," Dana called when she stepped onto the deck. "How did it go?"

Suzanne smiled at her friend. "Better than expected. I'm still alive and so are they." Then she stood. "There's still half a pot of coffee. Want some?"

"Yeah. I'll get it and meet you in the office," Dana said, picking up Suzanne's cup and then leading the way inside.

Suzanne went through the kitchen and into her office. She and Dana had gotten into a nice routine. Each morning Dana would get a cup of coffee, bring Suzanne one, and then get ready to take her notes.

While Dana was doing her coffee run, Suzanne would look over some of her old mementos from *And Baby Makes Five!* There were scripts, notes, and even some fan letters. She had other things as well, from when she'd returned to Hollywood as a teenager.

Today, unsure of what to talk about, Suzanne began to look through the scrapbook her mother had started, when Suzanne had starred in her first horror movie.

She opened the book to a random page, and saw herself, half dressed, with all but the very tip of her left breast exposed. She smiled. It wasn't even her body. She had refused to do any nude scenes in the movie, so they'd resorted to a bit of trick photography in their advertising. They'd put her face and neck on someone else's body.

"Found something?"

Suzanne turned. Dana was already sitting at her spot on the couch, yellow pad on her lap. The tape recorder was on the table between the two cups of coffee.

"I was lucky, you know," Suzanne said.

"Wait a sec," Dana asked as she leaned forward to turn on the recorder.

Suzanne stopped her. "No, I meant you. I was lucky that you answered that newspaper ad. I think that because we had been so close when we were in school, it helped me now. I don't know if I could have opened up in front of another person the way I have with you."

"Thank you. But how do you know I won't sell all your secrets to the *Star*, or the *Enquirer?*"

Suzanne gazed at Dana for a stretched out moment. "You won't."

"I hate when people trust me," Dana joked.

Suzanne smiled. "It's not easy to trust people, I'll tell you that. Now, let's get to work."

"Suzanne, do you still take medication for your allergies?" Dana asked suddenly.

She shook her head. "Believe it or not, by they time I went back to Hollywood, I'd outgrown almost all of my childhood allergies. Every once in a while I still have reactions, but it's pretty rare now. In fact, the first time we realized that I wasn't as allergic to things was when I took the screen test for the first movie.

"I'd been sweating my buns off because I was so nervous. At one point, the director had stopped the test and had someone come out to pat my face down. Right after she'd dried my face, and before I could stop her, she'd begun applying blush to my cheeks."

Suzanne shook her head ruefully. "I'd waited for a reaction, half hysterical that I was going to have a repeat of my last screen test, but nothing happened—as far as my allergies. But I did get the part . . ."

As she spoke, she lost herself in the past, and talked, paced, and remembered for three hours.

When she reached the end of the first movie, complete with all the gory details and all the secrets of the way they do blood and guts special effects, she said, "Time to break. Let's have lunch on the deck."

"The mail just came," Dana announced, looking over Suzanne's shoulder as the mail truck pulled away.

"You get the mail, I'll get lunch. Meet you on the deck."

While Dana retrieved the mail, Suzanne took the two tuna platters she'd made earlier to the table on the deck.

The day was warm, bordering on hot. The sky was clear, with only a few cotton ball clouds to break the unending blue expanse of sky. It felt good to be outside.

Returning inside, Suzanne got utensils, two glasses, and

a pitcher of iced tea. As she set them down on the table, Dana joined her.

"Anything?" Suzanne asked.

Dana shrugged and went through the envelopes. "A couple of bills, and this," she added, handing her a plain white envelope.

Suzanne looked at the envelope. Her name and address were neatly typed. She turned the envelope over. There was no return address. Using her knife, Suzanne sliced the envelope, opened it, and took out a single sheet of paper.

The words on the letter were typed as neatly as her name on the envelope. But when she read the type, the blood drained from her face. Her stomach lurched and her throat began to close. "No," she whispered. "No," she said again, her voice barely loud enough to be heard.

Screaming the word "No!", she flung away the letter. She sat down and hugged herself, rocking slowly back and forth as chills raced through her.

Tears formed and spilled onto her cheeks. "Please," she sobbed. "Please, no more."

The letter floated to the deck, face up. The words on it were clear and visible. Through the misty fog veiling her eyes, she saw Dana bend and pick up the letter.

She shook her head, but could not find the strength to speak aloud and stop Dana from reading.

YOU SHOULD HAVE STAYED AWAY! YOU SHOULD NEVER HAVE RETURNED! YOU ARE A WHORE! YOU ARE A HARLOT! I FAILED BEFORE, BUT I WILL NOT FAIL AGAIN. YOU WILL DIE SOON. I PROMISE THAT THIS TIME YOU WILL DIE!

Chapter Ten

Twenty minutes after Suzanne opened the hate letter, her doorbell rang. Dana rose and, motioning for Suzanne to stay put, went to the front door.

Since reading the letter, Suzanne could not get her thoughts to operate in a cohesive manner; rather, her mind jumped and skipped about with such passion that it scared her as much as the letter itself.

She knew she was allowing fear to control her, but she was powerless to stop it. Too many things had happened to her over the years. And it was all starting to happen again.

Her heartbeat sped up suddenly, and panic was setting in again. Closing her eyes, she took a deep breath, and fought again for control.

"Suzanne," Dana called from the doorway.

Turning, she saw Peter Wilson standing next to Dana. Although his face was partially obscured by the shadows, she saw his eyes clearly. He appeared as calm and relaxed as always. Somehow, she was able to draw on his quiet strength and ease her fears.

She stood and walked toward them. "I'm sorry to drag you out here, again."

He shook his head quickly. "That's not necessary. Where's the letter?"

Suzanne half-turned, pointing at the coffee table and the letter that was on it. The white envelope it had arrived in was next to it.

The detective went to the table, knelt on one knee, and looked at the letter without touching it. When he finished reading, he reached into his jacket pocket and pulled out a folded plastic storage bag.

He laid the bag on the table and, using a silver Cross pen he'd taken from his shirt pocket, he pushed the letter into the bag. He did the same with the envelope.

After sealing the plastic zip bag, he looked closer at the note. As she watched the policeman read the letter, Suzanne began to fade in and out of reality. One moment she knew where she was; the next, it was as though she was a hapless victim in one of those old film-noir detective movies. But when Peter Wilson spoke, the spell was broken.

"It was postmarked in New Jersey. Does that mean anything?"

When Suzanne shook her head, Peter Wilson's gaze deepened. It was as if he were trying to see into her mind. Strangely, she was not uncomfortable under his scrutiny.

"Can we talk?" he asked a moment later. His voice was gentle as he added, "It will only take a few minutes."

"Of course," Suzanne replied.

He glanced at the letter. "This isn't the first threatening letter you've received, is it?"

She stared at the letter for several seconds. "No, it's not." She looked up at him. "But it is the first one I've gotten since I left Hollywood."

"When you were doing your television series?"

"Yes, but I meant later, when I was older and making horror movies."

"But nothing recently?" His eyes did not waver when he asked the question and she saw nothing reflected in them other than interest.

"No," Suzanne said.

The assistant police chief turned to Dana Cody. "You haven't hidden anything from her, have you?"

"Why would I do something like that?" Dana asked, her voice a half octave higher than usual.

"To protect Suzanne? Please, don't take offense, I have to know everything in order to help."

While the detective spoke, Suzanne continued to stare at the plastic bag in the man's hand.

"Why?" she asked suddenly.

"Why what, Suzanne?" he asked.

"Why is this happening?"

Peter Wilson walked over to Suzanne. He stopped less than a foot away. "To answer that question, we have to find the person who sent this letter. And Suzanne, I'm going to do my best to find out exactly who that person is."

She looked into his eyes and found herself believing him. Her mouth was dry. She swallowed several times. "I . . . I need this to stop."

"The only promise I'll make is that I'll do everything I can to find this person."

She didn't know if it was the way he'd looked at her, or the words he'd used, or even the way he'd spoken, but her growing panic lessened and a sense of strength grew in its place.

She smiled at him. "I won't ask for more than that."

He lifted the clear plastic bag with the letter tucked safely inside. "I need to get back to the station so I can have tests run on this. I'll call as soon as I have the results. Probably tomorrow."

Suzanne led him to the door. "Thank you for coming."

Wilson smiled. "It's the least I can do. After all, I can never tell when my car might break down again and I'll need another ride."

She laughed softly. "What was wrong with your car that night?"

"The fuel filter was clogged. The car's fine, now."

"Good. And Peter, I mean it, thank you for coming today."

"You're welcome. I'll call tomorrow with whatever results we come up with."

"You don't sound optimistic."

"It's very rare that we find anything. Usually the fingerprints have been obscured by your own, or there weren't any to begin with."

"That's not encouraging," Suzanne said.

"No, but it is a start. We have materials that we can trace, and forensics usually comes up with some unexpected tidbit to help us along."

"I hope so," Suzanne said, fervently, as he turned and went out the front door.

It was almost seven o'clock. The sun was well on its way toward the horizon when Suzanne walked out onto her deck. She looked at the river, but could not get that good feeling she usually had when she watched the river flow by.

It was the letter that was stopping her from deriving any pleasure from her view. That damned letter had been haunting her every moment since she'd opened it. What had she done to this person? she asked herself for the hundredth time.

But no matter how often she asked, or how much she changed the language, she couldn't come up with anything that remotely approached an answer.

She'd never willfully hurt anyone. Nor could she remember a time that she'd been mean or vindictive to someone. It wasn't that she was such a perfect person for all those years, she admitted, it was simply that her life had been so well ordered and maintained that she'd never had to face people across adversarial borders. Script disagreements, lighting problems, and stage direction were not the stuff that made people want to kill.

She didn't think that this person was one of the kids she'd gone to grade school or high school with. And while she'd been a bit of a loner in high school, she'd had her fair share of fights and disagreements with the kids in school who had teased her about having once been a TV star. But there was no way she could believe that what was happening to her now was some sort of a holdover from a school feud or fight.

What was it? she asked again. The portable phone chose that instant to ring. Suzanne jumped. Then she stared at the phone and thought about that ominous and silent phone call she'd received the other night. Could it have been from the same person? Should she have said something to Peter Wilson?

She reached for the phone and, as she brought it to her ear, hesitantly said, "Hello?"

"Suzanne, it's Tim."

"Hi, Tim," she said. Although her voice was tight, her tension eased with the knowledge that she knew the caller.

"What's wrong?" he asked suddenly.

"Nothing," she said, quickly. "Nothing is wrong."

"You don't sound right. What is it?"

"Tim, really, everything is fine," she insisted.

"No it isn't. Suzanne, I can hear it in your voice. I'll be there as soon as possible."

"No. Tim, please don—" She stopped in mid-word. He had already hung up.

The last thing she wanted was company. "Damn!"

Forty minutes later, her front doorbell rang. When she opened the door, she saw apprehension in Tim Randolf's gaze.

"I'm fine, really. You didn't have to come out here," she said. Then, as she studied his face, she felt touched by his obvious concern.

"I know I didn't have to. May I come in?"

Suzanne stepped back to allow him entry, then took him into the living room. "Tim, this was very sweet, but you needn't have driven up from the city."

"I thought it was necessary. Suzanne, what happened?"

Tucking one leg under her as she sat on the couch, Suzanne shrugged. "What makes you think something has happened?"

"Your voice, the way you're not making eye contact with me right now. This is Tim. We've known each other for a long time, Suzanne. A long time. Level with me."

She looked over his shoulder, at a small oil painting she'd picked up in New Orleans a few years ago. It was a scene she'd always loved: a child running free in an open field. It had been something she'd never been allowed to do as a child.

Then she focused on Tim's face. "I got a letter today. I . . . . It was a death threat."

Tim moved next to her. He took her hands in his. The heat from his hands warmed her cold fingers. "Did you call the police?"

She nodded. "They took the letter and the envelope and are having them analyzed."

"Good."

Suzanne took a shuddering breath. Tim's grip tightened and she responded to his pressure. The human contact felt good and more of her tensions drained away.

An instant later her stomach make a commanding noise.

"Excuse me," she said with a smile.

Tim scrutinized her carefully. "When's the last time you ate?"

Suzanne thought back to the lunch she had not touched. "Breakfast. I've been a little off, since the letter came."

Tim Randolf stood and drew Suzanne to her feet. "Come on."

"Where?"

"To a restaurant."

She didn't feel like going out, but the last thing she wanted to do was to cook. So, rather than argue, Suzanne nodded.

A few minutes later they were in Tim's car. "Any place in particular?" he asked.

"Wherever," Suzanne said.

"I'm not that familiar with the area. But there's a great place a few miles from here. The Carlton House Inn. Know it?"

Suzanne remembered the restaurant from when she was in school. It served excellent food, but its reserved ambiance was not the type of atmosphere Suzanne wanted to be in tonight.

Shaking her head, Suzanne said, "There's a small place on the river. Do you mind?"

"Of course not. You direct, I'll drive."

Fifteen minutes later, they were seated at a table near the back of the restaurant. While Suzanne had never eaten in the restaurant, she'd been by it a few days earlier, when she'd gone exploring the waterfront area of Nyack.

The restaurant was decorated in understated tones of rust, beige, and browns that combined to give a feeling of warmth and comfort. The tables were spaced with enough distance to give each a modicum of privacy.

The light was more than adequate to eat by, and soft enough to be either romantic or just pleasant.

"Drink?" asked the waiter who appeared at the table. Suzanne shook her head, and Tim Randolf did the same. The waiter then gave them a verbal menu of the evening's specials.

Suzanne ordered the swordfish steak the waiter had described. Tim Randolf ordered the same.

"Wine?" Tim asked.

"With the fish. And a glass, not a bottle. White."

Tim held up two fingers. The waiter nodded and backed away.

Alone, Suzanne accepted the way Tim was so openly studying her. "Tell me about the letter," he said.

"There isn't much to tell. I opened it, I read it, and I fell apart. Tim, it was . . ." She stumbled in her attempt to speak and shook her head when she was unable to go on.

"Do you remember that time, on the set of . . ." Pausing, he snapped his thumb and middle finger together in an attempt to recall something, *"The Axeman Cometh—* God, where did they get the nerve to name movies that way?"

Suzanne took a ragged breath. "Titles were never our horror movie producer's strong point. And yes, I do remember that time."

"Was this the same?"

"No. That letter was different. It was made out of cut out magazine print. This one was neatly typed. Tim, can we talk about something else?"

"Of course. Have you caught my shows lately?" he asked, changing the subject without even blinking.

She smiled. "No."

"You can certainly be ego deflating," he said. "But I forgive you. Besides, you're probably better off. The last few shows have been a little weird—it's sweeps week, so my producer goes for the exotic."

"Such as?" Suzanne asked, not out of interest but out of her need for a conversation to keep her mind off the horrible letter.

"Well, one of the shows was called, 'Husbands who love their wives' brother.'"

Suzanne couldn't figure out what sort of a reply that type of show warranted. And, she saw by Tim's face, she wasn't the first person to react that way.

"Today's show," he went on smoothly, "was about teenage runaways facing their parents."

"That at least sounds interesting."

"It was. Suzanne, it's not that I want to do a freak show, but in order to do broader shows with real meaning and benefits, I have to do the sludge. The sludge builds audiences."

The waiter arrived with their meals. After he placed their dishes before them, and gave them each a glass of chilled wine, Suzanne said, "Why do you have to have the sludge?"

"I told you that the other day. The viewers want it. Just the same way that they read the tabloids. They want to live outside themselves. They want to see things that can titillate and even scare them, as long as it's on television, or in the tabloids, and not happening directly to them."

Before she could say anything, Tim went on. "And my show is really no different than what you're doing. By writing your autobiography, you're inviting all those people into your life and thoughts. You're going to be doing what I do, but you are the guest, not the host."

Suzanne stared at Tim. "No, that's not true."

"Why isn't it?"

"Because I'm not writing my autobiography for the public. I'm doing it for me."

"Which is what everyone believes when they take on this sort of project. But if you finish it, I'll bet odds that you'll publish it."

"Well," Suzanne said as she lifted her wine glass in an effort to derail the track of the conversation. "Salut."

"Salut," Tim Randolf said, raising his glass to her.

They ate silently, enjoying the well-prepared food. When they were finished and had declined dessert, Tim paid the check and they left.

The night was balmy. The clouds moved casually across the sky, filtering the pale moonlight downward upon the small river hamlet.

Breathing in the scent of the river, Suzanne turned to Tim. "Thank you. I feel much better now."

"It was my pleasure," he said.

He leaned close and Suzanne was afraid that he was going to kiss her. But all he did was open the car door for her.

When they drove back to her house, Tim stopped the car but did not switch off the ignition. Suzanne looked at the house and realized that she hadn't left any lights on inside.

Her lips were dry. She moistened them with the tip of her tongue. "Would you mind coming in with me, for just a moment. I—"

"It's all right. I understand," he said, leaving the car and coming around to her side. He helped her out and then walked with her to the front door.

She unlocked the door and started in. Tim Randolf stopped her and went in first. He turned on the hall light and continued in.

Suzanne followed him into the kitchen and turned on the light. "Do you want me to check upstairs?"

Shaking her head, she said, "I guess I'm just overreacting."

"You're allowed," he told her.

"The letter got to me. It was so unexpected. I just opened the envelope and there it was. Would you like some coffee before you go?"

"That would be nice," he said.

"Why don't you go out on the deck? I'll put up a pot and join you."

Following her bidding, Tim went outside while Suzanne prepared the coffee maker. When she finished that task and turned the machine on, she set up a serving tray with mugs, sugar and milk.

From the corner of her eye, she saw that her phone machine's red light was blinking. She went to it and pressed rewind. A moment later she heard Arthur's voice.

"Just wanted to remind you about our lunch date. Meet me at my office and we'll go from there. See you then." There was a click and two beeps. An instant later another message came on. "Suzanne, it's Peter Wilson. I just wanted to make sure everything was all right. I'll call back tomorrow with the results of the tests. If you need anything, please don't hesitate to call me."

"Thank you," Suzanne said in a half whisper. Hearing Peter Wilson's voice gave her confidence. She was glad that he was helping her.

Turning, Suzanne gathered the tray and brought it outside. Tim was standing near the edge of the deck, leaning on the railing. "It's beautiful here. I see why you moved here. In a funny way, it reminds me of California. It's very different, but there's a good feeling here."

"I know what you mean," she said after she set the tray on the table and joined him.

"Suzanne, about the letter. You can't let it get to you. And you can't take it personally."

She reacted with disbelief. "How else do I take a death threat but personally."

Holding his hand up to stop her, he said, "Don't misunderstand. It's a terrible thing to get a letter like you did, but I don't know anyone in our business—any celebrity—who has not gotten their share of hate mail and death threats. Suzanne, I get at least one a week."

"But I'm not a celebrity."

"Yes, you are! And you'll never escape from it! You were famous as a child. You became a celebrity again when you did that series of movies, and you're famous in Europe as both the wife of a celebrity and as a movie star."

"But not here, and not recently," she said. "I'll get the coffee." She went back inside, retrieved the brewed coffee and brought it out. She poured the dark liquid into both cups and then set the pot down.

She sensed Tim coming up behind her. "I'm sorry, I didn't mean to be short with you. And I do appreciate your coming here tonight."

"There's no need to apologize," he said as she turned to face him. "I understand what you're going through. I just wanted you to know that you aren't alone."

She smiled. "Please," she said, pointing to the coffee.

He took his cup and sat down at the table. "There's milk and sugar," she said.

He poured a little milk into the cup, but bypassed the sugar. After taking a drink of the coffee, he nodded. "Good."

"Why are you doing this show?" she asked suddenly. "Tim, you are a wonderful actor. Why did you give up the profession?"

He stared into the coffee cup. "Is this True Confession time?"

"Only if you want to tell me," Suzanne said, seeing that she'd touched a hidden nerve.

He spoke without looking up. "I didn't give it up, it

gave me up. I was eighteen when the series ended, and the times were changing quickly. There wasn't any call for my type of sweet kid actor. And as much as you were changing, physically, I was too. I was tall—too tall to play a sixteen-year-old any longer, but my face stayed too young to play anything else.

"Do you remember that period between the series and the horror movies?" Tim asked.

"No, I don't. I don't think you ever mentioned it," Suzanne said after thinking back.

Tim Randolf laughed. "You're probably right. I wasn't proud of the direction my once big career had taken. I was doing mostly summer stock and regional theater. They hired me because they knew that everyone would want to see the grown-up version of my *And Baby Makes Five* character.

"But when I landed that role in the first *Axeman* movie, I thought things were going to change for me. And they did. You were in the movie, and I had missed you. Halfway through the filming we started to date. Remember?" he asked, finally looking up from the cup.

"Of course I do," she said.

"What did we do, three movies that first year?"

"Two."

"And we had fun." Tim paused to rub at his forehead. "But the fun ended not long after that, when Larry . . . when Larry died. You ran away, and I faded into obscurity." He stared hard at her. "You broke my heart, you know."

"I was still a kid, and we just about stopped dating before I started that last movie."

Tim Randolf shrugged. "After you disappeared, things went downhill for me. I did a lot more Summer Stock. Six years ago, I ended up doing a stint as a late night radio DJ. At the same time, I got involved with a cable TV show. That was a bit of a break for me, because the man who's producing my show now saw me there and came to me with a proposition.

"The rest is history. Two years ago everyone in this country had forgotten who I was. The fall ratings had me placed as the number one daytime talk show in the New York area. And there's big talk that my show will go into national syndication."

"That's great," Suzanne said. "That's really wonderful. I'm glad that you were strong enough to overcome the difficulty that's always been a part of this business."

"And it's getting late," Tim said, draining his coffee and standing. "I've got to be at the studio early tomorrow morning."

Suzanne rose with him.

"Don't be afraid," Tim said as he came close to her. "If you need me, all you have to do is call."

Suzanne gazed up at him. She met his open gaze and knew that he was going to kiss her. She didn't back away; rather, she held still when his arms went around her.

When he kissed her, his mouth was warm and soft. The kiss lasted for several long seconds and she began to feel protected and safe. She tried to tell herself that what she was feeling was right. But when his kiss turned deeper, she stiffened.

The kiss ended then and she drew slowly back. "Please, Tim, don't rush me."

He looked down at her. His lips were parted and his teeth showed white between them. "That's better than the last time we were together," he said, his eyes unwavering. "I won't rush you, Suzanne, just don't push me out of your life."

Meeting eyes, she nodded. "I won't."

"Thank you," he said as he started out. Suzanne walked him to the door and, as he left without trying to kiss her again, she waved to him and securely locked the door behind him.

Then she went back out to the deck. She sat on one of the deck chairs and looked up. The moon was hidden behind a gauzy cloud. The stars danced in a shining proliferation of pinpoint dots.

She closed her eyes as her emotions rose. She missed Jan-Michael so much that it hurt. But he was gone, she told herself. He was gone and she was still here. She had to stop mourning. She had to start living again.

Was Timothy Randolf the right one? She had liked him when she was a teenager. She had thought she was in love with him for a while.

She opened her eyes. Was she wrong to not want to become romantically involved again? Or was she afraid that if she did allow herself to become involved, another person she cared for would die?

Peter Wilson looked at the one-page report on his desk. He'd spent a good deal of the evening on the computer, trying to learn if there had ever been any problems when Suzanne had lived in Springvale as a child.

The results, after four and a half hours, had been minimal. According to the computer, there had been a problem at the Barnes's residence, on the fifth of October, fifteen years ago.

Suzanne Barnes had been in tenth grade then. Her brother Arthur had been in his second year at Julliard. Lenore Barnes had called the police at eleven o'clock that night to report an intruder.

The police had arrived to find that one W. Harold Reilly had indeed broken into the Barnes house. He had done so as a fraternity initiation. His errand had been to get a pair of "Baby's" panties.

The police arrested him and held him overnight. They called his parents, who came and bailed him out. Lenore Barnes had dropped the charges a week later.

The report on his desk was a fax follow-up he'd received about ten minutes ago. It was from the FBI and it showed that W. Harold Reilly now resided in Chicago, and had been there for the last seven years. Mr. Reilly, married, with four children, was a partner in a chain of wallpaper stores.

Peter turned the report over and pushed it away. He was certain that Mr. W. Harold Reilly was not the man stalking Suzanne Barnes-Grolier.

Reaching out, Peter picked up a photograph of the right front undercarriage of Suzanne's car. It clearly showed the brake line that had been tampered with. There could be no mistaking the gash for something else. The line had been cut.

And the severed emergency brake cable left no doubt in Peter's mind that someone was out to get Suzanne Barnes. But who? That was a question he knew could take a long time to answer.

Shifting in his seat, he pulled a pad of plain white paper to him. He made a quick notation to remind himself, tomorrow, to send a letter of inquiry to France. He wanted to find out if there had been any problems in France.

He thought about the tampered brakes, and about the death threat. Then he pictured the gas fitting in his mind. Although he had not mentioned it to anyone yet, he now questioned whether the gas leak at Suzanne's house had been accidental. As an accident, the gas leak didn't fit into the overall picture any longer. No, he was now certain that the gas fitting had been tampered with, just as the brakes had been.

Peter leaned back in his chair. Why, he asked himself, would someone want to hurt Suzanne Grolier?

He knew the answer would not be simple. He'd spent too many years as a policeman to expect an easy answer. His only hope was that he would find the answer before the person stalking Suzanne Grolier completed whatever mission he had in mind.

Chapter Eleven

Stepping out of the shower, Suzanne wrapped herself in a large, beige and mocha towel. She walked to the window and looked out. The gray sky she'd awakened to and exercised with had not changed. From all appearances, it looked as though the sun would not be a willing partner for this humid day.

"But no rain, please," she asked aloud as she went about the business of drying and dressing.

When she finally reached the kitchen and opened the deck doors, she discovered that the humidity wasn't as bad as she'd expected. Leaving the heavy, glass deck door open, but closing the screen, Suzanne made herself a light breakfast and took it out on the deck.

She ate amid the pleasant mix of sounds created from nearby birds and distant traffic. A seagull wheeled over the river, not a dozen feet from the stairs that led down from the edge of her property to the river bank.

Not for the first time did Suzanne wish she had the freedom of the bird. It would be nice to fly wherever she wanted, whenever the need arose.

She wondered if seagulls worried about love, or the lack of it. She hoped not. It was easier not to be affected by emotion.

Hate and love, she thought, are two very different, yet similar emotions. One could love passionately and hate passionately as well. Could that be what was happening to her? Did someone hate her with so much passion that they wanted her dead?

And who hated her so?

She tried to think back to any circumstance where she had hurt someone, whether intentional or not. But, try as she might, she could not find a single instance where her actions would have caused such anger and hate.

She pictured the wrathful words of the letter. She remembered her fear and panic when the brakes on her car had failed. Why did someone want her dead?

Realizing where her thoughts were taking her, Suzanne stopped the unproductive search for a reasonable explanation of insane actions. Instead, she finished her breakfast and went back into the house.

The clock over the sink told her it was nine, which meant that Dana would be there in a few minutes. She filled her coffee cup, another for Dana, and brought them into the office.

Dana arrived within seconds and was ready for work a few moments later.

"I'm having lunch with my brother," she told her friend and assistant. "How much of the dictation has been typed?"

"Through yesterday," Dana said.

"Good. If you don't mind, I'd like you to set up what you've typed. I want to go over it all this weekend. But this morning I want to talk about that first horror movie."

Dana flipped the pages of her yellow pad until she came to a clean page. She put a fresh tape into the recorder, took a sip of coffee, and picked up a pencil.

As Suzanne watched her friend go through what she called "Dana's get it together routine," a warm sensation settled over her. She liked having Dana there with her. It was comforting to have someone in her life. And with Dana, it was safe as well.

"Ready," Dana said as she replaced the coffee cup on the table.

"I returned to California right after high school graduation. You went to Europe, didn't you?" she asked suddenly.

Dana's head bobbed sharply. "France, Germany, Italy. You were supposed to go with me."

"That's right. I hadn't thought about that in a long time. But I'd taken that screen test in the late spring, and a week before graduation I'd learned I'd gotten the job."

"Actually, I'm glad you didn't go. Jeez, Suze, that last year in high school you turned into Miss Body Beautiful. I would never have met the guys I did if you'd been there with me."

"You're welcome," Suzanne said with a wink that denied the dryness of her tone. Then she settled herself and said, "It was a strange time for me. Arthur had just left for England. He was set for a three month study program in London. I was excited and afraid about returning to life in Hollywood. I was anxious about returning to acting. I'd never forgotten all the good times I'd had during the TV series and the way the people had treated me when everything was going great. But I also remembered the end of the series, when things had fallen apart for me."

"What about hate letters? Did you get any of those during high school?"

Suzanne shrugged. "My mother would have intercepted any letters that would have come to the house. So I really don't know if any were sent."

"When you got back to California, did the letters start again?"

Suzanne shook her head. "Not right away, because the

producer's plan was not to let anyone know that I was in the movie until just before the release. Then they were going to flood the market with press releases about Baby starring in the horror movie."

Suzanne paused. Although she'd intended to talk about when she'd arrived back in California, she realized that the morning had been spent looking for an answer to the letter she'd gotten yesterday. Perhaps . . .

Standing, Suzanne started to pace. Her thoughts were twisting wildly as they navigated through circuitous paths until they finally reached the old memories. Suddenly she was eighteen years old again, and halfway through the filming of *The Axeman*.

Suzanne adjusted the tee-shirt with a self-conscious gesture. But nothing she did was able to change the effect of the shirt. She was braless, as Wardrobe had instructed. She shook her head slowly. The thin cotton was next to invisible. It clearly showed the dark circles of her nipples, which, she knew, was the exact effect the producers wanted.

Although she was only eighteen, Suzanne was far from stupid. There were several reasons she'd been given the lead in this movie. And while the single most important aspect for considering her in the part had been that she'd been a famous child star, the reality was that if her face had not been pretty, and if her body hadn't been fully developed and sexy, she would not have gotten as far as the screen test.

Her mother's advice, and Suzanne had agreed at the time, was that no matter what she had to do in her part, she would also have to act well enough to show both the audiences and the people in Hollywood that she was a professional actor.

"Okay, just forget what the men will be watching," she ordered herself as she turned from the mirror and went over to the small couch to wait the fifteen or so minutes before she would be called for the next scene.

Plunking herself down on the couch, she looked around the trailer she shared with several other actresses. The furniture was spartan, with two cots for quick cat-naps and two dressing tables with fully lighted mirrors.

There was a sharp rap on the door.

"Come in," Suzanne called.

The door opened, and Sam Harding, the movie's director, poked his head in. "Can we talk?"

"Sure," Suzanne said, shifting on the couch and trying to casually cross her arms and cover her breasts without seeming to be shy. She was puzzled and suddenly nervous at his visit. They'd been working on the movie for seven weeks, the filming was half over, and this was the first time the director had sought her out.

Entering the trailer, the director sat next to her. He was in his late twenties, tall, and a little pudgy. He had red hair and a youthful face. "I just wanted to say that I appreciate the job you're doing. I didn't know what to expect when we hired you, but I'm pleased that we did."

Suzanne was taken aback by the unexpected compliment. "Thank you. I . . . . Thank you."

"Did you get those script changes this morning?"

She nodded her head quickly. "I haven't had a chance to read them yet."

"They don't take effect until after today's shooting. But check them out as soon as you can. If there are any problems, let me know," he said as he stood.

When he was gone, Suzanne went to the dressing table. There were five drawers on one side. Each drawer had a label with a name on it. Her drawer was the second one down.

Opening the drawer, she extracted the brown envelope with the scene changes. She took the envelope back to the couch, opened it, and began to read.

The changes weren't major, but there were enough so that she would have to work for a few hours tonight. She put the script back into the envelope.

She'd have to break her date for tonight. She wondered how he'd react.

"Five minutes," came a familiar voice at her door.

"I'm coming," she said. She went to the door and opened it. "Let's go."

"All set?" Tim Randolf asked.

"As set as I'm going to be. But there are some changes on tomorrow's scenes. I'll have to study tonight."

Disappointment flashed across his face. "I understand," he said. "We'll make it Friday night, okay?"

"Great," Suzanne said with a smile.

"Tim," came a loud shout.

Suzanne and Tim stopped as Roger Grant, the film's executive producer, waved Tim to him.

"I'll catch up in a minute."

Suzanne smiled at his retreating back. Her first big surprise when she'd reported for her first day of work had been in finding that Tim Randolf, who had played her big brother in the TV series, would be her co-star in the movie.

But, unexpectedly, she'd found herself attracted to him. And, over her mother's constant objections, they had started to date.

"Suzanne, mail's in," called Robbie Carter, one of the ever present production assistants, as he came over to Suzanne and handed her a half-dozen envelopes.

The late morning sun was strong on this early September day. The temperature was close to eighty-five and the sky was clear blue and cloudless.

Taking her mail, Suzanne went to the base of the old

elm tree that was on the front lawn. She sat beneath the shade of its branches and, ignoring the hustle going on around her, she opened the first envelope. It was a form from the production company about a SAG meeting to be held next week.

Suzanne was a member of the Screen Actors Guild, but her mother always handled any SAG business. She set the form aside, and picked up the next envelope.

The envelope was very light, and she immediately recognized the British stamp. She smiled happily as she looked at the return address. It was from her brother.

She ripped the flap off and opened the letter. It was a short note, telling her that he missed her and the family and that he would be back on the fifteenth of September.

Suzanne frowned. Her stepfather had told her that Arthur had been accepted for additional study by the London Symphony.

But as she read on, Arthur wrote that he wasn't sure that he wanted to stay in England, and that he was coming home for a few weeks so that he could talk things over with the family.

Exhaling, Suzanne felt a knot of excitement begin to build in her belly. She had missed Arthur this summer. He'd always been her best friend and advisor. It would be nice to have him home again.

She set his letter aside and picked up the next envelope. It was the size of a greeting card, and she wondered what it was. There was no return address on it, but she had the sneaking suspicion it was from Tim Randolf.

He'd been sending her little cards and things since they started dating, three weeks ago. She sliced the flap with her nail and separated the envelope. She withdrew the card, and looked at its front.

It was a cute card, with a picture of a furry cat curled up in front of a fireplace. When she opened the card she found no pictures inside, only writing. As she read, the blood drained from her face, and her heart pounded wildly.

YOU ARE THE CHILD OF SATAN! YOU ARE A FOOL! YOU JUST COULDN'T STAY AWAY COULD YOU? QUIT! QUIT NOW WHILE YOU ARE STILL ABLE. FOOL! YOU SHOULD NOT HAVE COME BACK. RETURN, SPAWN OF THE DEVIL! RETURN FROM WHERE YOU CAME. GO, BEFORE I AM FORCED TO TAKE ACTION AGAIN. GO, BEFORE IT IS TOO LATE!

Suzanne hugged herself, stilling the tremor that had passed through her with the memory.

"How terrible. But if there wasn't a lot of publicity when you were making the film, how could someone find out?" Dana asked.

Suzanne looked at her friend. "Hollywood is never private. Nothing can be totally hidden or secret. By the movie's halfway point, the producers were gearing up for a low-grade publicity campaign that they hoped would mushroom of its own accord and become a full-blown 'event' by the time the movie was released to the theaters."

"So it was pretty well known that you were making a movie?"

"Yes," Suzanne told her friend. "But it had been seven years. My Lord, Dana, seven years had passed and this person was still there."

"Do you really think it was the same person?"

Suzanne laughed. The sound was unpleasant in her ears. "Who else could it have been? As soon as I read the card, I thought about that other note, when I was doing *Baby*. It had to be the same one."

"No," Dana said shaking her head. "I meant the letter you got yesterday. Do you think it's the same person?"

Suzanne stared at Dana. Her stomach twisted and the bitter taste of coppery bile crept into the back of her throat. She swallowed back her nausea. "That would mean that this . . . person had been after me for over twenty years. Dana, that's insane. I . . . . No! It can't be."

The phone's ring startled both women. Dana reached for the receiver and picked it up. "Ms. Grolier's residence."

Dana listened for a moment. "Right here," she said, and extended the phone to Suzanne. "Peter Wilson."

Suzanne took the phone and put it to her ear. "Peter?"

"Yes. Suzanne, as I thought, the tests on the letter were inconclusive. I had our lab overnight the letter to the FBI lab in Quantico. As soon as I hear anything, I'll call."

"Thank you, I appreciate your help."

"Are you all right?" he asked in a concerned voice.

"Fine," Suzanne said. "Thank you again."

After saying goodbye, she hung up and looked at her watch. It was 11:30. "I guess that's it for today. I have to get going. You'll take care of those other things for me?"

"I'll leave the typed pages on your desk. Enjoy your lunch and if you need anything over the weekend, call."

"I will. Thank you." She started out of the room, then paused. "Dana, what do you know about Peter Wilson? I mean, what kind of a person is he?"

Dana shrugged. "I really don't know. A good person, I would imagine, considering I've never heard anything negative about him. I do know he's been with the department for ten years. My husband thinks he's the best policeman Springvale could have. He also says that Peter Wilson will take over for Chief Loughlin, when the chief retires next year."

"What about as a person?" Suzanne persisted.

Again Dana shrugged. "All I can tell you is rumor, and there isn't much of that. He's divorced. It happened about eight years ago. She doesn't live around here anymore. The rumor was that he had been offered a position with a major corporation. The income was high, and the job was a lot safer than being a policeman. His wife wanted him to take the job. He didn't. I think she moved back to where she came from—the midwest. That's all I know. Why?"

"Curious," Suzanne replied, honestly. "He seems to have taken an interest in helping me. I just wanted to know a little more about him. See you later."

She was comfortable from the first moment she entered Arthur's office. The reception area was decorated in warm earthtones. The furniture was of classic design rather than the coldly modern decor that most contemporary businesses preferred.

After giving her name to the receptionist, Suzanne sat on a Chesterfield, crossed her legs at the ankle and looked at the paintings on the walls. There were three oils. One was a portrait of Beethoven. The second was that of a young boy sitting on a high stool, playing a violin.

But when she focused on the painting across from her, her breath caught. She hadn't seen that particular painting in over fourteen years. It was a study of two people. One sitting at the piano, his back to the artist, his head slightly turned to one side. He was looking at the teenage girl who stood at the side of the piano, watching the pianist.

The teenage girl was herself. The pianist was Arthur.

"It fits, doesn't it?" Arthur asked.

Suzanne pulled her eyes from the painting to look at her stepbrother. "Perfectly," she said, standing.

They hugged, and kissed each other lightly. "Come," Arthur said. He led Suzanne to the reception desk. "This is Margaret Hains. Margaret is my right arm. She does everything!"

Margaret stood and shook Suzanne's hand. "It's a pleasure to meet you. I've heard so much about you from Mr. Barnes."

"It's a pleasure to meet you, Margaret," Suzanne replied.

"No calls," Arthur instructed just before he led Suzanne into his office.

The office was decorated in the same manner as the reception area. The walls were a light mocha. There were two lithographs on the walls. Both were posters heralding past musical events. Arthur's desk was mahogany, the two chairs before the desk were mahogany wood covered with embroidered material. A computer stand, made of the same mahogany wood, was set near the desk. An oriental rug of greens and browns completed the look to perfection.

Behind the desk, windows looked out on New City. Suzanne walked behind the desk and gazed out the windows.

From the eighth-floor window of Arthur's office, she could see the county buildings a quarter-mile away. "Lovely," she said to Arthur. "The view and the office," she added when she turned to face him. "You've done very well."

Arthur smiled. "I'm trying. Look at this," he said quickly, pointing to the computer. "This is my pride and joy."

Following him, she watched as he hit several keys. A moment later a list appeared on the computer's screen. "This is my data base. I keep each of my artist's schedules in here so I know exactly what's happening without having to go through a million different records."

Suzanne watched as he showed her several examples.

Of the three clients he used, she recognized two names. One was already on the world class level, and the other had been mentioned in last Sunday's paper as a possible contender for conductor of the Met.

"I'm impressed," Suzanne said.

"Of course you are," Arthur joked. "Margaret has a computer terminal at her desk, which is connected to this one. We share a printer," he added as he switched off the computer and stood. "And you're hungry, I hope."

"Actually, I am."

"Good. We have reservations at a new restaurant."

"I guess things have changed since I last lived here. We need reservations for lunch now?"

Arthur winked. "Suzanne, you wouldn't believe how things have changed around here."

With that statement, they left for the restaurant. They took both cars because Arthur had an appointment following lunch.

The restaurant Arthur chose was called Cecilia's. It was set in an old white house, in the center of New City, on Main Street.

And, as Arthur predicted, the restaurant was jammed with people. Yet when the hostess spotted Arthur, she waved him forward. "Good afternoon, Mr. Barnes, your table is ready."

"Hello, Emily," Arthur replied. They followed the hostess into the main room, where the majority of tables were set up. The dining room was light and airy, and reminded Suzanne of a plantation style restaurant she'd once eaten at with Jan-Michael, on one of their holidays in the Caribbean.

The hostess led them to a corner table with a window that looked out on a terrace. There were another half-dozen tables outside. Each was filled.

"Like?" Arthur asked.

"It's lovely."

"The food is very good," he said as a waitress came over and handed them menus.

"Drink?" she asked.

"Nothing yet," Suzanne said.

The waitress left and Arthur and Suzanne opened the menu. It took her a half-minute to decide on a curried chicken salad. She closed the menu and looked at Arthur, whose menu was closed as well.

He met her gaze and held her eyes for several seconds without speaking. Then he said, "Is it working?"

She blinked, confused. "Is what working?"

"Your attempt to cleanse your soul. Your memoirs."

She didn't laugh. "Is that what you think I'm doing?"

Instead of answering, he echoed back her own words. "Isn't that what you are doing?"

"No. I'm not trying to unburden my soul on paper. But I am looking for some reasons for my life, not for absolution for the things I've done in my life. I'm also trying to find out what it was that I might have done that's made my life what it is."

"Are you ready?" asked the waitress as she stepped to the table.

Suzanne bit off her next words and looked at the young woman. "The curried chicken salad and iced tea."

"The cold salmon," Arthur said. "Iced tea as well."

When the waitress left, and Arthur looked at her with raised brows, Suzanne said, "Arthur, I'm just trying to survive. And I need a reason to do that. I'm digging up my life in an effort to find that elusive . . . . Oh, I don't know what to call it, an ideal perhaps? Whatever it is, it's something that will make everything fit into place and let me want to continue going forward."

"Have you found it yet?"

She shook her head. "I keep looking. I keep going back

to Hollywood to see if I lost it there. But I haven't found it yet."

"Perhaps it's something you aren't meant to find."

"I'll find it."

Arthur laughed. "That's one thing that has never changed about you. You are the second most determined woman I have ever met in my entire life."

"Who was the first?" Suzanne asked.

Arthur's eyes changed. "Your mother."

Suzanne reached across the table and took his hand in hers. She squeezed it gently. "It's funny. I never really thought much about how she affected you," Suzanne admitted. "It wasn't something I was ever aware of."

He returned the pressure on her hand. "Why should you have? Suzanne, you're six years younger than me. When you were eight, I was thirteen going on fourteen. By the time we moved back to New York, I was in college."

"But I should have had some sort of a feeling about that. I was able to sense how Father felt about me. And I know that he hated me."

"He never hated you, Suzanne. Never!"

The old emotions rose strong. She remembered the tirades and rages Raymond Barnes had always directed at her. "You were there when he went crazy on me. You used to get in between us. How can you say he didn't hate me?"

"He didn't. What happened to him was he was being pulled apart by the circumstances around him. He was torn between his need for his wife, and his desires to help his son. While his wife was championing his stepdaughter's career, he was crusading on his son's behalf."

Suzanne stared hard into Arthur's eyes. Her hand tightened on his, as if she were afraid he would fall away.

"But I took precedence. Arthur, you could have been a great pianist. You had world class potential."

"According to my father."

"Arthur, you were—"

"No," he interrupted, his eyes boring hard into hers. "Listen to me carefully, Suzanne, because we're going to put this whole thing to rest, right now."

He drew his hand from hers, clasped his hands together, and put them under his chin. He closed his eyes for a moment, and then, as he opened his eyes, he separated his hands and put them palms down on the table.

"I was a good pianist, there's no denying that. And I still am a good pianist, better than most. But I never had that . . . little extra something that would take me beyond good and make me great.

"Do you remember when I was invited to audition for the Halpern Music Conservatory's gifted awards program?"

Suzanne nodded.

"I was good enough to be accepted into the Conservatory's regular program, but not the awards program."

"Because we kept dragging you all over the country. If you'd been able to stay in one place, have one teacher, and had been able to practice regularly with the same—"

"Every word you've spoken is the dogma of Raymond Barnes. Suzanne, please believe me, I've never been on world class level, and no matter how many lessons or how much practice I could have gotten, I never would have become world class."

She fought her tears. She wanted to deny his words because they stung her so harshly. "You're wrong. You—"

"No! Damnit Suzanne, listen to what I'm telling you. I am not unhappy with my life. I'm doing the things I want to do. I play piano every week with a local orchestra, and

165

I enjoy myself thoroughly. I have a thriving business that is more successful than I had ever imagined possible.

"My artists look to me to get them somewhere in life. And I never do what my father did to me. I never give people false hope or lie about their talent. If a musician comes to me, and I listen to him and find that he has that rare and special quality, I will work with him. If that person does not have that quality, I tell them right up front and try to save them the years of their lives they would have had to sacrifice."

He took a deep breath. "But the most important part of all is that I like myself and I like my place in what I call the spectrum of life. I just wish you could find yourself so you could be happy as well."

Suzanne moistened her lips. "That was wonderful," she said. Her voice was husky with the emotions that had warred inside her. She had carried the guilt of usurping Arthur's rightful place in the world deep inside. Arthur's impassioned statement had struck at the very place inside her where she had been hiding that guilt.

"Arthur, I don't know what to say."

"Don't say anything. Eat, instead," he told her as the waitress placed her lunch before her.

As she waved goodbye to Arthur, she noticed that the car's clock read 2:15. They'd spent an hour and a half over lunch, but it had seemed like only a few minutes.

She pulled out onto Main Street, turned left, and headed home. She felt good, almost lightheaded. She knew it was the easing of her guilt. It made her feel good to know that Arthur did not view her as the person who prevented him from having a career as a famous pianist.

She came to a stop at a red light. To her left was a

health food store. Ahead was the intersection of the main highway that would take her back home.

She sighed. The phrase "back home" was starting to sound right. The light changed and she started forward. As she crossed the intersection, a jarring new thought rose up to disturb her calm. Had Arthur been completely honest with her, or had he said those things to help to ease her guilt and to close the gap between them, so that they could be brother and sister again?

Was he that good an actor? she wondered. It was possible. He had been her acting partner for years, helping her with lines she needed to learn for the television show, and later, he'd helped her with the horror movies when he'd gotten back from England.

Yes, he would be able to act the part he needed to be.

That thought led to another thought. This one was cold and sharp and painful. Could Arthur have been lying about everything? Could Arthur have twisted the truth around to fit her ears when he actually felt the opposite?

Could Arthur hate her? Could Arthur blame her for having been the one who had 'made it'? Could he be the one who had sent the letter? Could he have been the one who had cut her brake lines?

"No," she whispered. "Please, not him."

Chapter Twelve

Suzanne finished the last line on the page, made a small notation at the bottom, and put the sheet of white paper on the pile on the table. She shook her head, finding it hard to accept that the pages she'd been reading were actually the story of her life.

Although she remembered dictating the situations to Dana, the typed-out words came across in a vastly different manner. It seemed almost as though what she had read was a story told by another.

Of course, Dana had taken a certain latitude with the dictation, but nothing that she and her friend had not discussed. Yet the reality was that Dana was taking her words and creating a viable story with them.

While it was strange to see her life and her emotions laid out so neatly in black and white, it was a good feeling because she was doing exactly what she'd intended.

This first reading of her work was both frightening and revealing. And even though she had no intention of publishing any of it, she was very surprised to see how interesting it was.

She laughed lightly. The sound echoed on the kitchen. Of course it read interestingly. After all, she reasoned, all the boring real life times had been left out.

There was no need for the boring times—the safe times—she acknowledged; however, it was essential that she find out what it was that had gone so badly awry with her life. She had to learn what this terrible thing was that required she be punished over and over and over again.

Tears formed quickly. She couldn't stop from crying. What had she done? Why had so many bad things happened in her short life. She'd lost her husband and her son. People that she worked with, that she looked up to and admired, all died or disappeared from her life. It had started when she was a child, and it just kept on happening.

Why?

Wiping her eyes, Suzanne pushed her chair from the table and stood. She had to get out for a little while or she would surrender completely to this melancholy mood.

Before she could take a step, the phone's harsh ring shattered the silence. She allowed herself a long and slow breath before picking up the phone and saying, "Yes?"

"Suzanne, it's Peter Wilson."

"Good morning, Peter," she said, working hard to project her voice evenly.

There was a slight pause before the policeman asked, "Is everything all right?"

"I'm fine, thank you for asking." Even as she forced her voice to be even and calm, she wondered if she so was patently open that everyone she spoke with knew when something was wrong.

"Good. The results from the FBI came in a few minutes ago and—"

Seizing the moment, Suzanne interrupted him. "Can I come down and talk with you?"

"Certainly," he said. "Do you know where the station is?"

"I do, as long as it hasn't moved in the last twenty years."

"It's in the same spot," he said.

"I'll be there in a few minutes." Hanging up, Suzanne went to the coffee maker and shut it off. She took her purse from the counter, slipped her keys from the key ring on the wall, and went to the garage, grateful to have a real destination.

"As you see," Peter Wilson said, pointing to the highlighted parts of the FBI faxed report, "the only fingerprints on the letter are yours and Dana Cody's. There are three other sets of prints on the envelope, but the FBI has identified each as a postal worker."

"Which means that the FBI wasn't able to learn anything more than you, yes?" Suzanne asked.

"How long did you live in France?" the detective asked.

Taken off stride, Suzanne said, "Awhile. Why?"

"Because you have a certain way of saying things that is more European than American."

"Such as?"

Wilson smiled. Suzanne liked the way it softened his face. "The way you asked your last question. You ended it with the answer, but in such a way that it was still a question. That's very European."

Suzanne nodded. She understood what he meant. The English would often end a question, or even a statement with a "what?." The French tended to used the word "yes," and the Italians would do the same but say "eh."

"I guess I lived there long enough to pick up their habits," she admitted.

"It's not a bad habit," Peter said. "Anyway, there are a few more items that the FBI lab did find. The paper is high-grade copy paper. The printing was done by a laser printer. They weren't able to narrow things down to the manufacturer of the laser printer, but they did come up with a brand name on the paper."

Following the movement of his long finger on the fax, Suzanne read the name of the paper.

"The only problem is that this is the third most common type of paper sold in the country. It's not a lead. Sorry."

Suzanne studied Peter Wilson. He met her direct gaze without hesitation. She liked that, too. Too many people changed focus when they looked at another person. It was as if they were afraid that she could read something in their eyes that they did not want known.

"What do I do?" she asked.

Peter Wilson's shrug was eloquent, because it was reflected by his features. She saw, and sensed, that he was at a true loss to make a positive statement.

"You can hire a bodyguard to stay with you, or you could contract with a security agency for both home and personal protection, or—"

"No," she said succinctly before he could go on.

"Then I'm afraid there isn't much you can do, other than to be careful," he finally said. "You must always be aware of who is around you. And when you do go out, you should never go someplace where you'll be alone. You might also consider an alarm system for the house."

Pausing, the assistant chief of police leaned toward her. His light eyes darkened with urgent intensity. "And you never open a door to someone whom you do not know!"

"In other words, there's nothing you can do?"

"I'm doing everything I possibly can. But you have to help as well. And the best way for you to do that is by listening to what I've just said. Will you do that . . . for me?"

She moistened her lips with her tongue. She understood that he was telling her that as a policeman, at this stage in whatever investigation there might be, he was helpless. But, she also understood that he was telling her more—that he was saying that he was concerned and was going to somehow look out for her.

"Yes, I'll do that," she said. And ten minutes after saying those last words, Suzanne was home.

She parked in the garage and then walked back out and went to the mailbox. There was no mail, yet. She started back up the driveway, but stopped suddenly when she spotted a bright object on her front steps.

Angling over, Suzanne went to the steps, to the large and fragrant bouquet of flowers. Bending, she picked the small envelope from the center of the bouquet and opened it.

A flush of pleasure rose along her cheeks when she read the signature. The flowers were from Timothy Randolf. She lifted the vase to her nose to breathe in the fragrant blossoms. As she inhaled, there was a noise behind her.

Her muscles stiffened and a prickly sensation crawled along her spine. An instant later came the crunch of a footstep.

Fear sent a jolt of adrenalin surging through her body. She turned suddenly, and almost crashed into the mailman. The blue-uniformed carrier jumped up and back, his eyes widening in surprise.

"Jeez," he said, his voice strangely high-pitched.

"I'm sorry," Suzanne said immediately, trying to ignore the trip hammer beating of her heart. "You startled me."

"You ain't the only one," he replied as he extended a packet of letters to her.

"Sorry," she repeated as he turned and walked quickly away. She watched him until he put a batch of letters into her neighbor's mailbox. Then she returned to the open garage door and went inside.

When she was inside and the doors were locked, she breathed easier. She was overreacting, but she couldn't help it. Everything she did or saw or even thought about seemed to react adversely on her.

She set the bouquet of flowers on the kitchen table and sorted through the mail. Then she opened the rear door and went outside.

Suzanne walked across the backyard, enjoying the feel of the sun and the way it caressed her. When she reached the edge of her property and the old fence, she looked down at the Hudson River.

The river had a soothing effect. After a few minutes Suzanne began to question her unreasonable fear. She had reacted to a threat when there had been no threat. If she'd had a gun, she might have shot the mailman because he'd gone out of his way to hand her the mail.

It's time to get control, she told herself. She knew that if she couldn't control her fear, whoever was haunting her life would win. It wouldn't matter if he hurt her physically or not, because if every phase of her life was lived in fear of him, she would be a perpetual prisoner of that fear.

"It will not happen!" she said aloud. Turning from the fence, she went to the house and she made herself a pitcher of iced tea.

She took the tea and the typed manuscript pages out onto the deck, and went back to work.

When the telephone rang, Suzanne put down her pencil and picked up the receiver. The sun was behind her, just beginning its late afternoon descent.

"Hello," she said.

"Hi, Suzanne, it's Dana. I hope I'm not disturbing you."

"Not at all," Suzanne said as she stood and stretched.

"Tonight is the first night of the concert series at the

town pier. Greg and I are going and we wondered if you'd like to join us."

Suzanne didn't answer immediately. She wasn't sure if she wanted to venture out into the heart of Springvale's summer night life.

"Arthur will be playing with the orchestra."

She thought back to the last time she'd heard Arthur play. It had been almost fourteen years. "You twisted my arm."

"We'll pick you up at seven," Dana said.

Putting the portable phone down, Suzanne gazed toward the river. Although she couldn't see it from where she was, the town pier was not a half mile from where she sat. She pictured the wooden structure perfectly. She was also able to imagine the people who were working on it at this very moment, getting it ready for the evening's concert.

Looking up at the cloudless summer sky, Suzanne was sure that the evening would be warm and dry, and that the stars would smile down kindly.

The phone rang again. She picked it and said hello.

"It's Tim. How are you?" Timothy Randolf asked.

"Good, thank you. And thank you for those lovely flowers," she added, turning and looking back at the house as if she could see inside to where the flowers sat on the kitchen table.

"I was thinking that perhaps I could come by tonight. We could go out for dinner, or we could even order in. What do you think?"

"Oh, Tim, I'm sorry, but not tonight." She did not explain the plans she'd made with Dana.

"I see," he said, his voice going tight.

She sensed the hurt, and said, "But I'd love to have dinner with you tomorrow night."

"Great," he said. "That's great. I'll be by about eight."

"Perfect," she told him, trying to make herself sound as pleased as he was.

When she hung up, she wondered why she had so readily acquiesced to his need to see her. *And why not?* she asked herself. The confusion she was undergoing was far from comfortable. Receiving his unexpected gift of flowers had made her happy. But she'd not been as pleased when he'd wanted to go out tonight.

"Good Lord," she said aloud, "I'm starting to think like a teenager again. Please, spare me!"

And then she laughed as she decided not to worry about Timothy Randolf. She would let things just take their natural course, and see where it would lead them.

But she had plenty to do between now and tomorrow night. And, Suzanne thought, it was time to put her work away, and to get things together for tonight.

The concert ended at exactly ten. Suzanne, Dana, and her husband, Greg, remained in their seats when the crowd left the pier's amphitheater. They'd met with Arthur earlier, and had agreed to wait for him at the end of the concert.

The concert had been good: the choice of music exceptional and the handling of it top-notch. In all, it had been a very pleasant experience.

Arthur's piano, though, had been the high point of the concert. And, after having listened to him for two and a half hours, she could still not understand—no matter what he had told her about his abilities—how his extraordinarily talented playing was not world class caliber.

While they waited for Arthur, Suzanne voiced her feelings aloud to Greg and Dana. "I just don't understand it," Suzanne repeated to Dana and Greg.

Greg, who stood almost a foot above his wife, turned to

Suzanne. "Have you tried looking at it in a different way?"

Suzanne gazed at him. She raised her hands, palm up. "In what way?"

"Perhaps the issue is not that he doesn't have the ability to play on a world class level; rather, is it that he doesn't have the desire to compete on that level? Not everyone who has a talent has the disposition to use it the way other people want. Maybe, just maybe, Arthur is happier in the life he chose for himself, instead of having to live a life that someone else decided on for him."

Suzanne liked Greg Cody and his answer. There was a directness about her friend's husband that was refreshing. Unlike most people whose directness was usually based on personal opinions and prejudices, Greg's words made you think about other options without trying to force you to agree with him.

"You should have been a shrink," Suzanne joked.

When Greg and Dana both laughed, and then glanced quickly at each other, Suzanne felt as though she'd inadvertently stepped into a personal moment.

"That's funny," Dana said, taking Greg's hand and bringing it to her lips. She pressed it briefly to her mouth before releasing it. "Greg's father is a psychiatrist. He spent almost all of Greg's teenage years trying to—very reasonably—talk him into becoming a psychiatrist."

"He said I had a talent for it," Greg added with a smile. "Perhaps I did, but I didn't want his life."

Suzanne studied him for a moment. "So you became a hospital administrator instead. Which is still in the medical field and still means that you are helping people."

"But it is different. I love overseeing a hospital; I enjoy making all the parts work together, so that a whole group of people can benefit. I don't like the thought of playing god on an individual basis, the way my father did."

"Here comes Arthur," Dana said, interrupting Suzanne and Greg's dialogue.

They rose as Arthur reached them. "Did anyone see my father?" he asked.

No one had, so they walked through the remaining people, looking for him. When this proved unsuccessful, Arthur went to the phone. He spoke a few words into the receiver, and then gave everyone a thumb's up.

When he replaced the receiver and returned to them, he said, "He told me that he wasn't feeling well earlier, and decided to stay home."

"Is he all right?" Suzanne asked.

Arthur nodded. "Yes. I told him I was with you, but that I would come home. He told me that he was fine and not to rush home. So, how does coffee sound?"

"Like a perfect ending to the concert," Dana said. "As long as there's some cheesecake with it."

They all laughed as they walked from the pier and stepped onto Main Street. They walked two blocks to a small cafe that Arthur suggested.

The cafe was only partially filled. A piano dominated the far corner. The hostess greeted Arthur by name and took them to a table off to the side.

After taking their order, the woman left. "I've never been here before," Dana commented as she looked around.

"It's not the usual family style place," Arthur explained. "And in Springvale, there usually isn't much besides family places. But, I enjoy it here. And every once in a while, I book one of my jazz pianists here."

The coffee and cheesecake was served by a pleasant waitress.

They spent a half-hour over their coffee, and in easy going conversation. Arthur and Dana talked about the way Springvale had changed over the years, and of how even their neighborhoods had changed.

Arthur laughed when he found out that Dana's oldest son had the same gym teacher that he'd had in elementary school. But when Dana saw that it was getting close to eleven, she declared that they had to get home to relieve the babysitter.

"I'm glad you came to the concert," Arthur told them as they all stood.

Arthur reached for the check, but Greg got it first. He glanced at it and then put a couple of bills on the table.

Outside, Arthur turned to Greg and Dana. "You guys live off South Mackly, right?" When they nodded, he said, "Why don't I drive Suzanne home? It's on my way. And that way you can drive home directly from here."

"Is that okay by you?" Greg asked Suzanne.

"Isn't that what brothers are for?" she asked. "Boy, it feels like old times. Remember when Arthur used to drive us on our dates?" she asked Dana.

Dana's laugh held an uncomfortable echo. "The only reason I went was because you wouldn't go out alone, so you made your date find a boy for me."

Suzanne gazed at her. "I don't remember it that way. Listen, guys, thanks for inviting me tonight."

"Our pleasure," Greg said.

"See you in the morning. Nine," Dana added.

She stood next to Arthur as Greg and Dana walked back toward the pier and the parking lot that was adjacent to it.

"My car is this way," Arthur said, guiding her across the street and up the block. Six minutes after they'd gotten into his car, they were in Suzanne's driveway.

Arthur put the car into park, and said, "Dana's right, you know."

"About what?" she asked.

"I remember when the two of you used to go out on dates. You were both seniors. You had already changed from that fat girl you'd been, but Dana hadn't. She was heavy, and she never really kept herself up."

"So the guys asked her out to get to go out with me?"

"Basically."

Suzanne didn't know what to say, so she said nothing for a moment. "It's funny," she finally said. "I remember so many things from when I was in Hollywood, but I don't remember that much from when I was here."

"It wasn't the best of times," he reminded her.

"But it wasn't the worst either. It was kind of normal, actually," she added as she opened the car door. She looked at her brother, and felt that old familiar tug of attachment. "Want to come in?"

"Sure," he said. He switched off the ignition and opened his door.

They walked to the front door together and, after Suzanne unlocked it, Arthur opened it for her. Inside, Suzanne realized she'd left the air conditioner off. The house was hot and stuffy.

"Let's go out back. Want a drink? Coffee?"

"Nothing, thank you," he responded as he followed her into the kitchen and then out onto the back deck.

She turned on the lights that were mounted along the deck's handrail. The low-wattage lights gave off a gentle, yellow illumination that enhanced rather than detracted from the night.

A quarter moon hung over the bridge's dark span. Stars proliferated in the velveteen sky.

"It's so beautiful tonight," she said as she traced the Big Dipper's points.

Arthur stepped next to her. "It is. Suzanne, I'm glad you've come back."

Looking at him, she smiled. "So am I." Then she led

him to the long bench that was built into the side of the deck. She sat, patting the bench next to her. "I wish you'd met Jan-Michael. I wish you'd known him, and I wish you'd have known Allan."

Then, before he could speak, or her emotions could get out of control, she turned to him. "Tell me why you never married?"

Arthur laughed nervously. When he spoke, she felt the hesitation in his words. "Actually, I was almost married. But circumstances interfered."

"What circumstances?" Suzanne prodded.

"She was a nice girl. A cellist, actually. We were engaged, and we had even set a date for our marriage. It was to be January, four years ago."

Suzanne stared at Arthur as the import of the date struck her. "Mother died that December."

Arthur nodded. "And my father took it very badly. It was as if his world had stopped. I had to spend a lot of time with him. Francine understood when I had to postpone the wedding. But somehow, time slipped by, and one day she came to me and told me that she wouldn't wait any longer."

Arthur paused. He shrugged, and said, "And that was the end of that."

Suzanne covered Arthur's hand with hers. "I'm sorry."

"Don't be. It would never have worked." He squeezed her hand gently, released it, and stood. "I'd best get moving. I want to check on Father before I go home."

Suzanne stood. They went into the kitchen, where Arthur paused. She saw him look at the flowers on the table, and then at the small card that was leaning against the vase.

When he looked back at her and raised his eyebrows, she smiled. "Believe it or not, they're from Timothy Randolf."

"Really?" Arthur said.

"Really. We went out a couple of times since I came back."

"You went out with him?" Arthur asked, his voice strained and husky. "How could you go out with that . . . that publicity seeking fool?"

Taken back by Arthur's unexpected and angry vehemence, Suzanne said, "What are you talking about? Arthur, when we lived in California, you and Tim used to be best friends."

"I was a teenager then. Suzanne, he's not the same person he was. He . . ." Arthur shook his head. "Never mind. It's not my place to tell you who you should see."

"Not, at least, without an explanation," she said, aware that her own voice sounded harsh.

"I really do have to go," Arthur said as he turned toward the front door.

Suzanne walked with him, still puzzled about his reaction to Tim Randolf. When they reached the front door, Arthur opened it, and then turned to look at Suzanne.

She stood still while he stared hard into her eyes. She sensed he wanted to say something, but was holding himself back.

"What?" she asked gently.

He shook his head, started to turn, and stopped again. When he spoke, his voice was low but the words carried clearly to her.

"It was because of you."

Suzanne blinked. His words confused her. "What was because of me?"

"Why I never married. It wasn't because Father was having a bad time. That was only an excuse. It was because of you. Suzanne . . . I . . . Suzanne, I love you. I have since . . . God . . . it seems like forever."

Chapter Thirteen

Why did he have to do that?

Suzanne stared at a photograph on the far wall. It was a picture of herself, surrounded by her mother, stepfather, and stepbrother.

They had been a family for so long. But they had not been a family for the last decade. And now, just when they were coming together again . . . . Why had he done this?

She couldn't get his words out of her head. She could still hear him saying that he loved her, and that he hadn't married because of her.

"But you're my brother!" she'd said to him once the thundering shock of his words had lessened and she'd been able to speak.

"Stepbrother! Brother by marriage! We're not related by blood. And what I feel for you is not abnormal. It's love. Suzanne, I've loved you for years."

"No," she'd shot back. Her mind had been reeling, and her heart had been broken, again. She loved him dearly. She loved him as she could love only a brother. "Don't you understand? It doesn't matter whether we're related by blood or not. Arthur, you're my brother! You're my friend. But there can never be anything else."

He had reached for her then, and before she'd been

able to move, he'd caught her and pulled her to him. He'd kissed her, his mouth pressing hard upon hers. Rather than fight, she'd held herself still and kept her mouth still, unresponsive.

For all the passion he had tried to put into the kiss, she'd felt nothing. When he'd finally released her, he'd stepped back and stared hard at her. "I love you," he'd said just before he'd closed the door.

The instant the door had shut, Suzanne had locked it securely. Then she'd gone into the living room and collapsed on the couch, her mind a bubbling cauldron of hurt and confusion.

"Oh, Arthur," she whispered, her throat clogging with emotion. She'd lost so many things, and now she'd lost yet more. Tonight, she'd lost her brother.

Maybe not, she tried to tell herself. Maybe her harsh words of reality, while they had hurt him, had also helped him to see beyond his emotions.

Rationally, she knew that there would be nothing wrong should she and Arthur have fallen in love. But the way she felt about him was as a brother only. She remembered his expression when she'd told him that. She saw that he did not want to hear it or believe it. She could only pray that this would pass, and the brother she had always loved would return.

Was that truly possible? Could he go back to being her brother? Could she accept that, after he had vowed his passion to her?

She would try. Of that, she was certain.

She yawned, and realized that she was just short of exhaustion. Standing, Suzanne left the couch and turned the lights off on the first level before going upstairs to her bedroom.

She looked at her bed, and then decided to take a shower. Fifteen minutes later, wearing a light nightgown,

Suzanne slipped between the sheets of the now darkened bedroom.

As her head sank into the downy pillow, her eyes closed and she sighed softly. She did her best not to think as she waited for sleep to steal her thoughts away.

But her twisting and turning thoughts kept sleep at bay. And as she lay quietly in the bed, breathing evenly and concentrating on the silence, she heard a car drive by. A few moments later the sound faded into the distance.

She tried to think of pleasant things, the way her mother had always told her to do when she had been a little girl. But it was hard, for too many things had been taken from her, and she could not think the good thoughts.

She heard another car start by. Then the car's engine quieted. An instant later a loud crash came from below. At the same time, the car's engine revved up and its tires squealed on the pavement.

She threw the covers from her and raced downstairs. When she reached the first floor, she found a red and orange tendril of fire spreading across the living room floor.

Without consciously thinking about it, she went to the oriental carpet and, ignoring the smoke and flames eating at the area rug, began to roll the carpet up.

The smoke stung her eyes. She wiped at them as best she could, coughing badly as she breathed in the smoke. But she did not stop, and by the time she'd rolled the carpet all the way up, the fire was out.

Sinking to her knees, she looked at the shattered living room window and then at the smoke darkened ceiling. Her anger grew swiftly, filling her with strength at this newest violation.

She stood and, refusing to acknowledge the wobbling of her knees, went to the phone and dialed the police. When the phone was answered, she gave her name and address and said, "Someone threw a . . . a firebomb into my living room. Please send someone. Please."

"On the way," the operator said.

The strength suddenly drained from her body. She hung up, tried to take a step forward, but could not. Slowly, she sank to the floor.

Suzanne heard them come inside; she wasn't unconscious. She just couldn't raise enough willpower to move. But when she felt strong hands on her, she opened her eyes. Peter Wilson's light gray-green eyes looked back at her.

"Are you all right?" he asked.

She let him pull her to her feet before saying, "Yes. Who . . ." she began, but stopped as a fireman walked across the room.

"They're checking to make sure everything is out," Peter said, leading her into the kitchen. "Sit here, take it easy for a few minutes. I'll be right back."

When he was gone, Suzanne realized that she was in her light nightgown. She looked down at herself. What she was wearing did not leave much to the imagination.

The assistant police chief returned in less than a minute. He handed her the robe she'd left on her bed. He also set down a pair of penny loafers. "There's glass inside. You've already cut yourself," he added, motioning to the floor. There were several drops of blood near her foot. "We'll take care of that in a moment."

She stared at the blood with bewilderment. There was no pain in her feet. "How did I get cut?"

"It was a Molotov cocktail—a firebomb made of a glass bottle, gasoline, and a rag for a fuse. You were cut by the broken glass."

Turning, Peter Wilson went back inside. Suzanne

stood, slipped on the robe and, taking the policeman's advice, put on the shoes instead of looking at the cuts.

When she stood, there was still no pain. She went inside. Peter Wilson was talking to two uniformed policemen and a fireman.

She waited silently, listening as Peter told the policemen to take the carpet back to the station, and to then have all the pieces of glass imbedded in the carpet taken out and dusted for prints.

When they were gone, and the firemen had left as well, Peter turned to Suzanne. "I think you should check into a motel for the night, or—"

Suzanne shook her head hard. Her hair whipped about in emphasis. "I will not be chased from my home!"

"Suzanne, you look exhausted. Are you planning to stay up all night and keep guard in here?"

She met his challenge openly. "If I have to."

Peter sighed. A shadowy smile outlined his mouth. "All right, Suzanne, you win. Go to bed. I'll stay down here. Just tell me where the broom and dustpan are."

"You don't need to be here, babysitting me. You should be at home. You—" He held up his right hand, palm forward, and stopped her.

"I'm not here to babysit. I have a job, and it will take me a while to finish it. So please, do me a big favor. Let me take care of the cuts on your feet, and then I'd like you to go upstairs and get some sleep. I have work to do down here. So, until the window can be replaced," he added, motioning to the shattered picture window, "someone has to be here."

"Peter . . ." she began, but stopped. She smiled warmly at him. "Can I make you some coffee?"

"After we check your feet."

Nodding, Suzanne led him back into the kitchen. She

sat on one of the chairs and slipped her shoes off. Peter lowered himself to his knees and lifted her left foot.

His hands were warm and gentle and firm as he checked the foot for cuts. "Nothing," he said, lowering the foot and reaching for the right leg.

He raised the foot, supporting her calf with his left hand while he inspected the sole. "Only one small cut, here, on the side," he said, turning her foot so that she saw it. "I'll need some peroxide and a band-aid."

"There's some under the sink in the hall bathroom."

She watched him leave. Peter Wilson, she decided, was a very different sort of person than she was used to. She didn't quite understand him, and couldn't help but wonder why he was doing so much more than his job. Or, was this seemingly personal concern just another part of his job as a policeman?

He returned quickly and cleaned and bandaged her foot. "Now, why don't you go upstairs and get some sleep and I'll finish up my work here?"

"After I make the coffee. The broom and dustpan are in the utility room," she said as she went over to the sink.

A moment later, Peter Wilson emerged from the utility room with the broom and pan. "Do you have any sheets of plastic around?"

When she shook her head, he said, "Then I'll need a few large trash bags and some masking tape."

"That I have." She finished setting up the coffee and, as the policeman swept up the living room, Suzanne found the tape and brought it to him along with a half-dozen garbage bags.

"The coffee will be ready in a couple of minutes," she said, and then yawned. "Sorry."

"For being tired? You've had what I would describe as a tough night. Why don't you go ahead to bed? I'll take care of things down here."

She stared at him for several silent seconds. "Let's have the coffee first."

Peter put down the implements he was holding and walked into the kitchen with her. She pointed to a chair and he sat in it while she poured the two cups of coffee.

"Milk? Sugar?"

"A little milk, thank you."

She finished prepping the coffee and brought the two cups to the table. She sat catty-corner from him, and took a sip of the coffee.

"Have you received any more threats? Were there any phone calls before the bomb?"

Suzanne shook her head.

"Nothing happened out of the ordinary?"

Suzanne thought about Arthur, and his declaration of love for her. Would he call that something unusual? But Arthur, no matter how emotionally confused he was, was still her brother. And she knew deep inside of her that he would never harm her.

"No," she said slowly. "Nothing's happened."

Peter raised his cup, blew the steam across the top of the coffee, and then took a drink.

As he lowered the coffee cup, Suzanne asked, "Why are you doing this?"

He didn't evade her gaze, or the question. "It's what I do for a living. It's my job."

"No," she said. "You could have just as easily had a policeman sit in a car out front. You didn't have to volunteer to sit in my living room until daytime."

"No, I didn't."

"Then why?"

Peter Wilson rolled the cup slowly between his palms. His gray-green eyes did not once move from hers. "Some people believe that all crimes are basically equal, and should be handled equally. I don't subscribe to that theory.

Yes, a robbery of a store should be classified the same as say, a home burglary. But a murder cannot be treated the same as some petty thief picking someone's pocket at a concert.

"And I can't find it in me to classify a car thief the same way I would a person who stalks another human being." He paused to take a sip of coffee. When he put the cup down, he said, "And I will not permit this sort of thing to go unanswered. Until we can learn who this person is, there isn't a whole lot I can do. But as a policeman with a degree of authority above the average citizen, I must do something. And if it means sitting here until the window is repaired, then I don't mind doing that."

Suzanne was unprepared for the answer she'd received. She was surprised at his vehemence, and pleased as well.

"Thank you," she said.

He nodded. "And now that true confessions are over, why don't you go upstairs and get some sleep while I do my job? With a little luck I'll find a fragment of glass with a print on it."

"I hope so," Suzanne said.

An hour and a half later, Peter Wilson poured himself the remnants of the coffee, and then surveyed his handiwork. He'd sealed the window, using three garbage bags and half a roll of masking tape.

The job wasn't pretty to look at, but it did effectively cover the window. The living room floor was clean, and all the splinters of glass were in a garbage bag that was destined for analysis at the lab.

Turning, he gazed at the fireplace mantle, and the four gold statuettes that stood proudly upon it. He went to the mantle for a closer look. The engraving on three of the statuettes had Jan-Michael Grolier's name on them. Each had a title of a book as well. He recognized two of the titles, having read both books. The third title was unknown by him.

He looked at the fourth statuette. It had Suzanne's name on it. Although he had never seen any of her movies, Peter sensed that she was an exceptional actress.

She had to be, he thought, because she seemed to be an exceptional person.

He took a sip of coffee, and wrinkled his nose. It was old, bitter, and cold.

Shaking his head, he went into the kitchen to make another pot. He wanted to stay awake on the off chance that the bastard who was haunting Suzanne might just try something else tonight.

Even as he thought of it, he knew that it would not happen. But, he told himself, he could always hope.

She woke slowly, stretched, and then froze as she remembered what had happened. She flipped the cover from her and looked at the clock. It was nine. She'd overslept.

Leaving the bed, she put on the robe and the loafers she'd worn last night. She felt a little catch on her foot from the glass cut.

Although there had been no pain last night, it was sore this morning. She used the bathroom quickly and, after running the brush through her hair, went downstairs.

She found Peter Wilson sitting at the kitchen table talking with Dana Cody. "Morning," she said.

Dana stood and went to her. "Are you okay?" she asked, her eyes filled with concern.

"I'm fine. But I overslept. Sorry," she said to Peter.

"Don't apologize. You went through a lot last night."

"Did you find anything?" she asked as Dana poured a third cup of coffee and brought it to her.

"There were a couple of glass fragments that were large enough to be analyzed. I'll know something a little later. But for now," he added, standing, "I've got to get to the station and check a few things. Call if you think of anything that might help find this person."

"I will, and Peter, thank you again."

He smiled at her and Dana, then left.

"All right, what really happened?" Dana asked as Suzanne sat in the chair that Peter Wilson had just vacated.

"Didn't he tell you?"

"He told me that someone threw a firebomb into your living room. But that's all. Tell me what really happened."

"That is what really happened. I was in bed, trying to sleep, when I heard a car drive by slowly. An instant later there was a crash. I ran downstairs and found the living room carpet was on fire."

"And that's it?" Dana asked.

Suzanne bobbed her head once. "That's all there was to it." She paused, staring past her friend to the sunny sky outside the kitchen. "Dana, you've been here all your life. You know the people. Tell me about Peter Wilson. Why would he spend the night here, guarding me?"

Dana stared at her for a moment before answering. Suzanne thought she saw something in her friend's gaze, but wasn't sure. Then, before Dana could speak, there was a knock on the door.

"That must be the window company. Peter called them this morning."

"Of course," she said to Dana as her friend went to answer the door.

Leaning back in the chair, Suzanne drank more of the coffee. Peter Wilson was a mystery to her. But she was not unhappy that he was the policeman handling her case.

Dana returned a moment later. "They said they'll have

the window replaced before noon. Want some breakfast?"

"I'm not very hungry," Suzanne said. "I just don't understand why this is happening. Why can't I just live my own life?"

Dana took her hand in hers. "This will end soon and you'll be able to get on with everything."

Suzanne looked up at her. "Will I? It's been going on for so long now. So damned long."

Dana shook her head. "This isn't the same. Everything you've told me—all the tapes you've made—show a series of happenings. Yes, there were accidents, and some were very unfortunate. But what you've described to me all points to the fact that it was the circumstances surrounding the accidents that made things appear even worse. Except for those threatening letters you used to get, there was nothing that pointed to an actual person being after you."

Suzanne exhaled slowly. The sound was loud and drawn out. "I know. My lord, Dana, I know what happened. But it just never ends!"

"Isn't that the very reason why you're doing this? Wasn't your agenda to seek the past to free yourself from all your old ghosts?"

"Yes," she admitted.

"Then why don't we do that, instead of wondering who or what is going on right now?"

Suzanne studied her friend, and knew that Dana was very much that—her friend. "Maybe you should have been a shrink. What do you call that little chat, a 'let's think about the past and forget the present therapy?'"

"No, actually I call it the 'let's cut out the crap and get our butts to work' therapy chat."

Suzanne laughed. "Okay. Let's do just that, but outside," she added as the sound of drilling echoed into the kitchen.

Ten minutes later, Dana had the tape recorder set up,

and Suzanne was putting some marmalade on a slice of toast. Her appetite had returned a little.

"Do you know Peter Wilson, personally?" she asked Dana in between a mouthful of toast.

Dana favored her with that strange look again. "Not well. He's on the same softball team as Greg, but we've never socialized."

"What does Greg think of him?"

"That he's a hell of a shortstop, and a good policeman. He's mentioned both at different times. Why?"

"Curious," Suzanne responded.

"So am I," Dana said. "About what comes next. Our last session was . . ." She picked up her notebook and looked at a page. "The first horror movie. There was that hate letter."

Suzanne nodded. "Yes. But that was all. The rest of the production went smoothly. I started dating Tim Randolf at the same time, and things seemed to be going along well."

She took another bite of toast. "By the time we finished the movie, the producers had offered me a new contract."

"So things started to change then. They were getting better."

"It seemed so, for a while. We started production of the second movie a couple of months before the first one was released. I was glad that I was working, because the publicity was pretty hard. Most of it was directed toward me. They were using my past as a child star to promote the movie."

"Which had been their intention all along," Dana pointed out.

"It didn't make it any easier. They used me, and they used Tim. And it worked. By the second week, the movie was number three at the box office. It was going great guns, and the *Baby* publicity was plastered everwhere."

"I remember. Everyone wanted to see what happened to you. And boy, did they see!" Dana said, laughing.

"You mean the famous boob shot!"

Dana nodded, trying not to laugh. "There was so much publicity about that."

"Well, it wasn't me."

"Come on," Dana said. "It's not such a terrible thing. Almost every actress out there has ah . . . bared their . . . chest."

"It's more common today, and taken in context with the part, it's fine. But back then I was young and innocent, believe it or not, and I wouldn't show my breasts for anything. They used a body double in that movie."

"But not in all of them?" Dana pushed.

"Later, I did my own scenes."

"What are we going to cover today? The second movie? Were there any more letters?"

Suzanne let herself go back in time. "No letters," she said to Dana, who had turned on the recorder. "But halfway through the shoot, there was another of those . . . accidents."

She closed her eyes, and willed herself to remember every detail.

Production on the second movie had moved with lightning speed once the powers-that-be had seen the figures on the first movie.

Everyone was as happy as possible, and they were talking about the second movie outdoing the first. The entire production staff was the same, and half the actors were as well.

Timothy Randolf again played her boyfriend. This time, they did not hide the fact that they were dating. By the fifth week of production, they were a week ahead of schedule.

On the first day of the sixth week of shooting, Suzanne was in her trailer. Tim Randolf was with her.

"I'll go on ahead," Tim said, closing the script they'd been using to go over their lines. Tim brushed his lips across Suzanne's. Then he smiled and waved goodbye. When the door clicked, Suzanne closed her eyes. She was tired. They'd been out late the night before, dancing.

She'd come home at one, to face her mother's anger. But when her mother had started to chastise her, with her stepfather staring on, Suzanne had stood up for herself. "I'm nineteen years old, and I don't do this often. But I do have a life and I need some time to live it. Don't do this to me," she'd added before turning from them and going to her room.

She'd never talked back to either of them before, and their response had been a surprised and shocked silence that had continued through the next morning.

Suzanne knew that by the time the day ended, and she went home, she would apologize to her mother. Her mother would do the same to her. But, things would change, and she would have a life of her own. She was determined about that.

She picked up the open script, glanced at it, and decided to go out to the set. Standing, Suzanne adjusted the tee-shirt she was wearing. The shirt was dark, and not see-through, but her breasts were perfectly outlined beneath the material. The shooting script had called for a physical scene, where she would be doing a lot of running. And, while she also understood that the type of movie she was making was of the low-budget sex and violence genre, she refused to be used to simply titillate the audience by going braless. Instead, she wore a specially designed sports bra, which outlined her breasts but contained them at the same time.

Suzanne left the trailer, and walked swiftly to the high school gymnasium they were using for a sound stage. They'd been at the high school location for three days, and had two more shooting days left. It was important to finish the shoot in the two days, because the school vacation would end then, and they would not be permitted to stay during regular school session.

The inside of the gymnasium was divided in half. One half was set up for a school play. The other half was set up with what appeared to school hallways. Suzanne's scene called for her to be working on scenery. As she painted a prop, a stalking masked creature/killer would come after her. She would run, going into the second half of the gym, and race along the prefabed hallways in her effort to escape her hunter.

"Ready?" asked Sam Harding, the same director she'd had in the first film.

Suzanne nodded. "All set."

"All right, everyone, gather 'round," Harding called.

When the cast and crew were around him, he said, "I want to do this in one take. We spent half of the morning rehearsing. I think we have it down. So let's get out there and get it done. And remember, we've only got today and tomorrow."

He looked around until he spotted Tom Courtney, the actor who played the masked creature/killer. "Tom, don't be too heavy handed with that knife. I want to see movement, not just the blade.

The grotesquely made-up actor said, "No problem," as he raised his hand and made an okay sign with his thumb and forefinger.

Harding turned to the director of photography. "Your people all set?"

"Definitely."

"Then let's go people!" Sam Harding shouted, as he did before every important scene.

Bedlam exploded, but it was an organized chaos resulting in everything getting done at optimum speed. In under five minutes the second AD called for action and a moment later the scene was underway.

Suzanne, ignoring the heat and lights that flooded over her, picked up a brush and began to paint a tree. She was counting to herself, getting herself ready for the physical acting she would have to do.

"Just right," Tim Randolf said, giving Suzanne her cue.

She put down the brush and stood. "Of course it is," she said, leaning toward him. "Just like me."

Tim bent his head and kissed her.

"Hey," Suzanne said after the lingering kiss. "We're alone here. I don't want to get in trouble."

Tim smiled. "I know we are; I planned it that way." He drew her close, pressing her tightly to him.

She stopped him. "Wait, did you hear something?"

Tim looked around and then shook his head. "It's just us. No one but us," he said with a smile as he bent and kissed her. Suzanne responded as her part called for. Just as she did, a shadow fell on them. A half-second later a large hand reached out, grabbed Tim's hair, and yanked him back.

"What the—" Tim said, as he stumbled backward.

On cue, Suzanne screamed. It was a loud, howling wail that followed the action of the masked creature who was raising a knife toward her.

Tim's character picked himself up off the floor and launched himself at the creature. He rammed the creature's side, and the creature dropped its knife.

He turned and grabbed Tim. In that instant, the director shouted, and everything froze. The crew swarmed around them, and Tim was replaced by a stuntman who wore the exact same clothing. The difference was that beneath the long shirt he wore was a harness attached to an almost invisible cord.

The girl in charge of script continuity went up to the stunt man and the creature and placed each in the exact position that Tim and the creature had been in when they'd stopped the action.

Only when she was satisfied, and signaled to the director that everything was okay, did Sam Harding call for quiet on the set.

Thirty seconds later, action was resumed. The creature growled, lifted Tim's double, and threw him. The invisible cord lifted and swung the stunt man twenty feet in the air. When the cord was released, Tim's double crashed into the high school play scenery and lay still.

Suzanne screamed again as the creature turned its attention back to her. As it reached for the knife Tim had knocked away, Suzanne started to run.

The creature howled behind her as she reached the gym door. She pushed through and started to run down one of the hallways. Above her, the camera rolled along on a track that had been set above the three-quarter high walls. A camera man rode behind the camera on a special platform.

Adjacent to the cameraman was a special effects man. He was in charge of the things that were going to happen in the hallway.

Suzanne ran slowly. She knew that in the final editing, it would appear that she was running at full speed.

She reached the first turn, and then went to the second. She stumbled as she was supposed to, and looked back in the direction she'd just come from.

Then, scrambling up from the floor, she whimpered

and ran forward again. Finally, she reached a door and went inside. She stopped on the exact mark she was supposed to reach. She leaned against the wall, breathing rapidly and deeply as she stared into the camera set two feet from her.

"Here we go," called the AD. Suzanne tensed. While there was no sound track on this piece of film, she still held herself in the part with her loud breathing. She would breathe loudly again, later in the sound editing room when they dubbed the film, but for now she needed to stay in character.

An instant later there was a crash behind her. The wall vibrated, and she shook for the camera. And then, above her, she heard the special effects man call out.

Suddenly, a small section of wall, on each side of her head, exploded inward. Two hands appeared then, groping for her face.

Screaming as the hands touched her face, she dropped down and started to crawl away.

As she crawled, the wall disintegrated and the creature stepped through. She flipped to her back and started to scramble backwards, her feet convincingly slipping on the tile floor.

Suddenly Tim was in the room with them. He had a long pole, and was lifting it over his head, preparing to hit the creature.

As he swung the pole, the creature turned and deflected the wood. The creature growled again and took a step forward. "Hold!" came Sam Harding's voice.

Everyone froze. Tim's double reappeared and took Tim's place. When everyone was set again, the director called for action.

Suzanne was against the wall, three-quarters of her torso was on the floor, her shoulders and head were against the wall. She had one hand to her mouth. Her eyes were wide and frightened.

The creature lifted Tim's double, held him aloft, and began to shake him. The creature screamed, and then Suzanne heard a strange crackling sound from above.

She looked up just as the wood of the camera track support sagged. In less than a second, the camera platform holding the cameraman and the special effects man tilted. The camera fell straight down and the two men followed it.

Pandemonium erupted amid screams of pain and panic as the camera crashed down, hitting one of the temporary walls and sending that wall inward onto the creature and the stunt double. The cameraman and the special effects expert followed, screaming in fear as they fell straight down.

From above, several of the temporary wooden beams came crashing down at Suzanne. She covered her head and face as the pieces of wood rained down on her. Something heavy hit her across her wrists. She cried out. And then everything was quiet.

Galvanizing her muscles into action and ignoring everything that had happened, she raced to the center of the small room, where the main havoc had fallen. The camera was laying on the stuntman's leg. The leg itself looked strange and twisted. The angle from the knee was not natural.

The actor playing the creature lay silent. Suzanne saw a piece of wood sticking out of his shoulder. The cameraman was trying to stand. Blood ran down from his scalp.

She went to the stuntman. He was unconscious. She tried to move the camera, but could not get it to budge.

And then the rest of the crew was there, reaching in to help. Sam Harding raced over to Suzanne's side and drew her back from the mess. Turning her, he looked at her face, and then at the rest of her body. "Are you all right?"

Suzanne couldn't speak, but she nodded.

To her left, someone shouted to call an ambulance. Then the man said, "I need help here! Brian Keller's arm is shattered. The artery is cut."

Suzanne turned to help, but her legs started to give way. Sam Harding held her up. "Let them help. Come on," he urged, half carrying and half dragging her back to the main part of the gym.

"How terrible," Dana said when she shut off the recorder.

"It was. The special effects man lost his arm. The stuntman's leg was broken in three different places. The actor who played the creature had seventeen stitches in his shoulder and a dozen more in his scalp, and the cameraman had a sprained neck. I guess I was the luckiest one of all, because all I got was a few scratches and bruises."

"It must have been hard to go on from there," Dana said.

"But we did. Still," Suzanne said with a sad shake of her head, "it just adds another rung on that strange ladder of my life. I mean, really, Dana, I have to be cursed. Look at what happened, again. Things were going great. Better than they had in years. But, just like when I was on the TV series, and things went well, something bad happened, and people were hurt. I'm telling you, it's me."

"Stop it. You aren't cursed. It was an accident."

Suzanne stared hard at her friend. She studied Dana's face, and saw the concern and faith in her eyes. "Accident or not, it was my fault. And Dana, don't try to tell me it wasn't. Somehow, I know it was."

Chapter Fourteen

"I am sorry, but there was nothing on the glass," Peter Wilson said.

"Did you really expect to find fingerprints?" Suzanne was not trying to challenge him; rather, she was just confirming her own suspicions.

"It's not just the prints. There are other identifiable things that we look for. But we came up empty. I am sorry," he repeated.

"You tried, which is the important thing. And I do appreciate that."

There was a moment of telephone static silence before he said, "Would you do me a favor?"

Suzanne nodded. The telephone receiver bobbed with her head. "Yes," she said.

"Don't go anywhere alone. And don't go anywhere with someone you don't know well."

Suzanne laughed, albeit nervously. "The only people I would be going anywhere with are those who I know very well. And there aren't many who fall into that category. But thank you for your concern."

"I wish I didn't have to be concerned. Suzanne, if anything out of the ordinary happens, no matter how small or insignificant you might think it is at the moment—anything at all—I want to know about it."

"All right," she promised before hanging up.

After setting the portable phone in its base on the kitchen counter, Suzanne went into the living room. The smell of smoke remained distinct, but it was not as strong as earlier. She was certain the scent would be gone in another couple of days.

She looked at the dark scorch marks that marred the beauty of the light oak floor. She would have no choice but to have the floor refinished.

"In time," she said. She glanced at her watch. It was getting late and Tim Randolf would be arriving soon. She started toward the stairs, knowing that she would have just enough time to get ready for their date.

When Tim Randolf's car pulled into the driveway a half-hour later, Suzanne had changed the dressing on her foot and was just securing the last button on her pale pink blouse.

Glancing in the mirror, she pushed back a wisp of hair and went downstairs. She reached the door at the same instant that the bell rang.

She paused, took a breath, and opened the door. "Hi."

Tim Randolf smiled at her. He was holding yet another bouquet of flowers. This time it was roses set within an emerald-green sheath of fern-like leaves. He wore a dark blue double-breasted jacket, gray pants, and a gray shirt without a tie. She stepped back to let him in.

His eyes roamed from her face to her clothing and back to her face. "You look magnificent," he said at last. Then his brows furrowed. At the same time, he sniffed the air several times. "It smells like fire."

"My carpet," she said as she took the flowers from him.

"Your carpet?" he asked. "Did something happen?"

She took his arm and brought him into the living room, where she explained the previous night's events.

His expression went from surprise to shock to dismay. "My God, you could have been killed. You . . . . Why . . . . Did you call the police?"

"They're investigating, but there's nothing they can do without someone to go after."

"And until then you have to stay in danger?" Tim asked, incredulity etching his features.

"Basically."

"I won't have it!" Tim stated. "Suzanne, I . . . you can't stay here, not until they catch this nut case. You must come back to the city with me. You can stay at my penthouse for as long as it takes them to find this maniac."

Suzanne couldn't contain her spreading smile. "Will you be living there as well?"

His eyes left hers and shifted to the scorched area on the floor. "Well, naturally I would be. But I wouldn't expect you ah, us, ah . . ."

"And you'd be right. No thank you, Timothy," she said shortly. Then, smiling to ease the terseness of her reply, she held up the flowers. "Give me a minute to put these in water."

Without waiting for a reply, she retrieved a vase from the dining room, brought it to the kitchen, and filled it with water. After cutting the stems and arranging them in the vase, she set it on the dining room table.

When she returned to the living room, she found Tim Randolf still staring at the scorched floor. "I can't believe it."

"I'm ready," she said, ignoring his comment.

They ate at a small restaurant in Springvale, just off the river. Afterward, they took a walk along the waterfront promenade.

As they strolled, Tim took her hand. She did not pull

away. The contact was nice. She breathed in the night air, enjoying the fresh scents that came from the river and did her best to ignore the small amount of pain from the cut in her foot.

They moved slowly along the walkway, glancing into the windows of the various shops. But, a few minutes into their walk, Suzanne began to feel eyes on her.

She didn't know how she knew, or where whoever was watching her was standing, but the crawling sensation that rippled along her spine could not be denied. She knew that she was being watched.

When they passed a jewelry store, Suzanne pulled Timothy to the window. Pretending to look at the display, Suzanne carefully glanced over her shoulder. There was no one looking at her.

She turned back just as Tim said, "Isn't that a nice ring?"

She followed his finger to a magnificent diamond solitaire. "Yes, it would make a pretty engagement ring for some lucky girl."

"Yes, it would," he said before he turned and led her away. "Look. An ice cream parlor. Do you have room enough for a cone?"

She watched a young girl walk by licking a cone. The girl was all of fourteen or fifteen. She remembered back to when she was that age, and how her body had always reacted so terribly to sweets. "I'm sure I could fit one in."

They went to the parlor's outside window and ordered two cones. Suzanne got chocolate chip while Tim ordered coffee ice cream.

The took their cones and continued on. When they reached the pier, where Suzanne had been not more than twenty-four hours ago, they stepped onto it and walked to the railing.

Leaning on the railing, they ate the cones. But, again,

the strange and crawling sensation of being watched came over her.

"Excuse me a moment," Tim said suddenly.

Before she could stop him, Tim was on his way to a couple who'd just stepped onto the pier. She fought against the sudden rise of fear at being left alone and watched him greet them: there was a handshake for the man and a peck on the cheek for the woman.

Tim spoke with them for a moment, and then waved to Suzanne, urging her to join them. Rather than staying alone, she went to the small group.

"Suzanne, I want you to meet some friends. This is Kristen Bremmer and her husband Carl Hawks. They produce several shows for CBS."

"Suzanne Grolier," she said, extending her hand to Kristen and then Carl. "It's a pleasure to meet you."

"You look very familiar," Kristen Bremmer said, scrutinizing Suzanne carefully.

"Of course she does," Tim said. "Grolier is her married name. Her maiden name is—"

"Barnes," Carl Hawks said quickly. *The Axeman Cometh*. Great B flick. I loved it!"

"Thank you," Suzanne said, smiling. "Actually, the title was *The Axeman*. But the ad agency got carried away."

"It worked though," Kristen said. "But there's something else," Kristen said. Then she shrugged. "I'll remember eventually. Are you doing anything these days?"

Suzanne shook her head. "I'm taking life easy."

When Kristen's eyes hazed over, Suzanne knew she'd used the perfect phrase to turn off questions. A producer was interested in people who were either on the rise, or established and bankable stars and who were recognizable and utilizable for their box office draw.

Suzanne's answer had told them that she was not working or looking for work, or even being sought for work.

Within seconds of her admission, the conversation shifted to Tim's afternoon show. The husband and wife producing team had several people whom they thought would fit in well as guests on Tim's show.

While the three talked, Suzanne looked around. She glanced at the band shell and thought about the previous evening's concert. A murky sadness spread through her when she thought about Arthur's admission.

Suddenly, the sensation of being watched grew strong again. She looked around slowly, trying not to seem as if she were searching out anyone. All she saw were people wandering about casually. None pulled their gaze from her when she looked at them. She recognized no one and there were no suspicious looking people at all.

She wondered if she was undergoing some form of paranoia.

"I know," Kristen Bremmer said suddenly.

Suzanne turned to her, dreading that the woman was about to tell her that she remembered how "just wonderful and cute" she'd been in the old TV series.

"I feel like an absolute fool. You made that wonderful movie with Albert Moreau. I can't think of the title, but I've seen it several times. You were magnificent. I'm so sorry for not having recognized you."

Suzanne was doubly shocked that the woman had seen that movie, and that she'd liked it as well. "Thank you, I didn't know it had been released here."

"I don't know if it has been or not. I saw it in Paris, when it was first released. And I've been fortunate enough to have seen it several times on television when I've been in Europe," she said, switching to French for the last words.

Suzanne responded in kind. She felt better after the woman's words. And it was nice to be remembered for her adult work rather than her time as a child. But she still couldn't forget that until the producer had remembered her, she'd been dismissed.

They said goodbye to the producers a few minutes later and continued on. Suzanne finished her cone, and disposed of her napkin in a trash can. Tim did the same.

But as they returned to the promenade, the dramatic activities of the last few days finally caught up with her. She yawned.

"Tired?" Tim asked.

"Yes," she answered truthfully.

"Then it's time I get you home," Tim said. He took her arm and led her to his car.

In the car, Suzanne leaned her head back and closed her eyes. She opened them only when they reached her house and Tim had turned off the ignition. He walked her to the door and, as he stood there, he said, "The offer is still open. I've got plenty of room at my place in the city."

"Thank you," Suzanne said. "But I need to be here. Tim—" she began, but he cut her off by placing a finger over her lips.

She stared up at him. He didn't speak; instead, he drew her to him, bent, and covered her mouth with his.

He kissed her deeply, while drawing her closer to him. She felt his tongue press against her lips, and an instant later, pass through. But, just as she started to respond to his ardor, he drew away.

"Goodnight, Suzanne." He turned and went to his car. She stood there watching until he backed out of the driveway and drove off into the night.

Moving in slow motion, Suzanne opened her door and went inside. She closed and locked the door, and then leaned back against it.

His kiss had taken her completely by surprise. And, as the feeling of his heated mouth continued to linger, she realized she was not unhappy about what he'd done. In fact, it was nice to know that she could still respond on a physical level.

She yawned, wrinkled her nose at the smell of smoke, and went into the kitchen. She saw there was a message on the answering machine and played it back. It was from Arthur. He was concerned about the fire. He wanted her to call him, no matter when.

She was not ready to talk to him, not yet. She turned off the machine and went upstairs to her bedroom. After undressing, going through her bathroom routine, and getting into a fresh nightgown, she got into bed.

It seemed that the instant her head touched the pillow, the phone rang. She reached for it, reflexively, saying hello even before the receiver reached her ear.

There was silence. "Hello?" she repeated.

"You did it again, didn't you?"

Suzanne's breath caught. The voice was jarring, harsh, and mechanically twisted. "Leave me alone!" she shouted into the receiver.

"Not until you are dead, you spawn of Satan! You escaped again. You should have burned last night. And damn you to hell, you will! I'm going to make sure of that! And I—"

Suzanne could not listen any longer. She slammed the phone down and stared at it as if it were some vile and alive thing. Her breathing was tortured. Her chest rose and fell much too fast. Her heart rate was speeded up, and her mind was spinning.

Belatedly, she realized why the voice seemed familiar. It was a mechanically altered voice similar to a voice that had been used for a doll in one of her movies. The doll had killed people by setting them on fire.

Shivering, Suzanne curled into the fetal position and hugged herself tightly. She lay like that for a long time, until sleep finally took her from her fears.

* * *

"Accident or not, it was my fault. And Dana, don't try to tell me it wasn't. Somehow, I know it was."

Suzanne listened to her tape recorded voice, and shook her head. "I don't think there's much more to say about that production. We had to shoot around the injured people as best we could. And we used a lot of doubles work for the creature. But we did get the movie finished, and it was successful."

Dana wrote a couple of lines of notes, then she put her pad down. "Did they find out what happened?"

Suzanne shrugged. "The police were there, as well as the studio's engineers. They found nothing out of line. Everyone believed that there was a weak spot in one of the wooden beams. It gave way when the camera's weight was on it."

"How can you say it was your fault that that happened?"

Frustration bubbled in her. Hadn't Dana been listening to her? Didn't she understand? "Dana, it happened because I was there. I told you, accidents happen around me. I just have to be there, and something bad is guaranteed to happen!"

Leaning forward, Dana stared at Suzanne with unfeigned intensity. Then she looked at a spot over Suzanne's head.

Suzanne looked up, but saw nothing. "What?"

"I don't see it."

"See what?"

"The dark cloud hanging over your head. You know, that terribly malignant cloud that follows you and brings disaster to wherever you are."

Suzanne's cheeks burned. "Why are you making fun of me?"

Dana shook her head quickly. "I'm your friend. And I'm not making fun of you. I just want you to hear what you sound like. Suzanne, accidents happen. Sometimes they happen more frequently to some people than to others. But they aren't caused by you simply being there. And this isn't a horror movie where a curse of death follows the heroine wherever she goes."

Her anger eased. "I'm not so sure."

Dana started to say something, but the doorbell cut her off. "I'll get it," she said, standing before Suzanne could move. She returned a moment later with Peter Wilson.

"I hope I'm not interrupting," he said when he stepped into the room.

"No," she replied quickly. "Would you like some coffee?"

"Thank you," he nodded.

"I'll put up a fresh pot," Dana said.

"I won't be long. But I do need to go over some things with you."

She looked into his gray-green eyes. As she studied him, she got the distinct feeling that he was the type of man who did not give up a task until it was completed.

"I'll let you know when the coffee is ready," Dana said. Smiling at Suzanne, she left the room.

When they were alone, and after Suzanne brought Peter to the couch, and they sat down, Peter Wilson said, "Officially, you are listed in our records as case number 92113SG. Your case contains two reports of definite criminal actions. The first was the incident with the tampered brakes.

"The second report was of the fire bombing." He paused. "The department has done as thorough an investigation as has been possible. So far, we've come up with no leads as to who is behind these incidents."

"I understand," Suzanne said.

Peter Wilson continued to stare at her. "I've also been doing some checking on my own."

"Checking?"

His nod was almost imperceptible. "I don't like the things that happened to you. I don't like it when people hurt other people. I don't like it when one person makes another person a victim. And I hate it when I am made to feel helpless by some perverted mind who thinks they can do whatever they want to whomever they want, and do it with impunity."

When he paused for a breath, Suzanne took one as well. His impassioned words had held her in thrall. The fire in his voice was also in his eyes.

"So," he continued, "I started doing some checking on you."

Suzanne frowned. She didn't understand what he was getting at. "Why me?"

"To see if I could find out if there was something in your past that might point me toward a suspect."

"And was there?" she asked.

Springvale's Assistant Police Chief shrugged. He leaned slightly back on the couch. "I've learned a lot about you."

"I hope what you've found hasn't made you dislike me," Suzanne half joked.

Peter fell momentarily silent. His eyes held tight onto hers. "No. But what I did learn has caused me to be even more concerned about you."

A chill caught her. And then her stomach tightened painfully. "I don't understand."

"There seems to have been a lot of tragedy in your life," Peter said. "When you were making the television series, *And Baby Makes Five* there were some incidents at the studio. Is that correct?"

Suzanne nodded.

"And when you returned to Hollywood to make horror movies, there were several incidents, weren't there?"

Again Suzanne nodded.

"And there was another death. Larry Hartvale was—"

The memory of that day roared into her head. Suzanne closed her eyes as she felt the blood drain from her face. Her head spun, and although she was sitting down, she had to grab onto the side of the couch for support. "Larry was murdered," she said, interrupting him. "I killed him."

"No," Peter Wilson said. His voice was sharp, the single word was loud.

Her eyes snapped open and she looked at him. "I shot him. I squeezed the trigger and fired every bullet into him! I killed him!"

"You were playing a part. You had a prop and you used the prop. Someone else killed Larry Hartvale. And the killer is a sick and twisted person who used you."

Suzanne swallowed several times in an effort to raise some saliva and moisten her mouth. When she could finally talk, she said, "I've been through this with the Hollywood police, and through more shrinks than you would even want to count. But when it comes down to having to face myself, I can't deny that I was the person who pulled the trigger."

Wilson leaned forward. He took both of her hands in his. "I understand how you feel. But you have to accept one very basic point. You had no control over what happened—none at all! There was no conscious decision to hurt or kill someone. What it really comes down to is that you were the weapon that someone else used."

"But I was still—"

"No!" Peter said. "You were nothing more than a weapon. And a weapon, no matter how lethal it is, can harm no one by its own volition. A weapon can't be blamed for anything. It's the person who uses the weapon."

"Peter," she said, squeezing his hands, "intellectually, I understand what you're telling me. But inside, I . . ."

He smiled what Suzanne could only term a gentle smile, and released her hands. "You're going to have to learn how to intellectualize what happened, if you ever want to be free of it.

"But let's leave that for now. There are other things that I need to know."

"What things?" she asked as she attempted to control her emotions. She wanted to accept what he'd told her about her own feeling of guilt, but she'd been over all of it so many times before that she couldn't.

"Other than the letter you got the other day, and the two that are in the California police records, have there been any other threats?"

Suzanne looked from his face to her hands. "There have always been . . . hate letters. I got them when I was doing the TV series, and I got them when I was doing the horror movies too. But," she said, looking back at him, "everyone in my business gets them in one form or another." She paused and thought about Tim Randolf's reaction to her last letter. "Actors can't take them seriously."

A muscle twitched high on his cheek an instant before he said, "Why can't actors take them seriously?"

"Because it's just a way that people use to call attention to themselves."

The intensity of his features did not lessen with her answer. She saw the muscle on his cheek knot and unknot again. Then, he reached down by his feet and picked up a manila envelope. He opened it and withdrew some paper.

"Perhaps you should take these letters seriously." Then

he extended the sheets of paper toward her. "This is a report from the French police. It is the examination of your husband's car after the accident. There is some slight evidence that the blowout of the front tire was caused by a rifle bullet, not by a weak spot as you were told."

Suzanne blinked several times. She tried to speak, but could not. Then, forcing control on her emotions, she said, "What are you telling me?"

Peter Wilson did not turn from her as he said, "Because of the condition of the car, there was not enough conclusive evidence to prove the accident was not an accident. But one of the people who examined the remains of the blown out tire believes the possibility exists that a bullet caused the blowout."

"I . . . I just don't understand."

Wilson looked at her for a long time. His gray-green eyes were gentle as he reached out to take her hand. The movement was uncharacteristic and clumsy.

"I've put enough of your background together to believe that the accidents that have been plaguing you are not accidents. Suzanne, I think that these letters you've gotten over the years are all from the same person. I think that the strange accidents that have happened around you have been either directed at you personally, or have been intended to stop you from doing certain things with your life."

He reached out with his other hand, and captured her free hand. "After reading the reports and speaking with the French policeman, personally, I believe that your husband's death was not a traffic accident—it was a murder. And, Suzanne, I believe that someone is after you now, and has been after you for years."

Chapter Fifteen

She heard birds calling outside the window. She even heard Dana preparing coffee in the kitchen. But none of it made any difference, for Peter Wilson had spoken the unspeakable, and his words twisted inside her like a thousand little razor blades.

"This can't be happening," she whispered. Unbidden tears rolled down her cheeks with the thought that her son and husband had died because of her.

How much hurt, how much pain was she responsible for?

When she looked down, she realized that Peter Wilson was still holding her hands. When she looked at him, she tried to pull her hands from his.

His grip tightened and he shook his head and spoke in a low yet firm voice. "You were not responsible."

She stopped fighting his hold. "Of course I was. I was supposed to have gone with them, but I had to go to Paris. There had been a problem with the movie I was working on."

"But you weren't with them. You weren't even near them. So, by your own theory, you can't be responsible," Peter Wilson stated.

"I was supposed to have been in the car. Whoever

. . ." she paused, swallowed, and said, "whoever shot out the tire was trying to kill me."

Peter Wilson's eyes turned more intense and their gray-green color deepened. "No one can be held responsible for the acts of another person. Suzanne, you *must* accept that premise. If you can't, then whoever has been doing these things will win. He or she will one day attain their goal."

"To kill me," Suzanne said.

"Yes, and anyone else who might step between this madman and you."

Suzanne drew on the strength flowing from him to her. Returning the pressure of his hands, she then slipped her hands from his. "What do we do?"

"We do whatever is necessary to stop this bastard."

Dana walked into the office at that moment. "Stop who?" she asked as she set down the tray and began to serve the coffee. By the time everyone had their coffee, Wilson had given Dana an encapsulated version of the story.

"Can the Springvale Police Department protect Suzanne?" Dana asked the minute Wilson finished.

"To the best of our ability."

"What exactly does that mean?" Dana asked.

As he spoke, Peter Wilson looked from Dana Cody to Suzanne. "The Springvale Police Department is not a large one. In order to protect you, we would have to take a third of our uniformed officers—eight policemen to be exact—and put them on exclusive duty watching your house. We can't do that. It's not feasible. However, I've already scheduled patrols to drive by at certain intervals."

The assistant police chief held up his hand to forestall Dana's coming words. "But there is another avenue to pursue. My belief, and that of the French policeman I spoke with, that your husband and son were murdered, is only a theory. But that theory coincides with everything else that has been happening to you. What I intend to do is to try and find this person."

"How?" Suzanne asked.

"With your help. I need to know everything, and I mean everything, about your past. I have to know when you got your first threats, and I must know about every 'accident' that has befallen you over the years. What I need is to read your life story," Peter added, pointedly.

Suzanne looked at Dana. "How much is left to transcribe?"

"The last three tapes."

"Peter, I can have Dana make copies of what has already been transcribed. After she finishes transcribing the last three tapes, which detail my last movies in the U.S., I'll get them to you too."

"It will help me," he said as he stood. "How is your foot?" he asked, looking down.

"Much better, thank you."

As she walked him to the door, the bell rang. She opened it to find an overnight delivery man. After signing his computer clipboard, he handed her a box. She looked at the label and saw it was from Tim Randolf.

She went to put it down, but the policeman stopped her. "From now on, you don't just open anything that arrives. You check it first."

"I don't understand," she said, but was beginning to do just that. And she did not like what she was feeling or thinking.

He took the package from her and brought it into the kitchen. He placed it carefully in the sink. "You've had a bomb thrown into your house. Your brakes have been tampered with, and a gas line mysteriously parted from its connection. You've had threatening letters and phone calls. How do you know that this isn't from your stalker?"

Stalker! The instant he'd said the word, dread filled her.

"But it's from a friend of mine," she said.

Peter looked at her. "Is it? Or is it just that your friend's name is on the label?"

She was suddenly unsure about everything. Her stomach turned queasy when he motioned her away. Backing up, she stopped when she bumped against Dana.

She glanced at Dana and saw worried concern on her features.

Then Wilson lifted the package. He held it to his ear and shook it slightly. He set it on the counter. Then he took a twelve inch Sabatier knife from the knife stand on the counter and, grasping it by its black handle, moved it to the top of the package.

Carefully, he slipped the knife's tip under the split top of the box. He reversed sides and direction and did it again. Then he set the knife down and turned to Suzanne and Dana.

"No wires." He opened the top.

Suzanne held her breath as Peter's hands reached into the box. A moment later, he lifted an object out of the box.

"No bomb," he said, turning his now stoic face to her. In his hands was an almond-colored music box. Perched on top, in a classic pirouette, was a porcelain ballerina.

The assistant police chief handed her the music box and then took out a small white envelope from the box. He handed it to her as well.

She set the music box on the counter, opened the envelope, and read the enclosed note.

Behind her, Peter Wilson silently left.

Suzanne finished reading the note, folded it, and put it back into the envelope. She turned, and was surprised to find that Peter Wilson was gone.

She looked at Dana. "Where did he go?"

She shrugged. "Perhaps he was embarrassed."

"Why?"

She stared at Suzanne, then shook her head. "You know, opening a gift from another man."

Suzanne cocked her head to the side. "I don't know."

Dana smiled and said, "Well, at least it wasn't a bomb."

Suzanne walked into the Springvale Police Station at three minutes after six and went directly to Peter Wilson's office. The door was open, and she saw him sitting behind his desk, reading.

She knocked on the door's frame, stepped into the small office and set down the one hundred ninety typewritten pages.

"My life, as promised," she said glibly.

The policeman stood in greeting. "Please," he said, motioning her to a chair across from him. He pulled the pages to him and looked at the top page.

"Thank you," he said before setting the manuscript to one side.

"What do you think you'll find in there?"

"I don't know yet. But something has to be in there that will point me in the right direction." Pausing, he studied her. "I'm waiting for something from out West. It should be here in a little while. Have you had dinner yet?"

Suzanne shook her head.

"How about joining me? There's a decent place around the corner."

Suzanne was hesitant. Then she shook her head. "I should get back to the house."

"Is it hungry, too?"

"Excuse me?" she said, confused.

"You said you have to get back to the house. Is it hungry?"

Suzanne laughed, despite her downcast mood. "No, it isn't."

"Suzanne, I don't mean to be pushy, and I am used to eating alone. But I would really enjoy the company. I'm hungry, and it would give me a chance to get a head start on this," he said, nodding toward the manuscript. "I have some questions that I need to ask. By the time we finish dinner, my query should be here. It's about you."

His persuasion was just gentle enough to make her change her mind. "All right," she agreed.

The policeman took her to a small pub a block from the station. As they walked, she glanced occasionally at him. His stride was strong, and she saw that he didn't just look where he was going; rather, as he walked, his eyes took in everything.

The pub itself was a small place, with a dozen booths lining the wall across from a long, mahogany bar. It was half full, and the sound level was just below noisy. The music playing over the speakers came from a prominent juke box located in the rear. A distinctively English flavor underlayed the pub's predominantly American theme.

Peter guided her to a table halfway down the length of the pub. She started to sit, but he stopped her. "Would you mind if I sat there?"

She shook her head and switched seats. When he was seated across from her, she said, "Why is it that men need to sit facing the door?"

"I don't know about other men, and normally I don't care where I sit. But given the circumstances of the past few weeks, I'd just as soon see who comes through that door."

A chill glided along Suzanne's spine. "And I couldn't agree more," she said in a much lighter tone than she felt.

A few moments later, the waitress came over. She motioned to the blackboard hanging over the bar. "Drinks?"

"The burgers are great," Peter said to Suzanne before turning to the waitress. "I'll have a draft and a burger, medium rare."

"I'll have the same," Suzanne said.

The waitress left, and an old Elvis song came over the speakers. She looked at Peter. "If I closed my eyes, I could almost imagine I was in Paris."

"Why is that?"

"This place reminds me of Paris. There are a lot of little bistros there, like this one. It's quaint, and the old rock and roll . . . . The French really love it."

Peter smiled. Lines radiated from his eyes warmly. Suzanne realized that she'd never seen him smile that way before. She liked his smile. There was nothing hidden in it.

"Tell me about France."

"You've never been there?"

He shook his head. "The closest I've been to France was a couple of French bars in Saigon, when I was in the service."

"You were in Vietnam?"

He nodded. "In the late sixties and early seventies. France?" he reminded her as the waitress brought over their drinks.

He lifted his, silently toasted her, and sipped.

She matched his gesture, and then said, "France is different. It's hard to explain. The country is beautiful. I prefer it to any city. The people can be beautiful as well. In the country, outside the major cities, the people are the gentlest I've ever known.

"How long were you married?" he asked.

"Almost ten years."

"He was a wonderful writer," Peter said. "The first

time I read one of his short stories, I was so amazed at the way he could describe a scene, that I went to the library and took out every book of his that they had. His words were like pictures to me. Reading Jan-Michael Grolier's stories was like having a private screening of a movie written just for me."

Suzanne swallowed several times. Peter's words evoked strong emotions. Yet, she was pleased that Peter felt the way he did about Jan-Michael. For some unknown reason, it was important to her.

"I've always experienced the same things in his writing," she said.

Their food arrived then. After the waitress asked if they needed anything else, she disappeared.

They ate slowly, and their talk centered around Springvale, and the changes that had come since Suzanne had last lived there.

When they'd finished eating, and they'd each ordered coffee, Peter leaned back in the booth. He rested his head on the high wooden back and looked at her through half-lowered eyelids.

"Tired?" she asked.

He shook his head. "Relaxed, actually. I've enjoyed this dinner."

Strangely, she had, too: not the food as much as the company. She also felt safer than she had since . . . since Jan-Michael had died.

The waitress returned with their coffee and the check. Suzanne used the distraction to hide the emotions that had come over her so quickly. Across from her, Peter Wilson stayed in the same position for another few seconds before leaning forward to pick up his cup.

"We need to find out the *why*," he said suddenly.

"The *why* of what?"

"Why this person is after you. If we can find a reason,

we can find the person. With a little luck, it will be in your manuscript."

He drank some coffee and looked at his watch. "The fax should be in by now." He put a twenty dollar bill on the small black check tray.

Sensing his impatience, Suzanne took a quick last sip of coffee and nodded that she was ready.

They walked back to the station silently. The fax was on his desk when they entered his office. He picked up the top sheet and began to read.

When he finished the first page, he turned to Suzanne. "Please, have a seat and I'll explain in a moment."

She sat and watched his eyes flick back and forth over the paper. His face was set and intense. His lips were drawn almost to the point of disappearing. Only the barest line of white teeth showed from between his lips.

When he finally put down the last page, he exhaled slowly. Then he turned his attention to Suzanne. "That was a report from the L.A. police. It was about the threats you received when you were making the television series. And it was also about the shooting. It must have been difficult for you. The actor, was he a friend of yours?"

Suzanne took a deep breath. "We were all friends. These movies weren't big budget things. We spent a lot of time together, rehearsing, traveling in buses . . . that sort of thing. You either become friends, or you're left very much alone."

"I'm not trying to bring up painful memories. But I have to dig. It's my job, and it's important."

Suzanne tried to speak, but emotion clogged her throat. A few moments later, she tried again, and succeeded.

"It was . . . is difficult. I spent a lot of time in therapy, but it never helped. I always believed that it was my fault that Larry is dead. There should have been some way for me to have known."

Leaning forward, she tapped the report with her forefinger. "I know this says that it wasn't my fault. And, intellectually, I know that as well. But I just couldn't convince myself of that."

She looked up from the report to find Peter watching her carefully. "Jan-Michael helped me get through it before we were married."

Peter leaned toward her. "It is good to know that he was as good a person as he was a writer."

"He was that, and more."

"Suzanne, I need your help. Tonight, I'm going to start to read your manuscript—"

"I hope it won't put you to sleep," she said in a half-hearted attempt at humor.

He smiled. "While I'm doing that, I need you to make a list of all the people who have been around you when any of these 'accidents' have happened. And Suzanne, I need the names of all the people, no matter how insignificant you think they are. And that means the people from the time you were a child, and in that TV series, too. The people around you here in Springvale."

"I will," Suzanne said. "When do you need this list?"

"As soon as possible. Tomorrow?"

"In the afternoon? About four?"

"That would be perfect."

Standing, Suzanne smiled at him. "I'll see you then," she said.

Peter stood and came around from behind his desk. "I'll walk you to your car. And don't forget, if anything happens at home, or if you think that there is something suspicious happening—call! There will be a patrol car nearby throughout the night. And be careful on the drive home."

* * *

Suzanne drove slowly. Her growing paranoia, combined with Peter Wilson's words of caution, kept her eyes constantly shifting to the rear-view mirror to make sure that no one was following her. When she turned onto her street, she spotted the one thing she did not expect. Tim Randolf's limousine was parked at the curb of her house.

She chastised herself for not realizing that Tim would follow up his gift of the music box with a personal visit.

Too much on my mind, she told herself as she pulled into the garage and got out of the car.

Tim was already walking up the drive. She met him and they exchanged hugs and gentle cheek kisses. "This is a surprise," she said.

"A pleasant one I hope," Randolf replied as he handed her a bouquet of a dozen long-stem roses. Their deep, red color was made even more intense by the pale moonlight.

"Come for a ride with me. The sun roof is open," he said, pointing to the rear of the limo, "And the night is as clear as glass."

Suzanne raised her hand to his cheek. "Thank you Tim, for the music box and for these flowers. But I'm exhausted. I wouldn't be good company, I'd just fall asleep."

"I don't care as long as I'm with you."

She smiled and lowered her hand. "That's very sweet. But really, I am tired. The last few days have been very hard."

"Suzanne," he began.

She raised her hand quickly, pressing her forefinger to his lips to stop him from speaking. "Tomorrow night, Tim. Pick me up at eight."

His smile grew. He put his arms around her and drew

her close to him. The roses pressed against her even as his mouth covered hers and he kissed her deeply.

Then he released her and stepped back. "Tomorrow night," he said before returning to the limousine.

Before she reached the door, his driver had turned the car and started out. As the limo drove away, a blue and white police car turned the corner and drove slowly toward her house.

She unlocked the door, turned on the inside light, and then waved to the police car as it paused in front of her house.

She closed the door, locked it, and went into the kitchen. There, she lifted the roses to her nose. Their scent was fresh and strong and clean.

She put them down, and as she stared at them, the phone rang. She jumped at the staccato sound, her paranoia bursting forth. Would it be that mechanically twisted voice?

She didn't want to pick it up, and decided not to. The phone machine answered on the fifth ring. She stood there, waiting.

"Suzanne, it's Arthur. Please call me. I need to speak to you."

Suzanne closed her eyes. She shook her head. She had no intention of talking to Arthur. Not yet. Not until she could figure out what to say to him.

Pressing the off button on the VCR's remote, Suzanne put down the yellow writing pad and stretched her arms over her head. It was almost midnight, but she was not yet ready for bed.

Soon after coming home, she had decided to get to work on what Peter needed. She'd started her notes, but kept going in circles.

To aid her, she'd done something she hadn't done in almost a dozen years. She'd started to watch the tapes of her old television series in an effort to jog her memory of the people that had been around her in those days.

As she watched them, the time period came back to her with even more power than when she'd been dictating to Dana.

She looked at her list. There was almost a full page of names, and descriptions of each person's relationship to Suzanne. At first she'd tried to think of anyone who might mean her harm; but that was next to impossible. How could she know what another person was or had been thinking?

So, instead of just putting down the names of people she thought might harbor resentment toward her, she listed everyone she thought of as significant factors in her life. Then she concentrated on those people who had been near or around her whenever one of those "accidents" had occurred, just as Peter Wilson had asked.

She'd started with her family. Although she knew that none of them would ever harm her, she'd put down her stepfather's name and Arthur's name as well.

Then she'd followed things with chronological orderliness. The next name on her list had been Judd Malcome. Judd had been her agent from childhood until she'd left for Europe.

She'd put down Timothy Randolf's name, and several other actors from the TV series. Then she'd thought about the movies she'd done and added eight more names.

Finally, Suzanne couldn't think of another name. But as she started to stand, she stopped suddenly as one more name popped into her mind. Valerie Hartvale. Suzanne sat back. She closed her eyes and tried to squeeze away the sharp and painful memory.

Valerie Hartvale had been the wife of the man Suzanne had shot during the filming. Valerie Hartvale had accused Suzanne of murdering her husband for no other reason than publicity.

After the tragedy, the woman had spent months trying to get the police to arrest Suzanne for her husband's death. That had been another reason for Suzanne's decision to go to Europe. She wanted out and away from everything that reminded her of that terrible accident.

Slowly, almost reluctantly, Suzanne wrote Valerie Hartvale's name at the bottom of the list she would give to Peter Wilson tomorrow.

Then she closed up downstairs, and went up to her bedroom, hoping that tomorrow would be a better day.

I need one, she thought.

Chapter Sixteen

"I don't know what to say," Dana commented after handing Suzanne the yellow pad with the list of names. "I wasn't around you then."

"I know," Suzanne agreed as she looked out the window at the street. It was empty. Turning, she smiled at her friend. "I thought that you might have picked up something I missed. Besides taking all that dictation from me, you also typed everything. Perhaps . . ."

Dana shook her head. "Sorry. But maybe we can get some work done. What do you say?"

Suzanne studied her friend. "Trying to get my mind off of this craziness?"

"If I were, I wouldn't do it by asking you to remember it. Besides, we were going to get into that last horror movie. Tell me, which of these people were there?"

Suzanne took the list and studied it.

Across from her, Dana turned on the tape recorder and lifted her own pad.

"None of those people were there that day—at least not on the set." She paused to look at Dana. "My mother did get there, but later. My stepfather didn't even know what happened until I got home. Arthur had returned from Europe, but was in another part of the state.

"I know my agent was at his L.A. office, because I talked to him just before I did my scene. I'd been offered a major part in a 'real' movie, and we were deciding if I should take it or wait for something we liked better."

"What about Tim? Wasn't he in the movie too?"

"He was in town, but he wasn't working on that movie with me. His character had been killed in the previous movie. He was in pre-production for his next movie," Suzanne added as the memory returned.

"Tell me about that day," Dana said.

Suzanne stared at her, thinking that her friend was starting to sound like the shrink she'd wasted so much time with after the shooting. A chill raced through her. She hugged herself. She didn't want to go back to that day. She didn't want to have to remember.

Taking a deep breath, she shook her head and then exhaled slowly. "I don't want to talk about the shooting itself. I . . . I think what happened after Larry's death is important.

"The shooting was a terrible accident." Suzanne stood. She had to move. She couldn't sit still and relive the pain of that day.

"When I realized what had happened—what I had done—I fell apart. Immediately after the shooting, I was numb. It was as if my mind had shut down. I don't think I can string together five coherent seconds between discovering that I'd really shot Larry, and when the police started talking to me. It was . . . a nightmare," she said as her mind skipped back over a dozen years and returned her to the day that had changed her life, forever.

She sat on a chair, hidden behind several people. She was still in her costume, what little there was of it. Her hands were trembling and she could not stop them, no matter how hard she held them together. She looked at them and saw there was still some of Larry's dried blood on her fingertips.

She took another makeup wipe and began to scrub it off. She shivered, but not from being cold. Larry was dead and she had killed him.

Roger Grant, the producer, came over to her. "Suzanne, they want to talk to you, now."

Suzanne looked up and saw that the three police detectives who had arrived just after the ambulance were making their way across the floor. The detectives wore conservative suits. Their hair was short and their faces were clean shaven.

"The police? Didn't you tell them what happened?" she asked, not really caring. She was still sick to her stomach, and she couldn't think straight no matter how many deep breaths she took.

"Miss Barnes?" said the youngest of the three police detectives when they reached her. His face was hard though, not what she was used to, and his eyes were piercingly intense.

She nodded.

"We understand that it was you who fired the weapon?"

Again, she nodded.

"Why did you fire it so many times?"

Suzanne stared at him, and then blinked. "I don't understand."

"When you felt the difference, why did you fire it over and over again?" he asked, his eyes growing even more intense.

Suzanne looked from him to Roger Grant and then back. "Because that was what the script called for."

"What the script called for?" asked the second policeman, favoring her with a strange expression she couldn't read.

"Yes. I was supposed to fire the gun until it was empty and then keep on pulling the trigger."

"But when you felt the difference, why did you keep doing it?" the first detective repeated.

"I don't understand," she said.

The younger policeman shook his head. "Anyone can tell the difference between a blank set up for a movie and a full power shell. The recoil is so much stronger."

Suzanne stared at him with comprehension. "I . . ." And then she realized what he was insinuating. He was actually accusing her of killing Larry. Her stomach twisted. The nausea struck again. She tried to stand, but didn't make it. Turning from the detective, she bent.

Waves of nausea pulsed through her as whatever was left inside her came out. Someone's arm went around her, supporting her firmly as the dry heaves racked her body. When they ended, she straightened up and found that her mother had finally arrived.

She looked at her mother, tried to speak, but was unable to. "It's okay," her mother crooned. "It's okay."

"Are you finished?" Lenore Barnes asked the police detectives.

The younger man shook his head. "No, ma'am. There are still a lot of questions that need to be answered. And I'm afraid that we need to take Miss Barnes to the station. It's required under these circumstances."

"Are you accusing her of actually—"

"No, ma'am," said one of the other policemen, quickly. "But, when there's been a homicide—"

"Homicide?" said Roger Grant, the producer. "This was an accident."

The younger detective shifted his hard eyes from the producer to Suzanne as he said, "An accidental death is a gun misfiring. This was murder. Seven rounds were fired. The first four were blanks, but the last three bullets were live rounds. When your daughter fired those three nine millimeter bullets into Lawrence Hartvale's chest, she killed him. Therefore, we must bring Miss Barnes to the station in order to take a formal statement."

Suzanne watched him and his angry eyes. She shook her head slowly.

Her mother stood. "Are you telling us that you are going to arrest my daughter?"

"No, ma'am, that's not what I said. In any shooting, there are procedures that must be followed. That's what we're doing. However, if she doesn't voluntarily go with us, then we'll have no other choice."

Suzanne stood. She looked at the younger detective, wondering what had made his eyes so hard. "Can I change first?"

The man didn't lower his eyes from her face. "Certainly."

Suzanne took her mother's hand and they went to her trailer. The policemen followed behind. When the two women entered the trailer, the policemen positioned themselves at the door.

"They think I murdered him," Suzanne said to her mother as she went into her mother's arms. She drew on Lenore Barnes's always ample supply of strength, as well as the warmth of the close contact. "How can they think something like that?"

Her mother stroked her hair. "Because they don't know you. Don't worry, sweetheart, we'll take care of this. You change," she said, holding Suzanne tighter for a moment before releasing her. "I have to make a call."

While her mother dialed, Suzanne stripped off the tattered costume dress and pulled on a pair of pants. She put on a bra and a heavy tee-shirt. Then she went into the bathroom and washed her hands again.

When she came out, her mother was just hanging up the phone.

"It's all taken care of," Lenore said. "Judd Malcome is going to get Harvey Browner. They'll meet us at the police station. Come on, baby, let's get your hair brushed."

She stood still while her mother brushed out her hair and then, with the haunting vision of seeing Larry Hartvale falling down, over and over again, she followed her mother out of the trailer, and into the waiting police car.

Fifteen minutes after reaching the police station, her agent, Judd Malcome, and her attorney, Harvey Browner, arrived. A few moments after the lawyer entered the small room where she and the detectives were, she began to give her statement.

She finished an hour later. The statement procedure was not what she expected. She didn't give a statement of what happened; rather, what she ended up doing was answering an hour's worth of police questions.

Then, thankfully, the questioning ended and a short while later the typed transcript was brought into the interrogation room. Her lawyer took his time and read every page. When he finished, he handed it to Suzanne. "It's exactly what you said. You can sign it."

She took the pen. Before signing the statement, she looked at the policeman with the hard eyes. Then she turned to her lawyer. "He doesn't believe me."

Harvey Browner looked her straight in the eyes. "It doesn't matter what he believes. We know you, and we know what you did not do. Sign this and we'll leave. After that," he added, turning his gaze to the young detective, "I'll handle anything else that might come up."

She signed the statement and stood up. "I want to go home now."

Her mother came protectively to her side. Harvey Browner went to the other side. "Judd is outside with the car," the lawyer said.

As they went out, Suzanne couldn't stop herself from looking back at the detective. His eyes were on her, as she knew they would be. The instant she met his gaze, she felt his animosity again.

"Why?"

Suzanne shook her head and turned back to Dana. "I don't know why he hated me. I've given it a lot of thought, but I've never come up with the answer. At first I thought it was because he believed that the whole thing had been a publicity stunt gone bad. But in the long run, I'm sure it was because I was an actress, somewhat famous and well off. But all I know is that he spent five months trying to prove that I would have been able to tell the difference between firing real bullets and blanks."

"How could you?"

Suzanne sighed. "His theory was that if I had fired a weapon before that scene, I would have known the difference between blanks and real ammunition. So the detective tried to find someone who had seen me fire a gun. But I never had. This was the first movie that I used a gun as a weapon. And we'd never fired it until that scene. Even in rehearsal, we never fired the gun. I just held it and squeezed the trigger, but there were never any bullets in it.

"Eventually, he gave up. But I can still see his eyes . . ." She shook her head slowly.

"What was his name?" Dana asked.

"Why?"

"I want to put him on your list."

Suzanne laughed. "I think he had a problem with celebrities in general, not me in particular."

Dana put the yellow tablet down. "All right, what happened next?"

"Not much," Suzanne said as she sat across from Dana. "The movie went on hiatus for three weeks. Then we finished it up by redoing the scene with a different actor and a different ending. But we didn't use blanks this time. The sound was dubbed in."

"After that, I spent the next four months in intensive therapy. I spent an hour or two a day with a shrink. I couldn't go outside my house, because there were always reporters and photographers camped out there, waiting to take my picture and get a shot at a story.

"And slowly but surely, things started to fall apart at home. My agent and the shrink both wanted me to go back to work. My mother was pressuring me to do the same. And while what she was doing was no different than it had been all my life, Larry Hartvale's death had changed my life.

"It was strange, though," Suzanne whispered. "No one seemed to understand what had happened to me. They all believed that it was over and done, and that I should just go back to doing what I had always done, acting."

Suzanne exhaled. "The last thing in the world I could do was act. I'd killed a man. And although I know it wasn't my fault, I couldn't go on the way I had. I just couldn't!

"But my mother wouldn't stop. She just kept on pushing me. It's funny. I'd always known she was a strong woman, and that she was living a part of her life through me—the part she'd always wanted to have but couldn't get. And I'd never really minded it. But I had become different after the accident.

"My stepfather grew even worse than he'd always been. We'd never really gotten along, and he resented the fact that now that I was grown, he was back in California 'babysitting' me again, as he put it.

"He'd never liked the way I had always been put first and the family second. But after the accident, my stepfather was worse than at any other time in my life. He was always telling me about how much he had given up for me, and how I should be grateful to him and to my mother for everything and I should be back at work so that he and my mother could go back East where they belonged, and get on with their lives and their marriage."

Suzanne paused for a breath. Her heart was pounding with the memories of the last months in Hollywood. "It got so bad at home that the only time I even came out of my bedroom was when no one else was at home. I had stopped talking to my stepfather and I hardly said a word to my mother.

"A week after the shooting, Arthur had returned East. With him gone, the only buffer between myself and my stepfather was my mother, and she was having a hard time keeping us apart. Finally, I couldn't stand it any longer and went as far as signing a contract for a new movie."

Suzanne leaned back in the chair and closed her eyes. "But I couldn't. When I told my mother and stepfather that I was not going to do the movie, my stepfather snapped. He slapped me in the face so hard that I was knocked out of my chair.

"I left the next day. I ran away. I didn't tell anyone. I left a note for my mother and one for my agent, and I took the first flight I found to Europe, where no one knew me. I lived in seclusion and met no one as I tried to get my life in order. I didn't let anyone know where I was."

Suzanne opened her eyes and smiled. "And one day,

when I was shopping in a little grocery store, I met Jan-Michael. We were married a year or so later.

"I called my mother, a week before the wedding. We talked for almost an hour, and I finally explained it all to her. She flew to France and attended my wedding, but only after she'd promised that no one, other than herself, would ever know where I was or what I was doing."

The phone's ring stopped her from going on. She leaned forward, but Dana beat her to it. "Ms. Grolier's number, can I help you?"

Dana looked at Suzanne. "Just a second, Arthur."

Suzanne was shaking her head even before Dana had finished. "Not now," she mouthed.

"Arthur, sorry, Suzanne is tied up right now." Dana paused, nodded her head, and said, "I'll tell her. Bye."

She hung up the phone. "He'll call back this afternoon."

"I don't want to talk to him," she said.

Dana studied Suzanne for a moment. The question in her eyes was obvious, but she remained silent.

"There's a problem," Suzanne admitted a moment later.

"Brothers and sisters always have problems," Dana said. "You should see me and my sisters."

Suzanne worried her lower lip between her teeth. When she released it, she said, "I should be that lucky. Dana, you know that Arthur is my stepbrother—"

"Of course."

"Well, the other night . . . when he drove me home, he . . . . God, this is hard."

Dana remained silent, waiting.

"He told me that he was in love with me. I mean, he just flat out told me he loved me. I . . ."

"Jeez," Dana said. "You don't have enough problems yet, do you? What did you do?"

"Nothing. I haven't seen him or talked to him since. I can't. I don't know what to say to him. I love him, but as my big brother, the way he's always been."

Dana glanced at the list on Suzanne's yellow pad. "When did this happen?"

"The night of the concert, when we went out for coffee afterward. He drove me home."

Dana looked from the list to Suzanne. "The night of the fire bomb?"

Suzanne stared at Dana. Her head spun at the thought. Then she realized how ludicrous it was. "I've known Arthur almost my entire life. I've lived with him. These accidents are not being caused by Arthur."

Dana shrugged. "It fits."

"It's not Arthur," Suzanne repeated, adamantly. "Let's get back to work," she said. "Where was I?"

Suzanne poured steaming water into a cup and watched as it turned from clear to tan to a darker brown. A few moments later she removed the tea bag and set it in the saucer. She squeezed the small wedge of lemon, stirred the drink, and then sipped it.

Holding the cup, she leaned back in the chair. Dana had left a half-hour earlier and Peter Wilson was due at four, which was in twenty minutes.

It had been a long day, but a productive one. She'd dictated two chapters, and was feeling as though she was actually getting some place with her mind.

She was finding it easier to reach inside herself and bring out the things she needed to remember and to face. Also, the list of people and the list of accidents and tragedies that had always surrounded her was growing as well.

She glanced at the kitchen counter. The music box Tim Randolf had sent her was perched there. She smiled.

While she was looking forward to seeing him tonight, she was a little nervous about it as well.

Their last kiss had been passionate—more passionate than she had wanted it to be. And while she had responded to him, she was not sure that she was ready to give herself to another person, especially while these terrible things were happening.

She would never be able to forgive herself if something happened to Tim. The doorbell rang. She put down the tea cup and went to the front door. "Yes?"

"It's me," came a familiar voice.

Her chest constricted. She looked through the peephole and saw Arthur. Knowing that she would eventually have to face him, she opened the door and let him in.

"I've been very worried," he said as he gazed at her. "You haven't returned my calls, and that fire . . ."

"It was taken care of. Arthur . . . would you like some tea?"

"No. Suzanne, we have to talk."

"I know. Let's go inside." She led him into the kitchen. He sat across from her. His eyes were locked on hers. His mouth was a straight and tense line. His lips were pale from tightness.

"What happened the other night was a mistake."

"Yes, it was," Suzanne said immediately.

"I thought . . . . Damnit, Suzanne, my timing was never the best. But I thought that if you knew how I felt—"

"No," she said suddenly. She sensed that his apology was not going to be for what happened but for what didn't happen. "It was a mistake. We're brother and sister. We can't be anything else."

Arthur stared at her with pleading eyes. His features were taut and sad. "If I could take back what was said, I would. If I could find some way to undo what I did, I would. I don't want this to destroy everything we've had."

"But you can't take it back. You stepped over the line, Arthur. And for what?"

"For love! Damnit, aren't I allowed to have feelings and emotions? Aren't I allowed to love?"

His words pushed her over the edge. She could no longer hold back the emotions that writhed within her. "Yes, yes you are," she said, her voice rising sharply. "But not me! And not like that! I'm your sister. My God, Arthur, I've always loved you and respected you. And I've always looked up to you as my big brother. What you did was wrong. Even if you truly do feel what you said, it was wrong! You had no right to say it, none!"

"You're my sister in name, not in blood. And who are you to tell me I have no right to love you! I didn't choose to fall in love with you. It happened. If I could stop the way I feel, I would have, a long time ago. I . . . . Damn you!" he shouted.

Then he stood, knocking the chair back against the counter. "There's no winning with you, is there? No matter what I do, I just can't win, can I?"

Suzanne held his angry glare for as long as she could. Then she stood too. "I think it would be best if you leave now!" Her voice crackled with anger. "I don't want to talk about this any longer. Leave, Arthur, before we say things that will make it impossible for either of us to live with."

His nostrils flared. He started to speak. But instead, he turned and stalked out of the kitchen. Suzanne jumped when the front door slammed shut. A few seconds later, she heard his car race down the street.

She sat there, ignoring the tears that streamed down her cheeks. Would this never end? Would she ever find some sort of peace in her life?

Chapter Seventeen

Assistant Police Chief Peter Wilson rang the front doorbell promptly at four. Suzanne was thankful that there had been enough time for her to calm herself and regain her composure after the scene with Arthur.

The last thing she wanted was to explain to Peter about what had happened between herself and her stepbrother. Besides the embarrassment, she didn't want the policeman to be sidetracked by something as foolish as Arthur's misplaced emotions.

Giving herself a mental shrug, Suzanne smoothed her top one more time and opened the door. "Hi," she said, smiling and stepping back.

"Hi," he replied as he entered the house. He wore a dark blue suit, an off-white shirt, and a gray and red striped tie. His hair was brushed neatly away from his face. There was a manilla envelope in his left hand.

She brought him to the office and motioned to the couch. As he sat, she said, "Would you like something? Coffee?"

"Nothing, thank you."

Her yellow pad was on the small table. Her other notes were there too. When she sat and turned to him, she found that he was already looking at her.

"I read the chapters and found them very interesting. What I need to do now is compare what I've learned with the people you've listed."

Suzanne pointed to the pad. "That's everyone that I've been able to come up with."

He picked up the pad and looked it over. Then he opened his manila envelope and removed one sheet. "This is the list I compiled, from your manuscript."

He placed the pad side by side with his own list, and began to match names between the two lists. When he was finished, everything except two names matched,

"Let's start with Aaron Kolstein and Carter Reynolds. They were both around at the very first accident, when Buzz Carlyle was killed, right?"

Suzanne nodded, but she was also badly taken aback. "You don't think that Buzz's death was because of me, do you?"

Peter cocked his head to the side. "It was an accident that happened around you. Perhaps it was because of you. From the way you describe the accident, it may have been more than just a simple hit and run. I'm theorizing from your memories, but you said that this truck came out of nowhere as soon as his car had left the studio lot. The truck hit him and continued on without slowing or stopping, correct?"

Suzanne nodded.

"That could have been a hit—a professional hit that was intended to kill the man."

"Why?" Suzanne demanded.

"To stop you from making a movie? To interfere with your life? Who knows what's in the mind of a psychotic. But both Aaron Kolstein and Carter Reynolds were there that day, along with almost everyone else on your list," he added, pointing to the neatly scripted names on her yellow pad.

"But neither one of them would want to hurt me."

Peter favored her with so intense a look that she almost missed the concern reflected in his eyes. "Starting right now," he said, enunciating each word precisely, "you change the way you think. You will no longer assume that because you like someone, or trust them, that that person means you no harm. Someone is interfering with your life. Since your return to Springvale, this *someone* has tried to kill you at least three times. Your own autobiography attests that it's happened before. Please, don't assume, okay?"

His eyes softened on the last words, and she was able to relax again. "Okay."

"Now, tell me about Aaron Kolstein."

"There isn't much to tell. Aaron Kolstein was the business part of the team. He ran the business end—paperwork, setting things up, financing, etc. Buzz Carlyle was the creative one."

"Would Kolstein have benefitted from Carlyle's death? Was there something about you making that first movie that would have done something to Kolstein?"

Suzanne smiled. "Don't you think I was just a bit too young to know about those things? I was what . . . all of nine or ten?" Before he could answer, she went on. "But I do know that Aaron Kolstein was lost without Buzz Carlyle. The next two seasons proved it. And I've never had contact with Aaron Kolstein after the show was canceled."

"None at all?"

Suzanne shook her head. "After the show was canceled, we moved back East. When I returned to California, later on, I never bumped into him."

"What about Carter Reynolds? Could he have had it in for his uncle and you?"

"Why would he do something like that?"

"He hadn't wanted to be in the series to begin with."

"He was fourteen years old. He was a boy. Why and how could he arrange to have his uncle killed?"

"He was wealthy in his own right. Maybe he hated his uncle for using him in the show. He could have also hated you for having made the series so popular."

"No."

"We don't know that for sure," Peter asserted.

"But I do," Suzanne said. "Peter, you say you believe that whoever is after me has been after me from the very beginning, in Hollywood. Am I right?"

"Absolutely correct."

"Carter Reynolds loved horses more than anything else. The year after the show went off the air—I think he was eighteen—he was in a riding accident. He was thrown from a horse. He . . . Carter broke his back. He's been in a wheelchair ever since."

Peter Wilson picked up his pen and crossed off Carter Reynolds's name as well as Kolstein's. "All right. Our lists match, now. Let's start at the beginning. Tell me about each of them."

As Suzanne read the list, she tried to organize her thoughts. But so many different memories came to her that she couldn't concentrate.

She exhaled sibilantly. "I think it would be best if you ask questions. You know what you're looking for, I don't."

Nodding, Peter picked up the list. "Let's start with your family. You and your stepfather never got along, is that right?"

Suzanne waited a beat before answering. When she spoke, her voice was calmer than her mind. "We always fought. The older I got the more we fought." She remembered the memories she'd dragged up for Dana, earlier that day. "Part of the reason I went to Europe was to get away from him."

"Why did your mother put up with it?"

The question caught her off guard. She blinked. "Why wouldn't she? She loved him. It was Raymond who had backed her when she'd first gotten me going in show business."

"You mean he encouraged her to start you off in television?"

"No," Suzanne said, thinking back to several of the talks she'd had with her mother, after Lenore had fought with her stepfather. "It was as if they had two relationships. One was as parents of two children, the other was as lovers. Raymond loved my mother ardently. I remember it clearly. When they disagreed, it was always over me or Arthur. But Raymond always supported my mother in whatever she wanted to do."

Suzanne shifted on the couch to face Peter more squarely. "My mother wanted me to have a future, and never to worry about money or security. He had given her whatever she needed to get me going—primarily money and contacts. But he always worked with her, and always deferred to her."

"Even when it came to Arthur?" Peter asked.

Suzanne didn't want to think about Arthur. "Usually. But there were problems. Arthur was a very talented pianist. Raymond wanted him to have the same chance at success as I did."

"But it didn't work out. Was it that the family couldn't stay together with two talents?"

"To a degree. Arthur needed to be on the East Coast. I needed to be on the West. They tried to work things out for him in California, but it never happened, so they concentrated on Arthur whenever the series was in hiatus.

When the series ended, we moved back to New York. It was then that Arthur's piano work got better."

"So the end of the series was good for Raymond Barnes. It let him get his son back on track?"

"I suppose," Suzanne agreed. "But that doesn't mean anything."

"Not in itself. But it is an avenue to pursue." Peter leaned forward to jot down a note. "Tell me about your brother," he asked when he finished.

Suzanne glanced away from Peter. She took several shallow breaths before looking back at him. "What's there to tell? Like Raymond, Arthur has been around me all my life. But Peter, Arthur wasn't there when most of the accidents occurred."

"Are you sure?"

She nodded her head sharply, once. "By the time he was sixteen, he was away at school. And he had no reason to hurt me, or want me dead," she said. She knew he could not be the one. Especially not after his admission of love.

"You're forgetting what I said earlier," Peter reminded her.

"No, I'm not. But I know the circumstances of the things that happened. Raymond wasn't there most of the time, either. And, if you need to connect either of them to my husband's death, it can't be done. No one knew where I was."

Peter Wilson held her gaze. "We'll get to that later. First tell me about Timothy Randolf. He played your brother in the series. He was in the horror movies with you. And he's in New York and you've seen him recently. Tell me about him."

Suzanne stood. "I need something. Does coffee sound good to you?"

The assistant police chief smiled. "Yes, it sounds good."

She liked the gentleness of his smile. It bespoke volumes about him. "I'll be back in a minute."

She made a small pot of coffee. When she finished, she checked the kitchen clock. It was 4:30. Tim was supposed to be here at six. She shrugged. This was more important.

Returning to the office, she found Peter looking through one of the photo albums that had been on the shelves. "France?" he asked.

"The countryside," she explained.

"Your son had your eyes."

She went to him and looked down. Peter was pointing to a picture of Allan and herself. They were sitting on a blanket, a picnic basket nearby.

She remembered that day clearly. Allan had been three and they'd been visiting Jan-Michael's sister. Her throat clogged. She cleared it and said, "Why don't we continue in the kitchen?"

They took the paperwork and went to the kitchen, where Suzanne poured two cups of coffee before sitting across from the policeman. "Tim Randolf and I go back to my start in Hollywood. He played my brother in the series, and he played my boyfriend in three of the four horror movies I made. And yes, I have seen him since my return. But what would make you think he is the one who wants me . . . dead?" she said after a slight pause.

"I have to look at every aspect and every suspect. Of all the people who you know, your stepfather and brother, Tim Randolf, and your agent are the four people who have been the most constant figures in your life."

"I haven't seen my agent since I went to France," she argued.

"Which he may not be too happy about."

"Which is not a reason to kill me."

"Which you could be mistaken about," Peter countered. "In your world, you want everything to fit neatly the way you think it should be. But in my world, Suzanne, the reality of people is very different. In my world, things rarely fit so perfectly."

"But it doesn't make any sense. He has no reason to hate me."

"Unless he believes you've injured him," Peter explained. "And that injury could be real or imaginary."

She shook her head. "But I didn't. In fact, I did just the opposite. I made a lot of money for him. Even after I left the country, the reruns and syndications continued to bring him commissions."

"But you could have made him a lot more money if you'd stayed. Don't forget the possibility that he instigated the other 'accidents' to gain publicity and make even more money off of your notoriety."

"In show business, notoriety doesn't always make money. Especially if there are always problems on the set that slow down or hold back production. Besides, Judd Malcome didn't know where I was in Europe."

"How does he send you your royalties?"

"He doesn't send them to me. They go directly into the trust fund my mother set up for me when I was a child. No, it isn't Judd. Peter, he doesn't even know I'm back in the States again."

"So you think. How do you know? Maybe Tim Randolf told someone and it got back to him. After all, Randolf is one of the biggest talk-for-money show people in the country."

"It doesn't make sense. Why would people who have benefitted from what I've done try to hurt me?"

"Insanity is just another word for senselessness. Murder makes no sense, as you already know."

Suzanne held her silence. She wanted to see where he was leading.

"When you made that last movie, Larry Hartvale was murdered. His death was not an accident, and you know that."

Her stomach knotted. "But I didn't . . ."

"No, you didn't murder him. You were the weapon. That's the point I'm trying to make. His death makes no sense, unless it was used to hurt you, to punish you and to stop you from having your career, or to advance someone else's monetary stake in you."

"Why!" she half-shouted. "Why?" she whispered a second later.

"I don't know. If I did, it would make things easier." He reached across the table and covered her hand with his. "I'm not trying to make you upset. Think of me as an archeologist on a dig. I have to go down beneath the surface in order to find whatever facts might exist. And when I've ferreted out those facts, then I'll have something to give me an insight into this person's mind. Then, I'll be able to find him and stop him."

"You think it's a man?" Suzanne asked.

"It's possible, but I said 'him' out of habit."

"I understand," Suzanne said as he drew his hand back.

"You said that when you were in France you had no contact with anyone in the States?"

"That's right. My mother did come to France when I married Jan-Michael, but she never told anyone. She didn't even know where I lived. We didn't write. I called her every once in a while, but that was about all."

"How did you learn about her death?"

"My husband's attorney developed a relationship with my former agent and my attorney. When Mother died, I was notified through Jan-Michael's attorney."

"What was the cause of her death?" Peter asked suddenly.

"Cancer," Suzanne said as another surge of sadness touched her. So many of the people she loved had died. So many. "Sorry."

"No need," he said. "Were there any accidents in Europe? Anything with Jan-Michael, or even when you were making the movies in France?"

Suzanne shook her head. "There was nothing. Life was good, and it was fun. Nothing bad happened at all, until my mother died. And then, a year later . . ."

Peter Wilson took another sip of coffee. "When did you learn of your mother's death, before or after the funeral?"

"Before. I flew to New York for the funeral. Judd Malcome contacted Jan-Michael's lawyer. I was at her funeral."

Suzanne picked up her cup and took a drink. She made a face at the cold coffee and stood. She took Peter's cup with hers and got them fresh coffee.

When she sat back down, Peter said, "Whoever it is saw you at the funeral. I'll bet anything he somehow followed you back to France. It makes sense."

Suzanne nodded in agreement. It did make sense. "But who?"

This time Peter shrugged. "I don't know yet, but I will." He tapped the yellow pad. "And I'm sure the name is here."

His confidence made her feel better. There was something about him that made her feel secure. She only hoped that he was right, and that he would find out who it was, quickly.

"Any ideas?"

"A few," he said before he drained the coffee. Then he looked at his watch. "It's 5:30, I have to get going."

Suzanne walked him to the door. There, he turned to

her. "Remember, if you think of anything at all, call me."

"I will," she said, and suddenly found herself reluctant to have him leave.

When he reached for the doorknob, she tried to think of something to say that would stall him. Before she could speak, the doorbell rang. She jumped. Peter Wilson put his other hand on her shoulder. Then he turned the doorknob and opened the door.

Suzanne exhaled sharply at Timothy Randolf. "I know I'm early . . ." His voice trailed off as his gaze shifted from Suzanne to Peter.

"That's okay. Tim, this is Peter Wilson."

"Peter," he said, offering his hand, "I'm Tim—"

"Randolf, I know," Peter finished for him.

"And you are?" Tim Randolf asked as he pointedly looked Peter Wilson up and down.

"Peter is the assistant police chief," Suzanne said.

"Oh."

Peter Wilson looked from Tim Randolf to Suzanne. "Thank you for your help. I'll keep in touch. Remember to call if you think of anything."

"I will," Suzanne promised.

Peter left and Tim stepped inside and closed the door. "What was that about?"

"The problems I've been having. You're early," she said, changing the subject.

"Only a half-hour. Besides, I couldn't wait." He moved closer to her. She sensed he was going to kiss her and stepped back.

"Make yourself at home. I need to go upstairs and change. I'll be down in a few minutes," she added as she turned and went to the stairs.

* * *

Peter's car was parked on the street. As he walked to it, he passed Tim Randolf's vehicle. The car was a very expensive 560 Mercedes sports coupe with some fancy and superfluous ground effects that detracted rather than added to the car's usually elegant lines.

As he continued on toward the street, he decided that the customized car fit the actor. And then Peter decided he would also follow one of his hunches and make a very thorough background check on Tim Randolf.

Reaching his car, Peter opened the door but did not get in. Instead, he stood with the door open and looked at the house for several seconds.

He wondered if she would be safe with him. Then he stopped himself. Even if Tim Randolf was the man stalking Suzanne, she would be safe. Tim Randolf would not be stupid enough to do anything—at least tonight, now that he could be placed with Suzanne.

The police radio crackled, and Peter heard his code being called. He slid in behind the wheel, started the car, and drove off. As he reached for the microphone, he made a mental note to call the men on patrol tonight and ask them to keep an extra close watch on the house.

"The restaurant was wonderful, and so were you," Suzanne said, smiling as she unlocked the front door.

It was true. Dinner turned out nicely. They had gone to a pleasant little French restaurant in Westchester. She had kept their conversation focused on Timothy and his show, and he had been as entertaining and charming as ever.

Stepping closer to her, Timothy said, "I'm glad you enjoyed it. That means we can do it again."

Before she realized it, his arms were around her. He

drew her close and kissed her. His lips were warm and soft, and his body was hard against hers.

When the kiss ended, Suzanne drew slightly away. "Tim, I—"

"Don't say anything," he asked. His eyes roamed her face. "I know that things are happening quickly. But they are happening and I can't stop them. Suzanne, I love you."

She was unable to speak through her surprise. Her mind spun with the impact of his words. She shook her head. "Too fast," she whispered, thinking about Tim and about Arthur. What was happening? And why?

She pushed free of his embrace. "Tim, I'm flattered," she began.

"Suzanne, I'm not looking for anything. You don't have to tell me anything, just let things happen the way they should."

"Tim, I care for you, I do. But the timing . . ." She stopped talking as a police car drove slowly by. The car reminded her of the danger she was in.

"Let's go inside and talk." Turning before he could answer, she stepped inside. He followed obediently. After they were inside, she closed and locked the door and brought him into the living room.

"Suzanne, I—"

She cut him off before he could finish. "Tim, the timing is bad. There are things happening right now that make a relationship between us unfair to you."

He looked at her for several seconds. "Suzanne, we have a history together. And I can't stop my feelings for you. I've held them inside for over a dozen years, but I can't stop them. What I can do is slow things down. Just don't push me away. That's all I ask."

She sensed his need. She closed the gap between them and stroked his cheek. "All right. But Tim, it's not going to be easy. It's . . . complicated. And right now, things aren't going too well."

"Is it your writing?" he asked quickly. "If it is, maybe I can help."

"No, that's coming along," she said without elaborating.

He smiled. "Perhaps what you need is to go back to work—the sort of work that you really understand."

She laughed lightly. "What, do another sitcom? I could even be the mother this time."

"Yes," Tim said emphatically "Or, you could do something different." He paused for a moment, and then his eyes widened. "If you wanted to, you could test the water by doing a guest spot or two on my show. Wait, I've got an even better idea," he said tapping his forefinger to his temple. "Why not take advantage of me? You could guest host with me, say for a week or two. That would be a great way to test the waters."

Pausing, Tim nodded and smiled. "We could do a week of nostalgia."

"No," Suzanne said, emphatically.

Shrugging, Tim waved the idea away. "Well, think about it. I wouldn't mind doing it for you, especially if it would help you."

"I appreciate it, Tim, but I really have no desire to get back into the limelight."

"Your wish is my . . . . You know," he said with a wink. Then he looked at his watch. "Oh, oh, it's Cinderella time. I think I'd better get back. But, Suzanne," he said, stepping closer and putting his arms around her. "I meant what I said. And this time I'm not going to stay in the background like some love sick little puppy. I'm going to be around and I'm coming after you."

If his tone had been any different, she would have started to believe Peter Wilson's suspicions. But as she looked into the face she'd known for three-quarters of her life, she was sure that Tim Randolf was not her tormentor.

"I'm not asking you to stay away, all I asked for was time."

He brushed his lips across hers. "I'll call you tomorrow." With that, he turned and went to the front door.

When he was gone, she locked the door and went back into the living room. She sat on the couch, curling her legs beneath her. Would her life ever be calm? she wondered.

If it wasn't one thing, it was something else. But Tim was sweet. She knew his offer to guest host the show with him had come from his heart. Yet she was concerned about their possible relationship. Did he really love her as he said, or was this some sort of a hold over from when they had dated in Hollywood?

She tried to analyze her feelings toward him, but couldn't. She thought about the passionate kiss they had shared a few days ago. She had responded to him on a physical level. It had been a long time since a man had held her and kissed her like that.

But emotionally, she felt nothing. There was still a barrier that refused to let her go any further than to think that someday, something might happen between them. But not yet, not until she was able to get her life back together.

And Jan-Michael? Could she ever love another man the way she loved Jan-Michael? Standing, Suzanne willed her thoughts away from her problems and turned off the living room light before going upstairs to the bedroom.

The phone's harsh call dragged her up through a myriad of sleepy layers. She turned, fumbled for the telephone, and finally grasped the cool, plastic receiver.

" 'Lo," she mumbled.

"Suzanne?"

"Uh-huh," she said, still half asleep.

"Wake the hell up you stupid bitch!" shouted the voice as it changed and became loud and mechanically distorted.

Her eyes snapped open even as her heart began to pound. "No!"

"Yes, damn you! Yes, it's me again! Hey, hey, hey!"

"What do you want?" she cried.

"You! I want you. I want to see your lifeless body lying on the ground. I want to see your dead eyes staring up at nothing so I can laugh at you! I want you gone! I want you dead! And I'm going to make you that way! Oh yes, I'm going to make you wish you were never born, and then I'm going to make you dead!"

"Leave me alone!" she screamed into the mouthpiece. "Damn you, leave me alone!"

She slammed down the receiver. Then she lifted it again, moved it over the floor and dropped it onto the carpet.

"No more," she begged as sobs began to rack her body. "No more, no more," she repeated, turning her words into a litany that continued to fill the darkened bedroom.

Her body began to shake. She hugged herself tightly. Then she curled into herself, bringing her knees up to her chest and wrapping her arms around her legs.

And as she tried to banish the mechanically coarse voice from her mind, she also tried to stop her body from shaking. She lay there for a long time, her mind lodged in some dark and descending pit of hell, until exhaustion finally overtook her, and she released her consciousness and fell asleep.

Chapter Eighteen

She woke slowly, not wanting to open her eyes for fear of what she might find. The call that had dragged her from sleep was a sore, festering in her mind.

She had reacted to the call with terror. Fear had gripped her and had shut down her ability to act rationally. She'd been unable to think, or move, or do anything other than stay curled in a fetal ball.

She thought about Peter Wilson and how she had ignored his advice not once, but twice. He had told her that if she gave in to fear, she would continue to be a victim. Last night she had caved in to her fear. He had also asked her to call whenever something happened. But her fear had controlled her and she had not called.

She opened her eyes. The sun poured through the bedroom window. The sky was clear. She wondered why it mattered what Peter Wilson might think of her.

She snorted with impatience. She knew exactly what Peter Wilson would think of her. He'd be disappointed. She sensed that Peter Wilson, like her husband, was a man who had accepted a responsibility and always saw it through.

She retrieved the telephone receiver and replaced it on its base. "No more," she said in a low yet firm voice. Then she got out of bed and set her sights on the upcoming day. Dana would be arriving soon, and she wanted to get some work done.

The phone rang. Her newfound resolve threatened to desert her, but she rigidly maintained her control and answered the phone with an unwavering voice.

"Hello. It's Peter Wilson," he replied to her hello.

"Is something wrong?"

"No," he said quickly. "But I do need to see you again today. There are some things that I'd like to go over and get clear in my mind."

"All right. I'm working this morning, so how about after lunch? Say two?"

"That's bad for me. I've got several appointments later. If it's not too much of an imposition, why don't you meet me for lunch?"

"Okay," she said.

"There's a small cafe by the pier. Will that do?"

"That'll be fine. About twelve?"

"I'll see you there. Thank you."

She decided to wait until she saw him to tell him about the call. "You're welcome," she said before hanging up and going into the bathroom.

Suzanne parked the car in the municipal lot, a half block from the restaurant. She got out and looked up at the clear, blue sky.

The warmth of the early summer sun made her feel alive. Not even the last minute call she'd gotten from her stepfather was able to damper the pleasant feelings the warm day gave her.

And she had to give him credit. Raymond Barnes was attempting to make amends. He had called and invited her to his house, tomorrow. He'd been saving her mother's things so that Suzanne could go through them and pick whatever she wanted.

He is trying. But, she thought, it was a shame that he'd started only after her mother's death.

She locked the car and walked to the restaurant. The cafe was small, with the tables set in what seemed to be no particular order. The walls were light, decorated with the for-sale work of local artists.

Only about half the tables were occupied. She spotted Peter as soon as she started into the room. He was seated at a table by the window, looking out: his face a mask of concentration. His eyes were open, but as she drew closer, she knew that whatever he was seeing was inside his head and not outside the window.

She took a moment to study the slim policeman. Even with his face set so intensely, his outward appearance was that of perfect calm.

"I bet you were one of the laid-back and cool kind of guys when you were a teenager," Suzanne said, sitting across from Peter.

He blinked, focused on her, and smiled. "So I was told. How are you?"

"I'm good," she said as a waitress silently set the menus on the table and left.

"The reason I wanted to talk with you is that I need to go over my list, again. There are some things I need to get settled in my mind."

"All right."

"We should order first. I've never had anything bad here, but it isn't fancy cooking either."

"Then I'll enjoy it." When she opened the menu and looked at the entries, it took her less than a minute to decide on the cold lemon chicken.

After their orders were taken, the assistant police chief, and Springvale's sole detective picked up a manila envelope from the floor and removed a single typed sheet of paper. On it was the narrowed list of suspects that Peter Wilson had drawn up.

Suzanne edged her chair closer to his and studied the list. She tensed involuntarily when she read the names—all but one were friends or family. But every name on the list bothered her.

"Why Valerie Hartvale?"

"Why not?" he asked. His eyes locked on her, and he seemed to be trying to see past whatever was on her face.

"She wasn't around in the early days. How can she be a suspect?"

"Before I can explain that, you'll have to follow my thoughts." He paused until she nodded, then said, "First, we think about the person who put the real bullets into the special effects gun. Let's say this person was the one who has been after you for years. When Larry Hartvale died, this person's goal had been accomplished, to a degree. He ruined you and your career. Are you with me so far?"

She nodded. It wasn't hard to follow him.

"So, you have unwittingly killed a man. You've also made a terrible enemy out of the man's widow. The widow now takes up her own vendetta against you."

"But," Suzanne said, lightly patting the back of his hand to interrupt him. "She never threatened me with physical harm."

"No, but she spent five months trying to have murder charges brought against you. She gave interview after interview, charging you with murdering her husband."

"Peter, she lost her husband in a terrible way. And all she could think about was that I had killed him. Dear Lord, it was all I could think about as well."

"It became an obsession. She started sending you threatening letters. She would call you. Who can say that it didn't turn into some sort of psychosis?"

He took a breath. "Please, think about it. Isn't it possible that the person who originally was trying to harm you had actually found another weapon in Valerie Hartvale? By this person manipulating your life so that your hand was the instrument that killed her husband, he turned the widow into a weapon against you. I'm not saying that was the original intent, but it is feasible that such a thing could have happened."

"Twelve years ago, perhaps. But not now. I'm sure Valerie has realized what actually happened. And . . ." Her words trailed off when she realized that he was openly staring at her.

"What?" she asked, self-consciously.

"I'm finding it very hard to believe that you are real. Suzanne, you've lived a life that is truly amazing. You've reached levels of success and fame that most people would give their souls for. You've also been through tragedies that would break a lot of people, yet you sit here and defend someone who might be trying to kill you."

"Valerie Hartvale is not trying to kill me."

"We don't know that yet. But we will, soon. I'm in the process of checking on her. But that's not the point I'm trying to make. No matter what you think, it could be anyone from Valerie Hartvale to . . . to Dana Cody."

"No, Peter, these people aren't killers. These people are not the type to stalk me for years and years."

"You don't know that," Peter said, adamantly.

"I can't accept your way! Peter, the person after me is crazy! This person is insane. And he's using my old life to get me. He even used one of the voices to scare me, last night."

For an instant, Peter's relaxed and cool demeanor wavered, and she caught a glimpse of the intensity that underlay his features. "Last night?"

Suzanne sighed. "He . . . it, called last night. The voice

was altered to sound like a doll that was used in one of the first horror movies I did. He said things . . ." She paused to gulp some air as the horror of the phone call returned with its full impact. "They were terrible things. He said that he wanted me dead and he wanted to laugh at me when I was dead. I . . . . He also said that he was going to make me wish I was dead before he killed me."

She gulped some air and then said, "I guess I freaked out then. I just went blank until I woke up this morning."

She looked down at her hands. Her fingers were shaking. She glanced back at him. "I'm sorry," she said. "I know I'm not supposed to let my fear get out of control."

He reached out to her. His touch had a calming effect on her, and her hands stopped trembling. He said nothing until he released her hands. "It happens. Tell me about the call."

"I just did," she reminded him.

"No, tell me about his voice. Suzanne, you're a trained actor. You've been taught to listen and utilize inflection. Tell me about the inflections he used, the tone, the things behind the voice."

She closed her eyes and thought back to the call. She tried to pick out some peculiarity, but could not, except for . . . "Anger," she whispered. "Hatred was the dominant thing. That was what it was. Anger and hatred. But I can't equate that kind of demented emotion to anyone I know."

Peter nodded. "Whoever it is hides it well."

"What about those people who go after celebrities?"

The detective nodded, once. "I've been checking on that aspect. While there is a possibility that this person is some sort of celebrity stalking loon, I can't put a lot of confidence into the theory. To begin with, these people usually stalk current celebrities because they are trackable through the newspaper gossip columns, the tabloid papers, and newscasts on television. But you've been in none of them."

He paused as the waitress brought coffee and the check. When she walked away, he said, "On top of everything else, my instincts tell me that it's someone you know."

She held his powerful stare for several seconds. "And your hunches. Are they always right?"

"Usually."

The way he said it left no doubt in Suzanne's mind that he was talking from experience, not from an overstated sense of self-confidence.

"What do I do?" she asked.

"Exactly what you've been doing, but better," Peter said. "You keep working on your autobiography—it's my best chance at finding this person. You think back and remember everything, no matter how small the detail might be. Suzanne, the person we're dealing with is most likely psychotic, so rationality will not be his strongest suit."

He shifted slightly in his seat. "Perhaps in your remembering your past, you'll stumble across the thing that set this person off. It might be something as minor as a fleeting look you gave him in the space of a breath; or, it could be as deep and devastating as a death that this person believes you caused.

"But whatever the reason, this person has fixated on you, and will most likely keep being fixated until you're dead."

Suzanne tried to play down the severity of his warning, but could not. "Peter, I—"

"I'm not saying these things for their fear value. What I'm trying to do is make you understand that whoever is doing this to you is sick. We can't fight this person with the same logic we would use under normal circumstances."

"I do understand that," she said.

Peter's eyebrows rose slightly. "Do you?"

"Yes," she said truthfully.

"In that case, I want your word that if you get another call, you'll call immediately. If something, anything at all seems suspicious, you'll call me or the station to get help."

"You have my word," she whispered.

"Perhaps it would also be best if you stayed home until we find this person. I . . . we can't protect you if you go into the public. I can have a policeman do your shopping for you, and—"

"Why did you invite me here, if that would put me in danger?"

"There was an unmarked car following you here."

Her anger spiked, but she clamped it down. "I will not become a prisoner of my house because of this . . . this person. I will not be forced to spend my life hiding inside a house because someone *might* be outside and want to kill me."

"Just for a little while, until we're able to find him."

"I can't. This—" she paused, at a loss for the right word. "This bastard has spent years stalking me. You've told me that you believe he killed my husband and my son. Now you want me to sit in my house and wait him out? Peter, he's waited twelve years to find me, what makes you think he won't wait until the police lose the urgency of the minute?"

"We won't," he said.

She closed her eyes for a moment. When she opened them, she found that his gaze had not shifted from her. "You're a good man, Peter Wilson, but there are and will be other people who need your help. You can't be my full-time babysitter. And I intend to go on with my life as

I have been doing. I will not let this person stop me any more."

She saw that he was about to argue with her, and she held up her hand in warning. He nodded slowly, reached into his inner jacket pocket, and withdrew a wallet.

After putting money on top of the check, he said, "Let me walk you to your car."

She rose from the chair and walked outside with him. The day had not changed. It was still clear and blue and sunny. "Thank you for the lunch," she said.

"You're welcome. Will you do what I've asked?"

"Except for becoming a shut-in, yes."

"I need to see every page as you finish."

"You will," she promised as she unlocked the door and got in. She rolled down the window and leaned slightly out. "Thank you for your concern and for your help."

Smiling, he said, "That's what you pay taxes for. Drive safely," he added as he walked away.

She watched his retreating back. Somehow, she doubted that her taxes paid enough for the type of job Peter Wilson did. No, all of his actions served to confirm exactly what she thought, that Peter Wilson was one of the rare and unselfish men who did his job because he cared about the people he worked for.

Suzanne sat on the chaise and looked across the river to the east bank. A train was barrelling along the tracks. There were several boats out on the Hudson.

In all, it was a pleasant summer afternoon that should have made her feel good, but did not. Too many things had happened and were happening. Too much bad and not enough good.

And, she knew that if she didn't concentrate on digging

out all of her memories, the bad would just keep coming along, and soon that would be all there was.

She shook her head and reached for the tape recorder. She pushed the record button and, when she saw the small red light start to glow, began to speak.

"Okay . . . . Incidents that have happened," she said, thinking about what she'd already put down on paper. Then, she nodded to herself. "Okay, here we go. Of the four horror movies I made, the third one was without doubt the very best. It took the longest, had the best plot, and was actually a strong story as well as a scary movie. Although I had to dress scantily and act as if all women were made of were breasts and screams, the part actually let me do some acting.

"It was the last movie with Tim Randolf. We were dating, which made great fodder for the tabloids and the columns. But, it didn't really bother us.

"We liked seeing each other. It was fun, and it was romantic too, but our romance had not reached the level of our becoming lovers, no matter what the gossips had written.

"The movie was another sequel of the *Axeman* movies. Tim was my boyfriend in the movie. The first two thirds of the movie went smoothly. We were well into the production, when one of those strange accidents occurred. I don't think I ever put it together with any other of the accidents that had surrounded me throughout my career, because of its very nature."

Suzanne paused for a breath. When she spoke again, her words carried her back almost fourteen years.

"Let's get moving," called director Sam Harding. "Tim, stop hanging over Suzanne. Let's all get into the right positions, shall we?"

Suzanne moved to the mark on the floor that was her position for the scene. Ten feet from her, partially hidden behind a prop was the man playing the Axeman. His face and chest were covered by a special makeup that turned his skin into a mass of scar tissue.

Tim was on her left, two feet away. He was dressed in jeans and a tee shirt. His hair reached to his shoulders. There were cameras everywhere for this scene. One was on a track above the set, and there were three others on the floor level.

Her clothing consisted of a tight-fitting pair of jeans and a slightly torn halter top. Her hair was long and pulled away from her face.

The scene called for her and Tim to be in a boat house, hiding from their friends and making-out, passionately. Then as they made out, the Axeman would appear. He would rise above them, ready to kill them. But before he could bring down the axe, Tim would pull his feet out from under him and she and Tim would run.

The scene was simple, and she did enjoy those scenes where she and Tim kissed, because she was able to combine her acting with her real emotions, instead of having to build a set of emotions for a scene. And it helped to have Tim, because she was able to ignore the lights and heat and commotion that were always a part of the set.

"All right kiddies, let's get to it. Ken," Sam Harding said, motioning to his assistant director.

Ken Spalding stepped forward. He turned to the three actors. "Get on your marks." Then he pointed to the girl with the clap board. "Let's get it rolling. Quiet on the set! And . . . Action!"

Suzanne turned at the instant of the action command. Tim moved to her side. "I feel like someone's watching me," she said.

Smiling, Tim drew back and looked her over from waist to eyes. "Yes, me."

She laughed and pressed herself against him. They kissed. As they kissed, Tim lowered them to the floor. The scene went on, with them on the floor and the Axeman watching.

Tim started to undress her for the scene. His movements were slow and exaggerated for the camera, and before any flesh was shown, the Axeman stepped out from behind the door.

He walked toward them, his gleaming metal axe held high. Suzanne saw him move into position. She gave no sign of this because her part called for not seeing him.

He moved close to them and slowly raised the axe. On cue, Suzanne stiffened, tore her mouth from Tim's, and screamed.

As she did, the Axeman completed the art of raising the axe high. In that instant, there was a sharp cracking sound and the axe head snapped off and went flying backward.

The gleaming metal head spun crazily through the air. A half-second later came the sound of shattering glass.

Everyone froze, turned, and stared at the way the head of the axe had lodged into the lens of one of the cameras.

"What the hell!" screamed the cameraman as he stared at the destruction the axe head had caused.

Tim, looking from the camera to the Axeman, shook his head. "That was lucky. If it had waited until I'd pulled you down, that might have hit us."

Suzanne uncorked a bottle of Chardonnay and poured herself a glass to accompany her dinner of trout. She sipped the wine, took a bite of the fish, and thought about the afternoon.

She'd never connected the accident on the third film

with any of the other accidents. But it was a very distinct possibility that the axe had been tampered with.

She hadn't remembered the incident fully, especially Tim's comment about what could have happened if the axe hadn't cracked at that very instant, until she'd relived the scene.

She decided to have Dana transcribe the tape tomorrow so she could give Peter the hard copy.

The phone rang. Suzanne stared at it. She hoped it was Tim, or Peter, or anyone other than the "voice."

Putting her fork down, she went to the counter and picked up the receiver. "Hello?"

Her throat started to close the instant she heard the distorted mechanical doll voice. But she held herself firm. "Put on your TV. Put on channel 3. Do it! Do it now!"

She slammed down the phone and ran upstairs to where the television was. She turned it on, and put the cable selector on channel 3.

The television fuzzed, and she saw that there was a listing guide of the shows on television that night. An instant later the picture shifted.

Suddenly, she was staring at herself, twelve years earlier, watching as she raced up the stairs of the old Victorian house, taking them two at a time.

When the younger Suzanne reached the top, the sound of *his* feet came from the sound track.

A high-pitched mew bubbled from the younger Suzanne's mouth before she clamped her lips tight. She ran down the hallway into a darkened bedroom and closed the door behind her.

Low moonlight came through the window and seemed to spotlight her on the wall, clearly showing her effort to blend into the paint and the darkness.

Trembling, Suzanne watched her younger self inch along the wall until she reached a nighttable. Next, this young Suzanne's fingers found the ornate brass handle of the drawer and carefully began to open it.

Suzanne's breath caught. Her heart beat wildly as she watched this terrible picture from the past, knowing every frame that was yet to come.

The sound of footsteps in the hall came from the TV's speakers as the younger Suzanne pulled the drawer open. It squeaked and she froze. The younger Suzanne yanked on the drawer. It opened fully. She reached into it, searched around, and pulled out a pistol.

Then the bedroom door burst open and light flooded in. Suzanne screamed at the television as she saw herself raise the pistol and aim it at the man with the leather mask.

"No!" Suzanne screamed, more than twelve years later. "No! No! No!"

But nothing she could say would stop the events that were about to unfold as the creature moved toward her, the axe raised over his head.

"I'll shoot," Suzanne heard her younger self say.

The creature snorted, gave vent to a loud bloodcurdling howl, and charged. The upraised axe went all the way back in preparation to strike.

Suzanne's entire body shook fiercely as she watched herself pull the trigger, once, twice, three times.

With each shot, the creature grunted. Special effect blood spewed from his chest.

She fired again and again. Blood sprayed at her, hitting her in the face and arms. He was almost on her when she fired the last shot. It hit him in the face and knocked him off his feet.

He lay silently on the floor, blood pumping obscenely from the wounds in his chest. Suzanne watched herself drop the pistol and fall to her knees. But the sobs that came from her television set were low compared to the sobs that now racked her heart and body.

And then, through her torment, she heard that terribly twisted voice. She looked up at the television. The scene was frozen. She was on her knees. Larry Hartvale was dead.

And then the voice said, "You are a fool! You are a stupid, stupid fool to think that I can't get you whenever I want! And I will, soon, Suzanne! Very soon!"

Chapter Nineteen

The doorbell rang. Peter Wilson motioned for Suzanne to stay where she was while he answered the door.

Returning a moment later, he placed a battery operated portable VCR unit, wrapped in a clear plastic bag, on the coffee table.

"Just as we figured," he said, as he sat. "It was hooked right into the cable junction box that fed directly to your house."

Suzanne stared at the VCR. From the moment the voice had screamed at her, until now, she'd done her best to keep control. She'd worked at it, calling Peter as soon as she was able, and then holding herself together until he'd gotten there.

She answered each of his questions as clearly as possible, and then waited with him, as he gave orders to the police officers that had accompanied him.

After calling the cable company, he'd sat down with her and forced the conversation on to a variety of things other than what had happened.

But now, as she stared at the black recording unit, reality became brutally clear. "What will this do for us?"

The detective patted the unit with what could almost be deemed as affection. "With just the smallest bit of luck, we'll find something on it that will help us to identify your caller. Perhaps a fingerprint, or even a partial print could work. If not those, maybe we'll find out where it was bought and then by whom. There are a lot of different ways to proceed. We'll use them all."

Suzanne couldn't keep her eyes from straying to the recorder. She hugged herself against a sudden chill. "There won't be anything on it, you know."

"No, I don't know," Peter responded.

"You . . . . Oh, God," she whispered as another chill hit. Her mind filled with despair. No matter how she tried to think about the future, she came against a blank wall. She could not make plans for her life as long as the person who was terrorizing her was still on the street.

And then her wall of self-control gave way. Tears welled, and her body shook. "I . . . I . . . I can't do it!"

Peter Wilson put his arms around her, drew her head to his chest, and stroked her hair gently. "Let it out, Suzanne, let it free."

His gift allowed the floodgates to open, and her emotions spewed violently out. She cried, wailed, and sobbed. Her body trembled, and her tears spilled. Her agony was plain, and her grief monumental. She cried for herself, and for the pain she had caused others just by their being near her. She cried for her son Allan, for Jan-Michael, and for her mother.

She cried for Larry Hartvale, and she cried for her brother, Arthur, too, for she had lost him with his admission of love. She wasn't aware of how long she stayed with her forehead pressed to Peter Wilson's chest, but when her tears finally ended, she was drained and exhausted.

"I'm sorry," she said, her voice muffled by his jacket.

"There's nothing to be sorry about."

She straightened and wiped her eyes. "It's strange . . . that part of the movie, where Larry was . . . . That scene was never used in the movie. The writers had done up a completely different ending. Peter," she said, her eyes searching his face, wondering what effect her words would have, "the film clip I saw was from the original movie!"

"Which means our suspect is definitely someone who had access to the film vaults, or had access to the film at the time of the filming."

Her strength was draining rapidly. She yawned, and covered her mouth. "I'm sorry, I . . ."

"It's all right. It's been a rough evening for you. Why don't you get some sleep? We'll talk tomorrow."

He stood and smiled at her. "You did very well tonight. You didn't give in to the fear. If you hadn't called me as soon as you did, we might not have found this," he added as he picked up the recorder. "Get some rest, Suzanne. You deserve it."

When he was gone, and she locked the door and checked all the windows and other doors, she went upstairs. She was in bed within minutes.

She thought about the day, and then tried to focus on the tape of Larry's death, but her mind refused to follow that direction. Within minutes she was asleep.

The police station was buzzing with activity at ten in the morning. Suzanne was directed to Peter Wilson's office, but had to wait ten minutes before she could see him.

When he was free, and she was escorted inside, he greeted her warmly and showed her to the seat across from his desk. "You look as though you slept."

"I did," she replied as she sat.

"What brings you here so early?" he asked as he started to his desk.

"Impatience. I'm on my way to my stepfather's, but I didn't want to wait until later to find out if you'd learned anything from the VCR."

Sitting at his desk, he picked up a file folder and opened it. "Not as much as I'd hoped."

Suzanne shifted to the front edge of the chair. "What does that mean?"

"There were no prints on the recorder case or on the video tape case itself. The tape was a copy made on a store brand of tape. We've sent the serial number of the player as well as the tape to their manufacturers. With just a little luck, we'll get the store where it was sold."

"What good will that do?"

"If we find the store, then we may just find a clerk who remembers who bought the VCR."

"Oh," Suzanne said. "That would be good."

"Wouldn't it, though?"

She studied him, wondering if he was making fun of her or not. Not, she decided. "Was there anything else?"

He favored her with a confident smile. "Yes. I've been able to eliminate several people from our list. Judd Malcome, to begin with, is officially a non-suspect."

"I didn't think he was a suspect," Suzanne stated.

"No, you said it wasn't him. That's all. But you were right. He couldn't have done these things to you. He had a stroke shortly after your mother died."

Suzanne stiffened. Her heart went out to Judd. He'd always been fair with her. "Is he recovering?"

"It was a severe stroke for a man in his sixties. But yes, he is recovering. His son handles the business now. But Judd Malcome has started coming in to the office a few times a week. Even so, he would not be physically capable of doing the things that have been done to you."

Suzanne decided not to say "I told you so."

"Dana is off the list."

"Of course she is. She never was on it."

He held her stare. "She was on my list because she knew you before Hollywood, during both periods in Hollywood, and currently, as well. She could have somehow been involved."

"She's my friend; her husband is your friend."

Exhaling loudly, he nodded. "Which makes it a good thing that she isn't a suspect."

Suzanne gave a short laugh when she saw the shadowy smile he was regarding her with. "Okay, you got me that time."

"It helps to see the humor in the worst of situations. And Valerie Hartvale is off our list as well. She remarried four years after the accident, and has three children. She's living in Colorado."

Suzanne closed her eyes and gave a little prayer of thanks. Valerie Hartvale had suffered a great loss; she was glad the woman had recovered and had gone forward with her life.

"That leaves us with four suspects."

Suzanne pictured the list they'd drawn up yesterday. Her eyes snapped open. "Three. My stepfather, brother, and Tim. Which is actually none."

"No, I added someone else. Paul Driscoll."

Suzanne's jaw dropped. When she recovered from her surprise, she said, "How did you work that one out?"

"He's Timothy Randolf's director. And I did some extra research. Did you know that after *And Baby Makes Five* went off the air, your former director didn't work for almost five years? When he did finally get work, it was only the lowest of his profession's offering."

Suzanne shook her head. "No, I . . . . He was a good director. He cared about the show."

"But in the end, he was the one who'd been blamed for the show's demise. That and the fact that he spent years

278

trying to get a job might have turned him bitter. If that's the case, and he became fixated on the idea that you were responsible for his troubles . . ."

Suzanne was again saddened. "Paul Driscoll wasn't that kind of person. We all knew why the show had to end. I think it was just his bad luck that caused him not to get a job."

Peter exhaled loudly. "You're doing it again," he said. "Please, Suzanne, don't declare someone innocent until you know who the guilty person is."

She nodded, but refused to change her mind.

"It could also be what we spoke about yesterday. A crazy—someone who has become obsessed with you. A crazy, celebrity hunting killer who'll do anything to get what he wants. But," Peter said, his tone softening, "I'll bet everything I have that it's someone you know, and have known since you first went to Hollywood. The type of accidents, and the type of killing, all spell knowledge of you, your life, and your work."

Suzanne wasn't thrilled about his confidence as to who the killer might be. If he was right, then the person who was terrorizing her was someone she knew, and probably loved. "Whoever it is, please find him Peter, find him soon."

Peter stood as she did. "I'll do my best," he said, countering her pleading gaze with a look of strength and hope. "But you'll have to do the same. You'll have to work on your memories, and you'll have to keep yourself strong and watchful."

She parked the car and looked at her stepfather's house. She could see her mother's hand on it, although it had been two years since her death.

The house was painted a soft shade of beige. The trim

was a dark mocha. Evergreen bushes surrounded the house, and several tall trees lined the driveway. The lawn had been mowed recently, and the scent of cut grass lingered in the air.

Getting out of the car, Suzanne took a deep preparatory breath before starting forward. She had not been in her stepfather's house since she'd graduated from school.

The walk seemed endless, but when she finally reached the front door, her resolve to see this through had returned. She pressed the doorbell and waited.

A half-minute later the door was opened by Raymond Barnes. He looked the same as he had when he'd come to her house—older than his years. "I'm glad you could make it. Come in."

She moved toward him to give him a daughterly kiss on the cheek, but he was already turning and heading into the house.

Relieved rather than upset, she trailed him through the house, seeing even more evidence of her mother as they went. The furnishings were very much Lenore Barnes's taste, from the type of furniture to the color and quality of the carpeting and drapery.

Raymond stopped at a closed door halfway down the hall. He opened it and said, "This was your mother's room. She called it her 'office.' I've left it the way it was, for the most part. Look through it all. Whatever you want is yours." He motioned toward the far wall. "I've left a couple of empty boxes for you."

"Thank you," she said as she went into the room. Once inside, she stood in the center and surveyed it all. Her mother's desk, a Victorian secretary that Suzanne remembered from her own childhood, was against one wall. The accompanying ladderback chair was there as well.

Memories hit her hard. She could picture her mother seated in the chair and doing paperwork at the desk late at night. The memory was as comforting as was the furniture itself.

"Would you like a cup of coffee?" Raymond Barnes asked.

Suzanne shook her head. "Not right now."

"I'll leave you alone. If you need me, just call. I'll be in the kitchen."

She turned to him. The light from the overhead fixture caught him at a strange angle. Half his face was in shadows. It gave him a dark, almost malevolent look. For an instant, she thought about the list of suspects she and Peter Wilson had discussed.

Raymond Barnes's name was on that list. She tensed, suddenly afraid. Then Raymond turned completely toward her. The shadows disappeared, and he was once again the father she had known since her third year of life.

"Thank you," she whispered.

He paused. "For?"

"This," she said, spreading her arms to show that she meant the room full of her mother's things.

Nodding, he turned and left the room.

When he was gone, Suzanne reprimanded herself for allowing herself to think that Raymond Barnes could be the person who was trying to kill her. Their relationship over the years had not been close, but that was no reason for her to even consider the idea that her stepfather was out to harm her.

Shaking off the thoughts, Suzanne went to her mother's secretary. The first thing she saw was a picture of herself, at the height of her fame on *And Baby Makes Five*. The picture had been taken on the set, in one of her cutest scenes.

Next to that was another picture. This one had been taken in France, at her wedding. It was of her and Jan-

Michael and her mother, standing together in front of the church where they had been married.

She touched the photograph with her fingertips. She traced her mother's face and then Jan-Michael's. Then she realized she was crying.

She looked around again. There was a set of shelves built into one wall. She went to the white lacquered shelves.

On the top shelf was a large Minnie Mouse doll she and her mother had gotten at Disneyland, the first year she had done the television series.

As she looked at the items on the shelves, she spotted another memory. There was a small barrette she'd made in kindergarten. She picked it up. The top of the barrette was made of cardboard. She had painted it, and then written the word "Mom" on it.

She turned the barrette in her hand. The colors were almost gone, the word "Mom" faded but still legible. She took the barrette and the Minnie Mouse doll and put them in one of the boxes Raymond had left for her.

Then she started around the room, lifting, touching, reading, and feeling her mother's presence. A half-hour later she was done. She had one box packed with the things she wanted to take with her.

She brought the box into the kitchen, where she found her stepfather. The kitchen, too, had her mother's unmistakable mark on it.

The fixtures were all white, the rest of the kitchen was a combination of floral and earthtone colors. The white and earthy mixture had always been her mother's favorite.

"The house is lovely," she said as she put the box on the floor next to the table.

"Coffee?"

She shook her head. "You miss her a lot, don't you?"

His features were unreadable, his eyes dull. "She was my life," he said. "Everything I did, I did for her."

Suzanne swallowed. "I know you did."

"We didn't always get along, you and I."

"No, we didn't."

"But I made a good home. I provided."

"Yes, you did."

"We weren't like those other parents—the ones who took their children's money for themselves. We never touched your money."

"I know," Suzanne said.

His eyes came alive for a moment, blazing as he said, "You hurt her when you left."

Suzanne held his glare. "I know. But I was hurting, too. And I had to find a way to live. I couldn't go on the way I had been. Things were impossible for me. I didn't leave to cause her, or you, any pain. I left for my own sanity."

With her words, the fire in his eyes went out, and his gaze dulled.

"Thank you for letting me have these things."

Raymond Barnes stared at the single box. "That was all you took?"

"It's all I need," she said. "Thank you, again," she added as she picked up the box.

Her stepfather stood and walked with her to the front door. He opened it for her and stepped aside. She paused to look at him. She wanted to say something, anything, but couldn't think of a single thing. "Bye," she said at last.

She made the drive home in under ten minutes. When she entered her own house, she heard Dana working in the office.

"How's it going?"

Dana turned from the computer. "Fine. I've almost finished the last chapter you dictated. You've had a couple of calls. Tim Randolf called three times. He said it was very important and asked that you call him as soon as possible. And your brother called."

"I don't want to speak to Arthur," she said as she went to the phone and dialed Tim Randolf's number. His secretary answered, and transferred her immediately.

"Hi, beautiful," Tim said.

"Thanks, but I don't feel so beautiful today."

"You are, have no fear." Tim paused silently. Then, he said, "Suzanne, I would like to see you, tomorrow night."

Suzanne sighed. Things were moving in so many directions that she was feeling overwhelmed. "Tim, I . . . tomorrow night wouldn't be good."

"Suzanne, I need to see you. It's very important to me. Please," he asked in a low but persistent voice.

She shook her head. She didn't want to be pushed into things.

"Suzanne, are you there?"

"I'm here."

"Suzanne, I need to see you. It's very important to me."

"All right," she said, giving into the plea in his voice.

She heard the uplifting change in his voice as he said, "Great. I've got a special I'll be taping in the afternoon so I'll send my car for you, say at 7:30. I'll meet you at the restaurant. It's in Jersey. You'll love it. See you tomorrow night."

"Tomorrow," she said and hung up the phone. Why had she agreed to go when she really hadn't wanted to? Am I that easy? she asked herself.

"You okay?" Dana asked.

Suzanne turned to her and shrugged. She explained what had just happened, and her own trepidations.

"Ah, the life of the stars," Dana said.

Frowning, Suzanne was unable to hide the annoyance

caused by her friend's statement. "Is that what you think?"

"Isn't it?" Dana rejoined, meeting Suzanne's without flinching. "Really, Suzanne, you are a famous celebrity and you're dating another famous celebrity who's sending a limousine to pick you up. If that isn't the life of the stars, then I've spent my life reading the wrong books and seeing the wrong movies, because it certainly isn't anything that approaches reality or normalcy in my life."

Suzanne paused to think about what Dana had said. As she digested her friend's words, her indignation eased. "I guess you're right. I've never thought about it in that way. But I've never thought about myself as a star, either."

"You are, regardless of your own perception."

"I guess I am," she said, seeing herself through Dana's eyes. "But I don't feel like a star, and I would trade my life for a normal one and never look back."

"But you can't. How do you feel about Tim?" Dana asked suddenly.

"I don't know. I've known Tim a long time. I like him . . ."

"And love?"

Suzanne shrugged. She remembered her reaction to him when he had kissed her. "When we first started dating, I thought it might work, but . . ." She paused, not sure of what she wanted to say. "The other night he told me he loved me. I told him that the timing was bad, that my life was upside down right now. He asked me not to make any decision, but to let time do it for me."

"That sounds promising," Dana said with a serious nod.

"It's strange. How can I fall in love with someone at this point in time? Dana, there's a lunatic out there trying to kill me, and Tim wants me to fall in love with him."

Suzanne shook her head. "There's more. I have this

bizarre feeling that Tim is actually expecting me to fall in love with him. Truthfully, I don't know if I'll ever be capable of loving again the way I did with Jan-Michael. I don't even know if I want to be in love again."

"There will be someone, again," Dana prophesied as the phone rang.

Dana picked it up. A moment later she said, "I'm sorry, but Suzanne doesn't want to talk to you. She asked me to tell you to stop calling her."

Suzanne knew that it was Arthur on the other end. Why was he calling? Hadn't she made it plain enough to him?

"No, Arthur, I'm sorry. She just doesn't want to talk to you. You'll have to give her time. When she's ready to talk to you, she will."

Suzanne saw the exasperation on Dana's features as her friend listened to her brother. Then Suzanne realized she couldn't put this off on Dana any longer.

She strode across the room and took the phone. "Arthur," she began, but he cut her off.

"Suzanne, listen to me. We have to talk. We have to get things worked out between us."

"No, *we* don't have to do any such thing. This is the last time I will discuss it with you. Arthur, for the sake of the past, let things go. Please don't call. When I'm ready, I'll call you."

Without waiting for his response, she hung up.

"Are you okay?" Dana asked.

"No. But maybe one day I will be," Suzanne said.

Chapter Twenty

The sun fell below the far horizon, yet the sky was alive with brightness. Twilight was still a good distance away while Suzanne looked through the refrigerator, trying to change her apathy toward food into a desire to make something for dinner.

Before she found anything that piqued her appetite, the doorbell rang. She looked at the kitchen clock. It was 7:30. She went to the front door and looked through the peep hole.

"This is unexpected," she said, opening the door to Peter Wilson.

"I hope I'm not interrupting anything," he said.

"Only my attempt to figure out what to have for dinner. Would you like to come in?"

"In a moment," he said as he turned and motioned to someone with his arm.

In response, a blue uniformed policeman came up the walk. The policeman was in his mid-twenties, with bright blue eyes and a very serious manner. "This is Officer Stork. He'll be on duty until midnight. Another officer will relieve him then."

Suzanne nodded to the officer, who turned and walked away.

"I don't understand," she said.

"Let's talk inside," Peter suggested.

She stepped back so he could enter, and then she led him to the kitchen. "I decided to place an officer on watch throughout the night. I'm not happy about the way this investigation is going. And I'm especially not happy knowing that this person was able to get close enough to the house to set up the VCR."

"But you've had a car on patrol every night. Isn't that enough?"

He looked at her for several seconds before speaking. When he did speak, she sensed something deeper behind his remarks. "I've got a hunch that this . . . person is starting to move faster. I don't want you to be vulnerable."

"I don't know what to say. But thank you. I . . . . How about dinner?" she asked spontaneously. "Unless you have other plans."

He smiled. Again, she was taken by how the smile transformed his features from those of a responsive policeman to those of a warm and concerned friend, which was how she now thought of him.

"No other plans, and yes, thank you, that would be nice."

She went to the refrigerator again, but this time she did so with a mission rather than with apathy.

A half-hour later, Suzanne set a platter on the outside table, and turned on the deck lights. "Would you do the honors?" She handed Peter a corkscrew and a bottle of wine.

He looked at the wine, a Chenin Blanc, and then peeled the lead seal from the top. Suzanne brought the rest of the dinner out to the deck and Peter poured the wine.

"Looks wonderful," Peter said as Suzanne served a

pasta salad made of rollatini, fresh vegetables, and a light basil dressing.

"To a lovely night," Peter said, holding his glass and looking up at the star filled sky.

Suzanne raised her glass toward him. "Yes, to the night."

She sipped the wine, which was cool, dry, and light. As they ate, they talked about insignificant things.

Through the impromptu dinner, she was aware of the way he avoided any mention of what had been happening. When they finished the meal, she was surprised to find that she was pleasantly relaxed.

"That was delicious," Peter said.

"Thank you." She picked up her wine glass and drank what little remained. When she put it down, she realized he was looking at her. "What?"

He shook his head. "I was just trying to get into his mind."

She instinctively knew whose mind the policeman was talking about. "Why?"

"To try and understand him. But I can't. In order to do that, I have to have more. And it's hard to get into another person's mind when what is happening makes no sense."

"To him, it makes sense," Suzanne said. "Peter, you said you have a premonition that he's going to move faster."

"It's only a hunch. But I'm a cop, and I live by my hunches. I think by setting up the VCR, he's signalling his intention to push harder and faster."

"Why?" she asked. "Why doesn't he just come after me and get it over with?"

Peter slowly shook his head from side to side. "It's never that simple. If what we suspect is true, this person has spent over two decades stalking you. He wants you to be afraid—no, he wants you so terrorized that you won't be capable of doing anything other than being his victim. And it's all to pay you back for whatever it was that he thinks you did to him.

"He wants to turn you into a shell of a person, controlled by fear. Then, and only then, when he's reached the point where he thinks he's punished you enough, will he perform his final act."

Suzanne shivered. "I . . ."

"But I promise you this," Peter said, leaning forward. "I will not let him do this to you. I will not let anything happen to you. And I will stop him."

She held his fiery gaze for several moments and, as she let his words build inside her, her fear began to subside. She sensed that there was more to Peter Wilson's promise than just words. It was that knowledge that made her less afraid.

"And now, I have to go."

She walked him to the front door, and opened it. The moonlight blended with the outside house light to give the illusion that the night had yet to cross over from the other side of the house.

"Remember, if anything out of the ordinary happens, call. Don't forget that there will be a policeman outside, all night, every night, until we get him."

"I'll remember," she said.

For a lingering moment that seemed cut from time, she thought he was going to bend and kiss her. But he didn't; rather, he smiled and started down the walk.

As she watched him, she wondered if he really had wanted to kiss her, or if it was just part of the peculiar mood that had taken hold inside her head. Then she wondered what she would have done if he had kissed her.

* * *

Sinking gratefully into the hot water, Suzanne laid her head back on the tub's cool, porcelain rim. She thought about the day she'd moved into this house.

Her mind was playing tricks on her. While it seemed that she'd been here for ages, she hadn't yet gone through a single season.

True, she'd accomplished a lot: well over two hundred pages of her autobiography had been transcribed, and she'd begun to live as a person rather than as a mourner. But there was a price that she was paying for this new life, and that price was the *stalker*.

At the same time that she thought of the stalker, she was also aware that there was more substance to her life than there had been since Jan-Michael's and Allan's deaths.

She was dating Tim. And she was thoroughly enjoying that aspect, too, she told herself as she shifted in the tub. The water sloshed, splashing her in the face.

She wiped the water from her eyes. "All right, so I'm stretching it a little," she admitted to the silent bathroom. "But at least I'm doing something constructive."

That had been the reason she'd returned. She'd had to find a way to live again. Part of that way had been to relive her past. The other part was to confront all her demons, and move forward.

She opened her eyes and looked around. She suddenly understood what she'd expected Timothy Randolf's part to be in her life. When she had returned to Hollywood, Tim had always been around her. He had been eager to be near her and eager to love her. And now, she realized that he represented a safe harbor in her current life because he was a known commodity.

He was a safe person for her to start being romantic with. He was predictable, and she had assigned him the task of helping her to escape the past and step into her future.

Only it wasn't working—at least not in that way. And no romance would work until the maniac who was haunting her life was out of it, once and for all.

Understanding herself a little better, Suzanne decided that when she saw Tim, tomorrow night, she would do her best to explain herself to him, and explain why they could not go further.

For an instant, Peter Wilson's face flashed across her mind's eye. She was thankful for him, and thankful that he had taken a personal interest in her case. The policeman was an anchor in her life. He was keeping her sane.

She closed her eyes and tried to let the hot water do its work on her tense muscles. Her eyes snapped open a second later as she asked herself if she'd done the right thing in not telling Peter about Arthur's confession of love.

No, she knew she could not hurt Arthur any more. To tell Peter about Arthur could cause an intolerable amount of harm to him, emotionally as well as socially, should word get out.

"How about thinking of good things," she said to herself. She smiled then, and thought back to when she was barely ten, and she and her mother had played hookey and gone to Disneyland.

Officer Kevin Stork walked slowly from behind the house, where he had been checking the back door, and started toward the street.

He had not taken more then a dozen steps when he heard a noise in the bushes separating the Grolier house from its neighbor.

Turning toward the noise, Kevin held still. He searched

the area with his keen eyes, but saw nothing. Slowly, he started toward the spot.

When he reached the line of evergreen bushes, and followed them toward the street, he found no evidence of anyone. Then, as he reached the street, a car's engine started.

Headlights flared. The car moved forward. Kevin Stork watched the car go slowly past him. He couldn't make out the driver, but he was able to see the license plate.

As the car's taillights faded, Officer Kevin Stork carefully wrote down the license plate number on his note pad. When the pad was tucked inside his shirt pocket, he resumed his tour of the grounds around Suzanne Barnes Grolier's home.

Suzanne toweled herself dry and then put on a light terry cloth robe. She went into the exercise room and turned on the television. The news was on, and the weatherman was in the middle of his report. The five day forecast filled the background of the screen. The man was talking about how hot and dry the next week would be.

Suzanne watched the news until the sportscaster came on. He was an obnoxious young man with sapphire-blue eyes, a huge jutting jaw, and a look that said, "I'm a jock, don't you love me!"

"No," Suzanne said before pressing the remote control's off switch and going into the bedroom.

Suzanne exchanged the terry robe for a set of soft silk pajamas. She looked at the bed, debated about getting in, and finally decided that she wasn't tired enough for sleep.

She left the bedroom and started downstairs.

* * *

"Stork out," Officer Kevin Stork said after finishing his 10:45 check-in report. He released the transmit button and hung the hand-held police radio on his hip.

Turning, he started down the far side of Suzanne's property. He glanced at the house and saw the bedroom light come on. He thought about how pretty Mrs. Grolier was and found it hard to believe that the beautiful woman who lived in the house had once been that gawky kid on the television series he'd watched as a boy.

Just as he reached the front edge of the house, there was a crackling sound. He recognized the noise as a foot stepping on a dead branch.

Stork pulled his flashlight from its clip, turned, and began to silently work his way toward the other side of the house. He froze a half-dozen feet from the house's side door when he saw the silhouette of someone bending over the doorknob.

He considered calling for back-up, but discarded the idea immediately. Any noise he made would alert the intruder. Instead, he waited to see what the person would do. But, when he heard the click of a lock, he knew he could wait no longer. As the door opened, Kevin Stork launched himself at the intruder.

Suzanne set the kettle on the flame and started back to the kitchen table. Her tape recorder was already on the table, as was a yellow note pad.

Just as she started to sit, there was a distinct noise in the pantry. She froze, her heart starting to beat crazily. She waited, but there was nothing else.

She told herself that a can had fallen from a shelf. Then she reminded herself that since there was a policeman on guard outside her house, she had nothing to fear.

Going to the pantry, she reached for the door. But even

while she told herself that there was no danger, she was all too aware of the way her fingers trembled. "Stop," she told herself. Then, willfully, she grasped the doorknob.

"Open it," she ordered herself. She tried, but her muscles would not obey her. She was afraid that when the door opened, she would find something there that she did not want to face.

"Do it!" She closed her eyes and turned the knob. Then she opened her eyes and pulled the door toward her.

Her breath escaped in a loud whoosh when she saw that the room was indeed empty.

But her relief was short lived as the outside door rattled and a dark shape filled the door's window. She could not stop the scream from escaping as, an instant later, the door crashed open and a large, dark shape charged toward her.

She screamed again when the dark and hulking form came right toward her. Then, suddenly, another body slammed into the first. The two blurred together, whirled around, and after crashing into the shelves lining the pantry, fell to the floor.

Suzanne fought the almost overwhelming panic as she tried to back up. Her hand touched the door frame and, without realizing what she was doing, she turned on the pantry's light.

She blinked away the dancing spots that filled her eyes and looked down at the floor. Officer Stork was lying atop the intruder. He was in the process of putting on handcuffs.

A moment later, the young policeman was on his feet. Then, he bent and half pulled, half helped the shackled intruder to his feet. Slowly, the policeman turned the man toward Suzanne.

"No," she cried, shaking her head and biting her lower

lip as she stared into the face of her stepbrother, Arthur Barnes.

"It does make sense, sort of," Peter Wilson said. "He was jealous of your success and fame. He's probably been that way since he was a boy. Everything fits," Peter said as he slapped the back of his right hand into his left palm.

"Suzanne, you need to look at things in a different light. When someone loses their ability to reason and crosses over the line from reality into their own fantasy, they are no longer rational. When someone is fixated, the way Arthur has become fixated on you, it's a form of psychosis. Whoever and whatever that person once was has no bearing on what they've become. And I think Arthur Barnes crossed that line a long time ago."

Suzanne studied Peter's face. His eyes told her that he was certain. But she wasn't—not yet. "I just can't believe it. And he was never jealous of me, as a boy, or as a man."

He rubbed his jaw with a forefinger and thumb. "You wouldn't necessarily know that. He lived with you all those years. He had to have learned very early on how to hide his emotions."

She shook her head. "No. Peter, being jealous of a career is not Arthur's problem."

Peter Wilson's right eyebrow arched slightly. "Then what is his problem?"

Moistening her lips, she tried to figure out how to explain the situation. She took a deep breath and said, "Because he loved me."

"It wouldn't be the first time a brother hurt a sister. And he is a stepbrother."

"Not that way," she said, her voice almost a whisper.

His expression was guarded, his eyes showed puzzlement. "I don't follow you."

Suzanne forced herself to keep her gaze on his face as she said, "He didn't just love me. He was *in* love with me. And Peter, it was not the way a brother loves a sister."

"Whew," the tall detective said. "When did you find out about this?"

"I've known for a week or so. He told me—confessed would be a better word—about how he felt. He told me that he's been in love with me for a long time. I . . ." She tried to go on, but couldn't.

A flash of frustration crossed Peter's features, but disappeared as he took her hand. She felt the warmth of his touch, and accepted the comfort that it offered.

"Why didn't you tell me?"

"He's my brother. If I told you, you would have believed he's the one."

"It would have saved us time," Peter remarked. "We have a motive now, for what he's been doing."

She shook her head adamantly. "If Arthur loves me, why would he hurt me?"

"Because he couldn't have you, possibly. There could be any number of reasons. But at least you can relax now. You can get some sleep and know that there won't be any calls tonight. And by the time tomorrow gets here, I'll have spent a fair amount of time with Arthur and I should have some answers for you."

She squeezed his hand. "Peter, be easy with him. I . . . can't explain how I know, but I do know that Arthur is not the one who's after me. Arthur couldn't kill anyone, let alone my husband and son."

"A mind, especially the mind of someone who has emotional problems, is very tricky. I've seen things . . ." He shook his head slowly. "Suzanne, of all the links connecting the suspects in this case, Arthur Barnes fits into almost every category. He's had the opportunity, the motive, and the means."

"But he was in school when the early things happened," she protested.

"How do we really know? Did anyone see his school records, or was it just assumed? And what about after his schooling? What about then?"

"I don't know. Peter, do me a favor, please."

He cocked his head slightly askance. "If I can."

"Don't put all your money in the same bank."

When his expression went from puzzlement to comprehension, she added, "And don't cancel the policemen you have here."

He looked down at her hand, which was still within his, and released it and stood up. "All right. I'll call you tomorrow, when we've finished. Please, Suzanne, get some sleep. You can rest easier now."

After Peter left, Suzanne turned on the flame under the kettle. When the whistle trilled, she poured the steaming water into the cup that had been waiting for almost an hour.

She lowered the infuser into the water, and waited patiently until the tea was the exact shade of sienna she preferred. When she was satisfied, she took the cup and saucer up to the bedroom, where she turned on a late night talk show to keep her company while she drank the soothing brew.

Suzanne read the lighted numbers. It was 3:17. She turned again, searching for a comfortable position the way she'd been doing for the last two plus hours.

Finally, she gave up. She sat, leaning back against the headboard and drawing the summer weight comforter with her. She looked out the bedroom window.

The night sky was gray-black. A sprinkling of stars

dotted the distance. The house was silent and there were no sounds at all from outside.

She wished she could sleep, but her mind refused to calm itself. She kept thinking about Arthur and about Peter Wilson. The policeman was so positive that Arthur was the one who had been silently stalking her all these years.

Yet, there was something inside of her, telling her that her stepbrother would not harm her. She thought back to the days when he was her big brother-protector. She recalled the times when he'd walked her to the bus stop and waited for the bus with her.

She remembered, too, how he had played with her when she'd had no friends to play with; and, how he had covered for her when she'd gotten into trouble with their father.

But at the same time, she had a true and intuititive trust for Peter Wilson. He had taken on the role of protector and he was an experienced policeman who knew his job.

Was he right? Could Arthur's mind be so twisted that her stepbrother could love her as both a sister and as a woman he wanted to . . . . She stopped herself, knowing that to continue in that vein could only lead to more confusion.

She sought a way to make herself hate Arthur. If Peter Wilson was right, then Arthur was the person who had been haunting her all her life. If Peter Wilson was right, Arthur had done horrible things, not only to Suzanne, but to everyone around her.

She willed herself to think back. She did not think about the first incident—the hit and run truck that had smashed into Buzz Carlyle—but considered the possibility of the hate letters that had mysteriously gotten by the studio readers. She tried to think about the many accidents that had happened on the sound stage.

She remembered one, during a dress rehearsal for one of the last of the TV series. Everyone had been there: Arthur, her stepfather, and her mother. She was supposed to be baking a cake. The stove they used had no back, so a camera could shoot directly into it.

As she bent to check the cake, one of the lightbulbs used to increase the light inside the oven blew out. It shattered. Luckily, the fragments did not hit her in the eyes.

Suzanne shook her head. She'd forgotten the incident when she'd dictated her chapter to Dana. But how could someone arrange to have a lightbulb explode?

Who else had been there that day? Everyone on the suspect list, she realized. "This is crazy," she said aloud. Her voice sounded loud in the quiet bedroom.

She thought about Larry Hartvale. Where was Arthur then? Had he been in Los Angeles? She thought he had. Either there, or somewhere else in California, playing. But if he did love her the way he said, would he have done that? Would he have turned her into a murderess?

Balling her hands into tight fists, she slammed them down into the mattress. Who else could it be?

"Who?" she said aloud.

Tim Randolf had been in Los Angeles. She'd been dating him, but when she'd started that last picture, he'd also started another picture and their dates had become infrequent.

But she knew Tim Randolf well, and he was no more a killer than was Arthur.

She reflected on Peter's earlier words about what happens to someone when they cross the line between sanity and insanity. Could that be true about Arthur?

Could Arthur have learned where she was living in France, and come after her again? Could he have killed her husband and son? No, she refused to consider the possibility. Not Arthur. Not anyone she knew!

Another thought intruded. If Arthur's mind was so badly warped that he wanted to kill her and everyone involved with her, would he have asked her *not* to call their father to tell him what had happened?

She considered his reaction just before they had taken him to the police station. Arthur had pleaded with her to not call their father. He had not wanted Raymond Barnes to know what happened, because of Raymond's fragile health.

And Tim? What about Tim Randolf?

She stared up at the ceiling. She was supposed to see Tim tomorrow night. No, she corrected herself, it was already the next day and their date was for tonight.

And what about Tim? She had to tell him the truth. She had to make him understand that she was not yet ready for a relationship.

She yawned. Her mind began to fog up and her thoughts were having trouble arranging themselves cohesively. She slid down in the bed and turned on her side.

"Later," she mumbled, without knowing that she had spoken aloud. A few seconds later her breathing was deep and peaceful.

Chapter Twenty-one

"Tell me about the brakes," Peter Wilson said.

"What are you talking about?" Arthur replied. Dark circles shadowed his eyes. His mouth was stretched in a taut line that compressed his lips into pale thinness.

"Tell me about the way you sabotaged the brakes on Suzanne's car."

"I didn't. I want my lawyer," Arthur Barnes demanded.

"You agreed to this interview without a lawyer. Are you changing your mind now?"

Arthur stared angrily at Peter Wilson. "We've been doing this for three hours. You keep asking the same questions and I keep giving you the same answers. So either cut the questions or let me call my lawyer."

"Why, Arthur? Why have you been stalking your stepsister? Why have you killed all those people? You killed her husband and her son, didn't you?" Peter said suddenly, his voice rising harshly on the last words.

Arthur's face registered shock. He shook his head slowly. "I . . . . I would never harm Suzanne, I—"

"That's why you broke into her house, to *not* harm her?"

"We had a disagreement. I needed to talk to her in person, not over the phone."

"I don't buy it, Arthur. Let's go back a few years. Remember Larry Hartvale?"

Arthur's eyes widened. He stared at Peter for several seconds. "Yes."

"Someone killed him. Someone used Suzanne as a weapon to kill Larry Hartvale. I think the killer hoped that Suzanne would be charged with the murder and be sent to jail. Or, it's possible that the killer figured the actor's death would destroy Suzanne's career. At that point in time, perhaps that was all the killer wanted. What do you think, Arthur?"

Arthur Barnes moistened his lips as comprehension showed in his eyes. "I think that I want a lawyer. I think that I've finished answering questions until I speak with my lawyer. And I was always under the impression that I was allowed a telephone call after being arrested."

Peter Wilson nodded. "Yes, you are allowed all of those things, and you will have them, when we're finished here. Remember, you agreed to this talk."

"And I now withdraw my agreement. I want to speak with my lawyer."

Peter Wilson stood. "I'll make the arrangements. But first we have to finish the booking process."

"And that's as far as we got," Peter Wilson said as he shut off the television and turned to Suzanne.

"Did you get any sleep last night?" Suzanne asked as she studied his face.

Smiling, he nodded. "Enough to get by on."

"You still think it's Arthur?"

"Yes."

"Have you let him call his lawyer?"

Peter nodded. "The lawyer was here an hour ago, and has started the process to get Arthur out. Your stepbrother will be arraigned on Monday. Bail will be set then."

"Monday, not today or tomorrow?"

Peter shook his head. "The court is only open on weekdays. Since today is Saturday, he'll remain in custody until Monday."

"I'm still having trouble believing all of this," Suzanne admitted. "I just can't figure how Arthur could have been the one. How could he have engineered all of it?"

Peter's mouth tightened. His eyes became unfocused. "I haven't put it all together yet, but I will. Arthur made his biggest mistake last night. Now that we know where to look, we'll find each piece of the trail he had to leave, and the evidence we need to convict him will be there! It always is."

"You're so certain," Suzanne said. In contrast, she was a mass of painful confusion. She wanted her nightmare over; yet, she did not want the person responsible for ruining her life to be Arthur.

Peter nodded slowly. "I'm certain, yes, but you were right, as well, last night."

"About?"

"That no matter how confident I am that Arthur Barnes is the one, I need to get more proof than just catching him entering your house. So, until we have that proof, I will continue to have a patrol car going by your house, and there will be an officer on duty at night."

"Thank you," she said, not for the protection of the police patrols, but for the possibility that it might not be Arthur.

His next words made her think that he was reading her mind. "But I'm ninety-nine percent certain it is your stepbrother."

"Did he call his . . . our father?"

"Not that I'm aware of," Peter said.

"May I see him now?"

Peter studied her for several seconds. "Given the circumstances, do you think that's wise?"

Suzanne smiled for the first time since Arthur Barnes had broken into her house. "You and I have spent time together. We've talked. You know as much about my past as anyone. Now, what do I want to do?"

"I think you may be overestimating me, but," Peter said, as a shadowy grin appeared, "I've already made the arrangements for you to see him. I'll take you to him."

She put her hand on top of his. "Thank you."

He held her gaze for several moments. "You're welcome." Then he stood. "This way."

She followed him from his office, through the white and green hallway, to the elevator. They went down three flights to the basement level, which housed the small jailing facilities.

There, Peter Wilson brought her to a door marked, "Interrogation Room." "He's inside. Suzanne, regulation requires that either a policeman be present with you, or that the prisoner be secured. Do you want me inside with you?"

She shook her head. "I think that would be embarrassing for Arthur."

"After what you told me last night, so do I." He leaned forward and opened the door. "Knock when you're ready."

As the door swung open, she saw Arthur. He was seated at the same table that she'd seen on the videotape. His face was drawn and pale. His eyes, as they moved toward the opening door, reflected hope and fear.

His hands were manacled. He was in need of a shave.

Suzanne stepped into the small room and closed the door behind her. Her heart went out to her stepbrother, but caution ruled her emotions.

"Suzanne," he said and tried to stand. He rose only a few inches before he stopped. Suzanne looked down and saw that his ankles were secured to the chair's base.

She went to the table and sat across from him. "Why?"

He shook his head. "You wouldn't speak to me. I had to talk to you. I had to make you understand how I felt."

"I understood. Arthur, that's why I didn't want to see you or talk to you. Peter thinks that you're the one who's been trying to kill me."

"I know he does." Arthur held his eyes on her. "He's wrong. Suzanne, I would never harm you. I love you. I always have. But the reason I wanted to speak with you, was to tell you that I understand that your love for me is not a romantic love, and that I've come to terms with that."

She listened intently to his words, which sounded sincere. Yet, they were also very convenient. "So quickly?" she asked. "You told me that you loved me. You told me that I was the reason you never married. And after all of that, you can look at me and say that you understand how I feel and it's okay and you've come to terms with it?"

He looked briefly away. When he returned his gaze to her, he said, "Suzanne, perhaps it was a form of emotional catharsis. I don't know. But when I finally said what I had to, when I spoke about what I've been hiding inside me for all these years, something changed."

He took in a deep breath and let it out slowly. He looked down at his hands, at the handcuffs on his wrists, and shook his head. "It wasn't that simple. But once I spoke what was in my heart, and then after I confronted you the next day, I started to think, really think, about what I'd said and done. Suzanne, I kept going over it in my head. I kept thinking about what I said, and how I felt, and I started to realize that perhaps I was putting something more into my emotions and feeling than was really there.

"I'm not sure if I'm expressing myself properly. I'm better with the piano than with words, but what I'm trying to say is that our relationship is important to me. And that perhaps I used my feelings toward you to stop me from having feelings toward anyone else because it was safer to love someone I couldn't have than to love someone who might hurt me."

Suzanne wanted to believe him. She wanted him to be her brother again. But something was holding her back. "Why were you afraid?"

Arthur closed his eyes momentarily. When he opened them, Suzanne saw that haunted look reappear. "Whenever I thought about love and commitment, whenever I dated someone for any length of time, I started to think about the future. When I thought of the future, I also thought of the past. I remembered our parents' relationship, and how my father always reacted. He loved Mother, fiercely, and would do anything for her. But at the same time, he fought with everyone. My God, Suzanne, don't you remember what it was like? Don't you remember the fights and arguments?"

Wiping a hand across her brow, Suzanne nodded. "But I still don't understand."

"That was my only reference to a real life relationship between husband and wife. That, and your old show, which was so opposite of our lives. Don't you remember how perfect the *And Baby Makes Five* family was?"

"That was make-believe."

"Make-believe or not, it was all I had. Suzanne, that show was the only television I ever watched. Every other minute of the day was either spent studying or practicing piano. So those were my yardsticks," Arthur said.

The words bounced inside her head like billiard balls.

"Are you saying that you loved me because it was safer to love me than someone else?"

"To a degree, I think that's what I did. I didn't want to have the kind of relationship that my father had, and I knew that there was no reality in a relationship shown by a television series, so that if I loved someone I couldn't have, I wouldn't have to commit myself to someone who was real. But . . ."

"But I moved back to Springvale."

"Yes," Arthur admitted. "And I just let myself go. But Suzanne, I've never tried to harm you, or anyone around you. I couldn't."

Suzanne swallowed hard. She wanted to believe him. "Have you called Father yet?"

He shook his head. "I don't want to call him. I don't want him to know about this. Please, don't let him know."

"I won't," she promised. "Peter said you'll stay here until Monday. Have you spoken to your lawyer?"

"Yes. He's trying to get a special hearing set up. If he does, I may be able to get out by tonight."

"If you need anything, you'll call?"

"Then you believe me?" Arthur asked.

Suzanne looked into his eyes. "I want to Arthur. I want to. I only have you and Father. The two of you are my only family. I don't want to lose you."

"Suzanne, I swear it isn't me."

"Call me if you need anything," she said, standing. "We'll talk when . . ." she glanced at his handcuffs, ". . . when this mess is straightened up."

Suzanne studied the two dresses she'd laid out on her bed. She wasn't sure which one she wanted to wear. They were both similarly styled, with short sleeves and of a modest length. One was pale green, the other a deep blue.

She paused suddenly, wondering just what kind of a person she really was. Her stepbrother was in jail, and either he or someone else was trying to kill her, and she was wondering about which dress to wear on a date.

"Last date," she said, confirming her decision that seeing Tim Randolf was not what she wanted to do. He was a sweet person, and he was her friend, but she was not romantically interested in him, and was not going to let this go on any longer.

She looked at the clock. It was 6:30. She had to get moving. The car would be here soon and she still had to do her hair.

Choosing the pale green dress, she took off her robe and reached for the dress. Before she could put it on, the doorbell rang. She slipped the robe back on, secured it, and went down to answer the door.

When she opened it, Peter Wilson smiled at her. "May I?"

Stepping back, Suzanne said, "Please."

"I wanted to stop by and tell you what's been happening," he said as he followed her into the living room.

"I appreciate that," Suzanne said.

"I spent a couple of hours with the psychologist that the department uses. I explained the case to her, and went over the various aspects."

When he paused, Suzanne sensed he was searching for the right words. When he spoke again, she was certain of it.

"Dr. Hirsh agrees with me. When she went over the materials, and heard my explanations about the incidents, she said that all the indicators point to your stepbrother. So many of the incidents that occurred happened when a family member—your stepbrother—was either present, or nearby."

"What about the times when there were accidents and

Arthur was out of the country?" Suzanne asked quickly.

Peter nodded. "We discussed those as well. The very law of nature says that there had to be a few naturally occurring accidents. But by and large, Arthur was somewhere nearby when those things happened.

"Remember the chapter about the horror movie, when the camera broke from the track and there were a lot of injuries?"

"Yes. And Arthur was out of the country as well."

"No, not that time. You made a mistake. When we searched Arthur's office, I found his professional scrapbook. It had a listing of every concert he played, in America and in Europe. Arthur was in California—San Francisco to be exact."

Suzanne shook her head. She didn't want to believe him. She didn't, but it was becoming harder and harder not to.

"I'm sorry, Suzanne, but it does look as though it has been Arthur all these years."

Suzanne fought back her tears. Her world was rapidly crumbling, and she didn't see a way to stop it. "I'm sorry, too," she said, using every bit of the trade she had learned to keep her voice steady.

A moment later she became aware that Peter was staring at her, and his face showed his concern. "Things will work out, once this is behind you."

"I know," she whispered.

The tall and lean policeman reached out and squeezed her shoulder gently. "I have to go. But, if you'd like, I can come back later. Why don't we have dinner together? But this time I'll take you to a restaurant."

She knew he was trying to be helpful. She forced a smile. "Thank you, Peter, that's very kind, but I have a commitment for tonight that I can't break."

His eyes changed, and a second later they matched his

stoically unreadable features. "When will you be going out, and when will you be returning?"

She stiffened, but before she could respond, he held up his hand, palm toward her.

"Don't misunderstand. I need to know so I can alert the police who are assigned to guard you."

She ignored the flush that burned her cheeks. "I'm leaving at seven. I don't plan on being out a long time. I'm meeting Tim for dinner and then I'll be back. Probably by eleven."

"Tim Randolf?"

"Yes."

"Will you be in Springvale?"

She shook her head. "I don't know where I'll be—Jersey, I think he said. He's sending a car for me."

"I see. If you're in this area, please call and let me know where."

"I will," she promised.

"Thank you. Have a good evening." He smiled, went to the door, and let himself out.

When the door closed, Suzanne stared at it for several moments. Something had happened between them, but she wasn't quite sure of what. She thought she'd detected something, but could not be sure.

Shrugging, she returned to the bedroom and put on the green dress. She looked in the mirror, and took it off immediately. It looked much too good. She put on the blue dress, which looked wonderful, but not as inviting as did the green.

She looked at the clock. The car would be there in fifteen minutes. She went into the bathroom, knowing that she had very little time left.

She finished just as the doorbell rang. She gave herself a final look and went downstairs. With her purse in her hand, she opened the door, stepped outside into the warm evening, and followed the driver to the limousine.

Inside the air-conditioned luxury of the car, Suzanne leaned her head back and closed her eyes. Five minutes later they were on the Palisades Parkway, heading toward New Jersey.

A moment later, she heard the whirring of an electric motor. She opened her eyes and saw that a drawer was sliding out of the bar that was the barrier separating her and the driver.

On the drawer was a filled champagne glass, a gift wrapped box, and an envelope. She looked at the dark tinted glass barrier. All she was able to see was the dark outline of the driver's head.

Smiling, she leaned forward and retrieved the envelope. She opened it slowly, and withdrew a plain, white note-card. As she read the neatly scripted words, she tensed. She breathed deeply several times, and then re-read Timothy's note.

Nothing changed from the first reading to the second. The words were still the same. He had asked her to marry him.

She put the note back on the drawer and lifted the package. The note left no doubts as to what she'd find in the box. She debated opening it, and decided that if she didn't, Tim might construe it as a terrible insult.

The last thing she wanted to do was to hurt him. She opened the box and withdrew the black, velvet jewelry box that was inside. She opened the box, and her breath caught at the magnificence of the ring. She knew it was at least a five carat diamond, if not more.

Holding the ring up to the light above her head, she looked at it carefully. The ring, a solitaire engagement ring, was made of white gold. The stone sparkled with beauty. The diamond was as clear as any she'd ever seen, and its size was unbelievable. It was truly a remarkable ring.

Then she closed the box and set it next to the card and the untasted champagne. She leaned forward and rapped on the window.

"Yes?" came a voice over the intercom.

"I want to go back to my house," she said.

"I'm sorry ma'am, you what?"

"Turn around and take me home."

The driver's tone conveyed an underlying nervousness and confusion. "Ma'am, we're almost there. Another fifteen minutes. And Mr. Randolf was very specific about what time to get you there."

"Will you turn around?"

"Ma'am, I can't. Mr. Randolf is expecting you."

She realized that what she heard in the driver's voice was not nervousness; it was fear. For his job? she wondered.

She reached for the telephone set on the side of the bar. "Please pull over now and give me a number where I can reach Mr. Randolf."

The driver followed her instructions, pulled onto the grassy shoulder of the highway, and gave her the number. She dialed it immediately. The line was busy. For the next five minutes she kept on trying. Finally, she hung up the receiver.

She thought about again telling the driver to take her home. But that would only postpone the inevitable. She had to get the evening over with, especially now that Tim had gone this far.

"All right," she said, "take me to wherever it is we're going."

* * *

"Thanks Jim, I appreciate the help. See you soon," he added as he hung up. Swiveling in the chair, Peter faced the window. He saw nothing as his mind tried to fasten on the things he had just learned. It had taken longer than he'd expected, but his friend had finally come through.

Jim Meadows was a lieutenant in the Los Angeles Police Department. Jim and Peter had been in the army together. When they'd come home, Peter had joined the NYPD. Jim Meadows had done the same, but with the LAPD.

They'd both become detectives. Then, ten years ago, shortly after Peter had accepted the detective position with Springvale, Jim Meadows had been shot. He'd been seriously wounded and had almost died.

It had taken two years for him to make a full recovery, and when he had, the department had assigned him to desk duty. Jim Meadows had not liked it, but he'd been given a choice—desk or medical retirement.

In the years since the shooting, Jim Meadows had become the Los Angeles Police Department's liaison with the motion picture and television industry in Hollywood. It was Jim Meadows who set up street shoots and filming sites for the studios who were filming in Los Angeles.

It was Jim Meadows who knew everyone necessary to know in the acting business.

"Pete."

Peter turned at the unexpected voice. He found Amos Griggs standing at his desk. The assistant District Attorney for Springvale looked worried. "Judge Kornblute just called me. He wants to know why we can't treat Arthur Barnes with the respect due him. He wants to know why he isn't being called in to hold a special arraignment session, tonight."

"I'd like to know why he would be," Peter said as he straightened in the chair. "Amos, I know Barnes has influence in the community, but the law says that he has to wait for an arraignment proceeding, and that isn't scheduled until Monday."

"The judge says that if we remain unreasonable, he will come in and hold that arraignment so that Mr. Barnes can make bail."

Leaning forward, Peter stared hard into the ADA's eyes. "We can't afford to have him out, yet. Tell the judge that there is a strong possibility that Arthur Barnes is a multiple murder suspect. Tell him that."

"Peter . . ."

"Amos, do it. Stall, do whatever you have to. I need Arthur to sweat. And I need him in jail for another day or two."

"Why?"

Peter looked at the phone. What he'd learned from Jim Meadows made some sense, but not the kind of sense he had hoped. "So I can find enough evidence to keep him there!" Peter snapped, losing his patience for the first time.

"I'm sorry, Amos. This thing is getting to me. Please try to keep him inside."

"All right, I'll try," the ADA promised.

When the Assistant District Attorney left, Peter looked at the file that was on his desk. It was the Grolier case.

Jim Meadows had gotten him a lot of information, but most of it was hearsay. Yet, there were things he'd said that fit into the puzzle.

He opened Suzanne Grolier's file folder and reread everything. He looked at the reports of the gas leak, and of the brake problem on the car. Then he reread the fire bombing incident.

When he finished, he put what he'd read together with what he'd learned tonight from Jim Meadows. The problem was that while some of the information worked, some didn't.

Tim Randolf was still a suspect, as was Arthur Barnes. But there were two big differences between Arthur and Tim Randolf. The first was that Tim Randolf had not broken into Suzanne's house; and the second was that Arthur was in jail.

He closed his eyes. He owed Suzanne the strength of his promise that he wouldn't close the doors on any suspect even though Arthur was in custody. And Tim Randolf was still a good suspect.

Intuitively, he knew something was going to happen tonight. He'd felt it when he'd seen Suzanne earlier, and he sensed it now.

He reached for the phone and then dialed Tim Randolf's number, which Jim Meadows had supplied.

"Hello, I'm trying to reach Tim, it's extremely urgent," he said when Randolf's service answered.

"I'm sorry, but Mr. Randolf is unavailable tonight. May I take a message for him?"

"No, you may not. This is Robert K. Garnberry. I don't know if you've ever heard my name, but let me assure you that you will never forget it, if I can't get hold of Tim Randolf in the next five minutes."

"Sir, I—"

"Listen to me, young man. I am the vice president in charge of network programming. I must make a decision about Randolf's show, and that decision will be made momentarily. If I don't speak to him, he may very well be without a show. Do I make myself clear?"

"Yes sir, but I've already tried to beep him, and he is not responding."

"Then tell me where he is so I can call him directly."

"I can't."

"What's your name?" Peter asked, his voice rising another half-octave. When there was only silence on the other end, he wondered if he'd overdone it.

"He's at the Brigantine Restaurant in Fort Lee. You should be able to get him there," the young man said, his voice nearly breaking with nervousness.

"You did the right thing," Peter said in a softer voice before he hung up.

He knew the Brigantine. It was a very expensive restaurant set on a floating barge in the Hudson River, but anchored permanently.

He looked at the clock. It was a quarter to eight. The drive would take him a half-hour at best. After stopping at the duty desk to tell the sergeant where he was going, Peter went to his car. He was still sure that Arthur Barnes was the man responsible for Suzanne's problems. But, he'd made a promise to Suzanne and he would damn well keep that promise.

Chapter Twenty-two

When Suzanne stepped onto the barge, the maitre'd smiled and bobbed his head to her. "A pleasure, Ms. Grolier," he said. "Mr. Randolf is waiting."

She was not surprised that the maitre'd recognized her, considering everything else that Tim had set up so far. Holding the box containing the engagement ring in her left hand, she followed the tuxedoed man to a table overlooking the edge of the barge and the river itself.

The view was of the Manhattan skyline, and it was magnificent. But Suzanne paid little attention to it as she tried to prepare herself for the best way to tell Tim Randolf that her answer was no.

As Tim stood, and the maitre'd drew her chair back, she saw that Tim had already noticed the box in her hand, and that his eyes were sparkling with anticipation.

She sat and Tim followed suit. The maitre'd bowed to them and motioned for a waiter. The waiter appeared instantly, carrying a silver champagne bucket. He set it down in its stand, and the maitre'd whisked off the towel covering the contents.

Lifting a bottle of Moet, he displayed it to them both. A moment later, and with the accompanying flourishes, the cork was popped and the champagne served.

The maitre'd bowed one more time before leaving them alone.

Suzanne's entire body was stiff. She tried to relax, but could not. She caught her lower lip between her teeth when Tim lifted his glass and leaned forward.

"Say yes," he whispered. "Say yes."

Suzanne tasted her own blood. She realized that she had bitten her lip, but there was no pain. She ran her tongue across her lip.

"Tim, you've been absolutely wonderful to me since I've returned to New York. And our friendship means the world to me. But Tim, I'm sorry, I can't marry you."

A flashing, but unreadable expression flashed across his face. And then his smile returned. "Of course you can marry me. Suzanne, I love you."

She started to reach across the table to him, but stopped before her hand went an inch. "Please Tim, there's so much happening to me right now, I just can't marry you. I can't risk—"

"Do you mean you can't because of those attempts on your life?" He shook his head and made a dismissing gesture with his left hand. "Suzanne, we already talked about that. I thought you understood. Those things always happen. Suzanne, I can protect you. I'll make sure that nothing like that ever happens to you again, if you marry me."

She stared at him. Was it all that simple? Could he just wave a hand and all her troubles would vanish? "How can you promise that?"

"Bodyguards, of course. Twenty-four hours a day if necessary. Just marry me and you'll have whatever you need."

"Tim, it's more than that. I can hire bodyguards if I want them. I . . . . Tim, I don't want to hurt you."

He shook his head sharply. "Then why are you hurting me. If you keep saying no, you keep hurting me."

"I won't marry someone I don't love, and I don't love you," she said bluntly.

He blinked. "Suzanne, you can't mean that. Suzanne, I . . . I need you, Suzanne. I need you desperately. Please, I need you more now than I ever did before."

She tried to make sense of what he was saying. At the same time, she began to get nervous. Something wasn't right with Tim.

A flash of anger glowed in his eyes. He shook his head sharply. "You can't do this to me."

Suzanne pushed her chair back. "Tim, I have to leave."

Leaning across the table, he grabbed her wrist. His fingers tightened fiercely around her. "No!" he growled, his voice a low whisper. "You can't walk away from me. Not now. Not again!"

A wildness spread on his face. She jerked her arm sharply, and his fingers slipped from her. She pushed away, stood, and started out of the restaurant.

The maitre'd came toward her as she reached the doorway. She ignored his inquiring gaze and went outside to the parking lot.

As soon as she reached the parking lot, she ran toward the limo as fast as her heels would allow. She heard footsteps behind her, but concentrated on her destination. She was within a dozen feet of the long, black car when a hand clamped onto her shoulder.

Spinning in her effort to dislodge the grip, she found herself facing Tim Randolf. His features were twisted with rage. His eyes were wide and scary. "You won't do this to me again. Damn you, Suzanne! I need you now. You walked out on me once. You went away and left me hanging! You won't do it again. Do you understand me?"

he half shouted as his fingers dug cruelly into her shoulder.

"Tim, please!" she cried. She twisted and spun from under his grip, and made it another few feet before he caught her arm and yanked her toward him.

"I won't let you go," he said, his eyes wide and wild. "You will be mine this time. You will!" he shouted as he pulled her closer.

Suzanne knew that her life was in danger. She fought down the fear of what was happening and took a deep breath. At the same time she curved her free hand into a claw. Then, as his words registered through the fog of dread that was building in her mind, her own anger surged powerfully.

"It was you! All these years, it was you!"

A multitude of emotions washed across his features before his eyes narrowed into twin slits that spewed rage at her. "Yes! Yes, it was me! I loved you, and you walked away from me. But not now! Not ever again!" He jerked her, pulling her to him.

She let herself go with the pressure. But, as she moved toward him, she arced her hand upward at his face. Her clawed hand moved quickly. As he pulled her to him, she struck his face, raking her nails across his cheek.

He grunted loudly, released her hand and covered his cheek. Then, as he stared at her in disbelief, Suzanne started to run.

But again, Tim caught her. This time he hauled her to him, crushing her breasts against his chest. She tried to break free, but he kept applying pressure. All too soon, she could not take a breath. She had no choice but to stop fighting.

When she stopped struggling, Tim eased his hold slightly. "That's better. Don't make me act like this. Not out here. Not now," he added as he looked around.

What was he looking for? she wondered as she drew in a ragged and pain filled breath. Then she realized it didn't matter. She was with the person who wanted to control her life and end it at his whim. She had to do something; she had to get away.

"You will be mine," he told her when his eyes returned to her face. "You will do what I need you to."

"Yes," she said, knowing that her only salvation lay in making him believe he had won. "Yes Tim, I will."

"Good," he said. "That's better. We'll be married."

"Yes," she agreed. "We'll get married."

He nodded and smiled. "And then you are going to be on the show with me. We're going to do it together! Suzanne, we are going to become the most famous husband and wife team on television. We'll have it all. Oh, we will," he said, smiling at her.

She stared at his smiling face. Was he truly insane? Silently, she prayed for his grip to ease.

"Oh, yes, Suzanne, it's going to be perfect. Just the way I envisioned it when I saw that article in the paper and . . ."

His hold had eased while he spoke, and as it did, Suzanne attempted to slip away from him.

"No!" he shouted when she moved. His grip hardened and he pulled her tight again. "Don't try to leave me," he said, bending his face closer to hers. "Understand now that I will not permit that to happen."

Something snapped in her mind. Her thoughts blurred and her outrage roared forth. She screamed in fury, and somehow managed to get her hands between them. She pushed hard at his chest and fell back at the same time.

His grip was broken and he staggered. She spun and started to run. She heard him behind her. She pushed, forcing herself forward and trying to catch a breath. Then her hair was caught and her head jerked back sharply.

"No!" she screamed as her feet came out from under her and she fell hard to the ground. Pain spread up along her hip.

"I told you, you will not leave me!" His eyes were wide and his lips drawn into an angry death mask grin.

He bent toward her, reaching for her, when a shadow fell over both of them. An instant later the shadow grasped Tim Randolf's arm and spun him around. Tim gave vent to a loud and demented scream.

And then there was the loud thud of flesh meeting flesh. A half-second later Tim Randolf fell unconscious onto the parking lot pavement.

When Tim Randolf did not move, Peter Wilson bent and lifted Suzanne to her feet. "Are you all right?" he asked.

She gazed into his eyes and, ignoring the pain in her side and head, said, "I am now."

When Suzanne regained her composure, she stepped out of Peter Wilson's protective embrace and looked down at Tim Randolf. He was lying face up on the black surfaced parking lot. The parking lot lights, set high on poles and spaced unevenly around the perimeter, showered him with a yellowish glow that made his skin appear older and sallow.

He looked pitiful. How could he have acted the way he had and still professed his love for her? He was as sick as Peter had described the person who had been stalking her all these years.

And he had done all those terrible things in the name of love. Suzanne closed her eyes and shook her head. No, whatever Tim called it, it was not love.

Suzanne turned back to Peter. "I don't know what to say. I would never have thought that Tim . . ." She paused as another thought rose. This one was a happier one. "At least I was right about Arthur. It wasn't him."

When Peter Wilson started to speak, but stopped to shake his head, she sensed that all was not yet right. "What?" she prodded.

"Tim Randolf is not the one who is after you."

"But he—" she turned to look down at Tim. He was just starting to move. A low groan came from between his lips.

"I know," Peter said. He reached out and put his hands on her shoulders, making her turn to him.

"What happened tonight was not a part of what's been happening. I know it must seem like it, but I don't really believe Randolf would have ever harmed you. He lost it tonight, but not in the way you think."

"He was chasing me. He was crazy!"

"Yes, but for a different reason. Suzanne, I only learned about it tonight, from a friend of mine out on the West Coast."

Peter looked at Tim Randolf, who had pushed himself to a sitting position. His face was expressionless, his eyes vacant.

"My friend learned that Tim Randolf's career is dying. His show is the lowest rated local talk show on the air. He needed something to get the ratings up so that he could not only stay on the air, but syndicate nationally."

Suzanne stared at Peter. She tried to understand what he was saying, but couldn't grasp the intent. She glanced down at Tim and found he was watching them, waiting as she was to hear what Peter would say next.

"Did he ever ask you to come on the show? Work with him on the show?"

Suzanne nodded. "He said it would be good for me to get back to work. It would help me to sort out my life. He offered to have me co-host a week of nostalgia with him."

"You turned him down, didn't you?" Peter asked.

"Yes."

"That's probably when he started to woo you more ardently. Suzanne, the way I see it, having you on the show would have been a major coup. It would have boosted his rating, even if just for a week. But then, if I'm not mistaken, he came up with an even better plan. If he could get you to marry him and co-host his show, he would have it made. Even if the people only tuned in out of curiosity, there would be a good chance they'd continue watching the show."

Suzanne shook her head at the incredulity of the idea. "No," she said. She looked down at Tim. "Did you really think that I would do something like that?"

Before he could answer, headlights flared across the parking lot and the squeal of brakes resounded loudly. Suzanne turned to see a van pull to a stop.

She became aware of the small crowd that had emerged from the restaurant and was staring at the scene in the lot's center. Then Suzanne read the name on the side of the newly arrived van. It was a mobile news unit from one of the local television stations.

A cameraman emerged from the van, followed by a leggy dark haired woman dressed in a pair of jeans, a pale blue shirt and a lightweight blazer. She carried a wireless microphone and came straight toward Suzanne and Peter. She paused momentarily when she saw Tim Randolf sitting on the parking lot pavement, then shrugged and went over to Suzanne.

"Ms. Barnes," she said smiling. "I'm Amy Brooker, from WRDS."

Suzanne stared at her, wondering what the woman wanted. "My name is Grolier, not Barnes. And what is it that you want?"

The woman's expression turned puzzled. "I was told to

come here to interview you and Tim Randolf. We wanted to get the news of your engagement and of the new show you two will be doing, on the air, tonight."

Stiffening, Suzanne looked at Peter, and then down at Tim Randolf. "What kind of a person are you?" she asked him, her voice barely audible. "How could you do this to me?"

"Ms. Grolier," the reporter called.

Whirling toward her, Suzanne checked her temper before it exploded. "There is no engagement, there is no show, and there is no story either. Leave me alone."

Peter Wilson stepped close and put a protective arm around her. He turned and led her toward his unmarked car. Behind them, the cameraman's lights flared. Suzanne knew that the man was filming their retreat.

Once inside the safety of the car, and as Peter started the engine, Suzanne locked her door. When their seatbelts were on, Peter started out of the parking lot. They passed the growing crowd, and Suzanne saw that the camera was now focused on Tim Randolf.

A sad thought darkened her mind. Since returning from France, she'd lost one of her oldest friends, and her brother. "You were right. It was Arthur who has been after me all these years."

"I'm sorry," Peter whispered as he turned toward the highway.

She leaned her head back, tilting it just enough to look at Peter Wilson. It seemed that he was always there when she needed him. Then she remembered that she didn't even know where she would be tonight. "How did you know where I was?"

He laughed. "I called his service and told them that I was a network exec and if I didn't reach Randolf in the next few minutes he would not have a show, and they would not have a client."

She smiled, but the smile faded quickly when she thought of Arthur. "Couldn't it be a mistake?"

"Arthur?" he asked.

"Yes."

"No."

She hated the certainty of his answer. "Peter . . ."

Taking his right hand off the steering wheel, he reached across and covered her hand with his. He squeezed it gently before releasing it.

When he had both hands back on the wheel, he said, "I've been over it time and time again. Everything fits."

"He was too young to have arranged Buzz Carlyle's death. He didn't have the money or the experience."

"I agree. I've also talked to the Beverly Hills police. I've seen copies of the accident report. I think that perhaps I was reading too much into Carlyle's death, because of its connection to you. It very well may have been what it appeared to be, a hit and run."

"But it was the beginning of all the 'accidents,'" Suzanne protested.

"Yes," Peter agreed. "But it could be throwing us off. If we accept it as an accident rather than as an attempt to somehow harm you, then everything else follows along and makes sense.

"The letters you received on the set could have been smuggled in by Arthur. The small accidents—the ones that caused havoc without really hurting anyone, could all have been set up by Arthur. Suzanne, he was old enough at that point, and he was smart."

"All right. Say it was Arthur. The little stunts and accidents weren't that bad. But later, the physical violence. The things that happened . . . . How can you link Arthur to that? He was nowhere around."

Peter maneuvered around a slow moving car. When he returned to the right lane, he put on his bright lights. The green leaves of the trees lining the Palisades Parkway glowed in his headlights.

"The chapter where you describe the last audition you had in Hollywood, when you had the allergic reaction—Arthur was in town. It was summer. Arrangements had already been made for your family's return to New York. Arthur was scheduled to start the music conservatory in September. But, if you had gotten the part, everyone's plans would have been changed.

"Knowing that you would be made up with your own makeup, Arthur put something into it so that you would have a reaction and would not get the part."

Suzanne remained silent. She let his words spill through her head. His theory was sounding more and more like reality.

"Remember what happened when you returned to Hollywood? Arthur had just finished with his schooling in Europe. He was about to embark on his professional music career when you decided to try again for your own career."

"It wasn't just me. It was my mother," Suzanne started to explain.

"I know, I read the chapters. But that's not the point. He saw what was happening, and knew that he would be usurped again. He returned during your second movie, the one where they had that terrible accident from the overhead camera.

"I checked. Arthur was in California then. It was his first American orchestral work."

Suzanne stared out the windshield, her eyes fixed on the dark highway.

"And he was in California when Larry Hartvale died. Everyone on the set knew him, just as they knew the other members of your family."

"Peter, anyone could have done it. By today's standards the set was never heavily secured. If someone wanted in, they could get in."

"But they would have to have a reason. I've read all the reports on what happened that day. There is no indication anywhere that someone had it in for Larry Hartvale. He wasn't a gambler. He wasn't a womanizer and he wasn't rich or powerful. He was just getting started in the business. No, Suzanne, he was killed to destroy you."

A large green and white welcome to New York sign flashed by. That sign was followed by another, explaining that the gun laws in New York were so strict that if anyone was caught with an unlicensed gun they would go directly to jail.

"For jealousy? No, Peter, he never wanted publicity or to be in the limelight."

"So he says. But we don't know that for sure. Perhaps because of what he did, his own mind twisted back on him and his guilt stopped him from doing what he really wanted to do. I'm not a psychiatrist, but that could be a possibility."

"And Jan-Michael and Allan?" she said, her voice so low that she thought he might not have heard her. But, a moment later he spoke.

"That's the hardest part, and possibly the simplest. You kept in touch with your mother."

"Through the lawyers."

"Yes. But Arthur would have known that there was contact. Even that little amount of contact could have set him off and made him start to look for you."

"But no one knew where I was."

"They knew who you were, though."

She shook her head. "Jan-Michael was a well-known author. Because of that, we lived in a place that was listed under a different name. Peter, Jan-Michael had also tasted fame. But he had discovered, years before, that he needed solitude in order to create. Therefore, the only place that was ever listed in his name was an apartment in Paris. But our country home was under another name entirely. And there's no way that his family would tell anyone unless we gave permission."

"But someone who was accomplished in investigations could have uncovered it. And, Suzanne, you were making movies again. Maybe that combination set him off after all those years."

"Then there would be records of his being in France at that time."

"Yes," Peter agreed as he slowed the car and put on his turn signal. "I'm waiting for those records. They were supposed to have arrived yesterday. They'll probably show up on Monday. If they do place Arthur in Europe at the same time as your husband's death, then I think you'll have to finally agree with me."

Suzanne stayed silent as Peter turned off the highway, and started toward Springvale. Neither spoke again until they reached her house. There, Peter helped her out of the car and walked her to the door.

She unlocked the door and opened it. Then she turned to Peter. "Would you like to come in?"

Peter's eyes roamed across her face. "Yes, but I have to get to the station. I need to do some things."

She caught her lower lip between her teeth. A flash of pain reminded her that she'd bitten herself earlier. "I don't know what to say about tonight, except, thank you for being there."

He smiled gently at her. "You're welcome. I'm just glad I was able to help. And I'm glad that you're safe now."

Suzanne saw something grow in his eyes. She knew he wanted to say something else, but was holding back. She willed him to speak, but the silence lingered.

He stepped back. "Suzanne, now that this is over, I'd like to see you . . ."

"So would I," she said to help him overcome whatever barrier was holding him back. "When?"

"Tomorrow? Dinner?"

She smiled. "I'd like that."

He reached out and took her hands in his. He squeezed them gently, smiled, and released them. Then, without another word, he went to his car.

As he drove away, Suzanne went inside and closed and locked the door behind her. Turning on the lights as she walked through the house, Suzanne found that she was humming to herself.

She thought about it. Yes, she realized, she was happy. For the first time in a very long time, it seemed that her life was coming back together.

Chapter Twenty-three

Peter Wilson parked in his reserved spot and started into the station. He paused long enough to realize that the car that had just pulled away from the curb was Judge Kornblute's personal car.

"Damn." Turning, he ran into the station.

"The chief and the ADA want to see you in the chief's office," the duty Sergeant said. "And they're not in good moods."

"Thanks Ted," Peter said as he went to the stairs. Instead of going up, he went down to the cells. When the officer on duty told him that Arthur Barnes was still in his cell, he went to see the man.

Barnes was seated on the single bunk. He stared at Peter for a moment before returning his gaze to the floor. "Arthur, I've put it all together. By Monday I'll have enough proof to have you convicted. Talk to me. Arthur, if you level with me, I'll do everything I can to help you. I mean that."

Arthur looked at Peter again. The look was one of anger. "I've tried to tell you, ever since you arrested me, that I have never tried to harm Suzanne. If I'm guilty of anything, it's of loving her."

Peter stared at him for several more seconds before he

shook his head and left. Two minutes later he opened the door to the chief's office.

Seated behind his desk was Police Chief Loughlin. On the chair across from the chief was Amos Griggs, the Assistant District Attorney. "It's about time," Loughlin said.

"Is there a problem?" he asked, innocently.

"Being here on a Saturday night is a problem," the police chief stated. "Pete, Judge Kornblute was here."

"I saw him pull away."

"He held a quick session and set bail for Arthur Barnes."

Peter turned toward the ADA. "How much did you ask for?"

"The usual, but the judge felt that since Arthur has always been a model citizen, he is allowing Arthur Barnes out, on his own recognizance."

"Damn it! Well I'm glad I didn't pull the watch on the Grolier house."

"Maybe we're wrong on this one," the ADA said.

Peter looked from him to the chief. "Can we take that chance?"

"We have no choice," Loughlin said. "I just wanted to let you know before we release Barnes."

"Thank you." Holding back any sign of his anger, he stood and left the office. Once he entered his own office, he slammed the door shut.

He wanted to stop Arthur Barnes from leaving, but he couldn't. Nor could he follow Arthur wherever he went so that when the time came, he could catch the man and end his reign of terror against Suzanne.

"Damn!" he repeated, slamming his hand hard on the desk.

Instead of feeling the sting of wood against his palm, he felt paper. He looked down and saw an envelope. He picked it up. The postmark was from Washington. The return address was the State Department.

There was a note on it. It was an apology. The package had been delivered yesterday, but to the wrong department.

Peter opened it and withdrew the contents. It was the list of names and dates he'd been waiting for. He started on the first page, and began to scan the lists of names. By the time he'd read the last name and date, his mind was racing.

He thought back to everything he'd discussed with Suzanne on their ride back from New Jersey. He put the dates together, and even worked out the other intricacies.

He found the things he'd missed or had just dismissed as not necessary. And the report from the State Department was the final piece of the puzzle.

He put the papers down. It would be over in a half an hour and Suzanne Grolier would be a free person for the first time since she was nine.

Suzanne closed the photo album and sighed. Standing, she replaced the album in the bookcase and went to her desk. She looked at the chapter of the manuscript she'd been dictating.

She touched it, running her fingers over the typed words. Her work was done. The autobiography she had been writing was finished. The memories she had needed to bring forth had done their job.

Her life was back on track and she could now think about a future. Turning, she looked at the picture of Jan-Michael and Allan. She knew Jan-Michael would have approved of what she'd done, just as she knew he would have expected her to get on with her life and not live by mourning for the past.

She wondered if Dana would understand that all the work they had done would never be shared with the world. She had no intention of publishing her autobiography, nor had she any further need to finish the story.

Writing the story had done something else for her, as well. She now understood more of how Jan-Michael had felt when he was writing. He'd tried to explain it to her, more than once, but she had never comprehended his message. She smiled. It was simple. When you were able to transfer your innermost thoughts and feelings to paper, it made you feel good.

But, she also added in her silent dialogue, she liked the way she and Dana worked together. Perhaps she would continue writing, but on a novel, not on her life story.

The idea grew in her mind, and she found herself liking it. Maybe she had indeed found the next step in her life. Smiling, she turned, switched off the light, and left the office.

She looked at her watch and saw it was almost ten. She thought about making a cup of tea and decided against it. Instead, she decided to watch whatever movie was on television.

She checked all the locks and turned off the lights. Then she went to the stairs and started up. No sooner had she taken a step, than a sound came from the kitchen.

She froze, waiting to see if there would be another sound. But all she heard was the sudden pounding of her heart. "Who's there?" she called.

There was no answer. Then she realized how foolish she was being. There was a policeman outside. She'd seen him walking along the edge of her lawn, not twenty minutes ago.

She went down to the kitchen and, turning on the light, she looked around. There was nothing. She silently scolded herself for hearing things and started out.

The instant she reached for the light switch, she froze again. The hackles on the back of her neck stood out eerily. There was something there. She sensed it with every fiber of her being.

She tried to turn, but froze as cold waves of fear washed over her. Her heart beat rapidly and her breathing turned painful. Fighting the fear, she made herself look around the kitchen. It was empty.

"What's happening to me?" she asked aloud. Then she turned off the light and started out.

But her heart still pounded with the force of her adrenalin-laced blood. She tried to calm the fear that was so rife within her, but as she walked toward the stairway the sensation of being watched grew intolerable.

Stopping suddenly, Suzanne whirled to face the kitchen.

A scream of fear and surprise rose in her throat, only to come out as a strangled gasp when her eyes fell on the dark apparition standing in the center of the kitchen.

The hall light reached in just far enough for Suzanne to see that someone was indeed there. Then, as her eyes adjusted to the shape of the intruder, her heart sank. It was *him!*

"No!" she screamed at the apparition. "No! No!" she screamed again as the form took a step toward her. She saw the large axe in his right hand and at the same instant realized that it wasn't shadow that obscured his face, it was a leather mask.

No, it was *the* leather mask. It was her worst fear, her constant nightmare come back to haunt her.

Suzanne's eyes darted everywhere, seeking an avenue of escape. The door was out. It would take too long to unlock the two locks and take off the chain. She looked up and knew what she had to do. Galvanizing her fear-tightened muscles, she moved toward the stairs.

Reaching the stairs, she raced up them, two at a time. The intruder was closing in behind her.

When she reached the top, and she heard the loud sounds of his feet climbing the stairs, a high-pitched mew bubbled from her mouth.

She clamped her lips tight and ran down the hallway, into her bedroom. She closed the door behind her and turned off the light.

The low moonlight coming in through the window spotlighted her on the wall, where she tried to blend into the paint and the darkness.

Her mind sent her back a dozen years. She was reliving her last horror movie again, but this time it was not a movie. This time it was real.

Her breathing was fast and jerky. Her head spun and dizziness crept over her. She sucked in a huge gulp of air and held her breath. She fought furiously with herself, pushing back her fear, holding it at bay. She had to. It was her only chance.

Carefully, she inched her way along the wall, all the while listening for the sounds that would tell her where *he* was. Finally, her right hand touched the edge of the night table.

She froze and listened intently. There were no sounds.

She felt around the table until her fingers touched the handle of the drawer. Slowly, carefully, she drew the drawer outward.

Ignoring the footsteps in the hall, she searched through the drawer, looking for something, anything, to use as a weapon. But there was nothing, not even a nail file.

The footsteps in the hallway changed direction and came toward the bedroom. She bit her lower lip, using the pain to keep her mind clear.

Think! she commanded herself. Think! She moved then, running through the sitting room to the bathroom.

She didn't go into the bathroom; rather, she reached in, locked and closed the door, and dodged back to the wide closet that ran the length of the sitting room. She slipped inside, leaving the door a fraction of an inch ajar and then pressed her eye to the opening.

A quarter-minute later she heard the bedroom door open. The click of the bedroom's lightswitch followed, and a beam of light filtered into the sitting room. A minute later the masked Axeman stepped into the door frame of the sitting room. His head turned from side to side as he looked for her.

Holding her breath, she watched the masked killer step completely into the sitting room.

Her hands were shaking. Her legs threatened to give out their support. But she refused to cave in to the fear that was turning her mind dark and numb. Instead, she held herself in tight control as the masked man looked around the bedroom.

When his eyes went to the bathroom door, her heart pounded harder. He walked to it and tried the doorknob. He rattled it a few times and then laughed.

Taking a half-step back, he lifted the axe and slammed it into the door. Splinters sprayed outward from the door when the metal axehead bit into the wood. The sound crackled horribly in the room, sending shivers coursing along Suzanne's back.

She pushed the door open a fraction of an inch more when the crazed intruder struck at the bathroom door again. Then he pulled the axe from the door and laughed. "I'm coming for you. I told you I would and I'm here!"

She tried to recognize the voice, but the mouthless leather mask distorted the sound.

Then, in a fury of blows, he struck again and again and again. The thin wood could not stand up against the onslaught, and finally shattered and collapsed.

The instant he stepped into the bathroom, howling in glee, Suzanne opened the closet door and ran out. She didn't look behind her, or even think about what she was doing. She just ran to the stairs, and then went down.

No sooner did her feet touch the cold tile floor than she turned from the front door and went into the kitchen. She heard his footsteps on the ceiling. He was on the way to the stairs.

Stopping momentarily to grab one of the black-handled Sabatier knives from the countertop holder, Suzanne then went to the glass sliding door to the deck.

She reached for the lock and pushed it down. It wouldn't go. She grunted and pushed again. She almost screamed when her nail bent back and snapped.

She exhaled in pained frustration and tried again. This time the lock clicked and the door was ready to be opened. Then she heard him enter the kitchen. She pulled on the door, just as his voice reached her, and slid it open.

"Die!" he screamed.

Suzanne stepped sideways, away from the door, a heartbeat before he swung the axe. The axe's head crashed into the wood jam around the door. Reacting without thinking, Suzanne swung the knife at him.

She felt the blade hit his chest. She yanked it back and heard him cry out. He pulled the axe free and stepped back.

"Damn you to hell!" he shouted.

The phone rang at that instant, and momentarily, the killer froze. Suzanne, her mind dark with fear and rage, ducked her head and charged at him. The move caught him off guard and he stepped back, lowering the axe to protect himself.

She whipped the knife in an arc and struck his upper arm. She was rewarded with a pained grunt. She used that moment to spin from him and run out the door and onto the deck, the knife still clutched tightly in her right hand.

Peter Wilson got into his car. He slammed his hand against the steering wheel. He was too late. The killer had already gone.

He picked up the cellular telephone and dialed Suzanne's number. He let the phone ring ten times before he hung up.

Then he started the car and put it in gear. As he hit the gas, he picked up the microphone and called in. "Who's on duty at the Grolier house?"

"Perez," the duty officer at Central said.

"Patch me through."

A moment later Central was back on. "Lieutenant, Perez isn't answering."

"Send a unit, now!" he ordered as he put down the microphone and concentrated on driving. He was less than four minutes from Suzanne's house. He could only pray that he would make it in time.

Suzanne leaped from the deck and started toward the back of her yard. She heard the Axeman follow behind. Then her foot caught on something and she slipped and fell.

Twisting as she fell, she kept the knife away from her. She landed hard on her back. Her breath was knocked from her lungs.

As she lay there, she heard a siren in the distance. Intuitively, she knew it was Peter coming for her.

Then a dark shape loomed over her.

He stepped closer to her, spread his legs, and raised the axe over his head. "Now!" he shouted.

The moment he spoke, Suzanne rolled to her left. The whoosh of the axe was loud in her ear as it narrowly missed her and thudded into the soft earth.

She slashed at his leg with her knife, pulled her legs into herself, and kicked upward at his groin.

He screamed in pain even as he doubled over.

Suzanne got up and started to run again. She stopped, looked over her shoulder, and she saw he was straightening up. She glanced toward her house, but knew she could not get by him.

Then she looked toward the fence that lined the back of her property to prevent anyone from slipping over the edge. She realized that her only avenue of safety was to reach the gate and the stairway behind it so that she could get down to the embankment. There, she would have a chance. He couldn't swim after her with an axe.

She extended her senses. The sound of the siren was getting closer, but it wasn't here yet. She had to stall, she had to keep moving.

When the Axeman started forward, she started toward the gate. Then she realized that the man had anticipated her move and was already angling to cut her off before she reached the gate.

Putting her head down, she concentrated on pumping her legs as fast as she could. His footfalls grew behind her, but she refused to slow down enough to look for him.

Suddenly, she was at the fence. She looked to her right. She was five feet from the gate. Turning quickly, she put her back to the fence. At the same time, she brought the knife forward and gripped it with two hands.

The Axeman stopped. His loud breathing was tortured and strained. She knew he was tiring. If only she could

. . . . Headlights washed across the backyard as a car pulled into the driveway.

Hurry! she silently pleaded to Peter, willing him to hear her very thought.

Then the masked creature raised the axe over his head. His breathing was loud and strained and he started forward.

Suzanne looked around. There was no escape. Her hands shook as she gripped the knife tightly and faced him. "Stop, Arthur. Don't do this. Please, don't do this."

He laughed and took another step toward her. "It's over," he said. "Now you die."

He howled strangely, and then he charged.

Suzanne realized that she had only one slim chance to escape. If her timing wasn't perfect, she would die. Suddenly, she was thankful for all the dancing and fencing lessons her mother had forced her to take when she was a child. Those just might be her salvation.

She inhaled as he came inexorably forward. His momentum was building, like a steamroller let loose. When he was three feet away, Suzanne stepped sideways and then lunged forward in a classic fencing attitude. But, at the same time, she used the lunge to drop to the ground on her knees.

He twisted when she lunged, trying to swing the axe sideways at her while he rushed forward. His swing was off. The moment the axe passed harmlessly by her, she turned and thrust the knife upward.

The blade caught his shoulder as he fought to regain his balance. She pushed hard and the tip of the knife went deep into his shoulder. But when his momentum carried him past Suzanne, the knife was ripped from her grasp.

His scream of pain and rage tore through the night. Suzanne turned just as he crashed into the chain-link fence. He lay sideways against the fence, his head twisted so he could see her.

A second later he tried to push himself off the fence. But his legs were twisted together and he fell back on the fence. The fence groaned and sagged.

Moonlight reflected off the blade of the large kitchen knife sticking from his shoulder. The axe was still in his hand, but that arm was hanging limply at his side.

Before Suzanne could move, she saw him again turn his face toward her. His eyes widened insanely as he stared at her. He tried to raise the axe, but the movement was clumsy and put even more pressure on the fence, and it sank farther back.

Behind her, she heard Peter Wilson call her name. Then, the world turned into a slow motion picture as the fence slowly continued to give way to the weight of the masked man.

Seeing what was happening, Suzanne took a step forward. She reached out to him, her hand inches from his.

"No!" the man screamed in the last instant before the fence crumpled completely and sent the masked man tumbling backwards. The axe fell from his hand when he tried to find something to grip to stop himself from falling.

But there was nothing. In less than a breath, he was gone. His scream followed his descent and ended as suddenly as it had begun.

She went to the very edge of the palisades and looked down. He was lying half on the rocks, and half on the cement part of the dock.

From behind, Peter called her name. She turned and he was there. Willingly, she went into his arms. He held her against his chest. "It's over."

She wasn't aware of how much time had passed, but when her trembling ceased, she drew back from the safety and strength she had found inside Peter's arms.

"I can't understand how he could hate me so much. Peter, Arthur tried to kill me with the axe. He .... Dear Lord, he was truly insane."

Peter's lips were compressed tightly. His eyes were locked on hers.

"What is it?" she asked.

"I was wrong. That's not Arthur down there. It's—"

"But . . ." Suzanne began, then cut herself off. "Not Arthur. And it isn't Tim. Who .... I ..." Suddenly, she had to find out who it was for herself; she didn't want Peter to tell her.

She walked to the gate, opened it, and then went down the hundred foot wooden stairs. Peter was with her all the way. When she finally reached the man who had been haunting her life for over twenty years, she knelt at his side.

"Who are you?" she asked as Peter reached over her and began to take off the mask. But he'd done more than open the black velcro closure; she saw moonlight glint from a ring on the third finger of his left hand, and she knew who he was.

"Why? My God, why?" she asked as Peter removed the mask and revealed the face she already knew was beneath it—the face of her stepfather, Raymond Barnes.

Epilogue

The funeral had been simple and quick. Suzanne was glad it was over. She still did not understand why things happened the way they had, but the clear and uncomplicated truth was that with Raymond's death came her rebirth.

She had lost more in her short life than most people would ever lose. But that was in the past. Now, she had a future filled with hope rather than fear. She no longer had to awaken in the mornings to wonder who would be taken from her, or who might be hurt because of her presence.

She fought down a swell of sadness when memories of Jan-Michael and Allan rose up. Her sole consolation was that there had been nothing she could have done to prevent any of the tragedies of the past. And now, except for her memories of Allan and Jan-Michael, they were gone.

"Are you okay?" Peter asked as he moved beside her on the deck.

She looked at him for several seconds before she answered. She saw him as he'd been that first day when he'd come to her house in response to the gas emergency. His face was sober and his mouth firm. He was a handsome man, she thought. More so now that she had grown to know him. His features would be deemed rugged by a casual observer, but his expression as he looked at her was gentle.

"Yes, I'm fine," she responded truthfully. "I feel as though a weight has been lifted from me. I only wish that I knew why this had happened in the first place."

"Perhaps I can help."

Suzanne and Peter turned at the sound of Arthur Barnes's voice. Suzanne's stepbrother was coming up the stairs, and onto the deck. "No one answered the door, so I came back here to see if you were home."

"I don't know if this is a good idea," Suzanne said in a stiff voice.

Arthur stared at Suzanne. "It is if you want to know why my father did these terrible things to you."

"Then you knew all along?" Peter asked.

Arthur shook his head. He lifted a tan, covered book toward them. "No, I found this yesterday when I was going through Father's things. I didn't want to say anything until after his funeral. No matter what, he was my father and I owed him his burial, if nothing else."

Suzanne heard the grief in Arthur's voice, and her heart cried out for him. They had loved each other as brother and sister for far too long for her to hold any hatred toward him now. "Arthur," she whispered as she moved toward him.

He met her halfway there. They embraced, not as lovers, but as siblings. Peter stood silently at the railing, watching them with approval etched on his face.

When they parted and came toward Peter, Arthur again hefted the book. "My father kept a journal. Everything that happened is in here. He was insane, you know, and clever."

Peter nodded. "I know."

"Before we get into the journal, I need to explain about my father."

"Don't," Suzanne said, looking from one man to the other. "It's over. Let it be."

Arthur shook his head. "No. I think it's important that you know everything. If not, there will still be questions that go unanswered."

"He's right," Peter said. "You should know why it all happened."

Suzanne held Peter's gaze. She knew, intuitively, that what he said was right, just as she knew that he was telling her to listen to Arthur and to heal whatever breaches remained between them.

"Why don't we sit down?" She motioned toward the table and chairs a few feet from them.

And, as she sat down, and Arthur sat across from her, Peter cranked the umbrella open to shade them from the sun. Then he sat next to Suzanne.

Arthur looked at Suzanne and Peter. He moistened his lips with his tongue, took a deep breath and said, "Nine years ago my father had a breakdown. For almost two years he underwent private psychiatric treatment. No one knew about it, except for myself and Mother. He was out of work for only a few weeks. But he had sessions almost every day.

"The medical people were never able to learn the cause of his breakdown. But, eventually, he came out of it and seemed fine."

Arthur paused to tap the book on the table. "But last night I learned the reason for his breakdown. It was in here. Suzanne, what happened ten years ago?"

Suzanne tried to focus on that time in her past, but could not find a point that connected her to her stepfather. She shook her head.

Arthur opened the book to a page he had tagged with

a stick-on note and began to read. "She went to Europe to see her, but I don't know where. That damned spawn of the devil is taking my wife away from me again! She was gone for so long I thought she was dead. Damn her! She's back! Oh, please, Lenore, don't leave me again."

Arthur stopped reading. He looked back at Suzanne. "That was in April, when you married Jan-Michael Grolier."

Suzanne's stomach twisted horribly. She felt Peter's hand cover hers. His touch anchored her and helped her to regain her composure.

"He loved your . . . our mother deeply," Arthur said, as he closed the journal. "It was an obsession, the way he loved her. But he also loved me and wanted certain things for me. At the same time, he could never deny anything that Lenore asked him.

"It must have torn him apart. He wanted to give me everything he thought I needed, but at the same time he needed to give Lenore everything she needed. Part of what she needed was for you to become a famous actress." Arthur closed his eyes and rubbed the lids with his fingertips.

When he lowered his hands and opened his eyes, Suzanne saw how deeply saddened he was.

"I'm sure that if we were to talk with a shrink, and explain these things, that he would tell us that my father's insanity had been caused by his needs. I think that he was able to control himself, until that first picture offer."

"Buzz Carlyle?" Suzanne asked quickly.

Arthur nodded. "Yes, I think that it all started to fall apart for him then. He had already planned on coming east that summer, so that I could do some specialized studying."

"I remember," Suzanne said.

"But Mother wanted to stay because of the opportunity

it gave you." Arthur paused to tap his index finger on the journal. "There's a simple little entry, two or three lines. Basically, it says that Buzz Carlyle would never make another picture and it hadn't cost very much, either."

"He hired someone to do it," Peter Wilson stated. "I was right the first time. But I decided that it had been an accident because I didn't think you were old enough to set it up yourself."

"There are so many entries that go on and on about Suzanne and how she took his wife from him, and how she usurped my rightful place in the family and in the very world itself, and how my talent was being wasted because of her. I . . ." Arthur faltered. His voice crackled with emotion.

He drew in a deep breath and, after exhaling forcefully, went on. "I don't think anyone understood what was going on in his head. He covered it up so well. I . . . I spent so much time with him and I never knew. I feel like a fool."

"What happened to him would have . . . probably did fool an expert," Peter said. "You can't hold yourself responsible for his actions.

"How did he manage to change the bullets in the prop gun on the movie set?" Peter asked.

"According to the journal, he came to the set the day before, with Lenore. He hung around until Suzanne and Lenore got together and started to talk. Then he simply faded away. He got into the prop room and switched bullets for blanks. He was smart about it. He left the first few rounds as blanks and then used the live ammo for the rest of the clip."

"So that when the special effects people and the prop people checked the clip they would see the blanks on top," Peter said.

"He was behind everything? There were no accidents

at all?" Suzanne asked, her voice sounding shrill to her ears.

Peter Wilson tightened his grip on her hand, but remained silent.

"When you disappeared, he only used the journal a few times. Each entry told how happy and at peace he was, now that you had disappeared from their lives.

"But then," Arthur continued, "you asked your mother to come to your wedding. That's when he snapped."

Suzanne looked down at Peter Wilson's hand on hers. Then she lifted her eyes and stared at her brother. "And my husband and son?"

Arthur didn't answer right away. Swallowing, he looked at a spot above Suzanne's head. "He did that on his final trip to Europe, the one he'd taken before he retired."

"That was why I got here that night," Peter told Suzanne. "After dropping you off, I returned to the station. I had a talk with Arthur just before he was released. Then I went to my office and found the report I'd requested from the State Department. I'd been checking on Arthur Barnes, and had requested all data about his trips to Europe.

"Well, I not only got the information about Arthur, but the report included every trip by anyone with the name Barnes. Raymond Barnes's name was on the list, and it showed every trip that he'd taken to Europe. Suzanne, the date of your husband's death coincided not with a trip that Arthur took, but one that Raymond took."

"There wasn't much of an entry about that incident," Arthur volunteered. "I think that perhaps this time he wasn't proud of what he'd done. But there was a small paragraph that said that although he hadn't gotten Suzanne when he'd gotten the car, it had helped to pay her back for taking his wife away from him and for stealing my career, as well."

Then Arthur opened the journal and flipped through the pages near the back. Finding what he wanted, he flattened the book and stabbed at the page with his finger. "This is the last entry. Look at the writing."

Suzanne stared at the page. The lettering was large and crude, almost childlike. She could feel the hatred and anger with which it was written and, as she read the words, she shivered.

SHE'S BACK! SHE'S GOING TO TRY AND RUIN HIM AGAIN! I WON'T LET HER! I WON'T!

The sound of the journal closing was loud. But the very action snapped Suzanne out of the trance her stepfather's words had put her in.

"I'm sorry," Arthur said as he pushed the book across the table, not toward Suzanne, but toward Peter. "I imagine you'll need this for your report."

"Yes, thank you."

"I'm sorry," Arthur repeated to Suzanne. "I didn't realize how sick he was. I never made the connection between what happened to you, and him. I . . . . And I hope you'll forgive me for my own indiscretions. Suzanne, you're my sister, and I don't want to lose you. You're the only family I have left."

Suzanne smiled at him. "And I'm still your sister."

His face brightened. He smiled for the first time since stepping onto the deck. "Thank you." Then he stood. "I have to go. I've got an appointment at the lawyer's. I'll call you tomorrow."

"Please," she said as he came to her, bent, and kissed her cheek.

When he was gone, Suzanne turned to Peter. "I guess that takes care of it all."

He nodded. "I guess it does."

"And now that I've been saved, I suppose you'll have to find some other poor maiden to rescue from some terrible fate."

"I suppose," he said, his face stoic.

"It happens a lot, doesn't it?"

He blinked. "What happens a lot?"

"Your having to save people."

"Occasionally."

She looked into his eyes, and almost fell into them. Then she had a terrible thought. What if he said goodnight and never came back? She closed her own eyes for a moment to steady her thoughts. "Will I see you again?"

"That's up to you," he replied in a low and husky voice.

"Then my answer is yes," she said as she went to his side and surrendered to the warmth of his embrace.

Closing her eyes, Suzanne realized she was finally happy.

And at peace.